LIBERTY'S LIDO

RUBY LOCKHEART

Liberty's Lido

This book was first published in Great Britain in paperback during September 2020.

ISBN: 978-1-8382155-0-7

The inspiration for my book has come from a lifetime of living in the beautiful county of Cornwall. I've discovered the physical and mental benefits of swimming in the ever changing cold waters. Each swim washes away my anxieties bit by bit like peeling back layers of an onion.

I would like to thank my husband for supporting me, helping with the numerous edits, endless cups of coffee and encouragement to keep me going when I was feeling overwhelmed and didn't think I'd finish the book.

The characters are loosely based around swimmers I've met.

There is never a bad swim!

LIBERTY'S LIDO

Prologue 1928

Thirteen year old Liberty didn't really understand what was happening but the shore was becoming further away and she found herself facing out to sea. Tempestuous waves crashed over her as she kicked her feet, flailing wildly with her quickly tiring arms. The water closed over her and she felt the pull of the abyss dragging on her long and heavy clothing. Her lungs ached. She'd never known a fear like it. She was hurled to the surface and tried to take a breath, immediately inhaling icy cold salty water. Before she could cough, she was submerged by another wave. Once more, she was spat out by the sea onto the surface, this time managing to stay afloat long enough to gain half a breath before repeatedly plummeting under the unforgiving waves. Exhaustedly she fought her way to the surface only to disappear into the darkness.

"I'm going to die." She thought with trepidation, feeling the strength sapping from her arms and legs.

Sarah

Rachel Roberts was in that deliciously warm, snuggly half-awake cocoon under her cosy duvet and she was vaguely aware of the sounds of a coffee machine somewhere in the distance coupled with muffled voices, bird songs and the occasional vehicle passing her home. She was jolted awake from her sleepy contented thoughts when she remembered that today was Sarah's funeral. Heart pounding and with a sense of dread she pulled back her warm duvet and swung her legs out of bed trying to find her flip flops with her bare feet as she stood.

"Shit!" She stumbled as she tripped over her flip flops. She steadied herself and grabbed a mermaid print dressing gown from the back of the wooden bedroom door. Yanking back the curtains she blinked as the bright sunshine assaulted her sleepy eyes. She opened the window a crack and allowed the fresh morning air to fill her lungs slowly as she took a deep breath. She gazed blearily down out at her brightly coloured garden filled with daffodils, primroses and camelias; and out to the street beyond, a row of white former fisherman's cottages bathing in the early morning brightness. A pair of blue tits fluttered around a bird feeder while a group of sparrows chattered noisily from a neighbour's tree. A seagull started its loud cry from one of the roofs of the cottages. In the distance she could see the sun reflecting brightly on the sea's surface. With a turquoise blue sky and a few wispy clouds, it looked like it was going to be a perfect spring day.

Fifty three year old Rachel wandered downstairs and followed the aromatic smell of fresh coffee into the kitchen where her husband Tom, aged fifty seven, had just finished making her caffeine fix. He smiled at her, gathered her into a big, caring, all enveloping hug and kissed the top of her tousled brown head.

"Alright?" he enquired simply.

"Mmm yeah." She leant her face into his chest and took in his familiar comfy manly smell. "Gonna be a hard day today."

"Yeah." he agreed softly. "Drink your coffee."

Rachel sat at the kitchen table, sipping her drink but barely noticing the rich bitter taste as she looked at a card with all of the funeral details on it. Her phone pinged. It was a text from Poppy, Tom and Rachel's twenty one year old daughter, who was at Plymouth Uni studying Marine Biology, but had come home for a couple of days for the funeral.

"Better make that another coffee please Tom." Rachel said while gesturing upstairs. "Think Poppy might have overdone it last night catching up with her friends in The Ship."

Rachel texted a reply to Poppy that her Dad was bringing her up a coffee and some water and her thoughts turned to Sarah Rosehill, who she'd known for virtually all of her life and was her Grandmother, Liberty's, best friend. Liberty had been the first friend Sarah had made in Cornwall, second time around, when she arrived in the 1970s in her mid-forties.

Sarah hadn't been your typical old lady and she'd led an interesting colourful life. She started life in London and had been evacuated to Cornwall during the Second World War, aged ten, where initially she was lonely. An outsider, missing her parents and with a funny accent, but she gradually made friends, did well at school and grew to love Porthlowen, the endless summer days with blue skies and seas contrasting with the fantastic winter storms which churned the sea into a maelstrom of foam and crashing waves. Her landlady was Gladys Moon; and her husband Albert had been away in Africa fighting the Germans with Monty, the legendary wartime leader. Gladys and Bert had two sons, John a year older than Sarah, and Raymond, two years younger. Gladys had always wanted a daughter and so was kind and loving to Sarah, making her clothes when she could, singing to her while brushing her long blonde hair, baking delicious pies and cakes, rationing permitting. Gladys also introduced her to Nancy Glover, their next door neighbour, who Sarah had sat next to at the local school. Nancy and Sarah were best friends and spent a lot of time in each other's houses. Sarah had never really got on with John, who seemed to resent her presence, she a mere girl, but Raymond became like a younger brother to her, and he in turn looked up to her. They had an old piano in their front room which was Bert's but Gladys could play a little and she patiently taught both Sarah and Raymond how to play. All in all, Sarah's wartime in Porthlowen had been a reasonably happy one.

After the war she'd returned home to London and at twenty one she had become a model. She struggled initially but with her looks, style and a change of name to Rosie Rosselli she became one of the top models of the 1950s, appearing on the front pages of magazines like Vogue and Harper's Bazaar. Throughout the sixties and early seventies Sarah had worked with some of the top names in makeup and fashion, Quant, Biba, Revlon, Yves Saint Laurent and had dated several famous men before on a whim, and after a break up of a marriage with a former footballer, she packed a bag and drove back to Cornwall. Everyone in London took themselves so seriously and the famous men were so shallow and vain. She retreated from the bright city lights and retired from the fashion industry before taking up painting and throwing herself into the local surfing and art scene. Always looking effortlessly elegant her tall statuesque persona and slim figure meant she always carried herself with panache and style. With a whiff of French perfume, you always knew when she had been around.

Sarah had gone to Liberty's Lido for a summer swim one afternoon in that first week back in the 1970s and had got chatting to a local lady, who turned out to be the Liberty that the Lido had been named after. Sarah had remembered the Lido from her childhood although it had been shut during the war years, but as a child she'd walked past the boarded up gates, tatty walls and flaky paint. Her adoptive family had told her stories of the official opening in 1931 with King George V, bands and bunting. She'd always wondered what it had been like back then, and hoped it would open one summer so that she could see for herself. It never did in the time she was there and she'd forgotten all about the Lido until she'd been for a walk from her little bed and breakfast house one fine summer evening after a very forgettable meal at a seaside greasy spoon café on her first night back in Porthlowen. Pausing to look through the cast iron white painted gates she'd made the decision to go for a swim the following day, once she'd bought a swimming costume in the town.

First thing next day she'd ambled into Porthlowen after the guest house's rendition of breakfast; burnt bacon, rubber eggs, crispy thin sliced toast, insipid tea, brick hard scalloped rolls of butter but delicious homemade marmalade. She vaguely remembered and recognised the high street from her childhood and wondered what had happened to her school friends, especially Nancy, and indeed her adoptive family, lovely Gladys, surly John and friendly Raymond. She found a shop that sold swimming costumes and other summer paraphernalia. Another shop sold sandwiches, snacks and Corona glass bottles of Cola, Vimto and Lemonade, while next door was a WH Smiths that sold magazines and paperbacks. Loaded up she made her way back to the B & B as the temperature of the day started to soar. Now suitably dressed for her adventure she walked the short distance to the Lido, paid her entrance fee and found a space in the sunshine where she laid out her towel.

"Good morning." She'd nodded to the woman next to her who was reading the Times and they'd started chatting. Sarah realised that she'd forgotten to buy sun tan lotion in the town as she hadn't realised the deceptive heat of the sun. Liberty had passed her own bottle over without a qualm. They chatted most of the day, cooling down in the salty water of the pool at intervals and sharing their lunch, managing most of the Times crossword between them. They agreed to meet again the following day, weather permitting.

Sarah and Liberty became inseparable from then on and were the very best of friends, despite their differences in age. Liberty had been sixty in 1975. Over their many conversations in the early days Sarah had found out a little about her wartime adoptive family through friends of Liberty. Albert, who Sarah had never met, was killed in action in Africa. Gladys had never remarried and had died a couple of years ago. Her sons had both gone on to be in the Army like their Dad. John had married Nancy and they'd moved around with his military career and hadn't been back to Cornwall since Gladys had died. Nancy and Sarah had written to each other for a couple years after the war but the letters dried up as life moved on. Raymond had been killed in the Aden conflict in the 1960s.

Liberty had accompanied Sarah when she went to look for a home, eventually settling in a former fisherman's cottage overlooking the sea and since then they had celebrated many birthdays, Christmases, hot summers and wild winters together.

Sarah had been like a second Grandmother to Rachel, and the two of them had certainly shared secrets when she had needed advice and couldn't face talking to her own parents or grandparents, and once Liberty had died Rachel had met Sarah regularly for a coffee and cake. Sarah was one of those annoying people who ate all the wrong things but maintained her elegant figure. Rachel was going to miss the old girl, her friendship and wise advice, her memories of Liberty and her wicked, self- deprecating sense of humour. Today was going to be a hard day. Grabbing a piece of toast, she finished her coffee went to get herself ready for the funeral.

Rachel, like Sarah, was a member of an open water swimming club called The Liberty's Lido Ladies and Lads, shortened to four Ls and now simply known to the swimmers as "The Ls." The Ls met daily, all year round and swam in the sea just behind the Lido when they could and inside the Lido between April and October when they couldn't, perhaps it was too rough or the tides were wrong. They'd taken to wearing colourful fancy hats at any opportunity so as Rachel bent down to pick up the funeral invitation, she smiled to herself as she read the line "Everyone has to wear a bonkers hat." She finished putting festival glitter on her face, "Biodegradable of course darling." to quote Sarah, checked her makeup was on point in the mirror and pulled on a bright pink hoodie with the legend "Liberty's Lido Ladies and Lads" emblazoned across her back and a matching coloured sun hat with a wide brim.

"How do I look?" Tom asked, as he stood there in a dark suit, with a bright orange floral tie and a multi coloured jester hat.

"Ridiculous!" she laughed.

"Whereas you…" he grinned admiringly "Look gorgeous, as always." He gave her a quick hug.

"Selfie!" she demanded, holding her phone at arm's length. He dashed into the camera's focus, pulled some stupid faces and she snapped a few quick pictures. They laughed at the results.

Poppy appeared, coffee in hand, looking immaculate but wearing sunglasses to protect her eyes from the bright lights while recovering from a hangover from hell.

"Mum have you got any paracetamol?" she asked quietly.

"Yes. In the car." Rachel replied.

"Please don't shout." Poppy whispered in pain.

"C'mon. We'll be late." Tom said, grabbing his phone and keys. "Let's hope we can find somewhere to park."

Luckily Tom managed to nab the last space, allowing Rachel and Poppy to get out first so he could squeeze into a tiny parking bay. Awkwardly he angled his tall but slim body out of the car door and joined Rachel and Poppy as they walked to the church doors, enjoying the warm spring sunshine outside.

Sarah had many friends; her personality was effervescent and she was a popular member of the local community so the church was nearly full. As Rachel looked around nearly everyone was wearing colourful hats and bright outfits. She couldn't miss the Ls. Rachel laughed when she saw them all. This group was never one to hold back and they had really gone the extra distance for Sarah. Wearing their swimming group hoodies in every colour and even brighter hats she joined their ranks. Gazing around the church she recognised many local people and smiled at a few with their funny hats on but there were a few people she didn't know. In particular, sat, on their own, in the front aisle on the opposite side of the church from Rachel was a couple dressed in black.

"Who are they?" asked Tom in a low voice, following the direction of Rachel's gaze.

"No idea." She shrugged her shoulders. "Relatives maybe? I think Sarah had some nieces and nephews. She didn't talk about them much."

Despite this being a sad occasion, the losing of a dear friend, it was a celebration of an eighty eight year old life lived to the full. Sarah had continued swimming until the last couple of months before she'd become too frail and her legs just wouldn't carry her those few yards into the sea or into the Lido. In Sarah's inimitable style she had written and recorded her own eulogy a few days before her demise and she had the aisles of the church roaring with laughter as the congregation heard of her exploits and stories about some of the famous people she had known and men she had dated. Few of the congregation had associated Sarah Rosehill with the famous model Rosie Roselli. Abba's 'Thank you for the music' was the final song, which most people agreed was a fitting tribute to an incredible woman.

After the funeral Rachel, Tom and many of the swimming group joined the wake being held in the pub, The Ship Inn, across the road from the Lido and the sea. It was a loud affair. Sarah had organised her funeral and also the wake so had directed a seventies tribute band to play upbeat dance music and as Rachel entered the pub she could hear 'Dancing Queen' playing followed by 'Le Freak' by Chic.

Tom went to get Rachel a large G & T and a pint of Tribute for himself, turning to Poppy he asked "What would you like?"

"Same as Mum please."

"Really? You were dying two hours ago." He gave her a surprised look.

"Yes Dad, really! I'm a student."

Rachel had grabbed them all a pasty and made her way to where the rest of the swimmers were seated or standing, dancing and swaying to the music. It was a good party, one that did Sarah justice and many felt she would have liked to have been a part of herself. Many of the group were still chuckling and replaying some of Sarah's exploits as they toasted her.

After a couple of hours some people had started to drift away from the wake but one of the swimmers, Angela, because she had had too much to drink and never being one to avoid the limelight, declared "Wouldn't it be a fitting end if we all ran across the road, jumped off the wall while fully clothed and into the sea, otherwise we'll miss our swim today. The tide is in and it's calm out there. It'll be a laugh. C'mon Alice? Liz?"

Before anyone could say no, Angela stood up, dragging Alice and Liz, who had also drunk plenty of gin or wine, out of their seats and pushed them towards the pub door. Alice always followed what Angela did and Liz was always up for something fun. Rachel followed them, pursued by Tom with his mobile phone camera ready to record. Slowly everyone else followed, a couple of them moaning they didn't have their swimming costumes or goggles. Angela had grabbed a bunch of funeral flowers from the pub on the way out, kicked off her heels and climbed onto the sea wall. She threw the flowers onto the water and as they drifted away, she shrieked "To Sarah" and launched herself into the air. Alice, Liz and Rachel followed screaming as they hit the cold water. Everyone else just watched to start with, then phones, handbags and shoes were thrown down onto a pile of discarded coats and one by one the rest followed, laughing and shouting at each other while Tom, Poppy and a few other funeral goers, recorded the shenanigans. After several minutes they made their way back to the shore where, freezing cold and soaking wet, Sarah's friends shivered and giggled before making their way home.

Rachel stripped off in the car, sitting on her pink hoody and wrapping Tom's jacket around her. She and Tom talked animatedly as they drove home about the day, the funeral, the impromptu swim, the funny exploits that Sarah had recorded of her life, some of which Rachel knew about but many she didn't. They were alone as Poppy had met up with her friends.

"You jump in the shower while I stick the kettle on." Tom said as he parked the car on the drive.

The post had arrived while they'd been out and Tom picked the envelopes up from the mat as he'd opened the front door. Amongst the usual bills and mailshots to take out car insurance or change their broadband provider was an official looking envelope addressed to Rachel.

Rubbing her hair with a towel and dressed in her dressing gown Rachel came downstairs to the kitchen to a steaming mug of tea sat on the dining room table. Tom sat cupping his mug and taking sips while Rachel sat and opened the envelope. It was from Martins and Baker, a local solicitors' firm, concerning the estate of Sarah Rosehill and inviting Rachel to a meeting tomorrow afternoon at their office in Porthlowen.

"Wonder what that's about? Rachel pondered.

"She's probably telling you she's left all her money to a cats' home." Tom replied smiling.

"Doubt it. She's allergic to cats. Um. Was allergic I should say. Can't believe she's not here anymore." Rachel's face saddened.

"Can you go tomorrow?" Tom asked softly. "Haven't you got an appointment tomorrow or is that the following day?"

"I've got a hair appointment tomorrow afternoon but I'll rearrange it if needed. It's not urgent. Pass me my phone a minute and I'll quickly ring them."

Rachel didn't sleep well that night. She was hot, then cold. She woke around 2am with thoughts whizzing around her head. Why had she been summoned to the solicitors? What did Sarah want her for? She tiptoed into the bathroom then softly downstairs so as not to wake Tom and sipped a glass of water. She sat at the kitchen table drinking the water, gazing at the solicitors' letter again then flicked through some Facebook photos on her phone. She made her way back upstairs and climbed into bed beside Tom.

"Alright?" he murmured drowsily putting a warm arm around her.

"Mmm" she replied non-committedly and dozed fitfully while Sarah, Liberty and the Ls drifted in and out of her dreaming mind.

"You look like shit!" Tom announced when Rachel made her way downstairs the following morning.

"Thanks. Love you too. Bastard! Didn't sleep well last night and I've got a banging headache." She slumped into her chair and grabbed the solicitors' letter again. "This has been going around in my head all night." She said waggling the letter.

Tom placed a mug of coffee in front of her with a couple of paracetamol and a banana. "Breakfast is served." He gave her shoulder an affectionate squeeze. "I'd come with you if I could but I'm not invited and I'm on my way to work in a minute." Tom was a GP who worked at a local surgery in Porthlowen.

"Don't worry. I'll be fine, I'm sure once this coffee gets working and the paracetamol kick in it'll be ok. I'll jump in the shower in a minute, make myself more human and get to work on sorting this house out. Looks like a bomb has dropped. I'll go and see what this solicitor's letter is all about this afternoon and then I'll see who's about for a swim afterwards. The tides look ok and I'll think I'll need it later to clear my head. I'll fill you in on all the details when I get home."

"Ok I'll see you tonight." He kissed her head and made his way to work.

Rachel pulled some fish out of the freezer and placed it on the draining board to defrost for tea tonight while she stuck a couple of pieces of bacon under the grill, put some bread in the toaster and fished the ketchup out of the fridge. While eating, she put a note up on the Ls Facebook page saying she could swim down behind the Lido at around 5pm if anyone else was around. She finished her breakfast, sank the last of the coffee and made her way back upstairs to shower and get ready to make a start on the housework.

Liberty 1915 - 1924

Liberty had been born with mild Polio in 1915. Her left leg turned in slightly, was painful along with her back and hips, and slowed her down with a noticeable limp. Running around or playing with other children was difficult. With an elderly and strict governess, Miss Scrivener, and her father Sir Frederick Nancarrow engrossed in his work, Liberty was a loner in her younger years, especially after her mother Nancy had become ill and then died, of a weak heart, she'd been told. Liberty was only three years old when Nancy became ill and then just five when she was left without her mother. Nancy had been warned against having more children after having lost three babies during pregnancy but she wanted to present her husband with an heir to his land and fortune. So, Liberty was a rich but lonely, only child. Her bad leg caused her father to want to protect her and she was always told that she was a delicate child so rarely went out but if she did it was always wrapped up and taken in a horse drawn carriage.

Major Sir Frederick Nancarrow had inherited his house and estate from his father, Sir William, a bull of a man who, with a mixture of hard work, luck and an instinctive eye for an opportunity matched with an aggressive go getting style, had built up a huge business empire across a range of enterprises including mining, banking, shipping and fishing. Sir William had bought the land around the sea front of Porthlowen which encompassed a rich vein of tin, mined the land, reaped the rewards and built the impressive family home overlooking the bay while expanding the port too. Son Frederick had learned from one of the best and had, early on in his life, showed a natural flair for business, making important decisions in expanding the family empire with the purchase of two failing mines and making a success of them. As his father, Liberty's grandfather, started to age and have failing health he was assured that the family fortune was in safe hands before he died. When the resident Conservative Member of Parliament died, Frederick, as the largest local landowner, was approached and approved as a prospective parliamentary candidate. This was endorsed by a narrow victory in a by-election and then consolidated by the General Election in 1924. As a result, Frederick was often away on Parliamentary business and had to leave much of his local businesses in the hands of managers. However, the business was robust and managed to maintain profits despite national and international pressures.

Liberty took lessons and slow walks in the warm summer months around the spacious gardens with Miss Scrivener, her elderly governess, who had also taught Frederick's sister Maud, Liberty's aunt. Frederick had been sent to boarding school in Plymouth until the age of eleven when he then completed his education at Eton in Windsor. Maud had married an American merchant shipping tycoon then moved to the States but on a journey to Europe their ship was sunk by a U boat in 1917 and neither survived. Miss Scrivener was known to Frederick and when Nancy had died, and Liberty was five, her father sought out Miss Scrivener to manage the staff in his house and to educate Liberty into becoming a Lady. Miss Scrivener was a no-nonsense staunch Victorian who believed in hard work, virtue, politeness, duty, dignity, restraint and religion. A lot of her values were firmly entrenched in the nineteenth century and she struggled with many of the modern concepts of the roaring twenties. She disapproved of the antics of some of the younger staff, the frivolity and chatter, the fashion and the music. However, she was a competent, if somewhat stuffy, tutor and Frederick Nancarrow was satisfied that the day to day management of both his mansion and his daughter was in safe hands.

Much of Liberty's younger years were spent inside the house and only occasionally outside, apart from her twice a week visit to church, Sunday morning and evening. Once she was around nine or ten and she had time away from her governess she started to explore her local world.

"Don't go too far. You're too delicate." Miss Scrivener had warned her, and Liberty, being an obedient child, and not wanting to upset her governess or her father had limited her excursions outside but her curiosity was piqued. She went into the walled kitchen garden where she met the head gardener Mr Rowe, a kindly man in his late fifties with a brown wrinkled face, permanently dirty hands and greying hair. He stood up as she came closer and brushed the dirt off his hands.

"Hello Miss Liberty. Come to visit us, have you? Your father liked to come into this garden when he was a boy."

Liberty liked him immediately and she beamed at him. He smiled too and chuckled. "Now let's show you around." He walked slowly around the garden pointing out flowers, fruit and vegetables. Even a few birds. He made her repeat the names of some of the more unfamiliar items. "Make sure you remember the names and I'll ask you next time I see you. Now I must get on with some work or I'll be told off by your Miss Scrivener!" He winked at her and gave her a large red juicy apple.

The next couple of days were wet, cold and windy. Liberty could see the waves crashing out in the bay from the windows of the house which rattled in the strong wind. However, she'd tried to remember some of the flowers and plants in the garden. Miss Scrivener had encouraged Liberty's interest and had obtained permission from Frederick to use his copies of The Encyclopaedia Britannica in their studies. Liberty found the huge books fascinating and looked at all sorts of things. She leaned that the plants and animals all had Latin names as well as their English equivalent.

The next day was sunnier and dry, so once she'd finished her studies with Miss Scrivener, she went out into the garden again to find Mr Rowe. He was supervising a younger man weeding around the flower beds.

"Good morning Miss Liberty. This is Benjamin." He gestured to the young man who stood up and stopped his weeding. "C'mon Benjamin. Doff your cap. Don't you know a Lady when you see one?"

"Sorry Mr Rowe. Sorry Miss Liberty. Please don't tell your father." He spoke in a rush and blushed fiercely. He took off his cap and nodded his head.

Liberty realised that he was probably about fifteen or sixteen and she felt a little guilty. She nodded her head, smiled at him and dropped a small curtsy.

Mr Rowe smiled at her and sent Benjamin back to his weeding. "Now Miss Liberty let's see if you can remember what I told you last time."

Liberty named most of the plants and with prompting remembered some of the others. Some she'd completely forgotten. Mr Rowe introduced her to a few more plants and was delighted when she said that she'd been looking them up in The Encyclopaedia and learning their Latin names as well as their English ones. "I'm afraid I can't help you with the Latin names but maybe you can tell me them and I'll see if I can remember them although my memory isn't as good as it used to be."

Throughout that year Liberty ventured out into the grounds of her Father's estate when the weather was good and she learned all about the flowers, plants and fruit in the walled kitchen garden. There were so many other flowers, shrubs, bushes and trees to learn about around the estate too. Mr Rowe continued her education and she realised how knowledgeable he was about so many things and he delighted in having a willing, keen and intelligent pupil. However, that didn't stretch to his learning Latin but they agreed in the end that that wouldn't stop Liberty's natural history education. As well as outside she often saw Mr Rowe in the kitchen bringing in baskets or handfuls of fruit and vegetables and talking to Cook, Mrs Hitchens. Sometimes some flowers too, which then appeared around the house in attractive displays.

Benjamin always doffed his cap when he saw her and she always curtseyed to him and smiled but he was always too shy to say very much to her.

Liberty's exploration of her Father's grounds had also included the stables. When she was little, she'd always liked the shiny black horses that pulled the carriage when she went out anywhere. Elegant beasts, they'd always looked fantastic but they scared her, they were so big. Her Father occasionally rode a huge hunter but had fallen off once in front of Liberty when she was about six or seven. The hunter had reared up when a sudden gust of wind lifted the petticoats on Liberty's dress. There had been a lot of shouting and people fussing around. The horse had bolted into the woods, chased by one of the grooms. Her Father had been hurt and lay on the ground for a few moments before he was helped up by another one of the men. Liberty had been bustled inside roughly by one of the maids and put into her bedroom and told to stay there. She'd been frightened by the whole affair and had stayed well clear of horses from then on. She'd always thought it was her fault as it was her dress that the horse had reacted to, especially as her Father had been hurt. It wasn't long after, that the first Motor Car had appeared. It was her Father's pride and joy, a shiny black Bentley.

That had been four or five years ago and now she was older and her confidence in discovering things had increased so she decided to walk across to the stables. She could see the horses' heads looking at her over the tops of their stables as she approached and she counted six black heads. One suddenly whinnied loudly and she jumped. Her fears from when she was little resurfaced and she turned to run away.

"Don't be frightened Miss." A man's voice said. "They're only talking to each other. Just like us they are really."

Liberty realised that on the side of one of the stables a man had been standing in the shadows watching her approach. She recognised him as Tommy, a tall and strong looking man of around thirty. He often took the reins on the horse carriage when she went out with Miss Scrivener. He held hers and Miss Scrivener's hands when they got into or alighted from the carriage to assist them. Tommy emerged from the side of the stables, twisting his shoe on something on the ground and blowing a plume of smoke from his mouth. Liberty had been aware that Miss Scrivener and Tommy didn't like each other but she didn't really know why.

"If you come here, I'll show you the horses if you like." He approached her and she could smell smoke on him. She didn't like the smell and she turned and ran away. She could hear him laughing at her.

Solicitors

The sky was clear and the late afternoon sun still had some warmth in it, the day after Sarah's funeral, as Rachel hoisted her swimming rucksack onto her back. She shivered, as usual, after swimming as she made her way back to the car, parked in between the Lido, the Ship Inn and the church. The chill of the sea water initially had made her gasp and her friend, and fellow swimmer, Alice, had joked that her language was bad today. The cold water gave Rachel an "ice cream head" to start with until after a couple of minutes the two of them were able to swim properly. They swam hard through the clear blue water across the bay until, panting, they paused at a marker buoy two hundred metres from the back of the Lido.

"Oh, I needed this today." exclaimed Rachel. "Needed to clear my head and relax."

"We gave her a good send off yesterday." Alice replied.

"Yeah, we did. She would have liked to have been there."

"You were quite close, weren't you?"

"Yes, she was my Granny's best friend so I knew her throughout most of my life. I could always talk to her for advice or just to chat. She was just kind of …….. always there. She quite often came out when it was Granny's birthday or she'd be there when I called in to see my Granny. They were good for each other. They laughed a lot, ate cake, drank wine and laughed even more. Sometimes they just got the giggles, looked at each other and burst out laughing. It was infectious."

"I remember." Alice paused and smiled in reminiscence.

"C'mon I'm getting cold. Let's swim back." said Alice.

Dripping wet they changed quickly. "Gotta run. I'll see you tomorrow?" Alice asked, hugging Rachel.

"Yeah, probably. Thanks for the company. I'll see you."

Rachel looked out over the bay, the calm sea and gentle waves brushing quietly against the rocks. A few seagulls soared overhead squawking at each other while others bobbed up and down. On a rocky outcrop a couple of cormorants stretched and flapped their wings. Rachel thought she saw a seal popping it's head up but then it disappeared again so couldn't be sure. She took a deep breath and breathed in the cool salty air thinking about her appointment at the solicitors. After her swim she felt a bit calmer after the bombshell that had landed in her lap a couple of hours earlier.

She'd arrived a few minutes late at the imposing offices of Martins and Baker after being stuck behind a school bus then struggling to find a parking space in the small town centre of Porthlowen. Rushing to the parking meter she'd fumbled to find the change that she'd needed then promptly dropped her purse. Bending down, her hair had come out of its clip. Flustered, she arrived at the solicitors, tucking her hair behind her ears and rushing through the door. Doris Martins, the plump long haired secretary hadn't looked impressed, pulled her 1980s glasses down her too long nose and peered over the top of them at Rachel, making a point of looking at her watch.

Doris picked up the phone, pushed the intercom button and announced "Mr Baker? Mrs Roberts is here."

Rachel mumbled an apology and left Doris tucking into a packet of biscuits as she made her way up the stairs to the solicitor's office, thinking it was about time that Doris was put out to graze. With her portly figure and long blond hair, she certainly had a Muppet-esque look about her. Rachel suppressed a smile at the thought.

Tony Baker, one of the Ls, had originally set up the solicitors' office along with his lifelong friend Bill Martins. Doris had been their secretary for years and married Bill after her first husband had died of a stroke five or six years ago, "Probably to get some peace and quiet!" Sarah Rosehill had wickedly said, when it was being discussed down in the Lido one day a couple of summers ago. Bill himself had died a couple of years before, possibly for the same reason, and now Doris considered the solicitors as her own personal fiefdom. After Bill had gone Tony had decided the time had come to retire, to spend more time with his wife, and he'd taken up the wild water swimming as a way of keeping fit and socialising. Rachel liked Tony, the elder statesman of the Ls. He was always friendly and polite, would always talk to her and the others. Quick to smile and laugh, Tony was a popular member of the swimming group. He was often found talking to the other men about rugby, football, cricket and other sport.

It was a shame, Rachel thought, that it wasn't Tony she was being summoned to meet. However, it was his obnoxious son, Joseph, who was a few years older than Rachel and had been at school with her husband Tom.

Tom's opinion of Joseph, never Joe, was quite simple. "He was a knob at school and he's still a knob." His opinion of James, Joseph's elder twin, was quite different. "Good bloke."

Rachel knocked and opened the door of the office. Joseph had a haughty, overbearing manner, was bald and overweight. "Probably being fed too many biscuits by Miss Piggy downstairs." thought Rachel as she took the chair indicated by him, taking in the surrounding room as she sat in an old but adequately comfy seat.

"Thank you for joining us." he said in a tired and bored voice, as if he had much more important things to do.

Rachel had never been in this office before and she looked around as she took her seat. The office was simply decorated in an old fashioned style and comprised of a single large and imposing desk with paperwork, a desktop monitor and keyboard. Joseph took his place behind the desk and squeezed his portly frame into a rotating chair. A few nondescript pictures ordained the walls, mainly of local views. Ancient dark wooden shelves ran down one side of the room filled with books, probably legal stuff, thought Rachel. The carpet was a plain royal blue although slightly faded in places where the sunlight would come in, on bright and sunny days, through two tall single glazed sash windows on the opposite side of the room to the book shelves. Several grey metallic filing cabinets were behind the door. The ceiling and walls were white although evidence of the building's age showed in a slight damp patch high up in one corner.

"Us" comprised Joseph, behind his desk, and a couple that Rachel guessed were a few years older than her. They looked vaguely familiar and Rachel recognised them as being at the front of the church at the funeral.

"Malcolm Hudson and his wife Stella." Joseph introduced them with a flourish of his hand. "Malcolm is Sarah Rosehill's nephew."

Rachel knew of Sarah's family but if she'd met them before then she couldn't remember. Sarah had one sister several years younger than her, Beryl, but they'd never really had much to do with each other after the death of their own father, Arthur, back in the 1970s. Beryl made her life in Scarborough with her career minded estate agent husband Graham and their three children, Malcolm, Trevor and Julie. Sarah knew that Beryl had died after a stroke five or six years ago while Graham was in a nursing home with severe dementia, the weekly fees eating into any inheritance that Malcolm and his siblings may have expected.

"Hello." Rachel warmly smiled at Malcolm and Stella, shaking their hands.

Malcolm responded with a nod and a smile while Stella looked Rachel up and down with a look on her face that smacked of wasp swallowing. Malcolm was casually dressed in a work type shirt open at the neck, a jacket, jeans and lace up black shoes. Rachel remembered Sarah telling her that Malcolm had been a partner in the estate agents and continued as sole owner once Graham had retired in his sixties. He had the manner of competence and professional etiquette that his profession demanded. His thinning grey hair was tidy, his pale blue eyes gave him an intelligent look but the broken veins in his nose and saggy cheeks spoke of a liking for alcohol while the heavily lined frown lines showed a man under stress. He was overweight and looked like he needed to get outside and see some sunshine.

Stella had immaculately long blonde and styled hair, too much make up and fashionable clothing that would look better on a woman ten or more years younger. She'd never worked and, Rachel remembered, nagged Malcolm constantly. Whatever Malcolm earned was spent, lavishly, by Stella to maintain her appearance. She had a figure that spoke of lettuce leaf diets, tummy tucks and boob jobs; and a complexion that was maintained by holidays abroad and sunbeds. This lifestyle funding was probably part of Malcolm's stress.

Joseph proceeded to read out Sarah's will. A lot of it was in legalese with lots of "herebys" and "henceforths" but Rachel followed the gist of it.

"I Sarah Rosehill being of sound mind........"

It was relatively straightforward. Sarah didn't have any children and so her small local former fisherman's cottage had been left in equal shares to her sister's nephews and niece, Malcolm, Trevor and Julie. The first surprise was that Rachel was to be a joint executor with Malcolm and Joseph Baker. This had caused a sharp intake of breath from Malcolm and a long slitted eye stare from Stella towards Rachel. Rachel herself was shocked, her stomach did a flip and mentally she asked "Why me?" There was nothing to indicate why she would be asked to be an executor rather than one or other of the other family members. As far as she could tell Malcolm wouldn't diddle his siblings out of their rightful inheritance, Stella might have something to say about it, but Sarah was a wise old bird and Rachel was sure Sarah had her reasons and trusted her to make the right decisions.

The solicitor then "pulled the rabbit out of the hat", looked sternly at Rachel as he read out the final line. 'I hereby leave the contents of all of my bank accounts to ……." He paused for dramatic effect in the same way that presenters do when announcing the winner of a reality TV program….."Rachel Roberts"…… He paused again.

"What!" roared Malcolm, interrupting Joseph as he jumped to his feet, the professional manner discarded in an instant. He turned puce as he yelled "Give me that!" as he tried to lean forward and grab the will, unsuccessfully, from Joseph's hands.

At the same time Stella's blonde coiffured head spun towards Rachel and with vindictiveness hissed. "Bitch. We'll contest it. You've obviously been sucking up to her and persuaded her to change her will. We'll say she clearly had dementia and didn't know what she was signing."

Incredulously Rachel heard the shocking words from Joseph and gasped. Then was staggered by the reactions of Malcolm and Stella. She hadn't asked for this and had no idea that Sarah was going to make her a gift. It now made sense why she had been asked to be a joint executor. Stella wouldn't have let Malcolm give her, Rachel, a penny. It was going to be fun trying to negotiate any joint decisions. Not!

Joseph struggled to make himself heard and maintain order. "Please. Please. Sit down so that I can finish reading the rest of the will." He made calming gestures with his hands which almost made Rachel laugh as it reminded her of the Harry Enfield Scouse character.

"I think you've said quite enough already!" Stella turned her hateful gaze to Joseph.

Malcolm reluctantly sat down with an exaggerated sigh, Joseph cleared his throat and repeated. "I hereby leave the contents of all of my bank accounts to Rachel Roberts." It didn't sound any less of a shock the second time to Rachel but it was only accompanied by a shaking of the head and tutting by Malcolm and another evil stare in her direction by Stella. "I would like Rachel to take my place on the board of trustees of Liberty Lido and £50,000 of the contents of my bank accounts" Joseph continued "are to go to the Liberty Lido trust fund."

Again, he was forced to stop as Malcolm exploded "Fifty thousand pounds!"

Stella's voice rose "To repair that old white elephant?" Her voice was strained. "The old bat has lost her marbles. Have you two got a thing going?" She looked from Rachel to Joseph who stared at each other incredulously. "You've obviously both been buttering her up to be the executors and beneficiaries and taking our money." She turned to face Rachel. "And who, exactly, are you?" She looked Rachel up and down with distain. Rachel tucked her hair behind her ears nervously, feeling suddenly inadequate with her Primani outfit and hastily straightened hair compared to Stella's designer clothes and immaculate blonde locks.

"Well. Um…" Rachel began.

"I can assure you Mrs Hudson." Joseph blustered "that Mrs Rosehill made her will in this office over three years ago. She has been a client here for many years and we have represented her on a number of occasions. There is not the slightest doubt in my mind that she was of sound mind when she made her will."

"Well you would say that wouldn't you." Stella's withering gaze swivelled back to Joseph. "And you haven't denied that you and her……." She gestured towards Rachel leaving the words unspoken.

Rachel found her voice. "How dare you! Sarah was a very dear friend of mine." gaining confidence as she spoke. "And she was my Grandmother Liberty's best friend." The blonde hair swivelled back towards her. "There was nothing wrong with her mind. She was one of the smartest women I knew." Stella tried to interrupt her but Rachel's voice rose with determination and talked over Stella. "Mr Baker and I are happily married to our respective partners and if Sarah has written her will like this then there's a good reason for it. Maybe it's because you can't be trusted!"

"I've never been…" Stella began, an astonished look on her overly made up face.

"Spoken to that way before?" Rachel interrupted, raising her voice. "Well maybe it's about time someone did!"

She grabbed her bag and stormed out of the solicitors, marching down to her car, where she jabbed the keys into the ignition and, wheels spinning, raced out of the car park and sped towards the sea front where she parked up. She sat breathless in her car, tears pouring down her cheeks, gazing out at the sea but unseeing the view as she replayed her meeting in the solicitors over and over in her head until Alice knocked her car window, making Rachel jump and bringing her back to the present.

"Sorry." Rachel mumbled as she stumbled out of her car, wiping her eyes and cheeks with the back of her hands.

Alice handed her a tissue and gave her a hug. "I miss her too." she comforted, mistaking Rachel's tears.

"Thanks. C'mon I need this swim."

After Alice had left and Rachel was left alone with her thoughts, looking out over the bay, shivering but glowing with the after effects of her sea swim her phone buzzed. It was Tom texting her. "I'm just leaving work x."

"Can you pick up an Indian on the way home, I'm knackered x"

"OK. Vindaloo? Lol x"

"Lol. Usual x"

"Laters x"

Rachel drove home with the car heating on max, sorted her swimming bag, stuck two plates in the oven, put the defrosted fish from this morning into the fridge, opened a bottle of wine and was putting cutlery on the table as Tom arrived home. She rushed to him and hugged him hard and started crying again.

Over the meal, in between mouthfuls of curry, sips of wine and pauses for more tears Rachel poured out her emotions and details of the meeting at the solicitors.

Tom listened, interjecting with a "Wow." when Rachel said about the executorship. And an incredulous "What!" when told about the contents of the bank account. And then "How much?" when she told him about the fifty thousand pounds. When she burst into tears again as she recalled the horridness of Stella, Tom gave her a hug and held her tightly.

"Why me? Why have I got to be a trustee of the pool and an executor? And why will I have to deal with that bitch?" she sobbed. "Can you get out the old photos? I want to remember the good times." There were so many photographs and it made Rachel realise how lucky she was to be able to visit and swim in so many beautiful places with so many amazing friends. She selected half a dozen photos that included Liberty and Sarah on different swims and decided that she was going to buy a big frame to hang on her wall and show off the happy memories.

Over the rest of the evening, while looking at old photo albums the two of them discussed the will as well as memories of the Lido, the Ls, Liberty and, of course, Sarah. Eventually, exhausted, Rachel announced that she was going to bed. Tomorrow was Saturday and they had no weekend plans other than maybe a swim or a walk, bit of food shopping and general relaxation.

Rachel didn't sleep well as she replayed the meeting over and over in her mind and eventually at around five o'clock, she crept downstairs, made herself a cup of tea, and curled up on the sofa, with her legs under her and looked at the photos again. Tom found her asleep when he came downstairs later that morning. He carefully placed a blanket over her, removed the open photo album from her lap and quietly exited the lounge, easing the door shut behind him.

Rachel

Rachel was now what her friends called a "lady of leisure" but it was hardly that. There always seemed to be plenty to keep her busy at home. She'd been a primary school teacher for many years and had always enjoyed it immensely until a new head teacher, Mary Wood, arrived. For some reason Mary hadn't taken to Rachel at all. Everyone else at the school seemed to get on with her, or tolerated her. Mary was efficient enough, seemed to get the job done but always seemed to pick Rachel up on anything and everything. When Rachel talked to her work colleagues about Mary no-one else seemed to have a problem. If Rachel went into the staff room the conversation stopped, as if they'd been talking about her. Memos that went around to everyone else didn't seem to reach Rachel and then it made her appear stupid, or forgetful when she acted on the older information. It made her feel depressed and paranoid that maybe she was forgetting things so she'd talked to Tom and Sarah about it and they'd both said that she shouldn't let Mary get to her but Rachel couldn't help it.

Rachel still enjoyed working with the children and the majority of the other staff at the school but there was always the overhanging cloud of Mary. When it started to affect her health, initially she just put it down to the change and aging, now fifty, but as the doubts persisted, she developed aches and pains in all of her muscles, feeling like she had flu all the time, and her asthma became worse. She seemed to pick up every virus, cough and cold going and had to take time off work. Each time she returned to the school she'd had to have a "back to work" interview with Mary who'd always been less than sympathetic, had pointed out how much time she'd been off sick this year and talked about the pressure Rachel was putting on her work colleagues; and of course it wasn't conducive to the pupils' progress to have to keep on having relief teachers.

Rachel had thought it was the stress of the situation at work, bad back, stiff joints, ageing, the menopause and life stress in general. Poppy was also going through her GCSE's and then A levels and she had needed support through her own difficult and challenging times. She'd had a boyfriend, Ben, who was nice enough but he'd put pressure on her to spend time with him, or be on the phone to him, while she should have been doing school work, revising and doing exam assignments. Tom was also having his own crisis as his Dad, Rachel's father in law, recently widowed, was becoming increasingly difficult to handle as he'd developed dementia and was becoming a danger to himself and others, becoming lost, calling emergency services and Tom day and night with hallucinations of people in the house, the roof, the garage, including Tom's deceased mother. As Tom's two single sisters lived in Manchester and Birmingham and Tom's Dad lived just over an hour away from Porthlowen it was always Tom who had to sort out the latest mess.

During the long school summer holidays, the warmer weather had made Rachel's aching body less painful, her asthma was under control and she'd been without a cold for two months so life became much more enjoyable. Poppy had done well in her GCSEs and was working in the Lido café. Tom was at work as usual so Rachel had spent time catching up with friends for a coffee or lunch. On Poppy's days off they'd spent some girly time together and it had been an enjoyable summer. At Sarah's request and persuasion Rachel had joined the Ls for their daily swim around the back of Liberty's Lido. At first, she found the water cold but after a minute or two she acclimatised and really enjoyed the cool, refreshing sea. It was there she met and got to know, then became friends with many of the quirky group of open water swimmers, some of whom had been swimming all year round for many years.

Rachel had always enjoyed swimming and, indeed, had been a strong swimmer and represented her school back in the day but work, married life and bringing up a family had kept her busy. In the summer months she had gone to the beach or the Lido like other families.

She'd quickly learnt that most of the swimmers didn't wear wetsuits and went into the water in just their swimming costumes which they called 'skins'.

"What even in winter?" She'd exclaimed to Sarah the first time they went swimming together. "Just costumes?"

"That's right." Sarah had laughed. "Don't worry. You'll get used to it if you keep on coming throughout the year. We might make a small concession to warmth by having gloves and boots on to stop the extremities losing sensation."

Rachel introduced Tom to the group too and in the evenings and weekends they'd made their way to the Lido to get their dose of "Vitamin Sea." They found that if they didn't go for two or three days, they started to miss the exhilarating "bite" of the cold water, the bouncy waves, the abundant sea life above and below the surface, and the sense of achievement and togetherness of the group.

By the end of that summer it was with mixed feelings that Rachel had returned to the school. She'd relaxed and felt healthy and strong again. By having a break she'd regained some of her sparkle, purpose and determination. She had also obtained a sense of perspective about the Mary situation. She'd been looking forward to seeing her friends on the staff and to see how the children had grown over the summer. "Must be something in the air that makes them grow so much in the summer holidays." She was also looking forward to teaching her new group of pupils who were moving up from the year below. She knew most of them, of course, from the school but was looking forward to the challenges of teaching them this year.

However, on Rachel's first morning back, as she'd been off sick on the last day of summer term, she had to attend another back to work interview with Mary, who immediately made it clear that she'd taken Rachel back under sufferance, wasn't at all sympathetic and found that she was working with a different class, in a different classroom altogether. Immediately Rachel had been tense and after a week her body had gone into spasm again and she could hardly get out of bed. Reluctantly she'd persuaded her own GP to sign her off sick again, on Tom's advice.

"I just can't stand this anymore." She'd complained to Tom that evening as he'd patiently massaged her aching back and limbs. "I feel as if my life is just pain, painkillers and stress."

"You don't have to work, if you don't want to." Tom had replied. "I earn more than enough to support both of us, and put Poppy through Uni."

"Yes, but it's not just the money. It's my feelings of frustrations, letting her win, taking away a job I love, seeing and trying to inspire the children, my pensions, my self-worth, having my own money. It's so fucking unfair. I could smash her face in. Bitch."

She'd spoken to Sarah about the situation on more than one occasion and Sarah had agreed with Tom that Rachel's health was the most important thing. After being off sick for most of the autumn term, to preserve her sanity, reluctantly Rachel handed in her notice so she had started 2018 as unemployed. After various tests at the GPs there was nothing specifically being picked up and Tom, having done some research, concluded that her aches and pains must be polymyalgia.

Over the next couple of unemployed and frustrating cold winter months her health had improved slightly. She still picked up colds and viruses, and her polymyalgia varied on a day to day basis from bad to worse but the one thing that seemed to work was her regular sea swimming. Even though the water temperature varied from about seven to ten degrees throughout January and

February she managed ten or fifteen minutes most days at either Golden Rocks or other coves and beaches nearby. For those freezing moments she was able to forget her problems. It's difficult to concentrate on anything else when you can hardly catch your breath, you're so cold but it was exhilarating, exciting and she felt proud of herself. It cleared her head and it made her feel alive!

And so, a new chapter in Rachel's life began. Tom earned the money and Rachel spent her time investing in her health, looking at her diet, learning about different types of exercise, reading up all sorts of books and articles in order to learn more about living longer and healthier. She still missed working, the routine, the school, her friends there but she was more relaxed, healthier and possibly happier. She turned into a book geek.

Dip

The following day was Saturday and Rachel awoke from the sofa to the sound of the phone ringing. She flung off the blanket that Tom had carefully placed over her and raced to answer the call. She could see that the time on her phone was just gone 8am. It was Joseph Baker.

"Great!" she thought. "On a Saturday too."

"Good morning Mrs Roberts. There are some forms that need signing and we need to start sorting out Mrs Rosehill's estate, set up an executor's bank account, sort out your trustee position for the Lido and so on. Mr Hudson has to return home this weekend for work on Monday and I finish here at one o'clock today. He's arranged to be here at 12.30." His manner left her no choice.

"I'll be there." She promised. "As long as SHE's not there."

"Mrs Hudson you mean? This is a meeting for the executors only so there will just be the three of us. Mr Hudson, you and myself. Most of this, in the future will be by letter, email and phone. Today is just to commence the proceedings."

"OK. I'll see you later."

"Please bring your driving licence and/or your passport for identification purposes."

"No problem." She hung up.

Rachel put the phone down and relayed the message to Tom who had started to make some coffee.

"Shall I come with you?" he asked, setting the cup down on the kitchen table in front of her.

"No. Wish you could but it's the executors only. Just some forms to sign apparently." She took a sip of her hot drink.

"Tide looks good for a swim at Golden Rocks today at eleven if you fancy it? The webcam shows that it looks ok. Probably do you some good after the last couple of days."

"Yes, definitely although I want to come back home, shower, change and do something with my hair before my meeting with Joseph Knob at 12.30."

Tom smiled at her description of his fellow school pupil.

The two of them had breakfast, packed their swimming bags, made a hot flask to warm themselves afterwards and left the house. The sky was azure blue with lots of white fluffy clouds around. The sun was bright with a hint of warmth but they knew that the sea would be cold. It was mid March and the remains of winter were still hanging around, although the yellow avenues of daffodils gave a promise of better things to come. The sea wouldn't start warming up just yet.

Saturday was always the most popular day for the Ls and there was quite often a turnout of twenty or so hardy souls, even during the winter months. Today was no exception. Rachel squeezed into a space between Alice and Flo while they chatted about the funeral with Sally. Tom made his way down to talk to the other men about the England cricket team and the test match in the West Indies. The wind was light and southerly and standing in their multi layers the swimmers were quite warm but soon the air turned blue with profanities as they stripped off and entered the water. Some jumped or dived straight in while others faffed, posed for photos and delayed the inevitable painful entry into the clear blue water.

Rachel was one of the faffers as she could never jump straight in like Tom.

"Shit." She yelled as she dropped into the freezing cold water, her breath taken away as her heart rate soared upwards. "Fuck. It's cold." She bobbed for a couple of minutes acclimatising to the cold water and allowing her breath to slow down a little.

Angela and Alice joined her and posed for a couple of photos before the three of them swam together for five minutes out into the bay towards a marker buoy. The sun shone on the water, giving reflections, while the sea rippled gently giving a silky look to the surface.

"I've got brain freeze." Alice complained.

"Me too." agreed Rachel.

"I haven't put my face in yet." Said Flo who had joined them.

"It's so clear underneath. "Angela commented, emerging from the depths. "Just seen a starfish. What temperature have you got Alice?"

Alice had a waterproof camera that gave the water temperature. "9.2."

"Feels like it." Rachel said. She'd become accustomed to the temperature of the water now and relaxed in it's comforting gentle buoyancy. "Oh, I just needed this today. It's lovely."

They could see Tink and Liz out by the reef, their colourful swimming hats visible in the distance. They'd be in the longest, as always, they never seem to notice the cold. In the opposite direction Mike and Debbie, a couple of the newer swimmers, were together, their orange tow floats behind them as they swam the front crawl to the next buoy. Rachel could see many other coloured swimming hats in all directions. Closer to the shore a couple of the older women were already getting out.

Tom swam over to Rachel's group with Tony Baker, Joseph Knob's Dad. The two of them posed for a couple of photos with the others. Alice was the selfie queen of the swimmers and insisted on getting a photo of herself with the men, while Angela, never one to be outdone, followed suit.

"C'mon Rachel.' Tom said to her. "Come and have your photo taken with me. Then we better swim in."

The swimmers all shivered as they quickly dressed back into their warm clothing and sipped a hot drink. Rachel and Tom bade their goodbyes and scuttled back to the car, turning the heating up to maximum as they drove back home. Nearly thawed Rachel dived into the hot shower while Tom emptied the car and sorted the swimming bags. While Rachel dried her hair, Tom showered and dressed.

"Let's go for a walk after your meeting?" he suggested as Rachel came into the kitchen where he was loading the dishwasher.

"Yeah. Think I'll need it. Can you make up some soup for when I come back home please? You'll find some veg in the fridge. We'll eat, I'll get changed and we can go out for the afternoon." Rachel said as she pulled her boots on, shrugged her arms into her coat, grabbed her bag, phone and keys.

"Ok see you later. Good luck. Don't take any shit from Stella Artwat" He kissed the top of her head and was telling "Alexa" to tune into Talksport as Rachel walked out.

She grinned to herself. Men and sport. What was that all about? She didn't mind really. If he discussed sport with her for too long, she just asked him "Have you seen my latest glitter nail varnish?" He soon got the message that she wasn't interested.

Delicate? 1924 - 1927

Over the next two to three years Liberty found that she had increasing time on her hands as her Father was away more and more, both with business and his parliamentary work. Miss Scrivener, was becoming older and was also tied more to the management of Frederick's household. Liberty's studies continued in the mornings and then in the afternoons she was left to her own devices. She looked forward to these few hours of precious freedom and started to wonder more about the world outside the walls, fences and gateways of the estate. From the easterly facing windows of the dining room she could look down onto the Port and see the lorries and vans coming and going, taking things to and from the many small boats nestled side by side. Larger boats and ships would moor outside the small Port and the smaller boats would ferry supplies to them, before they made their majestic way to other ports near and far. Frederick's office and library also overlooked the Port so that he could glance down from his lofty perch and be aware of trading ships in the harbour. He kept a pair of Carl Zeiss binoculars which he would glance through from time to time if he wanted more detailed information. Sometimes exasperated blasphemous expressions could be heard and then he'd march down to the Port firing orders and dictating instructions to the merchants, warehousemen, drivers, sailors and anyone else unfortunate enough to get into his line of vision.

Liberty had her own set of binoculars which her Father had given her, at her request, on her twelfth birthday and she loved to look down onto the Port and beyond, near and far, the close bustle of the busy port and the distant horizon, with fingers of dark coastline edging into the lighter coloured sea and sky. She'd spend hours looking through them from different vantage points in the house, the dining room, the drawing room, her bedroom and so on. There was always something different to see. The ever-changing weather patterns, the infinite colours of the sky and sea, the constant motion of the waves and tides, and the boats, ships and people who lived and worked around the sea front.

It all fascinated the keen intelligence of young Liberty and she longed to find out about the greater world outside the confines of the house and the grounds of her Father's estate. She was fed up of finding out about life from The Encyclopaedia Britannica, or overhearing some of the staff talk about things going on in Porthlowen, in Cornwall, in England and even sometimes she'd hear about things happening in foreign countries. She wanted to see these things for herself. She asked her Father, on the occasional times when he was home, about going out and finding out about the local area.

"You're too young." He replied tersely, without looking up from his newspaper.

"But I'm twelve years old." She'd complained.

"You'll do as I say." He lowered his newspaper and fixed her with a stern look which left no room for argument.

She tried again a few days later, met with a similar response and then persisted with a further request. Frederick sighed and folded his newspaper, set it down on the breakfast table and motioned for her to sit next to him.

"Please listen to me carefully Liberty." He started in a not unkindly way, looking at her intently. "I don't want to upset you but believe me when I say that you really don't want to know what goes on outside these walls. The world is a rough, dangerous and harsh place and it's not suitable for a young lady like you. Miss Scrivener says that you've been asking questions about the trees, flowers, animals and plants in the gardens, and Mr Rowe asked her if it was alright to teach you about these things. She asked me and I said that it should be encouraged, to satisfy your curiosity and to help with your education. If you think that life is better or more interesting or more exciting out there" he gestured out of the window "then you're wrong. There's a popular song called 'The Grass is always Greener in the Other Fellow's Yard.' It means that sometimes things look better out there but when you get out there you realise that things were actually better back here. Since your mother died I only have you and she would want me to look after you. You're a delicate child and I want to protect you because I love you. So please think about what I've told you. Now I must drive down to the Port and get to work." He put his hand on Liberty's shoulder and gave it an affectionate squeeze before rising from the table and disappearing into his office. She heard the Bentley pull up outside the front door, heard Frederick go out, looked up and watched as Tommy, standing tall and erect, open the passenger door and then shut it with a bang once her Father was sat comfortably. Tommy then walked around to his chauffeur's door, jumped in behind the steering wheel and sped off.

Liberty sat at the table, in silence, for a long time pondering on her Father's words. She understood that he wanted to look after her, and he must know what he was talking about. After all, he went outside to the Port and further afield to places like London. Was he right? He must be. He went out. But then he was a man. A big man and a strong man, not delicate like her. She didn't like being 'delicate'. Was Miss Scrivener delicate? No, she was just old. Very old. She'd been governess to Aunt Maud and Aunt Maud was two or three years older than

Father. Father was quite old, maybe forty. His hair was mostly black but there was some grey just above his ears so he must be really old. So how old would Miss Scrivener be? Maybe fifty five or sixty? That was ancient. Liberty decided she would ask Miss Scrivener later. With her grey hair swept back in a tight bun, pince-nez spectacles, old fashioned long dresses, erect posture, tall and elegant frame, long nose and pursed lips and a walking stick Miss Scrivener was very different to the young maids Daisy and Dorothy. Liberty couldn't imagine Miss Scrivener ever being young like her. She wondered what a twelve year old Miss Scrivener had been like. Had she been delicate then? Liberty imagined that she would just look the same as now but with dark hair and no walking stick. Now Miss Scrivener was just old.

But then so was Mrs Hitchens, the cook. She had grey hair so she must be old too, but not as old as Miss Scrivener. She was plump, had rosy cheeks, always had her sleeves rolled up and always smelt nice, like pastry or cakes. She was kind and always good to Liberty but was she delicate? Liberty knew that Mrs Hitchens was a widow and that her husband, Robert, had died in the Great War. He'd been a young soldier in the Boer War at the turn of the century and had then come to work at Nancarrow House, as a groom. When men were conscripted to military service in 1916, he had no hesitation in joining up to fight for King and Country, along with many men from Porthlowen and the neighbouring villages, including Liberty's own Father, Major Nancarrow. They'd all served in the same regiment, The Duke of Cornwall's Light Infantry, and because of Robert Hitchen's previous military experience he became a corporal on Frederick Nancarrow's recommendation. Unfortunately, he became a casualty in the Battle of the Somme in 1917 while saving Major Nancarrow's life, coming back to drag the wounded Major into a trench but falling victim to a stray shot in the back of the neck just as he pulled the Major to safety. When Frederick returned home injured, he sought out Robert Hitchen's widow, Rosina, to tell her himself how sorry he was that she'd lost her husband and how grateful he was to her husband for saving his life. Seeing that she was struggling financially without her husband he offered her a job immediately in his home as assistant cook where she'd remained ever since, being promoted to Cook, when the previous incumbent had had a disagreement with Miss Scrivener and left under a cloud.

Liberty didn't think that Mrs Hitchens was delicate like her.

So, what about the maids Daisy and Dorothy? Dorothy was a farmer's daughter and had been working at Nancarrow House for five or six years. She was tall, with a large frame, and a round moon face. She was plain with big features and had a slow but deliberate manner about her. She had dark straight hair that fell just onto her collar. Her clothing never looked right, was always creased or a part of her hem had become unstitched. Things got broken when Dorothy was around as her big farm daughter's hands were sometimes clumsy and she easily became flustered, with permanently red and stressed cheeks. People had described some of the things that Dorothy broke as 'delicate' such as a cup or a vase, or even a flower in an arrangement.

Liberty didn't think she was like a cup, vase or flower. And nor was Dorothy. However, Liberty liked her as she was kind and polite to "Miss Liberty" and when she smiled her whole face lit up and transformed her features.

Daisy was short, petite and pretty. Her blonde hair was naturally curly and she always managed to look smart and tidy. She had an infectious laugh and was always giggling, which set Dorothy off too. She would hum and sing songs as she was working and would sometimes grab Dorothy and they would dance together laughing, until Miss Scrivener appeared and gave them a stern look or a telling off.

Liberty would hear Daisy's high pitched voice. "Yes, Miss Scrivener. No Miss Scrivener" after yet another telling off in the corridors or in another room sometimes. She would then hear Daisy's footsteps walk away from Miss Scrivener and then hear her mimic Miss Scrivener's precise, clipped tones. "Daisy, you must do better and pay more attention to your work." Then in her own voice "I told her yes Miss Scrivener, no Miss Scrivener, three bags full Miss Scrivener." Liberty then heard peals of laughter from both Dorothy and Daisy. Liberty laughed to herself. It was funny hearing Daisy mimic Miss Scrivener. Liberty hoped Miss Scrivener never heard Daisy, or she would be dismissed from the household. Liberty liked Daisy even though she called her "Liberty" and not "Miss Liberty."

Liberty, still sat at the dining room table after thinking about what her Father had said, decided to go into his office and look up "Delicate" in the Oxford English Dictionary, the collection of ten books that her Father kept in his office and she had occasionally used with Miss Scrivener's encouragement. She knocked the office door. No answer. She peered around the door and walked quickly to the shelves of dusty books, ran her fingers along them and picked out the book relating to D and E. It was quite heavy but she held the book firmly and pulled it out of its space.

She could hear her Father's voice in her head telling her to bring the book back when she finished with it. She shut his door quietly, the book tucked tightly under her arm.

She made her way to her study where Miss Scrivener was sat primly, upright as always.

"Promptness is a virtue Miss Nancarrow." She began sternly.

"But I was just…" Liberty started.

"Do not interrupt me when I am speaking Miss Nancarrow." Miss Scrivener looked fierce and her pale grey eyes bored into Liberty, who felt like she was about six years old again. "Promptness is a virtue in a Lady. One should be early to arrangements such as ours, as you know full well. I am respecting you by making myself available for your education on time and I expect you to show me the same respect. Now sit down and let us talk about the heavy book that you have in your arms."

"Yes, Miss Scrivener. Sorry Miss Scrivener." She looked away, smiling, as an image of Daisy came into her mind mimicking the elderly governess with her 'three bags full Miss Scrivener.' She daren't let Miss Scrivener see her laughing. She bit her lip and took her seat.

"Why do you have a copy of part of the Oxford English Dictionary under your arm?"

"I would like to look up the meaning of a word Miss Scrivener."

"Shall we do this together Liberty?" Miss Scrivener softened her tone. It really was no hardship teaching a willing pupil such as Liberty. Generally, Liberty conformed, did as she was told, undertook her studies diligently and asked intelligent questions, keen to expand her knowledge, with Miss Scrivener gently guiding and steering her protégé along the road to becoming a Lady, as would befit the daughter of a successful politician and businessman.

Miss Elsie Scrivener was forever grateful to Frederick Nancarrow for offering her a position within his House. After his sister, Maud, had completed her education Miss Scrivener had struggled to find regular employment. She lived at home with her widowed Mother and between the two of them, with careful management of Mrs Scrivener's savings supplemented by a partial governess's salary, they managed to be able to pay the rent, bills and buy food. Miss

Scrivener's life changed dramatically in 1920, shortly after Old Mrs Scrivener shuffled off this mortal coil, when Frederick Nancarrow, her landlord, arrived unannounced one Friday morning at her damp and cold house.

"I need a governess for my daughter Liberty and a live in house manager to look after the staff." He began without preamble naming a salary that was five times higher than that which Miss Scrivener had earned previously. "That's settled then." He was a man used to getting his own way. "I'll send my man to collect you tomorrow morning at nine sharp. Come straight to my office when you arrive and I'll go through your duties, show you your room, the study and introduce you to my daughter and the house staff. Good day to you."

Miss Scrivener was flabbergasted. She sat at her small table not believing her good fortune then chastised herself that she should feel pleased or happy when her poor Mother had only recently passed away. She slept very little that night and was ready to leave an hour before her carriage arrived, all of her belongings in two small bags. The roofed carriage was grand with a smart groom, and two shiny black horses pulling it. The groom had taken her bags for her, and held her hand strongly as he assisted her into the carriage.

Nancarrow House was huge, awe inspiring and a monument to the success of the Nancarrow family. Miss Scrivener had never believed that she would ever live in a house as grand as this one. That had been seven years ago and now Miss Scrivener enjoyed her status as chief housekeeper as well as governess to the child of such a well-regarded man as Sir Frederick. She admired him and was secretly in love with him, despite the fact that he was fifteen or twenty years younger than her. She did the very best that she could for him, hopeful that he'd never remarry, unless he married her, and she'd lose her position within the house and possibly her home too but luckily for her Frederick had thrown himself into his work and more or less left her to her own devices. She'd never regretted a day that she'd spent in the employment of Frederick Nancarrow.

She returned to the pupil in front of her. "What word is it you want to look up Liberty?" she enquired.

"Delicate." Said Liberty. "Everyone says I'm too delicate to do this and that and so I'd been thinking maybe you or Mrs Hitchens were delicate or maybe Dorothy and Daisy but I wasn't sure so I wanted to understand the word." She opened the big heavy book and carefully looked through the pages until she came across the correct place.

Miss Scrivener smiled to herself, glad that Liberty was growing more mature and self- aware enough to try and research things she didn't understand. She wasn't delicate herself but was aware that she was becoming older and needed her stick more and more. She asked Liberty to read out loud.

"Delicate. Very fine in texture or structure; of intricate workmanship or quality. 'a delicate lace shawl'. I'm not a lace shawl and I'm not of 'intricate workmanship'. Am I?"

Miss Scrivener smiled and encouraged Liberty to keep reading. "Easily broken or damaged. Fragile.' No that's not me. "She read on. "Subtly or pleasantly flavoured." She laughed. "Do I taste pleasant? I'm not food so that's not me either. "Sickly. In poor health. I cannot read this word." She pointed to the word 'susceptible'.

Miss Scrivener read it for her and made Liberty repeat it two or three times. "It means likely or liable to."

"Sickly, in poor health, susceptible to illness." She looked dismayed. "That is me. My leg stops me doing things and it hurts. I don't want to be delicate. I want to be able to run around and be strong and go out and not be sickly and sus, sus, sus oh I can't say it." She burst into tears and ran to her bedroom, burying her face in her pillow and cried. Life was so unfair.

Miss Scrivener let her go. Liberty needed to come to terms with her disability in her own time. She replaced the dictionary in Frederick's empty office and started to prepare for tomorrow's lessons and made a list of duties around the house.

Dorothy had been cleaning Frederick's room and came out when she heard Liberty crying. A kindly girl she hugged the child, stroked her hair and made soothing noises. "There there Miss Liberty. C'mon let's go and see Cook and see if she can find something nice for you to eat. If I get upset I always like to try and find a piece of cake or something sweet to eat."

Liberty held Dorothy's hand and meekly followed the huge lumbering housemaid to the kitchen where Mrs Hitchens dried her eyes, made her a cup of tea and found a piece of fruitcake which she placed in front of Liberty. After the sweet hot tea and the taste of the delicious fruit cake Liberty decided to herself that she wasn't going to be "delicate" any more. Enough was enough.

Paperwork

Rachel arrived with five minutes to spare at the solicitors and was there before Malcolm Hudson. Joseph was in the reception area with Doris, offered tea or coffee and took her to his office, gesturing her to a seat. He waved away her apology at her tears and rudeness the other day.

Malcolm and Stella arrived shortly afterwards. Stella striding into the room with purpose and strong perfume.

Rachel's heart sank. "Fucking terrific." she thought.

"Mrs Hudson!" Joseph said agitatedly. "This is a meeting between the three executors!"

"You and her got your story ready?" Stella indicated Rachel while still looking at Joseph.

"That's enough! What you are suggesting is slanderous. You are not permitted to be in here. You may wait downstairs."

"What concerns my husband concerns me too."

Malcolm interjected pleadingly. "Please would you leave us, darling."

"Don't worry. I'm going." She tutted, tossed her blonde hair dramatically and spun 180 degrees on her too high heels. "I've got the message. I'm going shopping if I can find anything to wear in this Godforsaken village. Ring me when you've finished here."

All three of them breathed a sigh of relief as Doris brought in the coffee. Biscuits were on the tray too, Rachel noted. Half a pack for them and probably half a pack downstairs for Doris.

Malcom stiffly shook hands with both Joseph and Rachel, apologising for his wife's outburst. "She's so very upset about Aunt Sarah's passing away. Please forgive her. Stella always looked up to Sarah and they were very close."

That was about as likely as Doris eating a salad, thought Rachel. Sarah had never said anything much about her niece and nephews and most of what she had said had been dismissive and disparaging.

Joseph pompously took charge and opened a file of papers. He briefly went through the will again, handing them copies. "There are two main things we need to deal with today. Setting up a new bank account to administer moneys in and out of the estate. That'll have to be done on Monday. I can get the details emailed across to you both for signing. Hopefully this will be sorted out shortly and the money in Mrs Rosehill's accounts can be distributed to Mrs Roberts including the £50,000 to go the Lido repair fund. Mrs Roberts have you thought about Mrs Rosehill's wish that you take her place on the board of trustees for the Lido?"

"Yes. I'll approach the trustees and find out when the next meeting is to try and get formally elected onto the board. I know Bill Chamberlain is one of the trustees so I'll contact him. I haven't told anyone about the £50,000 yet, apart from Tom, my husband."

"Tom Roberts? The GP? I was friends with him at school."

"Yes. He mentioned it." Replied Rachel, supressing a smile. That wasn't how Tom had described Joseph.

"Secondly, the contents and the property itself are bequeathed to Mr Hudson and his siblings. Do you have any plans for the property yet Mr Hudson?"

"We'll probably sell it. Any idea of its value?"

"We can get a couple of estate agents to give a more accurate figure but I'd guess in the region of £250,000."

"It's a lovely little old fisherman's cottage overlooking the harbour." Rachel interjected. "Probably be a good holiday let, or maybe a first home for a couple, or even a retirement place."

"Do you know the property Mrs Roberts?" Malcolm asked.

"Yes, I've been there many times over the years." Rachel reminisced. "Sarah was my Grandmother Liberty's best friend and when I was young, I used to go there with my Granny. As I got older, in my teens and early twenties, I'd go there on my own when I wanted advice but didn't want to talk to my parents or my Gran. She always kept my secrets. Once Granny died, I still used to go there sometimes." She paused, tears springing to her eyes. "Sorry. I'm going to miss her." She pulled a tissue from her bag, mopped her eyes gently so as not to smudge her makeup and wiped her nose. “Talking about Sarah has brought back memories of my Granny too.”

“Do you know who has the keys to the cottage Mrs Roberts?” Joseph queried, once Rachel had recovered her composure.

“Yes, I have a spare set but other than that I don’t know.” She sniffed, wiped her nose again and replaced the tissues in her bag. I’ll drop them in next week if that’s ok?”

The three of them completed the paperwork and formalities, shook hands and left the building.

Over lunch Rachel filled Tom in on the details of the meeting and he laughed as she did her impressions of Stella, Joseph, Malcolm and Doris.

“I’m Stella Artwat and I need to go shopping for new shoes.” She mimicked Mrs Hudson and tottered on tiptoe around the kitchen, followed by her rendition of blustering Malcolm.

“Well yes darling, of course you can.”

“Finish your soup.” He laughed at her antics.

He smiled and changed subject “Some of the Ls have kicked off on Faceache.”

“What now?”

“Diane and Ziggy have complained about people putting too many silly photos on the Facebook page.”

The swimmers had a closed Facebook group page so that members could have conversations about meeting arrangements, tides, weather conditions and so on. Some of the members uploaded photos of their swims, Tink often posted amazing underwater photos of starfish, urchins, crabs and other sea life. Some of the others also had incredible pictures of sunsets, waves and sometimes even seals. Most of the photos were taken of the swimmers themselves.

“Miserable cows.” Rachel looked at the group photos of today’s swim along with the comments. “They’re all up their own bloody arses.” There was the usual mix of wildlife and weather conditions, groups of swimmers and so on. Alice and Angela had been flashing their bums, sticking their V fingers up in front of themselves and having fun laughing and dancing around. Flo and

Rachel had joined in the dancing while Tom and Tony had clapped their hands. Debbie and Mike had watched smiling while Bill had looked on disapprovingly, Tink turned away tutting and was heard complaining to Sally and Diane about silly selfies. There was photographic evidence of most of this.

Diane had written that she thought that the Ls Facebook page was for information for members and not a platform for self promotion.

Ziggy had agreed and gone onto say that the selfie photos were unnecessary.

"She's not even back here yet. She's still in Germany but still commenting on photos from over there. Look, she's posing with Sally there." She indicated one of the photos. "Bloody hypocrite."

"Ah but it's a sensible photo." Tom said. "That's allowed apparently. And it is a photo from last year!"

"They're just mean girls." replied Rachel "With too much time on their hands and always complaining about something, very bitter keyboard trolls, they never say it to your face. Shame they can't practice Kindfulness."

"I like that." Tom said. "Kindfulness. A good word. Did you just make that up?"

"No. I read it somewhere. But I like it."

"Me too."

Rachel continued to look at the group's comments.

Bill had written in his own inimitable style "Someone could have slipped while dancing and got hurt and that would have meant the emergency services would be called out, wasting their scarce resources unnecessarily." Rachel read out from the Facebook post. Bill had been in the Army, was always quoting the rule book and wanted to do a risk assessment of everything.

"Sally Army more like." Angela had said once when some of the swimmers had been bitching about Bill one day.

Angela had taken offence at the negative comments about the photos and had, allegedly, taken to bed with a migraine. "I'm ill you know." She'd often say before hogging the limelight when the situation suited her.

“They’re like a bunch of bloody old women.” Rachel finished

“Most of them are bloody old women” Tom pointed out.

The two of them finished their lunch and went out for the rest of the day.

Normality

The next couple of weeks after the funeral were normal and Rachel's life went on with Tom at work during the week, swimming most days either at Golden Rocks or at one or two other coves and beaches locally, as well as life's usual chores of shopping, washing, cleaning and never ending paperwork. The weather was its forever changing pattern, some days that hinted of warmer weather to come while other days reminded everyone that winter wasn't quite finished just yet. Rachel had had some contact with Joseph about the will and its contents. The bank was still sorting out the executors account and Joseph was waiting for some correspondence from Malcolm Hudson.

She'd also spoken to Bill about Sarah's request that she, Rachel, take Sarah's place on the board of Trustees for the Lido. Bill, for all of his precision and sergeant major attitude, wasn't a horrible guy and had promised that he'd let her know when the next meeting was. She had no reason to doubt him. Bill had been a big fan of Sarah. She had a way of making you feel the most important person in the room and Bill, a confirmed bachelor, hadn't been immune to her charms. She would bolster his ego and say that his ideas and arguments were good and valid, then suggest another way of doing things which he'd then invariably agree to. Not for the first time Rachel wondered how she was going to fill Sarah's shoes on the Trust committee.

Rachel and Tom's daughter Poppy still had another week to go at Uni before she would break up for the fortnight's Easter holidays. Rachel was looking forward to Poppy coming home again.

"What the mess and the arguments? Tom had said.

"She's not like that at all. "Rachel had countered.

"Mmm." Tom had grinned and raised his eyebrows. "No. It'll be nice. Hopefully she's not working too much while she's here so we can go down to the Lido with her, and maybe take her out one night. I'll have four days off over the long Easter weekend."

"Yes, that'll be nice. I expect she'll want to have a girly day shopping too."

"I better apply to the bank for a second mortgage then." He made a face at Rachel.

"Get out of here. Go and get your swimming stuff ready then come and help me make up some lunch and the drinks."

"Yes boss."

Resolve 1927

As Liberty pulled herself together, she thanked Cook and Dorothy; and made her way to her bedroom where she sat on a window seat and looked out over the gardens of her home and beyond to the sea. Her south facing bedroom faced the sea but in the opposite direction to the port. From her higher vantage point she could look down at the beach with the huge golden coloured rocks, the never ending sky, the tides, the waves, the horizon and the headlands near and far. She could see birds soaring effortlessly or flapping earnestly. Automobiles, vans and lorries drove to and fro, up and down the roads, while cyclists dodged the vehicles; and there were people walking along the promenade.

After her resolve not to be delicate anymore she sat on the window seat quietly contemplating her life; looking out over at the sea, seeing but not really taking in the magnificent views in front of her. The window steamed up as she pressed her face to it, feeling the cool panes against her warm face. As her mind cleared and she relaxed, she wiped the steamy window panes and began to notice what was going on at the sea front. She wanted to look in more detail and needed her binoculars to do so she crept downstairs quietly and checked that Miss Scrivener wasn't going to make her start studying again. Hearing the strict tones of her governess berating poor Dorothy for finger marks on one of the mirrors in the dining room Liberty was safe for the moment. She crept into the study, retrieved her binoculars and quietly made her way back to her bedroom again. She opened her window and breathed in the cool morning air as she held the binoculars carefully and peered out towards the beach and the promenade. She followed the path of a red lorry as it made its way towards Trelyn fishing port and then swung back to a green bus making its way from Trelyn back to towards Porthlowen before turning away from the seafront. Her vision switched to an elegant white seagull as it flapped and soared across the sky, forever searching for food. Liberty dropped her vision to the promenade and could see people down on the sea front, singly or in pairs, nannies or mothers with prams, which Miss Scrivener insisted on calling perambulators, pushing infants along. Very occasionally Liberty had walked along the promenade with Miss Scrivener when she was younger but because of her polio she hadn't been able to walk very far or very fast. Tommy had pushed a large 'perambulator' which Liberty had been able to ride in if her leg became painful or if she was tired. The conversation between Miss Scrivener and Tommy was stilted and so most of the walk or ride was in silence. The rest of the time when she was out of the grounds of Nancarrow House it was nearly always with Miss Scrivener in the horse drawn carriage, again with Tommy tending to the horses.

On the rare times her Father was able to take her out it was in the black Automobile with Tommy driving. Frederick instructed Tommy where he wanted to go, Tommy mumbled an assent. "Very good sir." and they would speed off to their destination, again often in silence as her Father would be contemplating business, or would be reading papers, as they drove to their destination.

Liberty longed to be able to go out on her own, without stuffy Miss Scrivener, without the surly Tommy always in tow, even without her Father. Although she liked and admired Frederick, she was always a bit fearful of him and rarely initiated a conversation with him. If she did then she found he wasn't listening and would grunt non-committedly until she would give up and revert to looking out of the automobile window in silence wondering how this tedium in her life would end. She wanted to see things and places, meet new people and have some friends.

Over the autumn and winter of 1927 Liberty continued her studies but somewhat half-heartedly and couldn't wait until her formal lessons were over so that she could escape to her room and her views over the sea. She'd open her window and breathe in the fresh air. Sometimes it smelt of salt and occasionally she would swear she could even taste the salt on her lips. There she'd look out at the sea and the bay, the promenade and the people on it and make up small stories about them, imagining where they were going and what they were up to, giving them names. The boats and ships too, where they were going and which countries they were visiting.

"There's Miss Angove pushing a pram with baby Mary, she's going to Porthlowen to take the baby back home to its mother Mrs Penberthy. Mrs Penberthy is called Hortense and resembles a horse. Miss Angove is in love with Mr Penberthy and pretends that baby Mary is hers.

That's Michael Pascoe the butcher's son riding his bicycle to work. His father is bald and lazy and makes Michael do all of the hard work. Michael resents his father but knows that he'll inherit the butcher's shop one day so he does as he's told, begrudgingly.

That's fisherman Denzil Dyer on his way to catch fish on his boat "Pretty Polly" named after his daughter who was pretty when she was aged six but is now twenty six and is fat and ugly. The boat should now be called "Portly Polly." There's a fair wind today and lots of pilchards to be caught. Happy fishing Denzil.

There's sailor Samuel Semmens who will go on board the ship called "The Mermaid" and sail to Timbuktu in search of gold and spices and maybe a wife from Africa.

Miss Scrivener would scold her if she found the window open on a cold or windy day. "Good Lord child. You'll catch your death of cold." Daisy and Dorothy would also close the windows when they were cleaning or tidying.

Liberty wrote about things she saw and heard and with her vivid imagination created a fantasy world of people and animals, places and mythical beasts, dragons and mermaids. Sometimes she wrote about herself and a future in which she was safe and strong and well. And certainly not delicate. She would win the 100 metres at the next Olympic games; the first time women would be allowed to run at the Olympics. She would climb Mount Everest, the highest mountain in the world, and beat the men to it. She would captain a ship and sail around the world, gaining the Blue Riband at the same time.

Liberty would take advantage of any day when the weather was dry and especially if the sun was out to go into the grounds of Nancarrow House, making sure she was always wrapped up well. She would make sure that Miss Scrivener was busy with household duties before venturing outside. She'd talk to Mr Rowe in the garden and then she'd walk to the edge of the grounds and look down towards the Port one way and the promenade the other. She carefully stepped outside of the safety and security of Nancarrow House. The first time she took a few steps and then rushed back into the grounds shaking nervously. Getting her breath back she laughed at herself. That wasn't so bad. And she'd been out of the grounds before, either with Miss Scrivener or her Father, occasionally with Tommy and once with Daisy two years ago. She'd survived that. So now she'd survived going outside on her own. She grew braver and ventured further each time but always within sight of the grounds of her home.

Once she saw Tommy in the distance talking to another man, smoking as they both gestured towards the port and the sea. Liberty walked quickly in the opposite direction and back home. Liberty imagined that Tommy was once a fearsome pirate sailing on the seas with a patch over one eye and a long black beard.

Another day while looking down at the children on the rocks she bumped into Daisy, who was breathless and flustered.

"Oh. Hello Liberty. You haven't seen me here. Don't tell Miss Scrivener you've seen me will you!" And she rushed off before Liberty could reply. She'd been too quick for Liberty to ask Daisy not to tell Miss Scrivener either. What had Daisy been up to? Liberty wrote down in her notebook that she had imagined that pretty Daisy had gone to meet a tall dark handsome stranger she named Percival Pascoe, a man with good prospects as a clerk in a bank. Maybe they would elope and get married at Gretna Green. How romantic.

Polar Bear Ice Challenge

It was a keen wind when everyone met up for their daily swim the following day. Two of the Ls' members were just about to finish their last swim as part of their winter polar bear ice challenge (PB). This was a fun challenge completed between November and March each year. Liz and Tony were only allowed to wear a swimming costume and a special gold coloured 'Polar Bear Challenge' swim hat. No wetsuits, gloves or boots. This year they had gone for the Gold Challenge. This was to swim five thousand metres over five months during the winter season. Most of the others had completed this particular challenge the previous winter. The challenge had been started as a way of encouraging people to swim in the winter all over the world as long as it was cold. Swimming without winter gloves and boots could be hard especially when the temperature of the water dropped below eight degrees. Extremities hurt and go numb when the water is cold and then tingle with pins and needles when they come back to life again. Once the temperatures are down, they don't really come back up again until the weather improves, probably in April each year. The sea temperatures in March could be the coldest of the entire winter. After posing for photos as evidence of their swim, Liz and Tony slowly held onto a rail and walked down the concrete steps to Golden Rocks with the seawater lapping around and nipping at their icy toes.

Every day Liz asked herself the same question "Oh god. Do we have to go through this again?"

Every winter a question in most cold water swimmers' minds is "Am I going to be able to carry on swimming this winter? If you've done it once then you know what it entails. Good times and bad, usually the bad times when it's raining while you're getting dressed and trying to keep everything dry. However, that's always forgotten by the next time, the next day that you swim. Cold water swimming is like a drug where every single sense in your body is singing and your sight, smell, taste and sound goes into overdrive. Liz knows she's going to be feeling really alive later and that's what drives her every day to swim. She knows that being in the cold water cleanses her mind. No other thoughts can crowd into her mind as she feels the cold water washing over every limb. Today is no exception. Slowly walking down the steps she feels the cold water biting at her feet. Gradually, the feeling spreads up her legs and past her knees. For some reason that Liz has never understood she never feels the cold as much in her legs but the agony is far worse as the cold water reaches her stomach and always the last bit of getting your shoulders under the surface is hell. That last minute of faffing before ducking into the biting cold is hard.

Today it's exceptionally cold and she can feel the salty water stinging her arms and legs. Slowly she starts to swim. She knows to take it easy for the first few strokes as she starts to swim further away from the rocks, keeping her breathing slow and steady and not allowing the cold water shock to attack her body after peeling off the warming layers of her clothes. Now as her body feels more acclimatised and her breathing becomes easier, she feels ready to put her face in. It's so cold it is like a slap in the face but Liz is happy as she knows that this temporary feeling won't last but the energised euphoric feeling will linger all day, a short term pain for a long term gain. Liz knows this is the coldest time of the year but soon the warmer days will start to heat up the sea.

"Catch me up!" shouts Tony. Never one to mess around on the edge Tony is a swimmer who finds it easier to just get straight in, his bright orange tow float stretched out behind him like an umbilical cord keeping him tethered to the shore. "I'm going out to the second swimmers' buoy and back."

In the distance is an orange painted buoy in a matching colour to his float. He treads water waiting for Liz to catch him up, her bright pink tow float following behind her. She fished out her camera from inside her costume where it's securely attached to the straps with a nylon cat collar. Trying to take a photo she finds that the camera has turned itself off while swimming. Trying to get her fingers moving so that they regain their grip she turns the camera back on and bobbing in the water she accomplishes a selfie with Tony and herself. Carrying on their swim to the next buoy they swim faster to keep warm but steadily enough to make the distance back comfortably. They have swum this route so many times their bodies take over on autopilot leaving their minds free to clear. Stopping for one final photo they giggle as they try to lift both feet and hands out of the water to prove they've not worn boots or gloves. Tony always finds this particularly difficult as his head always gets submerged. Maybe he's not so buoyant as Liz.

Back at the steps and climbing out of the numbing water Liz feels like her blood has frozen in her veins. She's carefully left her robe and clothes in a certain order ready to get dressed as quickly as she can. Her skin is rough with goose bumps and she knows the cold is an efficient thief of body heat; and Old Man Winter's presence is causing pain in her muscles. On land Liz's daily struggles are apparent. She wears a supporting knee brace and several scars adorn her body, each with their own story from operations to accidents. However, in the water the cold relieves some of the pain and clears her head, making her feel more alive. Liz has an order of getting dressed. Firstly, she puts her blue towelling robe over her head and removes her costume. As quickly as she can she adds items of clothing, her favourite part is pulling on her soft pink onesie which she feels is like a big warm hug. Pulling on her black snow boots she knows she's nearly there. Her contrasting pink swimmers' hoodie is another layer of warmth. Finally, she reaches down for her thick heavy coat, the fluffy pink lining rubs against her face and the tough exterior of the coat is an instant windbreak. Pulling out a pink stripy woollen hat from her pocket she puts it on before reaching for her pink thermal flask full of steaming hot ginger tea. Taking a sip, she can feel the warmth running down her oesophagus and heating up her body from the inside out. She completes her dressing by pulling up the huge hood of her coat over her woollen hat.

Calling out to Tony "We did it! We've completed our Polar Bear Challenge." She walked towards him and gave him a big hug. Several of the other members of the Ls also come over to congratulate them. "I'll post the photos up on the Polar Bear Group page later on."

"Thank you, Liz. You've been a great swimming companion."

"Yes, thank you too Tony. You've been a great support, especially on the days when I really didn't think I could get in. Right I need to go. I'm feeling cold and I need to attend to all of the children at home."

"What children?" Tony asked looking puzzled. "I thought they'd all grown up."

"You know Tony. The spiders, the iguana and my dogs."

Tony gave her a knowing look.

"Heeeelloo Swimmers!!!" boomed a German accent. Everyone turned to look as they realised Ziggy had arrived for the summer. Ziggy owned a small fisherman's cottage along from the Lido overlooking the sea and always spent late March to October every year here after buying the cottage twenty years ago. Her place was in the same terrace as Sarah's cottage and the two of them had become friends. Sarah had been to stay with Ziggy in Germany a couple of times, that Rachel knew of. Standing at six feet tall and aged sixty three she gave everyone a hug. She was carrying a huge bag and everyone knew it would be filled with edible German treats that she would bring back every year to hand out to everyone after their swim.

Liz gave her a quick hug, explaining that she and Tony had just completed their PB challenge. The two of them disappeared while the others chatted to Ziggy, filled her in on the latest news and gossip and devoured her delicious treats.

Nature 1928

When Liberty reached the age of thirteen in the Spring of 1928, the weather was starting to warm up, the flowers bursting bloom in the grounds of her home, the trees were becoming greener by the day, replacing the bare branches of two months ago. Blue skies and warm sunshine gave a promise of better things to come and Liberty was by now an expert in sneaking outside of the grounds. Father was rarely home and Miss Scrivener was required to manage the house more and more giving Liberty increased free time. Liberty had now ventured down to the edge of the promenade and the beach and rocks. She loved to look closely at the ever changing colours and patterns of sea and sky, the high tides bringing waves close to the shore and then a few hours later the low tides exposing the rocks which were hidden earlier in the day. Every day was different yet there was also a regularity and familiarity to it all. Liberty knew that the tides affected a lot of things in this area, her Father had talked about the tides sometimes when she'd overheard conversations; and she knew that sometimes boats and ships couldn't sail because of the wrong tides or they were too low, and they'd have to wait until the weather improved or the tide was higher.

As her familiarity of the promenade improved, she started to see the same people using the facility to walk formally in their best clothes and then she'd see the same people in their working clothes. There were a lot of miners and fisherman walking, sometimes with women and children, to and from work.

Most of all she noticed the children, some older and some younger than her. They all seemed to have friends, brothers and sisters. Liberty longed to have had a brother or a sister or maybe both. A tall strong elder brother who would take over the family business, the Nancarrow Empire, after Frederick became old and then died. A pretty younger sister that she could play with toys and dolls; and write stores together, share secrets and take lessons with Miss Scrivener.

She would also have liked some friends to play with. She was envious of the easy friendship that the children seemed to have. The way they interacted and talked incessantly, and laughed and chased each other. Boys and girls together. She watched as they came down to the water's front to wash and bathe, their mothers barking instructions at them and smacking some of them. Then the children would cry but then a few minutes later they'd be laughing again as they chased a friend. They were filthy when they arrived, dirty from the mines, or from helping the fisherman down on the beaches where the boats landed.

They'd shriek when they entered the water. Some would ease in gently, shivering on the side as they stood ankle deep in the cold water while others would run and jump or dive into the oncoming waves. Liberty was surprised how young some of the children were when they walked alone or perhaps with an older sibling. She wasn't allowed out on her own and she was thirteen but some of these children seemed to only be five or six years old. Liberty was fascinated at the scenes before her, as it seemed in contrast to Miss Scrivener's comments, made as they walked along the promenade or rode past the families and viewed them from the lofty perch of the horse drawn carriage.

"Don't go near them. You might catch something, especially as you are so delicate."

That word again. It seemed to echo in Liberty's mind and reinforced her determined decision to become strong and robust. The younger children were able to run and walk and swim so why couldn't she?

Spring gave way to early summer and Liberty became more confident about going out of the grounds of Nancarrow House. Endless long hot days with azure blue sky, white fluffy clouds and golden sunshine. It seemed to illuminate everything and define everything in far more detail. Was this just Liberty growing up and becoming more aware of her surroundings or was there genuinely a difference in the air? Life seemed to flourish in the grounds of her home, the trees were so full of greenery, the flowers and plants in Mr Rowe's garden were full of colour, scent and insects indefatigably going about their business. As soon as she could Liberty would get outside into the gardens. She loved the daylight when she woke up and opened her bedroom windows wide to look out on the scenes near and far, rejoicing in the cool early morning fresh air, looking out onto the still or rippling sea, far out to boats and ships in the bay or on the horizon. She'd dress and make her way downstairs, through the kitchen, grabbing a piece of bread or fruit from Mrs Hitchens' worktops and out into the yard, through the garden and then find a quiet warm place on the eastern side of the House in the sun to hungrily devour her snack. She'd sit on a garden seat and look at the plants in front of her, feel the warming sun on her upturned face, closing her eyes and sniffing the sweet scents before her. She'd listen to the different bird songs, the chirping of the sparrows chattering to each other, pigeons cooing in the trees, buzzards crying, gulls mewing. She loved to watch the acrobatics of the swallows and house martins as they swooped after insects high in the sky then dive dramatically towards the eves of the House where they'd made their nests to feed their ever hungry broods. Sometimes she'd just stay there quietly, other times she'd walk through the woods or gardens but always looking at the splendour in front of her eyes.

All too soon it was time to return to the confines of the House and Miss Scrivener. Liberty would eat her breakfast then make herself ready for her governess' lessons. As soon as lessons had finished Liberty would go outside again while Miss Scrivener busied herself with chief housekeeper duties. The heatwave was getting to the household staff. It seemed that nowhere in the house was cool. The kitchens were always warm, even in the dead of winter and now Mrs Hitchens normally rosy cheeks were red with the heat. She was short tempered and always cross with Daisy and Dorothy. Dorothy also struggled with the heat while Daisy, as always, looked effortlessly cool. Miss Scrivener, insisting on continually wearing her starchy Victorian long dresses, gloves, hat and coats struggled the most and had to retire to her rooms most afternoons with the curtains drawn suffering with debilitating headaches.

Birthday

As was tradition the Ls would go out for the day when it was someone's birthday. The birthday person would always choose the location and this always varied depending on the time of the year. Today it was Alice's birthday and she had chosen to go to one of the most spectacular North coast beaches in Cornwall. Alice was Mum to her own two children and also Step Mum to her husband's two but now they were all grown up and living away. She had met her husband when she had started to work as a secretary for him at his successful estate agents. He handled sales and purchases for the rich and famous when they were looking for private secluded second homes in Cornwall. When he sold up and retired Alice had also stopped working. Her pride and joy now was her chocolate coloured Chihuahua called Coco that she liked to dress up. Coco had a wardrobe that was every girl's envy. Bling, diamante and glitter featured heavily.

Some of the group swam here on the North Coast in winter when the south coast was being battered by storms as it represented a small haven. It would always cause controversy and divided the group as some of the swimmers would choose not to swim at all when it was stormy, stating "We're loyal to the rocks."

However, those that really wanted to swim loved Parventon Bay beach and had nicknamed it "Parbados" as it looked positively tropical when the skies were bright blue and the sun was reflected on the shimmering turquoise ocean, even in the depths of winter on those cold clear frosty mornings when you have dragon breath when you exhale.

Meeting up in their unofficial "Swimmers' changing room" the group of ten or eleven had to walk past the glass fronted beach café, down the wooden sandy steps and towards the area that they used to change in, which was underneath the outdoor decked area for the café.

Dumping their heavy rucksacks on the wooden picnic tables everyone was wishing Alice "Happy birthday." But she was far more interested in the couple sitting on "their" picnic tables. She had a look on her face that translated to "This is our changing room." Poor people. They were only trying to enjoy a quiet coffee.

Liz rooted around in her bag and pulled out a box. Inside was the birthday hat carefully wrapped up in tissue paper. She'd made this hat many years ago from bright coloured felt material to look a bit like a crown. Tradition was that if it was your birthday you wore the hat, then took it home and added something new. It was in danger of becoming too well decorated and she joked that this hat needed retiring and she would make a new one, but she'd come up against lots of swimmers protesting that they couldn't retire the birthday hat. It was every colour of the rainbow and people had added feathers, sequins, shells, flowers and embroidery. It really was very beautiful.

The couple drinking their coffee decided it was time to go. The swimmers tended to take over with their multi coloured robes and rucksacks, now all stripped down to their cossies. As a group they were very loud and had shattered their peace and quiet.

Alice, wearing a new swimsuit decorated with ice lollies, declared "I will be wearing my birthday suit today!"

Angela roared with laughter "Well it has been known." she said winking at Alice. Everyone knew they like to skinny-dip if no one was around and had nearly been caught a few times by unsuspecting walkers.

"Parbados" was a photographer's dream and appeared in many brochures advertising Cornwall. Today was no exception and as the swimmers looked out at the cerulean blue sea the waves in the distance were sardine silver reflecting in the sun. The pulsing heart of the sea caused a gentle swell and the waves cascaded onto the shore unrolling like an old parchment paper in front of your eyes. A cormorant was flying towards the place where the sun and water met on the horizon. It really was bliss.

Angela looked out to sea, trying to see if she could spot a seal. Many of the swimmers had had close encounters with playful seals on this beach over the years. It was always really hard to spot which was a seal and which were birds due to the distance and the moving sea. If the seals were close enough to the shore it was easier when their bodies flashed steel grey and sunlight reflected against their wet shiny bodies. So many times, the swimmers had joked. "Is it a bird? Is it a seal?' Then just shortened it to "bird seal seal bird?" or a similar order depending on the dots bobbing about on the top of the sea.

Alice carefully took off her birthday crown and replacing it with her pink swimming hat declared she was ready, then started the brightly coloured procession down the beach. As usual they stopped on the shoreline, posing for their usual pre swim photo, underwater cameras tucked into costumes, producing odd shaped bulges in the figure- hugging attire. Turning around they noticed that the swell had started to build and the they could feel the energy as the waves reared up then pounded onto the sand with a thud. Cascading water washed up the beach leaving its white bubbling foam receding as the water drifted away, only to be repeated again and again. The sand having been caressed and assaulted sparkled brightly in the sunlight. The salty waves carried a faintly delicious scent of fresh air and new life.

Dawn had everyone in stiches as she regaled a story about her eighty odd year old neighbour, who unfortunately had dementia, but it had produced some comical escapades. "Brenda called me in this morning as she said her washing machine was playing up and everything was coming out brown. I had a look and it all seemed to be alright. Then she said 'I'm using the same washing powder that I always do, so it can't be that.' So, she showed me the box and what do you think the dozy mare was using? Coco-pops!"

The group roared with laughter. "No wonder her sheets were coming out brown." Dawn continued. "Last week she called me in to say that her cat wasn't eating his food, he kept leaving it. Well I'd wondered why it kept coming into my place pleading starvation, but I just thought it was being greedy. Anyway, I looked in the cat's bowl and she'd been feeding it bloody coco-pops. Poor thing. No wonder it was hungry. I secretly removed the coco pops and put some cat biscuits down but she'll probably feed it washing powder or something now. It is a worry. Poor old Brenda."

Focusing back on the sea as they approached the tide line Alice stated "Why do the waves always get bigger just as we're getting in the water?"

Tom was never fazed by the waves. He just ran into the sea and dived under a wave. Coming out the other side he shouted "Come on in. It's gorgeous."

Next in was Bill followed by Tony, two other non faffers, their three brightly coloured swimming hatted heads bobbing in a row as they faced the shoreline encouraging the rest of the swimmers into the bubbling and foaming sea.

First in from the ladies was Angela. The waves had diminished in intensity and she waited for them to wash past her legs before dashing through the shallow water; sending up a trail of white water behind her and just making it in deep enough that she could swim properly before the next wave arrived. Heather waded in quickly after her and followed Angela out towards the deeper water.

Alice was always nervous of waves, having being knocked off her feet and tumbled at the beach on many occasions. The waves started to ease a little and the sea became calmer so with a shriek she said “I’m going in. It’s now or never.”

Liz and Rachel were running in behind Alice holding hands for support, jumping up in the air as each wave rose higher up their bodies, yelling as the shock of the cold water hit the shudder zone.

“Made it!” Liz yelled moving back and forth, and bobbing up and down with the waves as she finally started swimming.

“Finally in.” Rachel gasped breathlessly before being nearly drowned out by the seagulls screeching in unison like a banshee choir singing in a ghost church on a Sunday morning. Sometimes Rachel imagined the seagulls were discussing how the humans had ruined the tranquillity of the beach or how stupid they were to go swimming in the cold. Her breath was rapid and her heartbeat had doubled so she relaxed and trod water for a few minutes to allow her body to acclimatise.

Tom duck dived under the water with only his feet showing. Rachel never knew how he could do this when it was so cold. She and the others were always head up breast stroke to start with. “Has anyone else put their head in yet?” Rachel shouted.

“Not me.” Angela shouted back.

“Nor me.” replied Alice.

“It’s too bloody cold.” yelled Liz.

“Okay everyone. After three let’s do it!” Angela. “One, two, three.” She lowered her face into the icy cold water, quickly lifting her head up and gasping “Done it” before slowly starting to swim properly, getting used to the cold water. After thirty odd strokes she lifted her head up shouting “I’ve got ice cream head.” The others all knew that feeling, the intense pain in the forehead from brain freeze. She gave herself in a few seconds for the pain to subside before carrying on with her swim.

The small group swam together across the beach, occasionally stopping to take photos of each other and to have a breather. The waves slowly started to calm down as the tide reached its lowest ebb.

While they were chatting Rachel shrieked, “I’ve been bumped” swiftly lifting her legs up in front of her.

The group knew what this meant and quickly looked around. They were used to seeing seals on this beach. The animals were curious and often followed them while they were swimming. The wonderfully inquisitive creatures would often swim up close and then go away and return, trying to work out who they were and what the blazes they were doing in their environment. Shy at first, the seals soon got used to the swimmers and would dash about playing with them. Young pups sometimes explored with their mouths trying to nibble inviting feet or fins. Some seals were very confident and would rub against your body when your legs were dangling down. It was always wonderful to see seals in their own environment. However, it was also scary when they bumped into you. Sometimes the seals would watch from a distance and just follow the swimmers but on this day the seals wanted to play. Shiny grey heads with big black eyes popped up near and far, gazing at the swimmers.

Alice exclaimed "They've come to wish me happy birthday. How exciting."

The seals were very stealthy and everyone felt more comfortable when they were in sight. When the seals dived, some of the swimmers lifted their legs up, not wanting to get bumped as it scared them. You never knew quite where they were until they either bumped you or burst up from the depths, sometimes just two or three feet away. Cameras were retrieved from unmentionable places within swimming costumes and the seals were snapped by the bathers.

Liz was nicknamed "The Seal Whisperer" by the Ls as whenever she got into the sea at this beach the seals came over and it was as if they "posed" for photos for her. She called out as she got into the water. "Hello my babies!" and she always got the closest and best photos. She'd even got one photo under the water of a seal blowing a bubble at her. Maybe the seals sensed she wasn't afraid and being so curious they had a natural affinity with her. As Liz swam with the seals so often, she had liaised with a marine charity, taking clear photos and helping to create a seal database. Lots of the seals often stayed in the same area and each of them had unique markings. Liz had names for them all. Two seals that always swam together were the twins, Hoodie was a young male that had black markings around his head that looked like he was wearing a hooded top while Black Beauty was a huge male that turned up occasionally. Alice thought he was about the size of a walrus and he scared her.

Often Liz swam over here with Heather and their two heads could be seen in the distance, far out to sea when the others arrived at different times, changed, swam, dressed again and left, as the two swimmers stayed in for so long.

Rachel joked that the seals were really mermaids trying to drag the swimmers off to the depths of the ocean by keeping them in the water far too long. Hypothermia could start to seep into every part of their bodies if the obsession to get the perfect seal photo meant that the duration of the swim was increased without realising the amount of time had passed while in the water.

"I'm heading in." Tom told the group, glancing at his waterproof watch. "I've been in twenty minutes and I'm starting to get cold." Rachel could see that he had 'dead man's fingers' where the ends of his fingers went white with the cold.

"Me as well." replied Alice.

"Five more minutes?" pleaded Rachel. "I want to get another photo of that little seal again."

"No." Tom ordered. "We've still got to swim back in yet." She knew he was right but knew that Liz and Heather would stay in longer as they just didn't feel the cold as much as the others and were quite often in for an hour even in winter. The peace and quiet of swimming with the seals was their solace time away from the pressures of their modern day lives.

The birthday team dried themselves and dressed quickly, tucking into the luscious moist chocolate brownies made and brought down by Alice's husband John, who, since taking early retirement from his estate agents had taken over all of the cooking in the house which he'd never had time to do when he was working. He'd surprised himself by being really good and Alice even joked he should enter the "Bake Off."

"Mmmmmm!!!! This is divine John. Thank you." Angela enthused. "If you ever want to rent him out, I would take very good care of him" she winked at Alice.

Before Alice could even reply Liz and Heather arrived to get changed. "Did you see the willies on the beach?" Liz shouted. Shivering and still wearing her thick swimming hat and with cotton wool in her ears she couldn't hear very well.

"What?" Replied Angela laughing.

The group was silent but looked over at Liz bemused. They were used to Liz coming out with random statements especially when she was over cold and slightly hyperthermic. She was a bit bonkers even on a good day.

Rachel replied, laughing "Define "Willies on the beach!"

Liz laughed. Taking her hat off and removing the cotton wool she repeated her statement. "Did you see the willies on the beach? Over there by where the seagulls are landing." She pointed.

The group looked over and could see several seagulls circling in the air and some more scavenging on the beach. Flashes of white contrasted with the blue skies, wings flapping as they retreated with full beaks, squawking as they made inverted arcs, calling out in celebration as other gulls arrived and dived in a frenzy, the air redolent of noisy seagull rush hour traffic.

All eyes moved back to Liz as she started to make sense even though her teeth were chattering, "I have taken photos so you'll be able to see later. After the storms the sand is much lower than normal and as the tide has gone out it has left behind lots of live sea creatures. And the ones I've seen today have animals coming out of the side of the shell and they look like willies." Liz now had her robe over her head and a hot drink in her hand. Lifting up her camera she got a picture on the display to show everyone. The group was starting to be reassured she'd not completely lost her marbles when she came up with another Liz-isms (Rachel had affectionately named them Liz-isms after the bizarre things that often came out of Liz's mouth). "Did you see the hair on that dark seal?"

"Oh god Liz I think you need some cake." Angela said, laughing, while picking up the box and offering Liz a chocolate brownie. "Sit down! Eat this! Then get dressed. You've obviously stayed in too long and drank too much seawater."

Between mouthfuls of cake Liz explained she'd seen a new seal and what she really meant was that the dark seal's markings looked like it had a dark fringe.

Tom picked up his swimming bag and put his hand on Liz's shoulder before saying. "It's a good job that Dennis is picking you up. I think you need to get dressed, have a bit more cake then get home and warm up." Ever the GP he was never off duty but he knew that Liz would be okay. She'd been swimming in the sea for over forty years and was experienced. Her husband Dennis's car would be nice and warm too.

Looking over at Rachel, Tom gave a nod of his head as the signal they were leaving.

Rachel followed Tom up the steps from the beach shouting over her shoulder "Catch you on Facebook later." All of the photos from today would end up on their group social media pages.

Sea 1928

Liberty took advantage of even more time unsupervised and stalked out of the grounds towards the promenade and the beaches. She wasn't immune to the heat and when she sat on the rocks, they were so hot she couldn't sit there for long. The heat of the sun seemed to burn down fiercely and there was no respite anywhere. There was no shade on the promenade, and few people seemed to be about today. Maybe they were at work or just sheltering from the blistering heat. Liberty's broad brim of her sunhat kept the sun from her face but it was so bright she had to scrunch her eyes against the reflective light. She made her way to where the families and children often congregated and looked out at the totally blue sea. Today there was no wind and the shiny surface looked like a mirror. A lone gull skimmed low over the water and Liberty could see its reflection in the water. It was so hot Liberty's light floaty dress seemed to cling to her. She looked around her and found a large rock that she could hide behind and not be seen from the promenade above her. Nervously she ducked down behind the rock, unlaced then kicked off her boots and took off her outer dress as she'd seen the other girls do. She pulled her stockings off and tucked them into her boots. Gathering her underskirt in her arms and pulling it to her knees she slowly made her way to the sea' edge. The sand squished under her toes and she relished the feel of it under her soft feet. As she approached the gently lapping waves the words of Miss Scrivener came to her. "You'll catch a disease. You're delicate."

Liberty gritted her teeth, took a step forward and allowed the slowly advancing water to cover her toes. It was cool and made her toes tingle. She laughed and took a big lungful of air then breathed out deeply, emptying her lungs and feeling her stomach muscles relax. She stood there enjoying the sensation of the cool water washing over her feet and ankles. She looked around at the sea, the sky, the rocks and the promenade above her then took another couple of small steps so now the small waves touched her knees. How long she stood like that she never knew. It was as if time stood still. After what seemed like an age, she was disturbed by the back firing of a car up on the promenade. She came to her senses and decided she'd better get back to the House or she would be missed. She vowed to return tomorrow. Her cold feet had now made the rest of her body feel cooler. She sat on a rock, drying her feet in the hot sunshine while looking at the rock in more detail. She noticed that the dark coloured rock had some smooth and some rougher edges. It was partly covered in white, yellow and green colours that looked a bit like moss. In damp crevices there were small reddish brown shiny round globules. She didn't know what they were.

There were some small snail shaped shells near to some small puddle of water on the rock. She picked one up and turned it upside down noticing something withdrawing slightly into the shell, probably the snail inside she decided. The she noticed some conical shells stuck to the rock but she was unable to pull them off. On the opposite side of the rock to her there were some rough fawn coloured areas that felt quite sharp. She wouldn't want to walk over those. Her feet would hurt.

Liberty brushed the remaining sand from her feet, pulled her stockings and boots on and made her way back to the safety of the grounds of Nancarrow House. She disappeared into the woods of the grounds and then sat there for a few minutes, recalling every enjoyable detail of her adventure, relishing her memories and smiling to herself.

"What are you looking so happy about?" remarked Daisy as she brought Liberty her lunch of cold ham and salad.

"I've just been in the gardens and woods enjoying looking at the birds and plants. Thank you, Daisy." She ate her lunch hungrily.

The following day was going to be another hot one. Liberty did the same as yesterday, Miss Scrivener still confined to her bedroom, and made her way to the sheltered part of the beach where she quickly pulled off her stockings and boots then sank onto the sand, noting the small sharp stones which occasionally would catch her unawares. She stood in the cold water and allowed the shallow waves to wash her feet and ankles. She closed her eyes, breathed deeply, smelling the saltiness and immediately felt herself relax, her stomach muscles seeming to melt a little and feeling the cooler air breathe life into her legs and arms and eventually her mind. She made her facial muscles relax, rejoicing in the new sensations this gave her. How long she stood like that she wasn't sure but when she opened her eyes the bright sunlight assaulted her eyes and then had to close them quickly before glimpsing out at the bay through slits. She took another couple of steps forward, lifting her skirts above her knees and gazed at all the sights before her as if seeing the bay, the sea, the sky for the first time. She gazed in wonderment at the blueness of the sky contrasting with the white fluffiness of the occasional clouds, the reflection on the sea, the ripples across the water, the gentle sounds of the sea washing across her legs and the beach just behind her. She heard the cries of the gulls, the soothing chugging of a small fishing boat meandering across the bay, the distant sounds from the Port, traffic motoring across the promenade.

Liberty didn't feel delicate. For the first time in her life she felt truly alive. She looked down into the clear water and saw green, brown and red weed undulating gently with the constant motion of the waves and she thought she saw a small fish dart across her feet.

Every day she got braver going further in and for longer as her new found love of the sea grew. Liberty took to sitting on the sand and rocks every day, looking out at the jewel blue water which she compared to a rippling blanket with a pulsing heart; and watching the perpetual motion of the waves cascading onto the beach. The rhythm of the waves soothed her and it fascinated her to see clumps of seaweed and other detritus washed up onto the beach and then taken away again. She was glad to get away from the hurly-burly of her life, her bossy governess and her busy sometimes domineering father.

Near and far she could see boats moving along, sometimes with their majestic full sails pushing the boats along at a fast speed in strong winds or lolling aimlessly when there was little or no wind, other steam boats chugging on tirelessly, smoke billowing from a funnel, a fire breathing dragon stowed away under the deck.

Liberty's imagination ran away with her as she understood the lure of sailing away to exotic lands with fierce warriors and strange animals. How exciting to see all these things but frightening as she imagined that many mariners ended up in a salty coffin after battles with wild seas and even wilder pirates. Liberty knew that sailors referred to their boats as "She" and a fully laden sail boat was as pretty as a maiden with her petticoats fluttering in the breeze. She'd heard tales of mermaids out on the horizon where the sea met the sky. She shaded her eyes from the sun and looked out to see if she could see any, listening to the call of the waves, imagining the songs of the sirens as they sang to the sailors beckoning them into the deep black bottomed depths of the oceans. She loved to see the elegant sea birds soaring low across the waves, admiring their skill and effortless poise, wishing she could join them, feeling the wind rush through their wings and fly up into the blue heights above and look down on the tiny people, houses and boats below. Gulls swooped and dived around the bay, their cat like calls filling the air as they followed a fishing boat while a darker coloured cormorant's wings were a blur of motion as it dived into the deep sea after fish.

Liberty came to recognise some of the children. She kept her distance, remembering what her governess had told her as she was too frightened to approach them but occasionally some of the other girls would wave to her if they saw her. Liberty never realised that the children who arrived every day and were around the age of about eight to fourteen years worked for her father in the mine. She saw them arrive every day and their clothes were filthy and had just assumed that this dirt was one of the diseases that her governess had warned her about. Liberty watched as every day they bathed in the sea washing off the dirt from the depth of the mines before heading back to their homes. Liberty watched the dirty, diseased children with fascination but she carefully made sure that her time in the water was completed before they arrived. They giggled and splashed and chatted with each other, friends, brothers, sisters or cousins maybe. Liberty envied their friendship and the fun they seemed to have together; as she was an only child and the only people that she knew around her own age were introduced to her as sons or daughters of business associates of her Father or whom she met at church. They never had anything interesting to talk about. The girls only seemed interested in clothes or getting married and having children while the boys looked at her as a potential wife, until they realised that she had Polio then swiftly looked elsewhere so she was never able to have a conversation about the sea, or birds, or even pirates or mermaids. If she started to talk about these things then they'd change the subject to something mundane or look at her as if she had two heads. In the evenings Liberty would be left to her own devices and during the dark winter evenings she'd write down her observations of these dull people and create stories about them, wickedly parodying or ridiculing them, and making them more interesting.

Closure?

Today was Saturday morning and the first day of the season at Liberty's Lido. The Lido opened daily from early April until late September each year and Rachel had many happy memories of years gone by when she'd spent endless hot days as a young child with her parents and sometimes with Liberty, then as a teenager with her friends, sunbathing, swimming, flirting with the local boys; then as a parent herself seeing Poppy grow from a little girl, then watching from afar as Poppy would be with her teenage friends and flirting with the local boys too. These days Rachel would meet up with the swimmers, sometimes with or without Tom, sometimes with other friends and they'd go around to Golden Rocks to swim, then return to the Lido to sit in the sun and top up their tans, chat, eat lunch, drink tea and coffee, read a book or just relax.

The first day of the season was always something to look forward to and this year was no exception. This year the Ls had decided to dress up in Hawaiian costumes and Rachel had taken a bag of hula hula paraphernalia as well as her swimming kit. Tom wasn't working this Saturday morning which they were both pleased about. The weather forecast had looked good with a light wind and only a few clouds about so it was a pleasant spring morning when the two of them woke. Pictures of the webcam of the sea front showed a gentle sea so it looked like it was going to be an ideal re-opening day.

Rachel made some sandwiches and packed some snacks and fruit while Tom made a flask of hot ginger tea and got their swimming stuff together. Parking the car across the road from the Lido and the Ship Inn, they grabbed their swimming bags and Hawaiian costumes out of the car boot. There a small crowd gathering outside the entrance as there was every morning in the summer except that today instead of everyone forming a queue they were huddled together and Rachel could see that in place of the usual anticipation and excited chatter of a new season everyone looked miserable but talking to everyone else in loud voices.

Flo caught her arm. "Have you heard? The Lido's shutting at the end of September. There's a notice attached to the gates." She pointed.

"What?" Rachel exclaimed and she pushed through the crowd to see for herself.

Attached to the gate was a yellow typewritten sign, laminated and tied to the gates.

Important Notice.

Unfortunately, due to the lack of funding the Lido will close permanently on 30th September 2019.!!!!!!!!!!!!!!!!!!!!

Rachel took her place in the queue with Tom and the others. "Short and not very sweet!" she thought. Where had the money gone? Her Grandmother Liberty had set up a trust fund for the Lido, giving them £20,000 a year and she knew this hadn't run out plus there was now Sarah's £50,000. The council had always paid money into the Lido along with the entrance fees, season tickets and profits from the café. Rachel would like some answers herself. Why hadn't Sarah spoken to her about this or hadn't she known when she'd become ill towards the end of her life. Maybe she hadn't been to some of the meetings over the winter.

The piercing sound of Angela's voice jolted her back to the present and she found herself amongst the rest of the swimming group who were listening to their unofficial leader and spokeswoman, in Angela's opinion, as the group shuffled towards the payment kiosk.

"Where's all the money gone? I knew this place was being mismanaged, it's obvious. Douggie is useless and I told him so. They drain the water at the wrong time. They close the pool when it's sunny or busy. The café's food is tasteless, the coffee too weak or too strong and too expensive. The queues are horrendous….. "Angela continued to rant. She had an attentive audience and some of the other swimmers chipped in with comments about the runny or frozen ice cream, food open to the elements, the untrained students who worked in the cafe, the teenagers, the litter, the seagulls, dogs being allowed in, dogs not being allowed in. Angela made sure she had their attention before concluding. "I offered to help and gave him some ideas but he didn't listen." Deep down Angela was very insecure and fearful of not measuring up to others so she constantly tried to elicit praise and approval from others to shore up her fragile ego by fabricating and embellishing her stories to sound more interesting and then striving for perfection and blaming others when things went wrong.

Rachel mentally switched off. It was hardly surprising as Angela's help was a bit like a badly tuned radio, full of interference. There were ways and means of dealing with people to get them on your side and Angela's manner of superiority and entitlement wasn't one of them.

Sarah had once said to Rachel, when Angela was venting her spleen against someone who allegedly was persecuting her, "She ought to write a self-help book. How to lose friends and disaffect people."

"I was so upset." Angela continued. "I went home and told Gerry. He agreed with me. I had to go to bed with a migraine."

If Angela wasn't the centre of attention, she'd have a funny turn, or feel sick or a migraine. Gerry was Angela's long-suffering husband. He found agreeing with her was the safest way for him to get into her good books. If she was blaming someone else, she wasn't blaming him. She had the ability to praise you and put you down in the same sentence. Rachel had once gone to the pub one winter's day last year wearing a fabulous new sparkly coat that Tom had treated her to as an early Christmas present. She loved the coat and Tom liked her to wear it. Angela had looked at the coat and said "I adore your coat. You look lovely in it. Those colours really suit you."

"Thank you." Rachel had said.

"You'd look even better if you lost half a stone." Angela had continued.

Rachel had thrown the coat into the back of the wardrobe and hadn't worn it since as it gave her horrible memories. Tom had mentioned it a couple of times over the winter when she'd worn her old coat instead of the new one but she couldn't see the coat without Angela's harsh words echoing in her head.

Rachel tuned back into the conversation as Angela said. "Well of course there will be a vacancy on the board of Trustees now Sarah has died. Maybe I'll apply. I'm bound to get in. Bill will vote for me, I know, then I can get things sorted out and I can tell them where they've been going wrong and I'll help them turn it around so the Lido will stay open."

Rachel decided to keep her mouth firmly shut and shook her head slightly as she fixed Tom with a steely gaze that told him not to speak about Sarah's request that she, Rachel, go onto the board. Her thoughts turned to the £50,000 that Sarah had bequeathed the Lido. What was going to happen to that now? She could hardly justify putting the money into the pool if it was going to shut but maybe that was in defiance of Sarah's request. She'd have to talk to Joseph

Knob about the legal implications. Maybe the £50,000 could help keep the pool open? And what was going to happen to the board of Trustees now? Would she, Rachel, even be needed anymore?

The gates swung open and the queue started to move down the concrete steps that had felt millions of feet skip or plod down it's whitewashed surfaces over the decades since it had opened in 1931, including Royalty. Rachel remembered the day that Prince Charles had visited to reopen the Lido after it had been damaged by the Winter storms of 2010.

Rachel reread the sign as she passed it while Tom paid for a season ticket for both of them. It didn't make any better reading the second time. She walked over to the rest of the group who were starting to get changed for swimming, all congregating together. There was an undercurrent of anger and frustration that this was going to be the last summer at the Lido and Angela was doing her best to whip everyone up into a frenzy and finding someone to blame. Rachel listened as everyone was trying to talk at once, each member had their own theory.

"It's Brexit" said Tink. "It's the fucking Germans trying to take over Europe by the back door. They failed in two World Wars and now they want to take Europe by stealth." She then had a furious argument with Ziggy, a German widow, who'd been married to a local Cornish artist for thirty years until he passed away a couple of years ago. Rachel heard the word "Sauerkraut." being shouted by Tink. Oh dear.

"Greedy Conservative Council cuts." said Diane. "If Labour had got in…"

"If Labour got in our Council Tax bills would be double." Tony Baker interrupted.

Sally pointed out that the money the Council saved from propping up Liberty's Lido was minimal compared to the cost of the NHS paying for diabetic patients and people with mental problems. "The pool helps people both physically and mentally."

Flo chipped in "There's only so much in the Council's pot. It's a question of priorities."

Diane sat down on a bench, her tie dye skirt fanned out around her, looking like she was perched on an odd coloured blanket. Her reduced mobility meant she needed to rest while the others continued standing and talking, all putting their two penneth in.

The group was getting louder so Rachel decided she needed to find out exactly why the pool was shutting and went in search of the manager, Douggie.

Scared 1928

As Liberty became stronger, she would venture further afield, the gorgeous hot summer weather keeping her busy and out of the house while Miss Scrivener was still struggling with the heat. Each day, getting braver and braver, Liberty went deeper and deeper into the sea. Today Cook had wrapped up a sandwich for Liberty and she sat on the warm golden sand while taking off her shoes. The shimmering sunlight made the sand sparkle like thousands of tiny jewels under her toes. Eating her sandwich, she could feel the warmth of the sun on her body and it made her leg hurt less. Lying back on the sand she could feel herself relaxing it was so peaceful with only the occasional screech of seagulls flying above her. The salty smell travelling up her nostrils gave her a flood of happiness and she forgot all her pain for a short while. She awoke to the sound of a seagull close by and didn't realise how long she had been asleep. Feeling hot she arose and decided to have a paddle. Taking off her outer dress and folding it up on the sand by her shoes she stepped into the turquoise sea feeling the now familiar contrast as her warm skin came into contact with the cool water. She stood there for a few seconds allowing her skin to acclimatise so that it didn't feel quite so cold on her toes. Whether she was still sleepy she'd failed to notice that the wind had got up; the waves were a little more choppy and she quickly found herself chest height in the water which was much further than she'd ever been before There was a strong undercurrent and she could feel herself being dragged out as she started to float. Suddenly Liberty could no longer feel the beach, then she felt the sea swirling around her, lifting her up then dropping her down quickly so she was just touching the bottom with tiptoes. She didn't really understand what was happening. The beach was becoming further away and she was facing out to sea. Waves swirled over her as she kicked her feet and flailed her arms. The water closed over her and she felt the pull of the swell dragging on her long and heavy clothing. Her lungs ached. She'd never known a fear like it. She burst to the surface and took a breath, but immediately inhaled icy cold salt water. She couldn't cough as she was submerged by another wave. Once more, she emerged but managed to stay afloat long enough to gain half a breath before plummeting under the unforgiving waves. Again and again she fought her way to the surface only to disappear into the darkness.

"I'm going to die." She thought with trepidation, feeling the strength sapping from her arms and legs.

Suddenly she was aware of strong hands grasping her clothing and arms underneath her armpits supporting her, dragging her roughly through the waves. She felt a body under her and legs kicking strongly beneath her.

“Kick your legs Miss!” a male voice told her and then heard his breath panting as he tried to keep her above the waves and then coughing and spluttering as he went under the water. She kicked out and caught the legs beneath her. It hurt her foot and she stopped.

“Keep kicking Miss!” he implored, in between breaths. “Don’t give up!”

She kept inhaling water, and coughing but kept trying to kick although her legs ached like never before and the muscles in them burned like fire.

The man kept encouraging her. “Keep going. You’ve got to keep kicking. “

Just when Liberty thought she couldn’t kick anymore she felt her toes touch land. She kicked hard again and then felt herself fall backwards with the man holding her as he gave a final heave to bring her to safety. He helped her to her feet and the two of them stood in the shallows panting, coughing and retching, their heads down and hands on knees.

Liberty felt weak, her legs felt like jelly, her arms ached, and her lungs and throat hurt. Gradually her breathing slowed and her heart stopped racing.

“Are you alright Miss?” the man asked, a concerned tone to his voice. Liberty pushed her hands on her knees and stood up, taking a look at her rescuer. It was a boy. He was as tall as a man with sopping wet brown hair but had a thin body as his wet torn dirty stained clothes clung to him. He ran a black hand over his face and pushed his hair from his eyes. Liberty correctly guessed he was a few years older than her.

“Yes. I think so. Thank you.” She was suddenly aware that her long wet underdress was clinging to her body. The words of her governess echoed in her head “You’ll catch a disease. You’re too delicate.” And now this boy had touched her, half carried out of the water.

He was looking down and pointed. “Your leg is cut. Would you like me to look at it for you?” He reached down to touch her leg.

A look of horror crossed her face, this boy’s hands were still covered in dirt despite being in the water, he’d held her and now he wanted to see her leg. This was the leg she was always conscious about, the leg that was thinner than the other due to polio muscle weakness and wastage, and this leg was now covered in blood. She might catch a disease. It was all too much for Liberty. She knew she had to get home and was starting to panic about what she looked like. She was wet and cold and knew that if her governess or her Father found out she had been in the sea let alone talked to a dirty boy she would really be in trouble.

Neither of them had noticed that the sky had turned black and the wind had become much stronger now. A few heavy drops of rain started to fall.

"I've got to go home!" She exclaimed rudely, starting to shiver.

"Let me look at your leg, it's bleeding."

"Leave me alone!" She hurried to her clothes, shoes and hat, grabbed them and walked barefoot as quickly as she could away from the rocks, the beach and the promenade, hobbling as she went. She had to get away from the boy with the diseases. By now the rain was very heavy and after a couple of minutes small rivers of water were running into the gutters and puddles were starting to form.

Luckily, she didn't meet anyone on the way home, as everyone was sheltering from the squall, and she quickly hid amongst the trees of the grounds of Nancarrow House, brushing her feet off as best as she could, pulling her shoes on and cautiously making her way to the back of the house.

Arriving home Liberty tried to sneak in via the kitchens with the idea that she could make her way quietly to her room, to change, wash the blood off herself and her clothing, and to sort her hair out, which was a sodden mess. However, unfortunately, she bumped into Mrs Hitchens, the Cook, who took one look at her and marched her out into the scullery, fetching her a towel and telling her to strip off her wet clothes.

"What happened to you Miss Liberty?"

Liberty started to cry and shiver. "Please don't tell my Father or Miss Scrivener but I fell asleep in the garden and then when the rain started, I rushed to get some shelter and slipped and cut my leg."

Mrs Hitchens made soothing noises and promised not to say anything. She didn't ask any more questions and Liberty wasn't going to divulge her secrets. Cook made Liberty a cup of hot sweet tea and found her a piece of cake; and while Liberty ate and drank, she dried Liberty's hair with another towel. She wiped the blood from Liberty's leg which was only a superficial cut and wouldn't be noticed under stockings while scooping her wet clothes into a pile and placing them in a pile of other dirty washing.

Once Liberty felt better, she was just about to make her way to her room and was at the bottom of the stairs with Cook, when she looked up to see her father looming over her, casting a shadow through his open office doorway.

Mrs Hitchens heaved her ample figure out of the way, nodding her head at her employer. "Sorry Sir" and went back to her job of preparing the evening meal leaving Liberty shivering at the bottom of the stairs even though she was wrapped up in a big fluffy towel. Part shock and part cold she just wanted her Father to wrap his arms around her and reassure her, so she could feel safe in his arms like he used to when she was a little girl, and he would stroke her hair and she would breathe in his manly smell and listen to his voice rumble in his chest where she'd placed her head.

"What in the Lord's name has happened to you?" he began.

"I fell over and cut my leg." She showed him.

"How did this happen?"

"I don't know. I just slipped."

"Why is your hair wet?"

"Um. I..... um." Liberty was just thinking about what to say when the telephone in Frederick's office began ringing and he strode purposely towards it, slamming the door shut behind him.

Saved by the phone Liberty hurried upstairs to her room, dressed herself, rearranged her hair and spent the rest of the daytime there replaying her nightmare ordeal over and over in her head, thinking of the possible repercussions. Would her Father find out? Would her interrogate her? Would he ask Cook? Would Cook ask questions? Would Cook tell Miss Scrivener, or Daisy, or Dorothy? Would her Father stop her going out? Or arrange a chaperone to escort her everywhere? Liberty's mind was in turmoil then her thoughts turned to what had actually happened at the sea front. She had been scared of the power of the sea, and had momentarily thought that she might die until the boy had saved her. Who was the boy? How lucky he had seen her or she would have died. How dare he look at her poorly leg! She was being ungrateful and uncharitable. The boy had saved her life and had risked his own life to do so. She'd heard him cough and choke on the water like she had and she knew that it hadn't been easy to pull her back to shore. She made up her mind to apologise for her rude behaviour and thank him properly when she saw him next. She suddenly found herself looking forward to seeing him again. And she surprised herself with those thoughts. What was that all about?

Liberty was disturbed from her thoughts when heard the motorcar drive past her window to the front of the House. She crept quietly from her room to the edge of the large window above the front door. Peeking around the edge she saw Tommy stand erect in the rain, holding the passenger door open for her Father, who emerged from the house holding an umbrella, then firmly shutting it once Frederick had taken his seat. Tommy then disappeared into the House, re-emerging with two suitcases which he placed in the large boot of the motorcar, closed the boot, jumped into his seat, slammed his door and sped off.

Liberty heaved a sigh of relief. Her Father was going to be away and so she hoped he would have forgotten her exploits by the time he came back home again, if he hadn't already. She gave it a few moments and then quietly went downstairs. She saw Dorothy in the hallway, about to go into her Father's office to start cleaning.

"Has Father gone out?" Liberty asked innocently.

"Yes, Miss Liberty. He asked me to tell Miss Scrivener that he was called away to London urgently for a few days and he'd left written instructions in a letter on his desk."

"Very good Dorothy. Thank you." Liberty entered her Father's office and saw the letter on his desk addressed to Miss Scrivener. Dorothy followed her in and started dusting and cleaning.

The rest of the day Liberty spent quietly in her room, only venturing down for dinner which she ate alone, not for the first time. That night Liberty didn't sleep well. Whenever she closed her eyes she could feel herself bobbing up and down in the waves, then she'd sleep a bit and dream about not being rescued then wake up in a panic, the dreams feeling so real, then she'd be drowning and her Father would be the one rescuing her, then scolding her and keeping her prisoner in her own room. Over and over, round and round her mind kept going through the events of the day. Finally, at around five thirty, she decided she wasn't going to go back to sleep so she swung her feet out of bed and padded to the window. She pulled back the curtains and opened the window quietly. The rain of the previous day had washed the world clean again and the cool early morning air smelt fresh and earthy. She sat on the window seat looking at the pink sky transform gradually to blue, contemplating the sea view before her, listening to the birds in the gardens reaffirming their territory and hearing distant traffic sounds as the early morning sun started to climb in the sky.

Liberty made her mind up. She decided that although she had enjoyed being down by the sea it was too dangerous, and she would leave it to the dirty families. She'd been given a second chance. She'd had a fright and she'd been lucky that the boy had rescued her. She was grateful to him but she was going to grow up to be a Lady, and Ladies didn't go into the sea.

Douggie

Douggie had managed the pool for the last thirty years and even though he was in his sixties he still kept himself fit and swam one mile every day, weather and tides permitting. There were photos of Douggie around the pool diving off the high board in his twenties and Rachel could see why he'd been very popular as a lifeguard with the girls and he hadn't lost his personality as he'd aged. But today he looked ashen faced and had aged several years since she had seen him at Sarah's funeral. When he saw Rachel, he looked like he was going to cry but pulled himself together. He kept apologising saying Liberty would be upset and Sarah would be turning in her grave.

"I will be blamed by everyone, the swimmers, the town, the rest of the Trustees."

Rachel remembered that along with Bill, Douggie was one of the Trustees of the Lido. "Do you know why the Lido is going to shut?"

"Just a simple matter of economics. I only found out yesterday. Letter from the Council." he replied. "Too much going out, not enough coming in. It's been run at a loss for the last two years and the Council simply can't continue propping up 'a lame duck'. We need a really good summer to bring in the money. And then of course there's the repair bill after the winter storms. That's more this year than the last few years. There's some major work that now has to be done that's been put off by successive Councils and can't be put off any longer." He looked like he was going to burst into tears again. "I've been coming here for all my life, as a child, then a teenager and I've worked here since I was about sixteen, nearly fifty years."

"It's not your fault Douggie." Rachel empathised and gave him a hug. He'd been there ever since she could remember. He'd been a lifeguard when she was in her teens meeting her friends in the school holidays and at weekends. And he'd still been there when her own daughter Poppy was in her teens too. It had been his life and even more so since he lost his wife to cancer five years ago. He spent many hours here both before and after work, and during the winter months too. Occasionally he came swimming with the Ls when the Lido was shut. She reassured him that he wasn't to blame. So many big businesses had shut and many major famous high street shops had long gone. Times had changed and with Brexit hanging over everyone's heads people were nervous. "When is the next Trustee meeting?"

"It's scheduled for the end of May when we need to find a replacement for Sarah."

That was nearly two months away. With a 30th September deadline it was imperative that the Board meet so Rachel could donate Sarah's £50,000.

"In light of this news would it not make sense to have an emergency meeting to bring the Trustees up to its full quota and see if we can come up with some ideas to get some more funding." she said persuasively.

"We?" he looked at her curiously.

"Well. Um. I'd like to throw my hat into the ring to become a board member. I have some ideas."

"I see." He looked reassured. "I'll get word to the other trustees and see if we can get it brought forward."

He became business like and put his game face on as he said "We're not shut yet. The show must go on and I need to get on with my work." He strode purposefully towards some of the other lifeguards as the first day of the season was always busy. Rachel watched as he talked and laughed with a couple of families then crouched down and talked to a little girl with blonde pigtails and a pink bikini who had an inflatable unicorn hanging off one arm.

Hula

The Lido with its attached café was one of the meeting points of the town as it connected everyone during the summer months. The pool was open daily from 10.00 – 18.00 from the opening day in April until the 30th September. Rachel would often not see some people at all during the winter. It was as if they hibernated like squirrels and reappeared bright eyed and bushy tailed for the summer season. She recognised some faces who were settling down on their towels with their clothes and bags as she made her way back to the Ls.

"It's all kicking off here." Tom rolled his eyes "As usual their opinions are like assholes, everyone's got one!"

Rachel laughed.

"What's Douggie got to say?" Tom continued.

"He blames himself." Rachel replied. "I'll tell you more later. C'mon let's get our fancy dress costumes on."

"Rachel. Darling you look fabulous as always." A French accent assaulted her ears. Pierre the café manager flounced by her. She did a double take. Any excuse to wear a dress, Pierre looked amazing in a long dark wig, full make up, short hula skirt and high heels. A part time Zumba teacher and lover of dance, he pirouetted perfectly on his heels and teetered off to the café. Pierre was often seen with Summer, his bestie, also a Zumba teacher. With her long blonde hair, slim tanned figure and fashion conscious image she was a lovely girl. Rachel remembered teaching her many years before when Summer was aged eight, a pretty girl then, she'd developed into a beautiful young woman. And now Summer was teaching Rachel in the Zumba classes she attended. Pierre often joined the classes or covered the instruction if Summer was away for any reason.

Pierre wasn't a swimmer but he was very much a part of the furniture of the Lido. He ran the café and everyone loved him. Aged just thirty and hailing from Paris he oozed confidence, charisma and charm along with stunning good looks. His French accent was sexy and Sarah had once heard Angela saying it was wasted on him being 'one of those' He lived with his husband, a local older businessman, who spent lots of time away from home so the café was Pierre's baby and he took really good care of it. Pierre's husband was called Bernard, or Bernie, as Pierre called him. No-one would ever have put the serious balding unfit businessman with the flamboyant much younger Pierre as a couple but it seemed to work for both of them.

Pierre exuded joy and enthusiasm about life and was genuinely upbeat. Him working in the café was good for the community. He always made everyone feel like the most important person in the room. He worked hard and it made the café a happy place to eat and work.

Today there was a buzz starting to develop as everyone was getting ready to dress up as was tradition every year on the opening day. Most swimmers were happy to just turn up and swim in the pool but some of Rachel's tightknit group of hardy swimmers were always up for fun, dressing up and generally making idiots of themselves. Some of the swimmers moaned about the hilarity and frivolity, namely Tink and Ziggy, or Doom and Gloom as Sarah had once christened them, privately to Rachel.

This year's theme was Hawaiian dress so everyone was wearing bright coloured grass skirts, flower necklaces and headdresses and there was plenty of laughter when the men also sported hula skirts and coconut bras. Angela and Alice emerged from their changing cubicles dressed identically, as usual. The local newspaper was always there on opening day and this year was no exception. The photographer took lots of the swimmers posing while Alice was in charge of selfies, as usual.

It was decided that the group would all jump in together after posing for the paper first, lining up on the side of the water. Everyone assumed a pose before holding hands, leaping into the air and shrieking as they all hit the ice cold water in a large and loud splash. They came up laughing and started to retrieve parts of their costumes which had fallen off. Ziggy mournfully retrieved a couple of flowery wrist bands holding them up to see who's they were and complaining about them littering the pool. Lots of items of clothing were floating on the surface and after they were reunited with their owners everyone got together still laughing.

Tony Baker had lost his coconut bra while Tom was singing the song "I've got a lovely bunch of coconuts" while pushing his own bra up and down in time to the music. It was hilarious.

The more Ziggy moaned the more Rachel and Alice laughed.

"Big ones, small ones, some as big as your head." Tom continued.

“That bra will block pumps.” Ziggy moaned as she ducked down again and again trying the retrieve the offending article.

Mike Higgins swam up towards the others. He’d found Tony’s coconut bra and had put it on his head.

“Tit head.” said his wife Debbie, laughing.

“I was doing the ‘breast’ stroke.” He looked indignant. Then laughed with the others.

“Now it won’t block sea pump!” said Ziggy looking like she’d been sucking a lemon.

The Ls climbed out of the pool still laughing and smiling. They changed then sat around chatting while drinking a warm drink and eating some food. Even though the swimming group swam in the sea every day they based themselves at the pool during the summer months and some members enjoyed the pool swimming when the tide was too low for them to scramble down the rocks into the sea, or those that could only swim in the pool due to mobility issues. However, they all enjoyed the social side it bought, the company and the swimmers’ cake that was handed around afterwards.

Domesticity 1928

Liberty deliberately stayed out of the kitchen for a couple of days to keep out of the way of Mrs Hitchens. She still enjoyed the outdoors but kept to quiet garden seats rereading the novel "The Wonderful Wizard of Oz" then finding fascination in a new book called "The Midnight Folk" where the character looks for his grandfather's treasure. Every night at midnight the hero embarks on an adventure where he encounters witches, pirates, flying horses, mermaids and talking toys. She loved escaping into a fantasy world.

A few days later after her morning lessons had finished, Miss Scrivener now back to resuming her teaching, Liberty found herself at the beach again in the afternoon. She'd not consciously set out to go there but had walked around the grounds of Nancarrow House, then it seemed as if her feet had a mind of their own and she found herself looking down from the promenade onto the scene of her adventure. It seemed impossible that it was just five or six days before. It seemed such a long time ago and yet the memory of nearly drowning was so vivid it was as if it were only yesterday.

Liberty stood on the promenade for a long time deciding what to do. She'd been frightened by her experience and yet the sea was a draw. She'd loved the way that she had felt before the near tragedy. The feeling of calmness and relaxation that the sea had given her. Was it the sea itself? The warm sunshine? The fresh air? Or maybe just being in nature? She enjoyed being out in her garden, looking at the sights and taking in the scents of the plants and flowers, watching the birds and animals, delighting in the ever-changing colours of the seasons but the sea was something different. She didn't know exactly what it was but she knew that she had felt truly alive when she was down by the sea.

She made her way down to the shore and removed her boots and stockings, feeling the cool sand on her bare feet. It reminded her of the sensations she'd had before, the cold water, the sand squishing up between her toes, the small stones and pebbles she could feel underfoot. She lifted her skirt to her knees and took a couple of small steps forward so that the small gentle waves lapped her knees.

"I'm just paddling." She told herself. "Not too far out." A calmness descended on her. She breathed deeply, closing her eyes to relish the sensations of the ebb and flow of the waves against her bare legs, the smell of the sea, the sounds of the waves gently dropping onto the shore. She relaxed and knew she was back. It was like as if she'd returned home to her true self. She felt the tension in her neck and shoulder muscles dissipate, the warm comfortable feeling she had inside felt like sunshine in her stomach. She was aware of the blood pumping through her body as her lungs filled with the clean salty air and a fogginess in her brain, that she'd been unaware of, suddenly lifted to leave a sharp focus and heightened awareness. This was true happiness.

Cake

The swimmers' cake was made by Liz White, aged sixty six, slightly bonkers in a nice way but her cake was legendary. It was filled with both dried and fresh fruit, plus it was a pretty shade of sunflower yellow due to the turmeric she added. It was very welcome especially in the winter when the swimmers were shaking with cold and teeth chattering. When it was only eight degrees Centigrade, "that wind" was blowing a hooley and numb fingers couldn't work enough to get dressed quickly; a hot drink and a piece of cake took away the pain. And it had the added bonus of a fruit portion!

Liz was laughing and apologising today that she'd put too much ginger in it. "Sorry, my hand shook as I was putting the ginger in so there's twice as much as usual in it."

No-one noticed. It was delicious and always hit the spot.

Ziggy sometimes made cake too but generally it was inedible, usually either raw or burnt, sometimes both. She tried to force it onto everyone who politely declined, suddenly turned gluten intolerant or became busy looking into their swimming bags.

"Never mind. I bring again tomorrow." She'd chime in her broken English.

Mike Higgins was always too polite to refuse until his wife, Debbie, had overheard Flo telling Angela that Ziggy had once made a carrot cake and the only oil she had at home was infused with garlic plus she had used garlic butter to make the icing. Another time she had half a tin of baked beans left in the fridge which had been added. Interesting taste!

"It's amazing what you can put in cake." Ziggy had said.

Since then Mike made a beeline for Liz's cake which was always delicious, then claimed he was full when Ziggy held her cake box under his nose.

Tom, always the GP, had looked online at the many physical and medical benefits of cold water swimming, stimulating the vagus nerve, improving the lymph system, helping with depression, the physical exercise and wished he could put it onto prescription, but Rachel always felt that the social side of the group helped too.

Many of the group were single through divorce or bereavement and so it gave them a purpose to get out of bed each morning and to meet up with their friends. There's something bonding about standing together, reluctantly undressing, freezing cold, shivering then leaping into cold water, swearing loudly, unable to put your head under as it's too cold, swimming for ten or fifteen minutes, then agreeing it was all good fun and we'll do it all again the same time tomorrow. Madness! But cold water swimming had been proven to develop resilience, give a mental toughness and made you better able to cope with the challenges that life throws up.

The group had temporarily forgotten about the end of season deadline and enjoyed the rest of the day while the photographer went around Liberty's Lido taking photos of locals young and old. Slowly some the group dispersed and went back home while others stayed there, met up with family and friends or just sat reading books and magazines. Luckily the weather stayed warm and dry, people had a good time, the Lido and café were busy and took lots of money. Maybe things could be turned around.

Tom and Rachel made their way home and she filled him in on her conversation with Douggie. "I don't think I'll be any good on the board." She stated. "I'll worry about everything too much."

"Rubbish." Tom comforted her. "You'll be brilliant."

"I don't think so."

"Sarah thought so. You'll be fine, people like you. They'll listen to you."

"Angela doesn't."

"Angela doesn't listen to anybody. Anyway, she's not a trustee."

"She wants to be. You heard her."

"You'll have to make sure you get on the board then won't you."

"Mmm."

Trustee?

Sunday was dull and the forecast was showing rain for the afternoon, worsening over the evening.

"Let's get our swim done this morning but not hang around afterwards then we can do a few bits in the house this afternoon to catch up a bit. I've got some paperwork that needs sorting." Rachel indicated a pile of envelopes and letters on the end of the dining room table. After breakfast she and Tom got ready for swimming and made their way down to the Lido.

"Morning." Rachel called to Flo as they got out of their car, pushed some coins into the parking meter, grabbed their swimming bags and walked across the road to the whitewashed posts either side of the wrought iron gates of the Lido. There was a smaller queue than yesterday but again there was a huddle around the gates. A new sign had appeared alongside yesterday's bombshell notice.

"In light of the news of the shutting of Liberty's Lido an extraordinary meeting of the Board of Trustees will be held on Tuesday evening in the cafe at 7.30 pm."

An agenda was attached. Rachel felt a sudden shudder of apprehension as she read that item one was to elect a new trustee. Applicants should apply in writing and be prepared to give a short presentation as to why they should be elected. Although she'd been vaguely aware that this would happen sometime in the future after the will reading the poster made it more real and she doubted that she could fill Sarah's stylish shoes on the Board of Trustees.

As usual Angela was filling the air with her piercing voice, promoting herself in a way that would do a presidential candidate proud. "I've spoken to Bill and he said that he would vote for me. I'll kick this lot up the bum and get them to keep it open. We'll make the Council see sense. It's been here for years and there's no reason why it should shut." Some swimmers and other locals nodded. In some ways Rachel agreed with some of what Angela was saying. "Vote for me and I'll keep this Lido open." Angela concluded to cheering and clapping.

The gates of the Lido swung open and the Ls, along with Rachel and Tom, as well as members of the public, made their way through the entrance turnstiles and down to their favourite perches.

Douggie approached Rachel and said. "Morning. Have you seen the sign about the meeting on Tuesday?"

Rachel concurred.

"After I spoke to you, I agreed with you that it would be a good idea to have a meeting sooner. I spoke to Bill and some of the other board members and they agreed too. I told them that it was your idea."

Angela approached them both as she'd been eavesdropping. "What's a good idea?" she intervened.

"Rachel suggested we have a Trustee board meeting sooner than the normal one in May after the sudden news that we're going to have to shut the Lido at the end of the season."

"Not if I have anything to do with it. You can't shut this place. I won't allow it. I told Bill we needed to replace Sarah on the board sooner rather than later. He said he'll vote for me. You will too won't you Douggie? You'll want to keep your job here so the best way is to vote for me on Tuesday. Tony is keeping his cards close to his chest and hasn't said he would vote for me but he also didn't say he wouldn't either. He's known me for years and I was friends with his wife. I phoned Millicent Angove too. She said we must keep the Lido open at all costs."

Millicent, the Treasurer, Rachel knew, was a former County Councillor and current Magistrate. Born and bred in the town, her father Cedric had owned a jewellery shop in the main street. He'd been a town Councillor and then Mayor and was a well-respected pillar of the community. Millicent's mother had died when Millicent was just fifteen, so Cedric made her his consort and she attended various mayoral functions, learning the ropes of local government and had later been a Mayor herself ten years ago. Always Millicent, not Millie, she had never married and had remained in the family home when Cedric had died in his eighties. Despite her somewhat old fashioned and frumpy appearance she was an intelligent, no nonsense woman with a penchant for reading the Times, mastering most of it's crossword, devouring a wide range of books; both fiction and non-fiction and loved cream teas, always 'jam first' of course. A regular churchgoer, she abhorred television, despaired at celebrity culture and was a regular listener to Radio 4. Interestingly she loved rugby and loyally turned up each Saturday afternoon to watch and cheer on the local team, as she had with her father when he was alive, then go into the bar, drink pints of Real Ale and vociferously argue rugby tactics with other club members. She was on the committee as treasurer for the rugby club and was fiercely supportive of funding for the youth and development teams.

Sarah had always approved of Millicent being on the board of Trustees for the Lido. Although she wasn't everyone's cup of tea she got things done, people listened to her and her opinions were generally sought and acted on. Indeed, it had been Millicent who had approached Sarah to apply for a place on the board when a previous Trustee had resigned, but had then abstained from the vote so that no-one would think that she was favouring Sarah. Since then they'd had an unlikely friendship, the former model and the frumpy spinster or "Beauty and the Beast." as one of them had overheard someone say in Muffins coffee shop in the town one day. Millicent had roared with laughter, and after initially being embarrassed, Sarah had joined in too. Sometimes the two of them finished the Times crossword together.

"Are you coming to the meeting on Tuesday evening Rachel?" Angela asked, looking down her nose at Rachel.

Angela never seemed to believe anything that Rachel said. If Rachel was talking about a television program or something from a magazine about health, fitness or diet, Angela would ignore her, but, then could then be heard spouting off about it a few days later to the rest of the group as if it was her own news or ideas.

"Well of course I'm gluten free, everyone knows that its healthy for you." Angela had chimed a couple of years ago when Rachel had been gluten free herself for a number of years before that and had found that many people had dismissed their griping stomach pains to wind or the weather or a day with a Y in it."

"Mmm, it isn't necessarily healthy for you Angela." Tom had said to her. "You could eat an unhealthy diet like pizza or pasties even though they're gluten free."

"Of course. Doctor Tom, you know best." She'd schmoozed, resting a hand gently on his arm.

"Yes. I'll be there" Rachel said simply, not wishing to elaborate further. She didn't want to antagonise Angela.

Jack 1928

Jack Pender saw Liberty as he was on his way home from her Father's mine Wheal Trencrom. He was the boy who had rescued her a few days ago. He was eighteen, the eldest of five children and the man of the house, since his own Father William had died three months ago in a mining accident when a tunnel had collapsed. His three younger brothers also worked at the mine with him, twelve year old James down in the pit, ten year old George and seven year old Henry working above ground, while his youngest sister, five year old Bessie, worked with Jack's Mother Agnes down at Trelyn Fishing Port, lifting baskets of fish from the boats and sorting them into different types and sizes of fish. Jack was a good worker, young and strong and when his Father had died, Jack had approached the foreman to take over William's position working on the tin face. Initially the foreman had refused, not wanting a boy to take a man's job, with other men also after William's better paid position.

"Please give me a chance. Let me work a month at the same rate of pay as I am now and if I'm good enough and prove myself then you give me my Father's position."

The foreman had reluctantly agreed to give him a trial but when Jack's productivity was better than most of the other workers, he had no hesitation in giving him the job. An always likeable and trustworthy employee, his ready smile and good nature, won over the doubters amongst the older men underground and he became a reliable colleague to work alongside. His gentle demeanour hid a determined inner steel and leadership skills that encouraged the men around him to work harder, with the result reflected in higher pay packets for all of them at the end of each week. The men deferred to their younger colleague and marked him as a future leader of men.

As he was older than the other children he started earlier and left the mine later and was often on his own as he made his way to and from the mine. He enjoyed the solitude of his walk as his home was a small, damp, cramped cottage, his brothers always fighting and arguing with each other, Bessie often in tears because they'd bully her and his Mother a broken woman since she'd lost her husband, her childhood sweetheart William Pender. When Jack was at home, he'd have to sort out his brothers, help his Mother and comfort Bessie, who liked nothing better than to sit on Jack's lap and listen to him telling her stories.

He was tired, hungry and dirty and was desperate to get home and eat but he needed to clean himself up. The mines, hot at the best of times, had been unbearable during the summer and the dirt had stuck to the sweat. He never seemed to get clean. In his solitude he sometimes talked out loud to his dead Father as he walked; other times he liked to listen to the sounds of nature, the wind, the birds and the sea as he walked. Occasionally he'd dream of owning a big house, with a beautiful wife, handsome sons, pretty daughters, staff to do all the menial jobs, and driving a shiny motorcar. His Father had sometimes talked about the Great War, his horrific experiences there and how it had changed the world afterwards, how the men had come back from the War and then the growth of the Trades Unions.

There were a couple of pretty girls and several plain ones at the mine and down in Trelyn and Porthlowen who had made no secret of the fact that they would like to go courting with Jack. Molly Masters had walked out a few times with him and he'd even kissed her when he'd thought they were alone but her eighteen year old brother had spotted them then punched Jack a few times and told him to leave his sister alone. Since then Jack's Father had died, he'd had to take on the responsibility of his family, and he didn't want to be punched by outraged brothers or fathers, so he'd ignored or politely declined the none too subtle offers he'd had.

Liberty fascinated him. With her long golden hair, her fair complexion, and her beautiful dresses he thought she was like an angel. He'd first spotted her from a distance when he'd come out of the water. He was a naturally strong swimmer, had learned when he was young, when he came down with his Father after their long shifts at the mine. He liked to walk quickly into the water and dive straight into the breaking waves, swimming strongly until he was forced to take a breath, then would lie on his back in the water, enjoying the sensation of floating. He would then swim back to the shore and scrub his hands and arms using the rough sand to remove the grime of the mine. He swam in his clothes so that some of the dirt would come off. He was behind some rocks when he was aware of someone along the beach from him standing knee deep in the water. She hadn't noticed him.

Liberty stood up gazing out to sea; Jack could see her long blond hair was blowing gently in the breeze, her wet clothing was now stuck to her and he could see a small pile of clothes further up the beach just out of the reach of the exiting tide. She stood there for a long time, hardly moving and he wondered what she was doing there. He decided not to approach her and kept his distance, wanting to go into the water himself but waiting until after she had left. He wondered who the angel was. He thought she was beautiful and she was obviously a young Lady, the way she carried herself. He kept hidden and watched as she dressed, pulled her boots and stockings on, and then walked away from the promenade. He followed her at a distance, and watched her as she made her way furtively towards Nancarrow House. As she entered the grounds of the House, he realised that either she worked for or was related to Frederick Nancarrow, the owner of Wheal Trencrom mine where Jack worked. Perhaps it was his daughter.

Jack blew out a sharp breath. It was one thing to be punched by Molly Masters' brother for kissing her but Lord only knows what would happen if he was caught kissing Sir Frederick's daughter. And why was he even thinking about kissing this girl? He hadn't even met her.

Jack noticed the girl a few more times over the weeks that followed but always kept hidden from her view. One day when he was returning from the mine, looking forward to his swim and hopefully spotting the Nancarrow girl, he noticed that there was a change in the air, it smelt differently, the wind had risen and switched direction, the waves had white tops and had grown in size. It was still hot and he thought that perhaps a storm was brewing. He'd have to be more careful with his swimming today, perhaps just a shallow swim to remove the dirt, staying closer to shore before the rain came.

As soon he arrived at the beach, he could see that the girl was in trouble. Firstly, she was further out than she normally was. Now she was out of her depth and disappearing under some of the waves. Without a second thought he kicked off his boots and dived straight into the waves, powerfully swimming towards her. With the waves crashing over his head he reached her, panting with the effort of swimming fast and continuously without pausing for a rest. He grabbed under her arms and urged her to kick, doing the same himself and pushing her upwards to try and keep her above the water. It was a real struggle to swim holding someone else and he didn't know if he could do this. She kicked him and it hurt his foot but he encouraged her to carry on kicking. His arms and legs ached, his lungs felt like bursting and he kept swallowing water but still he swam and kicked and implored the girl to do the same. When at long last he felt his feet touch the bottom he put an arm around her waist and gave a big heave, losing his footing in the process. She landed on top of him and awkwardly they both rose to their feet, spitting salty water from their mouths and stood, hands on knees recovering their breath.

Jack being fitter and stronger recovered first. He looked over at the girl and realised that her leg was bleeding. He offered to look at it but she reacted strongly, grabbed her clothes and stormed off towards her house, barefoot and hobbling. Jack just wanted to hold her, protect her and look after her but because of her reaction he thought she'd probably tell her Father and Jack would lose his job at the mine. He wandered around for hours in the rain until tired and exhausted, upset and worried, cold and wet he turned up at home and told Agnes, his Mother, what had happened.

"Oh Lord. What have you done?" exclaimed Agnes, wringing her hands. "We'll lose the house and all starve."

"What was I to do?" he retorted. "Watch and let her die? That would have been worse if someone had seen me and reported back to Sir Frederick. No. I did the right thing. I saved her life." He sounded convincing but not believing his own words. He still expected to be hauled over the coals for his actions and manhandling the mine owner's daughter. He kept a low profile at the mine for a few days, silently going about his work and being chided by his fellow workers for his abnormally subdued manner. He kept replaying Liberty's rescue over and over in his mind. Would he have done anything any differently? Could he have let her die? No obviously not. But then maybe he shouldn't have questioned her about her leg? It was the right thing to do wasn't it? It had been an automatic response for her concern. He would ask the same about his brothers and sisters and fellow miners or a neighbour but maybe not the thing to ask a Lady. He couldn't get it out of his head. He didn't sleep and felt awful, not only for himself but for his poor Mother and his siblings. Oh, what a mess. Even the normally cleansing sea failed to heal the ongoing chatter in his mind. His productivity dropped and the supervisor called him to one side at the end of one particularly gruelling shift.

"Here it is." Jack thought to himself. "I'm going to get the sack and we'll lose the house. I'm going to be summoned to see Sir Frederick." He listened, looking at the floor, expecting the worst.

"Don't know what's got into you boy but these last few days you've been next to no use to me at all. If you don't buck up your ideas, I'll have to replace you at the sharp end. You've been a good worker and the other men look to you for inspiration. It's not only you, but the whole shift productivity has gone down. Sort yourself out by the end of the week or you're gone. This is your last chance."

Board

On Monday morning Rachel contacted Joseph Baker and consulted him about the £50,000. He'd heard over the weekend, probably from Dad Tony, that the Lido was going to shut at the end of the season. Joseph was a local and would have grown up going into the pool as a youngster and had been seen occasionally down there with his own wife and children. He would know all about its historical place in Porthlowen.

"I know it's supposed to go to the Lido but now it's going to shut at the end of the summer the money would just go to the Council, or to pay off debts and I'm sure Sarah wouldn't have wanted that. She would have wanted it to have an effect and a purpose."

"I would just wait for the moment." Joseph advised "and see what happens with the Lido. I agree you shouldn't just pump the money in without finding out more information. It doesn't say when you have to pay the money into the Trustee fund and although it is legally binding it can be contested and I would say that this a fair and reasonable set of circumstances. Obviously, you can't have the money yourself but donating to a local charity, like the RNLI for example, might be something Mrs Rosehill would have approved of. I did know her a little bit and Dad always spoke highly of her so let's just sit tight. You may know more once you're on the Board. Any idea when the next meeting is?"

"Tomorrow night. I'll keep you posted as to the developments. If I get voted in and then how much I'm allowed to say." She hung up.

By Monday evening Rachel was a nervous wreck. Over the weekend she and Tom had discussed some of the ideas that they'd had for the Lido. She'd written down her ideas on cards and practised her presentation a few times in front of Tom, becoming more confident after three runs through. He'd played Devil's Advocate and quizzed her hard on some of the issues and Rachel got upset. "Better to think of some of the objections you're likely to get now and you have your answers planned."

"I'm not sure I want to do this." She'd complained.

"I believe in you. So did Sarah." Tom said softly. "When you're giving your presentation just think of the other members as eight year olds. Deal with them like you used to do with your pupils. You didn't take shit from the eight year olds so don't take shit from this lot. You're used to standing up in front of people, like when parents used to come to watch their little darlings at Nativity plays and things like that. Be calm. Speak clearly and with authority. If they interrupt, tell them off. If I could be there I would but it's just the trustees and the other candidates."

"They're bound to vote for Angela. She's such a strong personality."

"She is but she'll piss them off too." Tom argued. "Can you imagine her at the trustee meetings. She'd have them all trying to dance the can-can if you let her! Just picture Bill Chamberlain or Millicent Angove trying to dance the can-can."

Rachel laughed out loud, the tension released. "Tony and Douggie might though."

"What about Doris Martins? Isn't she the Trustees' secretary?"

"She is the secretary and I can't imagine her doing the can-can either." She giggled at the thought.

"Who else is on the board?" Tom asked, smiling at his wife.

"Nigel Merlo-Banks I think. I don't know him. I've met his wife a couple of times though. Obnoxious cow. Fiona Fortescue Banks. Very OK Ya! From London and I think she went to the same boarding school that Princess Diana did, obviously not at the same time"

"Don't they own the Scooby Doo house up by the golf club?"

"That's right." Rachel filled Tom in on the details. Nigel had made his money setting up an online hotel booking company and spent his time flitting between London and Cornwall. They'd bought and renovated a huge cliffside house which in the swinging sixties had been somewhat of a den of iniquity. There were rumours of loud and raucous parties there for several years, where pop stars and famous people mingled with prominent locals in the Art/Surf scene. Drugs, alcohol, prostitutes both male and female, some under age, were all present. After a tip off the police had raided the property and caught several people in uncompromising positions. After a massive furore the big house was boarded up and became empty. Over time it became derelict and squatters took over. They wrecked the inside using the internal doors to build fires to keep themselves warm, the flickering flames inside giving the house a spooky ghostly glow from a distance, looking like something out of a Scooby Doo episode, and gave the house it's nickname. Eventually in a drunken or drug induced stupor the squatters set fire to the whole property which survived thanks to local firemen and since then it had been abandoned to nature.

Many years later Fiona Fortescue was playing a golf match at the club, noticed the huge derelict house next door and had made enquiries, did some homework and found out that the house was for sale. She persuaded Nigel to buy the house, employed a team of specialists and renovated it to a high spec with the latest modern features. Fiona described herself as a professional Mummy but actually did little parenting, turning up occasionally at Portlowen's private school in her latest car, a Porsche or Range Rover, for functions bearing home-made cakes that "Cook" had lovingly made. Most of the parenting was done by Nanny while the professional Mummy spent her time at the Spa, doing lunch and attending yoga classes, or having lessons at the golf or tennis clubs. Shopping featured heavily in her itinerary. Her two darlings, were Phoebe and Freddy aged ten and seven respectively from her first marriage to Timothy Fortescue, a London barrister. Phoebe Fortescue rode a show jumping pony called Muffin most evenings in either an indoor or outdoor riding school while younger brother Freddy attended rugby training and judo classes.

"Just treat him like an eight year old too." Tom had advised.

Meeting

Rachel didn't sleep well that night and despite Tom's reassurances she awoke with a sense of icy dread in her stomach. She spent most of the day in a panic, practising her presentation in front of the mirror several times. She ransacked her wardrobe trying to find the right outfit. Suit? Too formal. Dresses were discarded as too sparkly, too frilly, too summery. Jeans? Too casual. In the end she settled on a plain dark skirt with a matching coloured pair of shoes, a bright top and a jacket, looking reliable and efficient, as Tom described her.

"I'll be here waiting. Good luck. Go and smash it!"

Rachel drove with trepidation to the car park between the Lido and the Ship and saw Beryl, the Ship's landlady, shuffling across from the pub towards the Café in the Lido, bent over her stick. "Hi Beryl."

"Oh. hello dear." Beryl looked up, speaking in a voice that had been honed from decades of abuse from smoking and neat gin.

"Are you going to the Trustees board meeting?"

"Yes. I'm going to be a trustee. Thought I'd throw my hat into the ring. You never know do you?"

Rachel shook her head. "No. You don't."

Beryl continued. "If we could get the Council to give free parking outside the Ship then that would be good wouldn't it?"

Rachel agreed. "Free car parking would be good for both the Lido and the Pub."

Pierre was on the gates of the Lido and let them both in. "Rachel you look so smart and efficient." He gushed in his flamboyant style. "Just like a glamourous secretary."

"Thanks Pierre." Rachel blushed.

"And Beryl. What can I say?" He offered his arm and Beryl took it, smiling up at him like a lovestruck teenager.

Rachel supressed a smile and followed the unlikely couple into the café.

The two of them were the last to arrive. Pierre showed Beryl to a seat and Rachel sat next to her. The others were around a square of tables pushed together. Tony Baker, a member of the Ls, looked up and smiled. Doris Martens, Jacob Knob's secretary, looked up and frowned. Angela was deep in conversation with Millicent. Pierre went into the back room of the café and shut the door. He wasn't a trustee member but he would lock up later at the end of the meeting and bring out one of his famous chocolate cakes when needed.

"Good evening Rachel and Beryl." Bill Chamberlain looked up from sorting his notes. "Tea and coffee on the side if you want any?" He indicated a table to the side. "Help yourself."

"Anything stronger?" Beryl said in what she thought was a low voice to Rachel but everyone heard.

Rachel sniggered. "Tea? I'll get them."

"Black. Four sugars please."

She made her way and looked around the room. The café looked a lot different in the evening. The big windows that overlooked the Lido, normally brought in lots of light onto the whitewashed walls, the counter was normally groaning with food and there was a hustle and bustle of a combination of busy staff and chatting customers. Douggie sat alone quietly and looked worried. She gave him what she hoped was a reassuring smile. He was sat next to a man she didn't know who was wearing a work suit and tie. His stripy shirt clashed with his paisley tie. He had a full head of greying slightly too long hair. He looked like a bank clerk that lived at home with his elderly Mum.

Rachel was joined at the table by another man who she didn't know. He was tall and elegantly dressed, with a fashionable shirt, open at the neck and a tweed jacket. He had light brown chinos that led down to brown laced boots. His blonde dishevelled hair was down to his shirt collar, his skin was tanned and his handsome face had craggy smile lines around his green eyes. He looked like an advert for a surfing movie.

"Will you be Mum Rachel?" He grinned and passed his cup to her.

"How do you know…? She started and then realised that Bill had wished her good evening.

"I assumed you're not Beryl?"

She smiled back and obligingly poured tea into his cup. "Sorry I don't know your name?"

"I'm Nigel." He said simply.

"Hello Nigel. I think I know your wife. We've met a couple of times."

"Shall we?" He gave her an "after you" gesture.

Bill cleared his throat, shuffled his papers importantly and welcomed everyone to this extraordinary meeting of the Board of Trustees. He ran through the agenda and advised that the first item was to elect a new trustee member following the unfortunate demise of Sarah Rosehill, while the second item was to invite Simon Grayson from Cornwall Council to discuss the reasons behind the shutting of the Lido at the end of this summer. So, we have three written applications here, he held them up, from Beryl Trebilcock, Angela Edwards and Rachel Roberts. We will hear from each candidate as to why they think they should be elected. Ladies, you should also expect questions at the end. Beryl, would you like to go first?"

Beryl supped a mouthful of cooling tea through the gaps in her missing teeth. "We need the Council to give us free parking out here." She gestured in the opposite direction to the car park. "Then more people would come into the Lido." She paused her wheezy breath then coughed for what seemed like an eternity to Rachel. The rattling chesty cough was deafening. "The more people who come in, then the more profitable it is. Simple economics." She stopped, breathless then coughed again.

"Anything else?" Bill Chamberlain looked incredulous.

Beryl shook her head still coughing.

Nigel waited patiently until she had stopped, then asked. "Beryl. If the car park was free do you think that more people would come to the Ship too?"

"They might do." Her rheumy eyes smiled. "I'd not really considered it."

Everyone laughed except Bill, who cleared his throat noisily. "If you've nothing more to add then we'll move on to the next candidate. Angela?"

Angela stood up and pushed her chair back noisily and launched into her spiel. "It's obvious what's wrong with this place I was only telling Douggie the other day." She pointed to poor Douggie who tried to shrink into his chair. "This place has been open since before my Dad was a lifeguard here. There are pictures of him on the high board. This place isn't run properly. The food is cold or burnt, there's food out all day in the sun." Her voice became higher pitched. "It's too expensive, they close the pool on busy days, they don't clean it properly, people can't bring their dogs, it opens too late, it closes too early." She ranted. "Douggie needs to keep his job and so does Pierre, I'll sort this place out." She paused for breath and looked around. The other trustees were looking at the desk in front of them, trying to dodge the diatribe as it rained around them. "I won't allow them to close the Lido. Vote for me!" She looked around at everyone expectantly, waiting for applause or cheers, as she'd had on the steps of the Lido a few days before. When there was no response she sat down with a huff. The only sound, apart from Beryl wheezing was Doris Martens scribbling furiously on a note pad.

"So, what would you suggest Angela? Millicent broke the silence softly.

"Haven't you been listening?" Angela raised her voice. "Vote for me and I'll sort it out. I'll make Sarah proud. I'll get Douggie to keep his job…"

"But how would you do it?" Nigel interrupted, his cultured voice gently goading Angela. "How would you 'sort it out'" He made an inverted comma sign with his fingers in the air. "You've told us what you don't like and if we voted for you, then you, single handedly, will sort it out but you haven't given us any constructive ideas or concrete proposals that we could discuss, debate or negotiate."

Rachel listened intently. Nigel wasn't just a pretty face, there was a shrewd business mind working overtime underneath his surfer boy looks. He continued smiling pleasantly at Angela. "There are, of course, several others of us here who have ideas about how we should proceed together and try to make this place more profitable. But we want to see if you have any ideas yourself."

Angela sat with her arms folded, lips pursed, looking like a scolded schoolgirl. "I've said all I have to say."

Bill stared at Angela for a moment then cleared his throat. "Rachel?" His gaze changed from Angela to Rachel.

Heart pounding Rachel quietly stood up, paused and looked around the room. Apart from Angela who was looking downcast, pairs of eyes looked expectantly at her. She took a small bunch of prompt cards from her jacket pocket. "They're just a bunch of eight year olds" she thought to herself.

"Thank you, Bill." She started softly. "Thank you for giving me an opportunity to put my case across." Bill smiled at being complimented. She took a deep breath and continued. "I agree with Angela on certain things..."

Angela's head shot up, smiled and looked at Rachel. "Told you." She said and looked around the room triumphantly.

"Angela please don't interrupt me." Rachel said quietly but firmly.

Nigel and Tony looked amused.

"I think that there are things in the café that could be improved. I think that there are days when the pool opens too late and shuts too early."

"I said that!" Angela interjected accusingly. "You're just pinching my ideas."

"Angela!" Rachel looked at her. "I was good enough to listen to your proposals without interruption. Please accord me the same decency." Angela looked stunned.

Rachel paused. "We need to think of ways that the pool could be open longer for example 7am to 7pm, or even longer when it's still light at 8 or 9 pm. There are swimmers who swim when the sun comes up all year round, weather permitting, just behind the Lido on Golden Rocks. If the sea is rough then they could swim in the pool so they don't miss their swim. We could also extend the season by opening at the beginning of March and keep going until the end of October half term. Quite often we get Indian summers when the weather and the sea is still warm but the pool is shut for the winter by then. Now the café....."

"What about staffing?" Nigel asked.

"Please don't interrupt me. I'm still speaking." Rachel looked directly at Nigel, thinking "Oh shit. I've blown his vote now!"

Nigel grinned and smacked the back of his other hand. "That's me told."

"The café..." Rachel continued, smiling, warming to her task, raising her voice and speaking quickly, with passion and conviction. "Could be improved by selling breakfasts and maybe evening meals too as well as the usual snacks, coffee, cakes, lunches. I know we have odd days at the moment where we promote fun days like a dog day and an inflatables day, and they're always popular and make money but we need to think of multiple ways of getting multiple income streams so that it's profitable all year round, every year, regardless of good or poor summers. Could the café space be cleared and used for other things? Dance classes? Yoga classes? Talks? Demonstrations? Needlework and craft classes, art groups and so on. Could any areas outside be used sometimes? The Lido is a great selling point for the town but needs to be promoted through all types of media, both conventional types and on social media. Get the local businesses, hotels, B and Bs and caravan sites to advertise cheaply here and in return their customers get cheaper entrance tickets. Once they're here they'll spend in the café, and…" she stole a glance at Beryl, who'd gone to sleep, "…maybe visit the Ship as well. Liberty's Lido is part of this town, is iconic, has been here for nearly one hundred years, and with careful management will be here for future generations and for another hundred years." Exhausted she slumped to her chair.

Tony winked at her and nodded his head, grinning. Bill smiled and Millicent stood up clapping, Nigel joined Millicent, stood and clapped with thunderous applause. Tony and Douggie took to their feet too while even Doris smiled and stopped taking notes. Beryl woke up with a start, shuffled to her feet and had a bout of coughing. Simon Grayson, the County Councillor, sat impassively. Angela clapped, nodded her head and mouthed "Well done."

Rachel met Tom in the Ship after the meeting. Beryl treated Rachel to a large G and T when she arrived another hour or so after the vote had elected Rachel unanimously to the board of Trustees. Rachel relayed the rest of the meeting to Tom. After the vote Pierre had escorted Beryl and Angela from the café and Rachel took Sarah's place on the board of Trustees.

Simon Grayson had stood up and in an expressionless, emotionless monotone had said that there was a deficit in the Lido's coffers. Every year there was always a repair bill but after the previous winter's bad storms there was urgent work that needed doing. However, the Council were unable to continue propping up a loss making enterprise however iconic, historical or popular it was; and unless £400,000 was found by the 30th September then the Lido would have to shut forever!

When quizzed further he became defensive and tried to shift the blame away from himself and the Council. Nigel and Millicent, mainly, had questioned him ferociously, demanding answers. Tony had chipped in with intelligent questions too while Doris had continued to write notes furiously. Rachel kept quiet, for as the newbie, she just observed how the Board worked, but she had felt quite sorry for Simon, however unpopular the Council's decision was. He was, after all, only the messenger. The decision must have been made by faceless names at the Council, accountants and pen pushers. In a nutshell the Board of Trustees had to raise £400k and submit a robust business plan of sustainability and profitability not just for the next twelve months but for at least five years and beyond. There was a possibility that the money, once raised, could be match funded by the EU and other grants but with Brexit looming on the horizon there was no guarantee of this.

There was an offer on the table from a firm of property developers who had submitted outline architectural plans to rip out the heart and soul of that part of Porthlowen and replace it with a 21st century modern hotel with car parking underneath, exactly where the pool was now. Rachel was horrified. However, sentiment would have to remain at the door. Hard, factual business decisions were needed to move forwards beyond the 30th September or Liberty's Lido would be consigned to the history books.

Having dropped his seismic bombshell Simon Grayson left the café, leaving the Trustees in a state of bewilderment, frustration, anger and shock. Bill suggested a ten minute comfort break while Pierre was summoned from the café kitchen to brew fresh tea and coffee and deliver that cure for all sorrows, cake. Rachel needed to clear her head and slowly walked around the perimeter of the pool, inhaling the cool, fresh salty air. As she returned to the café she could see Nigel, deep in conversation with Millicent, overlooking the diving area. Nigel was smoking a cigarette and was emphasising his point by flamboyantly moving his hand, still holding the glowing stick between his fingers. Douggie stood a few yards away from them, alone, and smiled at Rachel as she returned to the fold. Doris appeared at the door of the café to summon the members back to the meeting.

Bill looked as if he hadn't moved and shuffled his papers importantly again. He cleared his throat. "Can I call the meeting to order?" Everyone collected fresh tea and coffee, a piece of delicious cake and made their way back to their seats.

"Can I make an amendment to the agenda please Mr Chairman?" Millicent asked, looking at Nigel.

"Um yes, I suppose so Millicent." Bill looked annoyed. "This is highly irregular you know."

Nigel interjected. "For Christ's sake Bill. We've got about four months to raise four hundred thousand pounds and come up with a workable plan that's going to sustain this place to the Council's satisfaction for the next five years. Now is the time for action, not petty nit picking."

Bill looked aghast at being challenged. Doris stopped taking notes.

Millicent interjected. "Gentleman, please!" She looked around the room. Everyone looked at her in silence and anticipation. "I propose an amendment to the agenda."

"Seconded." Nigel chimed in. "Any objections?" He glared at Bill, daring him to object. "Millicent?"

"I propose that we meet back here in one week with ideas as to how we are going to raise the money. These are firm ideas. Not just vague ideas but as detailed plans as to how we are going to put these ideas into action. Nigel, Tony and myself have business contacts that we can use to chat up to get them on our side. Rachel? Nigel and I were chatting outside and we believe that you have the passion and drive to be able to put some of your proposals into action. We had thought that the pool and café haven't been used to maximum efficiency, no offence Douggie." She looked at Douggie who nodded in silent acknowledgement. "Rachel's ideas matched some of our own, and this now needs to be put into action. Quickly. Our decision has a deadline. We propose that you and Douggie, together with Pierre, look at the pool, the Lido, the café and this room." Millicent indicated the whitewashed walls. "We want a detailed plan, staffing, costs, proposed revenue and so on. If you need help, ask. Is that alright with you two?" She looked at Rachel and Douggie, who looked at each other and assented.

"Can I have everyone's contact details and email addresses please? asked Rachel. They agreed and she wrote it all down.

"I don't think there's any other business?" Nigel asked Bill.

Bill shook his head and agreed a time and date for the next meeting, in one week's time. The meeting broke up and Rachel walked to the Ship.

Tom listened to Rachel as she recounted the events of the evening. "Phew. You've got your work cut out. Sarah would be proud of you. I'm proud of you too. She knew that you were the right person to take over from her. You've got passion and ideas. We've just got to get these plans into action."

"But I don't know about staffing and costs of food. There's health and safety issues around opening the pool longer hours and I don't know about some of the legal side of things either. Contracts and stuff like that"

"That's why you have a committee. You're not doing it on your own. Tony's an ex solicitor. He can advise on the legal stuff and if he's not up to date then Joseph Knob will be, or know where to get the information. Douggie employs Pierre, doesn't he? And the other lifeguards and café staff? So, arrange to meet both of them individually in the next couple of days, tell them what you want. It's in both of their interests to come up with a workable proposal as if the Lido shuts, they'll both lose their jobs. Tell Pierre you want a good value, no nonsense menu together with a staffing rota for seven days a week, breakfast, lunch and evening meals. Tell Douggie to do the same for the lifeguards from 7am to 7pm, costs of that. Both will need more staff and/or extra hours, they'll probably need deputy managers or shift managers as they both can't be expected to be there 24/7. If you're doing evening meals, you'll need a proper chef. They will both need to advertise for extra staff so build the costs into the proposals. Talk to them. They may have some ideas themselves. Talk to the Ls. They use the pool and the Lido. Get Angela on board. What do they want from this place? Will the Lido need to advertise itself in local paper and on social media? What will be the cost of that?"

"Wow, you sound as passionate as me."

"I am. I want this place to succeed just as much as you do."

They ran ideas back and forth between themselves and decided to get back home so they could jot down the ideas and make a plan. By the time it was bedtime Rachel's head was buzzing but she felt inspired and couldn't wait for the next day to come so she could put her plan into action. She had to get Liberty's Lido to survive.

Apology 1928

Temporarily reprieved Jack hurried homewards towards the sea and the promenade, determined to have a quick swim and wash, resolving to get back to work properly the following day, the storm having not cleared the air at all, it was as hot and sticky as ever, as he arrived at the beach. He stripped off quickly, kicked his boots off and dived straight into the cooling water. He swam hard and fast through the waves, pushing himself hard, swimming aggressively until, panting hard, he finally relaxed, lay on his back and looked up at the blue and white picture above him, an occasional seagull gliding across his vision. He breathed deeply, feeling the knots in his neck and shoulders dissolve. With his ears under the water he could hear very little and enjoyed the peacefulness both externally and within himself. He didn't understand why he felt like this but it felt good. An escape from all of his problems, work, family and the golden haired Nancarrow girl. He just wanted to float forever. After a time, he started to feel cold and so slowly turned over and swam gently towards the shore. He reached the shallows and bent down to grab sand to rub the grime from his arms, hands and face. As he stood, he saw Miss Nancarrow watching him from a distance. She was standing in the shallow water, the cool water lapping over her feet.

"Oh no." The tension in his stomach resumed. He slowly made his way up the beach to the rocks where he'd left his jacket and boots dreading what she would say, or had said to her Father. He stood where he was drying himself and she slowly and shyly paddled towards him. He left his clothes on the rocks and walked towards her. They stood a few feet apart not sure what to say to each other. He not wanting to offend her and she wanting to apologise for her rude behaviour but not sure how to start.

"I just wanted to say…" She began. "You first.."

"I'm sorry I…" He started at the same time. "You first."

They both stopped, looked at each other, smiled awkwardly then laughed. Liberty recovered first. "I'd um like to thank you um for saving my life. I'm sorry I was so rude to you and ran away."

"Anytime." Jack replied grinning.

"What run away? Or be rude to you?" She laughed gaining confidence and taking the lead.

"Rescue you I meant." He smiled but still wasn't sure of her.

"What were you going to say?" She encouraged.

"I didn't mean to offend you when I asked you about your bleeding leg." He said softly, not sure if he would upset her again.

"No. It was my fault. I shouldn't be so sensitive. It was kind of you. I know you were concerned but it was only a scratch. I had polio when I was a baby and that leg isn't as strong as the other one and it looks different too and…" She stopped, realising that perhaps she'd said too much and he wouldn't want to talk to her anymore if he knew she had polio, like some friends of her Father's who had sons and daughters who wouldn't play with her or talk to her anymore once they knew she had polio, as if they were going to catch it.

"I hadn't noticed." He said honestly. "It was only the blood that I noticed that day."

"I was very silly to go into the water that deep. I hadn't realised that the sea could do that so suddenly."

"You have to respect the water. It's much stronger than us and it's unpredictable."

"You were very brave. You could have died."

"But I couldn't just sit by and watch you get washed out to sea."

"You could have got help."

"But you could have drowned before help arrived. I could see you were in trouble as soon as I arrived at the prom." They suddenly ran out of things to say and while Liberty looked at her feet Jack took the lead. "I could teach you how to swim." He blurted out. She looked at him curiously. "Just so that you stay safe." He continued giving her a cheeky smile.

Liberty wasn't sure what to say, so Jack sensing her nerves carried on the conversation. "I can meet you here after I finish at the Mine tomorrow if you're free. We can go at your pace." He smiled trying to put her at ease, really not knowing what to say and how to behave around the mine owner's daughter.

Liberty thought for a few seconds before asking Jack "Do you feel as free as I do when you swim? As if all of your worries go away?"

“Yes.” replied Jack after a pause, thinking about what she’d said and thinking about how he’d been wanting to float away earlier “And a lot cleaner.”

Liberty looked down at his wet and dirty clothes and laughed. “I do want to swim like all the other children. Will you really teach me?” She asked.

“Yes definitely, I think you need some help.” Suddenly realising that he might have overstepped the line he looked embarrassed and it was his turn to look at his feet. “Sorry.”

Liberty laughed again and replied “I think you might be right about that. We start tomorrow”.

“Right you are Miss Nancarrow.” He smiled at her.

She spun her head towards him. “How do you know who I am?” She asked softly.

“I watched you walk away last time into the grounds of Nancarrow House.”

“I could be one of the maids there.” She teased him, smiling.

“I don’t think so Miss. Your clothes are not that of one of the maids.”

“They could be my Sunday best.”

“It’s not Sunday.” He laughed.

“Yes. I am Miss Nancarrow. Liberty to my friends.”

“Am I your friend? May I call you Liberty?”

“You may. And you, brave Sir, what is your name?”

“I’m Jack Pender Miss. You may call me Mr Pender.” He laughed, forgetting his station for the moment. He enjoyed the banter with this young Lady.

“Well Mr Pender.” Liberty pretended to be affronted, putting her hands on her hips. “I shall see you tomorrow.” She laughed and leaving Jack on the beach she headed towards home.

Fundraising

Rachel didn't sleep well that night. She kept waking up and thinking of more things to add to her list. In the end, thoughts whirring around in her mind, she got up, silently grabbed her dressing gown and made her way downstairs to the kitchen, leaving Tom softly snoring away. It was still dark and as she put the light on she glanced at the clock. Ten past five! She grabbed a glass from the cupboard and drank cool water from it as she put her ideas to paper. She was still scribbling away and making notes on her laptop when Tom appeared nearly two hours later.

"How long have you been here?"

"Since about five o'clock. Been awake most of the night. I've tried to get our ideas in some sort of order. I thought that in the café...." She rattled on and Tom held his hands up in protest.

"Woah. Just give me five minutes to wake up. Coffee?"

"Please."

Tom held his mug in his hands and took that first, all important, mouthful. "Aaaagghh" he breathed out deeply. "Do you remember when Poppy used to copy us with her drinks?"

"Yes" Rachel smiled. She ran through the new ideas while Tom agreed, disagreed, interjected and offered advice. Finally, she typed up the notes and printed them out. She wanted them to be easy to read when she saw Pierre and Douggie.

As the two of them had breakfast and got ready for their day they discussed the Lido some more and Rachel added pencil marks to her notes.

Tom said "Why don't you swim first and then stay down at the Lido for the rest of the day if you need to. That'll give you a chance to talk to Douggie and then Pierre if they're not too busy. They'll have ideas too. I'm sure Douggie will have been thinking about this overnight like you, as he was at the meeting and Pierre was out the back so I'm sure he may have overheard some of what was said. Douggie may have spoken to him too. The swim will clear your head, especially after not much sleep."

Rachel agreed. "Yes. Ok. Good idea".

Rachel parked her car and made her way through the gates of Liberty's Lido and down to where the others were congregating.

Today they were discussing how much fun the opening day had been before the conversation turned back to the shock news that this was going to be the last season.

Seeing Douggie at the far end of the Lido, overlooking the sea, Rachel changed quickly, put her towelling robe over her swimming costume, grabbed her swimming goggles and hat and walked over to him.

Douggie greeted her with a warm smile. "Morning."

"Morning." Rachel replied brightly. "Will you have some time free today to discuss the plans from yesterday's meeting? Possibly with Pierre too?"

"Yes. I've spoken to him briefly. He's going to put his thinking cap on and come up with some ideas. I've suggested we meet together in the café just after we shut. It'll be quiet and we can thrash out some ideas. Are you gonna be around about that time?"

"Yes, that's ok. No problem. I'm here for the day and I'll see you in the café later."

She rejoined the rest of the Ls as they walked around the Lido to the rocks. After the usual shrieks and swearing she enjoyed her swim, relaxing in the sweet clean water. Body glowing and with a clear head she made her way back to the Lido with Sally, telling her about Poppy's life at University.

As everyone started to sit on the wooden benches in the sunshine with their drinks after getting dressed, shivering after being in the cold sea and eating Liz's legendary cake the topic soon returned to The End. £400,000 was such a lot of money to raise and in such a short space of time. Could it be done? How would they raise the money? And who would do it?

A bout of coughing interrupted the proceedings as Tony had forgotten about Ziggy's infamous offerings. She'd overheard Liz talking about putting extra ginger in her cake, by mistake and everyone loved it. Ziggy had decided to make a rhubarb and ginger pie but had put far too much ginger into it. And it was still slightly raw. Ugh. Poor Tony had been persuaded by Ziggy to try it and as he liked ginger cakes and puddings, thinking he would be alright today. Wrong! He excused himself, gasping for air his face turning redder, apologising to the group he rushed to the Gents to get some cold water. Ziggy looked affronted.

Angela shrilly continued talking over everyone, eventually everyone fell silent and only her voice could be heard. This annoyed several swimmers as they felt their voices were never heard. Even though she was seventy two Angela was fit and very determined already helping other charities and rescuing seal pups that had been abandoned or injured, turning out in all weathers. When she had everyone's attention, in an excited voice she announced "We can raise the money."

Nobody spoke!

Then fifty two year old Belle who everyone called Tink after the character Tinkerbelle from Peter Pan but was more like the character Eeyore from Winnie the Pooh started to laugh hysterically. "What raise £400,000 in four months. That's £100,000 a month and £25,000 a week. Really? We live in a poor area where nearly everyone is paid minimum wage and you're expecting to raise £400,000 in four months. That's the funniest thing that's come out of your mouth in weeks." She looked around at her cronies for approval.

Angela looked at Tink like she wanted to kill her. Tink was always the most miserable person in the group and being an artist sometimes this showed in her work. Most of the time her painting were of what she saw under the sea and she had an avid following of buyers for her work, but every now again she'd paint a picture of a morbid dark scene that was a reflection of her thoughts and she was known for throwing paintings out of her upstairs studio window, in temper, down onto the pavement just outside her gallery, as she was such a perfectionist. How she had never hit anyone or a passing car was incredible. Her dark moods would come crowding into her ever busy mind. Depression is unseen, unheard and you can't escape it no matter how hard you try. It follows you around like a black shadow, like death patiently waiting to envelop you. Tink's tongue could be vicious and when she was under death's spell, she couldn't care less what she said or how she acted. She was too consumed by her own thoughts and retreated into her studio for a few weeks, emerging on a very low tide as the sea started to beckon her back to its watery depths. It was like a rebirth, Tink used the sea to cleanse her body and mind. It was like she'd pushed reboot in the studio and now all systems were go again.

Angela pulled herself together and looking Tink in the eye said "Couldn't you organise an exhibition and get some of your arty friends to donate work?

That'll make some money for the Lido." She was almost mocking Tink as she said it, challenging her through eye contact and body language.

Rachel could see things were escalating between the two women so chirped up quickly and stepped in between them. "Why don't we ALL meet in The Ship Inn in a couple of days time and discuss if we can start the ball rolling and try and fund raise some of the money. For those of you who don't know I'm now one of the Trustees and I'm looking for ideas as to how we can save the Lido. I've got to take ideas to the rest of the Board of Trustees next week. I haven't got the monopoly on ideas. Let's work together. We're a strong group of people. I want this Lido to stay open and I'm sure you do too. C'mon. Put aside your differences and let's do this for Porthlowen." She looked around at everyone, amazing herself with her passion and caught Bill's eye. He winked and nodded encouragement. She continued. "How about everyone writes some ideas down and I will post a note on our Facebook Group page letting everyone know time and day. I'll talk to Stan and liaise with him too. I'm sure he'd be up for a large group of people coming to his establishment and spending money."

Most of the group laughed although Tink turned away muttering "Fucking waste of time." She picked up her swimming bag and stormed off.

Tension broken the group broke up and went their various ways, off to spend their day with their families, children and grandchildren, shopping, chores at home, out for walks, lunches and so on.

"I'm just going to check on Tony and then I'll get some coffee." Dawn grinned at Rachel. "Poor bugger. He never learns. Does he? Wonder what Ziggy did this time?"

Flo piped up laughing. "She's probably confused tea spoons and table spoons again. She's done that before. Then after everyone loved Liz's extra ginger cake last time she thought she'd put in an extra table spoon or two of ginger. That pie was probably as spicy as a vindaloo."

Rachel and Dawn laughed.

Alice joined them. "What are you lot laughing at?"

Flo told her. The three women settled down to sit in the sun. The others had gone now while Dawn went off to find the unfortunate Tony. She returned with coffee and reported that Tony was fine and was heading off home now to tend to his lawn.

After a pleasant day catching up on the gossip Rachel relaxed and as the pool was closing, she dressed and found Douggie and Pierre in the café. Tom arrived for a quick dip after work then took the swimming bags and arranged to meet Rachel in the Ship when she'd finished.

"Talk to Stan and see if there's one evening this week that's free for him to have the meeting in the Pub, then can you stick a note up on our Facebook page letting them know date and times and tell them to bring their ideas plus an open mind."

"You're not asking for much are you?" Tom grinned at her as he swung the bags up onto his broad shoulders and climbed the steps out of the Lido.

Agenda

As Rachel walked into the café Pierre was just wiping down the tables as the last customers drained their cups and glasses. He rushed over to give Rachel a hug and for the first time she noticed he looked slightly vulnerable. She'd never seen him like that before and she was slightly taken back. Pierre always oozed charisma and confidence and she thought to herself that maybe the pool closing and possibly the café too had made him take it personally. He loved the Café. It was his passion and she found herself giving him a reassuring hug and saying "it will be ok".

Douggie arrived and the three of them sat down with mugs of coffee and some left over chocolate fudge cake. It was Rachel's favourite and she wondered if Pierre, being the kind person he was, she had come to realise over the years, had saved it especially for her. It really was divine and in her head, she could hear Pierre's words "the edible glitter sprinkled on the surface just makes the calories disappear." Rachel smiled to herself at the thought and knew she needed to give both of the men some hope. She didn't have a magic wand but she did have some ideas. Opening her notebook, she found the page with her handwritten scrawl from that morning. Bullet points, each with an idea and she proceeded to read them out loud.

- Longer pool opening hours 7am-8pm (9pm in June and July)
- Longer season First March – end of half term in October
- Café open 7am for breakfasts, lunches, evening meals – all summer, query close 10pm
- All year round food, drinks, cake, snacks, soup – maybe restricted menu? Maybe weekend evening meals? Sunday lunches?
- Meetings, stitch and bitch, yoga, other clubs, Christmas market? Craft clubs, food markets
- Hired out for private functions. Art gallery, business meetings?
- Dog day
- Children's Parties
- Corporate advertising in the changing cubicles
- Share scheme

Drawing breath, she stopped, aware of the silence. She was starting to like bringing her ideas to life. It made her realise how much she missed working. The planning, delivering the ideas, the nurturing of others.

When Pierre started to talk it brought her out of her little planning bubble. "Wow" he said with a big grin. The little bit of doubt was starting to fade from his persona and she could see the confident Pierre starting to emerge again. "I love the ideas." he continued. "Douggie." He turned to look at his manager and said "I told you Rachel was the right person for this job."

Douggie was still quiet. "I'm not sure I've got the fight in me. Maybe I'm getting too old and I should just retire and let a younger person like you, Rachel, take control".

"Absolutely not!!!!" both Rachel and Pierre said in unison. It broke the tension and they all laughed.

Rachel continuing said "Douggie we need you to be on board. You're part of the furniture. We need your experience and knowledge. This place wouldn't be what it is without you. Your soul and the Lido are one". She carried on "If you leave then I don't think I can do it because I'm relying on you to help me out with all the technical bits and the everyday running plans. I'm here to support you, not the other way around." Rachel realised that she had stood up as she was speaking and getting more passionate. She slowly sat back down on her chair and drew breath.

There followed a silence before Pierre stood up and said "Group hug". Rachel standing up walked over to Pierre.

Douggie still sitting down was still trying to process the last few sentences.

"Come on Douggie" called Pierre, "Don't leave me hanging." offering his free arm and making Rachel laugh in the process.

Douggie rose slowly from the table, with a look as if the cogs in his brain were still turning. He joined Pierre and Rachel and squeezing them both tight Pierre whispered "We're going to be ok".

Rachel's phone beeped and disturbed the moment. Reaching down she saw it was a text from Tom.

"Thursday evening is free so shall I put a message up on Facebook with a 7.30pm start?"

Rachel replied with a yes and a couple of kisses. Looking up she said “Tom has arranged a meeting for Thursday evening 7.30 PM at The Ship, so that everyone can share their ideas before the next Trustees meeting.”

“Good.” replied Douggie. “We need lots and lots of good ideas.”

After a minute Rachel continued. “Right Douggie. What I need is a detailed plan by the next Board of Trustee meeting of kiosk and lifeguard rotas, cleaners, costings and so on. You’ll need deputy and shift managers as you can’t be expected to be here seven days a week. New staff will need to be employed and they’ll need training. Build the costs into your plan please. OK?”

Douggie nodded assent.

“Pierre.” Rachel continued. “Summer and Winter menus, breakfasts, lunches, coffee and cake, soups, evening meals, drinks license, costings of the food and staffing levels too. Like Douggie you can’t work seven days a week so you’ll need managers and also training. Alright with you?”

“You’re a task mistress aren’t you Rachel?” Pierre laughed. “Yes, of course I will. I’d started to think along those lines after listening to you at the Board meeting.”

Rachel pretended to be shocked and waved a stern finger at him. “Pierre. That meeting is supposed to be confidential and you’re not supposed to listen in.”

Pierre pretended to look told off.

Rachel continued. “Right. If you need any help then ask me or ask the other Board members. I’ve got their contact details if you haven’t.”

They drained their coffee mugs with Pierre returning them to the counter. Walking out together, Pierre locked the café doors and set the alarm before they all went their separate ways. Rachel joined Tom in the pub.

Swimming 1928

All day during her lessons Liberty thought about Jack and learning to swim. She wasn't sure if she was more excited about learning to swim or meeting Jack, continually asking herself in her head if this is what it's like to have a friend.

Miss Scrivener noticed that she was distracted "Liberty! What on earth is the matter with you today? I've told you about this French verb three times and you're just not listening. It's like I'm talking to Daisy."

"Nothing Miss Scrivener. Sorry Miss Scrivener."

"You'll sit here until all of this work has been completed." droned the starchy governess.

Liberty focused her mind. She didn't want to miss her first lesson with Jack. Lessons dragged on but finally they were finished for the day. She tried to busy herself in her room and then outside in the gardens and grounds of Nancarrow House but she couldn't settle to anything. Eventually she walked through the kitchen on her way out to grab a sandwich.

"Please may I have an extra sandwich today as I'm feeling really hungry." She asked Cook.

Mrs Hitchens smiled, glad that Liberty had a new found hunger. "Of course you can Miss Liberty, just give me a couple of minutes. Another cheese sandwich?"

"Yes please." She replied watching Mrs Hitchens cut a couple of thick slices of homemade bread, spreading butter, deftly adding some tomato, lettuce and onion to the concoction, wrapping it in greaseproof paper and tying it up in a white cloth. Liberty left the kitchen, made her way through the gardens and headed towards the beach, excited and with butterflies in her stomach.

Jack was already lying on the beach his face turned towards the sun like a sunflower. Spending so much time in the dark, cold, wet underground tunnels of the mine his body craved the warmth. Quietly Liberty sat down on the soft sand next to Jack. He didn't stir and she could hear his rhythmic breathing as his chest underneath his tatty dirty shirt rose and fell. It gave Liberty a chance to really look at him without feeling embarrassed. He had short dark hair which was tainted with the coal dust, the grime from the mine covered every inch of his body and the dirty water stains impregnated his clothes. Her eyes moved to his tanned but smeary face, his strong and determined chin, his bare throat and his Adam's apple moving rhythmically as he breathed deeply. His bare arms were tanned and muscular, scarred and cut from a hundred scrapes under the ground. The back of his hands were filthy, one had blood on the back of it her eyes noticed and they continued their downward passage. Jack's trousers were encrusted with dirt and his battered boots had several gouges on the top of them. Jack opened first one eye then another. He was tired from his work and the warmth of the sun had relaxed him to the point of sleep. Still lying down he propped himself up on one elbow. Firstly looking at Liberty, then looking at the tied up white cloth he asked "What's inside?"

Having being caught staring at him she blushed while unwrapping the food. "It's something to eat." Liberty answered. "I asked Cook to make an extra sandwich in case you were hungry. Would you like one?"

Jack sat straight up, grabbed the offered sandwich biting off a large chunk and before swallowing his first mouthful he bit another piece off. Liberty watched transfixed; she'd never seen anyone eat so fast before. He then bit off another piece and she was worried he would choke as it didn't look like he had swallowed any of the sandwich. Before she had even started hers he had nearly finished his.

Taking her first bite Liberty observed "You were hungry."

Jack finishing his last mouthful uttered "I've not eaten anything since before work."

"What time was that?" Liberty asked.

"Five o clock this morning" Jack replied watching her eat.

"I'm still asleep at that time" she replied, embarrassedly after swallowing a mouthful. She gave him the rest of her food and he wolfed the second sandwich as quick as the first.

Jack jumped up "Come on. Let's swim". He stripped off his shirt, kicked off his boots and ran down the beach, his suntanned arms, neck and face contrasting sharply with the milky white skin of his torso, even though he was covered in coal dust. Running into the water up to his waist he dived into an incoming wave and out the other side. As he broke up through the surface of the water, he ran his hand through his hair and out of his eyes. Liberty stood on the edge not sure what to do,

"Come on in." shouted Jack. "It's lovely and warm."

The water felt cool after the heat of the sand. The beach was full of debris from the previous week's storm. Liberty was walking on crushed shells and seaweed. The weed felt squishy between her toes, contrasting with the occasional sharpness of the shells as she entered the water, hobbling slightly. Jack swam back towards her and they met when Liberty was waist deep.

"I think it would be a good idea if you learned how to float" said Jack and he showed her how to float, "Just lie on your back and relax. Don't worry I'll support you. If that's alright Miss?" he added, remembering his station.

Liberty nodded assent, concentrated firmly, shut her eyes, bent her knees and leant back. She could feel the sun on her face, hardly noticing it but was fully aware of Jack beside her, his hand supporting her head and her lower back. After a couple of minutes, she put her feet back onto the seabed and stood up.

"How did that feel?" asked Jack.

"Amazing." replied Liberty. "That was so good I'm going to do it again".

Again, Jack supported her. After a few times he removed first one hand and then the other. The first couple of times she sank quickly and emerged coughing and spluttering but laughing as she brushed her sodden hair from her face.

"Let's try again" She said in a determined voice.

They tried a few more times and Liberty was starting to relax but still couldn't quite master the art of floating. Jack noticed that she was starting to shiver so suggested they both got out.

"But I want to learn to swim." She said adamantly.

"And you will." He replied gently. "You're cold and so it's time to stop. You've got to listen to your body and also respect the sea."

"But…"

"No buts." He interrupted, taking charge. "The sea is dangerous. If you get really cold you'll be in trouble." She looked cross and upset. "You've done really well today."

"But I still can't swim."

"You will. Be patient."

"I don't want to be patient. I want to swim like you."

He laughed. "How long do you think it took me to learn how to swim?" She hadn't thought about that. "How long did it take you to walk properly?" he added softly.

"Ages." She sighed. "You're right. I'm just impatient."

"Let's go and warm up." He suggested.

They waded back out of the sea and sat on the warm rocks, drying themselves and allowing the early evening sun to slow down the shivering.

Ideas

The Ship was buzzing for a Thursday evening. The tourist season hadn't really started in earnest yet so it was usually only the diehard regulars who frequented on a week night. Stan Trebilcock, the Landlord, had run the pub for twenty odd years having taken over from his Father Frank, who had died when Stan was just twenty one. Initially he'd helped his Mum, Beryl, to manage the pub but over the years he'd taken on more and more of the running of the pub while Beryl had basically retired. Now seventy two she did the occasional shift behind the bar when they were short staffed or it was a busy time of year. Living upstairs, the pub was her home and social life. Having been behind the bar for over forty years she knew everyone in the town and was a terrible gossip. Sometimes in the summer she'd join the Ls for a swim or a chat over in the Lido. Stan was always stylishly dishevelled, looking as if he frequented the beach surfing most days. You never found him not wearing sunglasses. Even if it was the evening they were on top of his head. Dressed in a black tee and jeans he was chatting and smiling with a couple of girls sitting the other side of the bar. He was born with the talent to flirt and charm. One of the girls he was talking to straightened her posture and tried to make herself more alluring to him. He noticed her reaction while running his fingers through his hair then looked up and saw Rachel. She had known Stan for years as he was the younger brother of her friend Catherine, one of her college friends. Catherine's family had lived above the pub and Rachel had gone there to hang out, listen to music and meet boys. Stan was the annoying little brother who was always being told to sod off by Catherine but he'd been a charmer even then, eleven years younger than the girls. Rachel had always said hello to him back then and he'd asked her to be his girlfriend once but Catherine had thrown a cushion at him and told him to get out. He was aged six at the time!

He gave a quick wave before walking towards her at the bar.

"Hi Rachel what can I get you?" he smiled as he surveyed the busy pub.

"A G & T please."

"Your usual?" Always a Bombay Sapphire with a twist of lime and tonic. "Or would you like to see our gin Menu?"

"What? A gin Menu?" Rachel gave him an enquiring look; thinking are there that many gins?

"Yes! A gin menu." He grinned and produced a spirits menu with a flourish including a list of gins. He went on to explain that he'd recently been to visit friends in London and gin bars were everywhere. It had come a long way from 'Mothers ruin' thanks to all the cool craft distilleries sprouting up all over the country including some in the area. He was hoping to attract some of the new class of drink artisans who visited on holiday and upon glancing at the menu she was impressed.

"Be rude not to." She perused the menu, selecting a rhubarb and lime gin with her bottle of Fever Tree tonic and paid £2 extra for the privilege. Grinning that Stan was onto a winner, or was that a grimace at the price, she walked over to join the swimming group who were already discussing the Pool closure.

Sitting next to Diane Pengelly, the seventy one year old glanced over and smiled before returning to her note book. Diane carried on scribbling notes. She could always be relied upon to put pen to paper and was often commenting on Facebook about various articles. Her views were very "Left Wing." She was always arguing that the rich should help out the poor and that taxes should be raised and the wealth distributed. A bit like a modern day Robin Hood.

Rachel took a sip of her gin, approving of the fusion of juniper, rhubarb and lime and listened to the general chatter.

Angela was trying to out speak everyone, boasting about her fund raising efforts from the past. Rachel could see that Tink was getting fed up and some of the group were drifting off to the bar.

Spotting Tom had walked in she relaxed. He'd just finished work and he was good at dealing with Angela. Rachel often joked that Tom was Angela's handler. He was one of those people who had a natural smile on their face all the time. He looked like he enjoyed life and was strong and dependable. Angela also noticed Tom had walked in. Sitting back in her chair Rachel took another sip of her gin, enjoying watching Angela start to move towards him, almost pushing Alice out the way in the process. Desperate to buy him a drink she was heard to say. "How could Rachel have not jumped up straight away. You work so hard for this community and it was the least I could do."

Rachel didn't worry. She knew that Angela thought of herself as the top person of the group and she liked to control everyone and every situation. Angela seemed to stumble as she turned and Tom caught her "Are you ok?" He asked

"Oh yes Doctor Tom. I've been feeling a pain in my back recently." She simpered.

Tom knew this was her way of getting sympathy and validation. He had said to Rachel in the past, "You pour positive, supportive words in at the top and they just flow out the other end no matter how much you tried to help her." He knew she was very insecure and her constantly trying to elicit praise from others was her way of trying to shore up her ego. He took his drink off the bar and walked towards Rachel and the others, followed very closely by Angela.

Rachel started to address the group regarding why they were there to fundraise. "Thank you all for coming tonight at short notice but you all know that we have to try and raise £400,000 by the end of September or Liberty's Lido will close." She paused as the murmurs of discontent rose in volume. She raised both hands and her voice. "Please let's be positive and do what we can." The room went quieter. "We don't agree with the decision and we can all have opinions on why it isn't right or isn't fair but talking isn't going to change a thing. We need action!"

She summarised that they needed lots of ideas and they ALL needed to be proactive and helping to secure the Lido's future. People pitched in with ideas while Diane wrote furiously in her note book trying not to miss a word.

"So far we have a cake sale, pencilled for Easter Saturday, an auction of promises, a masked ball and I'm going to set up a Crowd Funding page. Does anyone else have any more ideas?" Nobody did so Rachel brought the meeting to a conclusion and said that if anyone thought of anything then they could add them to the groups Facebook page.

Tink whispered under her breath "We won't raise even £500 with these ideas" before slinking off home.

Planning

Yesterday Rachel had collected Poppy from University for Easter. Poppy was excited to catch up with everyone, be home again and swim in the sea. She was twenty and was slim with long blond surfer hair. As a child she'd had an effervescent personality that had children and adults hanging on her every word while she was totally oblivious of her charms. Practically born on the beach she was a natural mermaid and had learnt to walk and swim at the same time. Rachel had once mentioned to someone that Poppy enjoyed swimming more under the water than on the surface to which her friend had replied, laughing. "Isn't that drowning?"

Growing up, Poppy had belonged to the local swimming club in the Lido and when she was old enough had joined the Porthlowen Surf Life Saving Club. While studying for her A levels she had become a beach lifeguard in the summer and all her spare time had been spent surfing, working or attending Zumba classes with Billy and Summer. She had been selected to represent the County in Surfing and everyone thought she would go down this route so it was a total surprise to Rachel and Tom when she said she wanted to follow in her Dad's footsteps and become a Doctor.

You could tell Poppy was back home as there was a trail of clothes and makeup all over the house, and the bathroom and her bedroom looked like a bomb had hit it. She had only been home for ten hours, but Tom and Rachel loved it. The house came alive when term ended and Poppy returned. They both realised how much they missed her.

"Mum I hope you ordered me one of Eunice's pasties from the café. I've been dreaming about one for weeks. I'm so tired on some nights after study I just eat super noodles."

"Yuk. I couldn't eat those." Rachel said. "They remind me of worms."

"Taste like them as well!" added Tom.

"You haven't eaten worms!" Rachel stated.

"I don't tell you all my secrets." Tom winked.

Eunice was the oldest pasty maker in Porthlowen, probably Cornwall and possibly even in the UK. Now aged eighty five she had been making pasties for over seventy years. Every day she would make twenty five for the cafe and one extra for herself. Any extra pasties the cafe needed were bought elsewhere. The swimmers were sure to order in plenty of time as the pasties always sold out long before Eunice bought them to the cafe every day at eleven thirty on the dot. Eunice was a tiny woman with a huge personality. She had ruddy cheeks, grinned with teeth missing but had blue eyes that still twinkled of mischief. Her wizened and wrinkled old face showed that she smiled and laughed a lot. She wore her knitted hat throughout summer and winter and nobody knew if she had hair or not. It was rumoured she even wore her hat in bed. Tom had once joked that she probably pulled on a shower cap over her hat when she was bathing. You could set your watch by her. Eleven thirty at the Lido café, one o'clock she arrived back home for her own pasty, four thirty in 'Muffins, the small high street tea room for afternoon tea and then at seven PM she would have a swift half of Guinness in The Ship Inn. Eunice seemed to be related to everyone in Porthlowen and knew everybody, and everybody knew her. She was fond of telling tourists she had never been over the Tamar bridge as she didn't have a passport. Nobody knew if she really hadn't been to Plymouth or not. She had once famously said that she would like to be buried at sea but thought that wasn't a good idea as she couldn't swim.

Today, as there had been a slower start due to the heavy spring rain, it had given Pierre a chance to think about the forthcoming cake sale, which would coincide with the Easter weekend when Porthlowen would be heaving with holiday makers.

He'd typed out an events page on the swimmers Facebook page along with a further post on the café and Lido page telling everyone about the event.

Easter Saturday

Cake sale

2pm

Help support Liberty's Lido Fundraising

Bake a cake or buns and bring along on the day

Pierre printed some posters before leaving the café to put them up around the Pool and then continuing into town to generate some more interest.

Before swimming each day, the Ls would gather at the Lido for 10.45. The first person there each day would grab several of the cubicles depositing clothing, bags and towels so that all swimmers could be together. Outside the cubicles were two wooden benches that they hastily draped their towels and hoodies for before and after swim chats. Lots of life had been put to rights on these two benches over the years. As they were such a large group, they were probably intimidating to holidays makers who usually looked at the swimmers and walked by to other seats around the pool. Today, while Pierre was putting up posters about the cake sale around the pool, he stopped for a chat with Diane who explained that she wasn't very good at making cakes but her daughter had offered to make a vegan chocolate cake. After chatting for a few minutes Pierre left the group, air kissing as he went and headed into town.

They became aware of laughter and looked over to see Angela and Alice going into each of the cubicles. Tink was standing a little way from them but watching them with a smile of her face. Both of them were holding small yellow bits of paper in their hands and giggling uncontrollably. When the others arrived, they took great delight showing them. Instead of adding items of her belongings to the cubicles as normal and finding she never had enough items for the ever growing group, Tink had made little laminated signs saying 'Reserved for Liberty's Lido Ladies and Lads.'

Angela having finished displaying the signs walked up to Tink saying "You make me laugh." before walking off to show the latest arrivals.

It was still chilly and everyone was wearing their colourful club hoodies with the words 'Open Water Swimmers Liberty's Lido Ladies and Lads' on the back and their own names on the front. The sun was starting to break through and would hopefully dry up the wet ground from the earlier rain as everyone started to get ready for their swim.

The swimmers' costumes and hats were an array of colours, hot pinks, sunny yellows and lots of sky blues. Everyone was also wearing equally brightly coloured towelling robes. They started to drift off in twos and threes chatting about life, all heading towards Golden Rocks, aptly named due to the natural colour of the rocks, which when the sun shone, brought out the true golden colours.

Out of the Lido entrance turning right, then following the concrete footpath, before reaching the Art Deco railings, Rachel thought to herself that she had walked this route so many times she felt like she was on auto pilot so she decided to hold back from the group and practice her mindfulness, being in the moment, and only thinking about the now. With fresh eyes she looked down at the path noticing that it had recently been jet-washed as she could see the little bits of green algae still left where the workman had missed. Raising her eyes up a bit she noticed the railings and realised she'd never looked at their beauty before. Lattice artwork left shadowed patterns on the pathway where the sun shone. Freshly painted for the season in turquoise blue, a recent sign still attached to the last pole saying 'wet paint' was a give-away. The railings carried on to her left side in a slight curve leading her eye around and on past the Cenotaph monument, before reaching the popular public swimming and fishing area.

Even though the Lido was a salt water unheated pool, the regulars enjoyed swimming in the sheltered bay, often seeing fish, sea urchins and starfish by swimming out to the reef and diving down at low tide to take photos. Tink based her whole gallery business around her photos and paintings of the wonderous goodies under the sea as well as the amazing waves above.

The sea temperature was at its coldest in March and was only now, in mid April, that it started to warm a little to ten or eleven degrees after the harsh winter of storms and snow. The group all developed "Swimmers' Swearing" as they entered the water, screaming and cursing. Everyone had their own style of getting into the water. The brave jumped or dived in depending on the tides, either their feet or heads getting the icy blast first. The others stood on the steps, faffing, with a queue of swimmers forming behind them before bravely slipping into the sea with shrieks of shock and swearing. The rest just walked down the steps and swam straight away from the word go. Diane was a typical "Swearers' Swimmer". She would faff on the steps and as she entered the water her language was loud and colourful. On calm days before entering the water the group got together on the rocks to take photos of each other. There was a group pose mastered over the years and every new member would have to join in. Everyone chanting together "Turn to the left side! Hand on the left shoulder of the person in front of you! Front leg slightly raised! Stand up straight! Smile and work it!"

"Teeth and Tits!" Alice would shriek, leading the group every time while someone would take a photo. Even the men joined in sometimes.

Everyone had their own time limit in the freezing cold sea water. Some only lasted five minutes, just long enough to get the euphoric feeling while some stayed in longer to swim to the only two remaining buoys left in the sea for the winter. The other brightly coloured buoys had not been put back in yet due to the bad weather and being freshly redecorated for the season by fellow swimmers. In the past they had been decorated as seahorses, starfish, mermaids and other sea creatures. Each one was a certain distance across the bay to measure how many metres the bathers had swam.

Every swimmer had the same agenda after getting out which was to get their towelling robe on as fast as they could and get dressed as soon as possible, clothes having been left in a careful order so that you could get warm quickly. No faffing here! A hot drink quickly followed. Some that could manage it would have a hot shower back in the Lido, but Rachel was one of those that after being out in the cold felt like it was burning her now sensitive skin.

The cutting wind of winter, described by the swimmers as 'That wind' was evident today. Blowing across the bay from a North Easterly direction, it had been a bouncy swim, choppy waves whipping up the sea. The sea was a grey colour against the dismal skyline.

Back at the Lido after everyone was dressed the conversation turned to next week's cake sale at the café. Everyone was chipping in and talking over each other, and even though Ziggy's English was very good, when they started to talk faster and at all once she looked confused. Angela just pointed to the poster and felt this would help. Liz told everyone she would bring one of her favourite swimmers' cakes, jam packed with fruit with added turmeric and was so delicious and moist. Liz was known for soaking the fruit in brandy before making her Christmas cake. Plump juicy raisins were so tempting and they often joked that one slice was enough to keep you under the drink drive limit but two slices might not be.

Ziggy announced that she would, of course, make her 'speciality' cake, to her secret German recipe. Looks of horror crossed the others faces. Nobody ate her cakes, they'd all succumbed to her offerings in the past when they weren't any the wiser.

Angela nudged Alice and whispered "Its ok we can hide the cake. We'll have plenty of others."

Awareness 1928

Every day Liberty turned up and slowly she learned to swim confidently, her new found friendship started to flourish; and her confidence and strength started to grow. It felt like she had always known Jack. They talked about his job in the mine, and she began to realise how hard he worked. Every day she would turn up with an extra sandwich and in return Jack helped her to swim. She felt really alive, perhaps for the first time in her life. She laughed more, chatted more and was generally more animated. Her hair shone and her complexion benefitted from the fresh air. She took more of an interest in life in general and asked more questions of her governess about the sea, the coast, the boats, foreign countries and peoples. She had a thirst for knowledge that her governess couldn't always answer. She became distracted from her studies by asking endless questions about the much wider world.

Her Father took daily delivery of the Times Newspaper which he read silently while eating his breakfast before he went to work. Occasionally Liberty joined him at breakfast and she'd never been allowed to talk to him while he read, or if she did, he grunted and was generally non conversational. As she became older, she could read the odd headline which never really made any sense to her and now as she entered her fifteenth year, she started to understand a little of what it said. Once her Father had read the paper it was left on the dining room table and one of the housemaids took it while she cleaned and tidied. Liberty knew that old papers were used to light fires in the house as she'd seen Dorothy do this sometimes. Liberty took the paper up to her room and tried to read it but there were unfamiliar words and she struggled at first. But as she kept reading, day after day, her knowledge increased and the names and topics became more familiar. Conservative party, Labour party, Liberal party, Government, Suffragettes, Trades Unions. Macdonald, Baldwin, Industry, Economics, Foreign policy, Capitalism, Communism and so on. Her father had a collection of ten books, the Oxford English Dictionary, and when he was out Liberty went into his office and looked up the unfamiliar words as well as many others she'd heard and even used without fully understanding their meanings. Gradually her understanding of the topics of the Times improved and she learned there was more to life than that of Porthlowen, Cornwall and even just England. She was surprised to learn that Frederick Nancarrow was the Member of Parliament for the West of Cornwall and was a leading light in the Conservative party.

She asked her governess about the paper and some of the headlines but the governess either didn't understand it or was unwilling to discuss it.

“It’s your Father’s business. Men’s work. You don’t need to know about things like that. You need to learn how to be a Lady like your Mother.”

“But surely there’s more to life than just being a Lady. I don’t want to just sit there sewing, or speaking French or going to call on other ladies to discuss pointless things. And just waiting for Father to announce that he’s found an appropriate and suitable husband for me to find that he just wants me to look pretty and wear nice dresses, while entertaining other wives. What about the women that have died trying to get the vote or those poor men, women and children who work in awful conditions? There’s so much in this country and other countries I just don’t know about and I want to learn.”

“I’m sure I don’t know about that. Now shall we concentrate on your poetry?” The governess said in a manner that left no room to discuss it any further.

“I’ll ask Father.” Liberty decided. But she didn’t want to upset him, or know how to start the conversation with him, and maybe it really was men’s business and so avoided the topic. However, she continued her swimming with Jack throughout the rest of the Summer and into early Autumn while maintaining her studies with her governess, continuing her own private reading of the Times and writing her observations of the day in her diary.

Progress

The Trustee board members had been busy in the intervening week. Each member presented their ideas together with handouts. Each point was fiercely debated but with all sides working to a common goal it was an exhausting but productive meeting. They agreed to put the plans into action with immediate effect. Each would support the others if requested. Emails were sent to each other summarising their actions, Millicent co-ordinated everyone in an efficient manner. They agreed to have regular fortnightly progress meetings, emergency meetings could be convened if necessary. Things were starting to take shape.

Cake Sale

Luckily the weather was dry but there was a cooling easterly wind and Pierre was just finishing his chocolate Easter cake ready for the cake sale. It was a showstopper, four layers high and filled with praline icing. The top was crammed with small chocolate eggs and halves of gooey cream eggs. He'd added as much as he could without the cake collapsing and had been up since 6am getting the café decorated with bunting and other Easter decorations. He was feeling nervous as this was the first event of the season. He really wanted it to be a success and raise lots of money for the fund. He looked back at the café, giving it an admiring look before he went to open the doors. He'd been so absorbed by his work he hadn't noticed the crowd gathering outside and peering in, so many people ready to bring cakes in. Pierre had cleared the café counter top and had set up several cake stands in readiness. In a whirlwind of cake boxes, people and energy the cakes were taken out of their boxes and displayed ready to be sold. More and more people arrived and it really did feel like there wouldn't be enough room inside. People began spilling out onto the pool terrace where the hot patio heaters were waiting to keep everyone warm. The members of the Ls kept the cakes and drinks flowing and more people were arriving with even more cake, Lemon Drizzle, Coffee, Chocolate, Victoria Sponge. It was turning into a delicious culinary event to rival the Great British Bake Off. Even when Ziggy turned up with her offering everyone was too busy to notice. Cake after cake was being sold and the pennies were mounting up. Just as it started to get a bit quieter with a lull so they could catch up with the washing up, more people would arrive and Ziggy took her turn behind the counter to help, placing her cake out on a glass cake stand right in the front. Nobody had noticed as it was so loud, warm and busy. Several of the swimmers had gone to clear tables inside and onto the terrace to collect cups and plates while other members were speedily trying to keep up in a conveyor belt of washing up. The cake sale was proving very popular.

Along with the locals there were a huge amount of holiday makers, some had been swimming in the pool so were very hungry. A tall athletic man had made his way to the front of the queue, his hair still wet from swimming, shivering a little and blowing on his hands. He was looking at the cakes and as Ziggy had pushed hers to the front he asked her which cake she recommended along with a steaming hot Cappuccino. Angela, Diane and Flo were bringing more clean cups and plates from the back kitchen when they noticed the familiar uneven slightly strange colour of Ziggy's cake which was being cut and plated up. The man picked up his cake and coffee and walked away to find a place to eat it.

All three gasped as the man took a bite of cake, slowly placing it into his mouth. He started to chew and as he was hungry putting in a second mouthful, before chewing slower as the insidious flavours started to hit his taste buds. He smelt the cake then recoiled quickly. He stopped chewing but realising he was in public he had a slight panicked look on his face. He grabbed for his serviette before choking the cake out at such a force people turned around to look at him.

Angela knew what she had to do so she placed the plates on the counter pretending to slip and pushed Ziggy's cake onto the floor. It landed in a mushy heap with the cake stand on top. "Oooh. Silly me. I'm so sorry Ziggy."

With Ziggy now distracted trying to clear up her cake, Diane quickly cut a large piece of lemon drizzle cake and headed towards the poor man, asking if he was alright before handing him the plate. He looked worryingly at the cake and was hesitant to take it from her. "Don't worry. This one is ok to eat." she said reassuringly. As she walked off, she saw out of the corner of her eye the man sniffing the cake and after suffering Ziggy's cake she didn't blame him. Flo and Ziggy cleaned up the sticky mess together but everyone could see there was tension between Ziggy and Angela. Angela apologised quickly to Ziggy and offered £10 towards the cake sale funds as compensation. Ziggy didn't have time to answer before more people arrived.

The cake sale lasted into early evening and due to the amount of cakes still left they ended up selling slices for people to take home for the next day or to freeze. Everyone was caked out. By the time everyone had cleaned up it was 8pm when Pierre, appearing from the café office, could hardly contain himself. He was all smiles as he flamboyantly strutted up to the counter before announcing they had made............. £1050.46. A big cheer went up.

"Here's to the start of Liberty's Lido Fund!" shouted Angela.

Cooler 1928

The cooler and shorter Autumn days of 1928 had made swimming more difficult. When Liberty looked out from her bedroom window across the bay she could see the differing colours of the sea and the sky. She noticed multi coloured tinges of blue but also all shades of green and grey and white, sometimes within a few minutes. While the water was still relatively warm and on some days the sun shone brightly there were other stormy days when she wasn't able to get into the water, or even venture outside as she'd get soaked. A couple of times some very heavy showers had left her clothing saturated and while it was exhilarating and exciting to feel the cool rain on her skin she started to worry that the weather and the cold sea water would stop her doing something she enjoyed so much. She still continued to meet Jack, feed him his sandwiches and they'd talk. She'd slowly come to realise over the summer that boys and girls like Jack and his siblings were working down in her Father's mines in appalling conditions for little money. Jack had said the heat of the summer was unbearable below the ground sometimes while in the winter he couldn't feel his feet when walking the five or so miles to the mine. When Liberty herself went anywhere she went in a carriage. She found it very cold inside there even though she was well wrapped up against the cold and it was dry inside there. Tears came to her eyes sometimes when Jack described his life and felt guilty that her lifestyle was paid for by the fruits of his and his family's labour. She was appalled when she found out that there had been a tunnel collapse and three miners had been killed, one of which, Billy, was only thirteen like herself. Billy had been the main breadwinner for his family as he'd lost his father in a similar accident three years before. Another miner had survived but both of his legs had been crushed and then amputated so he would be unable to ever work in the mine again. Jack had been the one that had pulled Billy's body from the rubble. That was four families directly affected by the loss of the major wage earner while the whole mining community mourned the loss of some of their own. Jack was somewhat stoical about it.

"But that could have been you!" Liberty exclaimed. "You were in that tunnel when it collapsed."

"Well it wasn't my turn today." He grimaced. "Just a fact of life. Mine owners don't care about their workers as long as we're making money for them." He then realised that he was talking to the mine owner's daughter. "Oh. I'm sorry Miss. I didn't mean to say that. I'm getting above my station." He reddened and rushed off apologising as he went. Liberty sat on the shore above the beach and cried with the unfairness of it all and made up her mind to challenge her father about it.

However, Liberty's father, Frederick, had problems of his own and was busier than ever at work and seemed to be at home less and less. He was regularly attending meetings in other towns and cities in Southern England including Plymouth, Exeter, Bristol and occasionally London. As a land and mine owner he'd been affected by increasing activity by Trades Unions in his mines and as a result was having to pay more for his workforce who were becoming more militant. The General Strike of 1926 had given the working class a voice and they weren't afraid to use it. Things had changed quickly after the Great War, the rise of Socialism and the Labour party while in Europe and beyond the League of Nations, with its Treaty of Versailles, was affecting worldwide trade including mining. Frederick wasn't happy that he'd lost two days money and production from his mine during the tunnel collapse which he blamed on the ineffectual underground managers. He was also ever mindful of the reporting in the Times that the continued record highs on the stock market in Wall Street in the United States of America would inevitably lead to a downturn. "What goes up must come down." seemed to be the general consensus amongst politicians on both sides of the House. He was even more short tempered than usual in the rare times when he was home and Liberty sometimes found herself intimidated by him and his blustering manner.

One morning at breakfast, not long after the tunnel collapse, he was, as usual, hidden behind the Times when suddenly he threw the paper down. "Blasted Trades Unions." He exclaimed.

His outburst startled Liberty and she looked at him. "What do you mean?"

He looked at her. "You wouldn't understand. You're just a child." He said dismissively, reaching for his cup and draining its contents. He stood up and threw his napkin onto the table.

Liberty looked him in the eye "How do you think Ramsay Macdonald will deal with the Trades Unions?"

He looked at her, suddenly seeing her in a new light and sat down again. "What do you know about Macdonald?"

"He's the leader of the Labour party and the new Prime Minister in a minority government supported by the Liberals."

Frederick looked at her incredulously. “How do you know that?”

“I’ve been reading the Times.” She said confidently.

“How? When?” he blustered.

“When you have breakfast you read it and I didn’t understand the headlines on the front of the paper that I could see when you’re hidden behind it and I didn’t like to ask you as you’re always busy so when you go out to work you leave the paper here or in your office and I pick it off the table before Dorothy or Daisy clean it away.”

Bunnies

The next day, Easter Sunday, was a special day on the swimmers' calendar as everyone dressed up as Easter bunnies. Most of the swimmers had attached fluffy bunny tails onto their costumes and wore bow ties, bright coloured wigs and long ears. A few had painted their faces with whiskers and teeth. The group was feeling positive following a successful fund raiser. Rachel had set up the Crowdfunder page and the £1050 had been added along with £250 of donations. It was a stark contrast to the opening day of the season with everyone now upbeat. Nobody mentioned Ziggy's cake.

Liz told the group that her special swimmers' cake was available to eat after their dip in her cake box left on top of her bag. "Just help yourself if I'm not out of the water."

Everyone moaned about how much cake they'd eaten the day before but she knew they would soon be buzzing around her box as they had "earned" their cake. She convinced them that it was 'healthy' and each slice really was a 'fruit portion' and 'one of their five a day.'

"After all it is Easter." She finished.

The yellow place cards that had caused so much amusement yesterday had been removed by Douggie after complaints from a stuffy local lady. He apologised but pointed out that the Lido was for the benefit of everyone not just the Ls. They grumbled a bit but did as they were told.

Angela picked up her bunny ears and was getting everyone organised so they could all walk out the pool gates together and around to the rocks. Everyone was wearing a colourful robe and bunny ears which made for funny viewing by anyone walking or driving past. The sun was shining and as Easter was later in the calendar this year the sun was warm and for a change the wind was still. The sun was sparkling like diamonds where it reflected on the rippling sea.

Alice took a deep breath taking in the warmth and the salty sea air. She breathed out while saying "It looks like a summer's day. We're so lucky today with none of "That wind."

Turning around she saw that Angela was getting everyone to line up, one behind the other, hands on the person in front's shoulders then all looking over their own shoulder. Some of the men were also wearing tutus,

"Men just love to dress up as women, don't they." said Diane.

Pierre was dressed as a sexy bunny girl from Playboy. He wasn't swimming but had still dressed up. He was wearing a long black wig and had borrowed one of Summer's pink sequin bikini tops with added chicken fillets and a sparkly pink tutu. He was wearing six inch black heels and was walking around like Beyonce so confident and assured of himself.

Rachel thought to herself "How does he manage to strut along in those shoes?" thinking of the struggle she had to walk in just a little heel."

Angela took the group photos, then she and Alice quickly swapped positions so Angela was also included.

Pierre was the selfie Queen and with his height and long arms he took the perfect shot and posed with everyone before heading back towards the Lido café.

The group had a loyal following on their Facebook page with both swimmers and non- swimmers saying the crazy photos cheered them up and they were a huge advocate for the mental health charity "Mind." Cold water swimming had been proven to help anxiety and mental health problems. The sense of "Being in the moment" was a powerful feeling. The friendship of the group was definitely a significant draw. On this particular occasion the camaraderie was a very big part of the day and every swimmer was aware that isolation can be deadly. Diane had lost her husband four years ago and with her adult children all living away from home she often found it hard to cope, but when she felt she was at her darkest, she found that dedicating a swim to a particular past memory helped clear her head and she usually felt more positive afterwards. All of the swimmers had been drawn to the group in one way or another. Some for the exercise, some for health reasons or the challenge of jumping into ice cold water, but most of the Ls had joined for the mental health benefits.

Confidence 1928

Liberty's new found confidence hadn't gone unnoticed by her Father. While he was always busy with work either directly at the mine or indirectly by meeting prominent business men he'd noticed that his little girl had suddenly become a young woman. He had noticed a new found confidence with Liberty which he'd put down to her growing up and becoming more mature while he'd been away so much. She looked much like his beloved wife, Nancy, especially as she'd grown older. While he loved his daughter greatly, especially since he'd lost Liberty's mother, he'd thrown himself into his work and business and rarely talked to her properly. She was provided for and to him that meant he was doing the right thing. Childcare had been designated to nannies and then Liberty's governess but he still regarded her as a child.

"Well I never." He said softly. He looked at her again, seeing the confident woman starting to emerge from the child. He quizzed her about some of the other things in the paper and realised that she did have a grasp of some of the news in the papers, and the goings on around the world.

They chatted amiably adult to adult and then he asked her where she headed to everyday after her lessons with Miss Scrivener. Liberty had been lulled into a false sense of security and feeling confident she started to tell him about her adventures on the beach. Leaving out Jack for fear of getting into trouble she told him about the rocks, the sand, the cool water and how she has learnt to swim.

"You take your clothes off? In public?" Frederick roared. "You're a Lady. Ladies don't swim!"

"They do actually. I read in the Times that Ladies are allowed to swim at the Olympic Games." Liberty retorted, standing her ground.

"They swim in especially built pools, with changing facilities, not in public with fishermen and miners walking around, and not in the sea. And don't contradict me. You might think that reading the Times means you're grown up but you're not. You're a child, living under my roof and you'll do as I tell you. No more swimming in public." He blustered, turning puce with anger.

Liberty looked crestfallen, her bottom lip started to quiver and she slowly sunk lower in her chair. Tears came to her eyes and she rushed out of the dining room towards the stairs to go to her bedroom hearing her Father's voice following her out of the room saying "No more swimming! You'll be telling me next you're playing with the mine children next". His office door slammed shut.

Crawling into bed Liberty pulled the covers over her head sobbing and feeling that the end of the world had arrived. Her happy place already a distant memory. The conversation with her Father went around and around in her head. How could she have been so stupid? Why on earth did she tell him about swimming? She replayed everything over and over in her mind, feeling worse and worse. She lay in bed not wanting to move. How would she see Jack? When would she go swimming again? Tears started to well up in her eyes. For as long as she could remember she'd never felt so happy, she had felt free. Her leg started to hurt and she hadn't noticed that for a while. It was a reminder that swimming had been good for her and made her forget that she was disabled. She fell into a troubled sleep then woke with a start, her worries immediately coming to her mind. What would she do? What could she do? She stayed in her room all of that day and night eventually falling into an exhausted dreamless sleep in the early hours of the morning.

It was around eleven o'clock when she awoke and having missed breakfast Liberty wandered down to the kitchen, feeling sick but not really sure if she wanted something to eat or not. Enticing smells wafted towards her as she entered the large room, Cook's domain. She was still in her night dress; her long golden hair was an unruly mess and her bare feet felt cold on the stone floor of the kitchen.

Mrs Hitchens seeing her looking unusually dishevelled and miserable came over. "Are you not feeling very well today Miss Liberty?"

Liberty looked down at her feet, burst into tears and mumbled something that Cook couldn't understand. "I .... can't go again .... I'm not allowed near the sea........... I won't see...... Jack.........."

Cook led Liberty over to the big window chair, sat her down, gave her a hug and made soothing noises. "There there. Tell Cookie all about it."

She'd been in Liberty's life since Liberty was a five year old child and after her Mother had died Mrs Hitchen's natural maternal instincts had taken over and they'd always enjoyed a much closer relationship than Liberty had with the matronly unfeeling Miss Scrivener. Being a Mother herself she'd always plenty of love to give and Liberty had often divulged her secrets to Mrs Hitchens, where they remained safe.

Making her a Special Cook's Hot Chocolate 'the drink to sort all problems' she asked Liberty why she was so glum. Through sobs and sips of the sweet beverage Liberty recounted her summer of swimming, freedom and meeting Jack, describing him to her confidant.

"Is that Jack Pender?" Cook asked.

"Yes" replied Liberty "Do you know him?"

"Why he's my Sister's boy, my nephew, eldest of four, fine young man, proper handsome chap he is isn't he?"

Liberty blushed "You won't tell my Father. Will you?" She added hastily.

"Of course not, but I did wonder where all the sandwiches were going" Cook said giving Liberty a wink.

Mermaids

Squeals of excited laughter greeted Rachel as she arrived at Liberty's Lido that morning. There was a huge queue of little girls aged between three to nine years. Nearly all of them were dressed up as fairies, princesses and mermaids to celebrate the Lido's annual mermaid day. Reluctant brothers were queuing with their sisters and parents although one or two had joined in with the dressing up. Rachel had temporarily forgotten it was today and she smiled to herself remembering the days when she brought her own daughter and how excited Poppy had been before each mermaid day, trying on her outfits from her dressing up box before deciding on her favourite.

Meeting a mermaid was very serious business when you are a little person and outside the Lido was a big sign saying that the mermaid of St Tresen would be there at 1 o'clock today. However, mermaiding wasn't just for children and Rachel realised she forgotten her tail so scrabbling in her rucksack she pulled out her mobile phone and dialled Tom's number.

"I've forgotten its mermaid day today. Please can you bring my tail and crown to the Lido? They're in a box in the garage."

Tom had gone into town early to get his haircut and was going to be following her down to the Lido later with the lunch. "Yes, no problem. I will just nip home. Anything else you need? If not, I will see you in about twenty minutes."

Joining the other Ls Rachel noted that several had bought their mermaid tails and had started to hang them over the Lido rail in front of 'the bench.' Although none of them could really swim properly with them, most of them had either made or bought the tails for a photo shoot a couple years before; when a University photography student had asked them pose on Golden rocks behind the Lido dressed as mermaids and mermen for her portfolio. Angela was recounting the day of the photo shoot. It was autumn and the event had already been rescheduled due to bad weather and literally as soon as they finished taking photos, the heavens had opened with an icy blast and heavy hail arrived.

Rachel shivered remembering that day but hopefully today would be a polar opposite as it was promising to be a hot one. The Lido was busy already and catching sight of a slightly harassed Douggie across the water she knew how he felt. Every bit of the Lido had been used to maximise enjoyment. There was a stall selling mermaid paraphernalia, a photo booth, a mermaid face painting station and plenty more.

And then Rachel saw her, a walking mermaid coming towards the group, her golden long curly hair shimmering in the sunlight like a flowing waterfall stopping its luscious flow just above her waist. Rachel was spellbound but confused. This wasn't the usual mermaid of St Tresen! Where was her swimming tail? Also, this mermaid wasn't made for swimming. This mermaid was gracefully stylised, her bikini top had sequins and jewels attached and flowing out behind her was a sparkly train. On top of her head was a beautiful shell crown. The swimmers fell silent as one by one they noticed this tall beautiful creature gliding towards them. No one knew who it was. Flo who had been applying eco glitter to everyone's face and shoulders stopped talking. With her brush in her hand she followed everyone's gaze.

"Who is that?" Angela said, but before anyone could answer, the mermaid had arrived and started talking to the group.

"Oh my god. It that you Pierre?" Alice shrieked. "I recognised your voice but, but, you look sensational. I'd have never have guessed it was you until you spoke. Your make up is incredible. How did you create the scales on your face, neck and shoulders?" She continued.

Pierre replied "I can show you if you want. Just let me get my makeup bag. I love this!" He excitedly clapped his hands. "You're all going to look amazing." Pierre shrilled and with a flick of his hair the mermaid strutted off towards the café.

"Did that just happen? Did I just see Pierre dressed up as a mermaid?" Angela exclaimed.

"You certainly did." replied Alice.

"Wow, she looks amazing." Tony stated. "The mermaid is much taller than usual. Those legs.....Wow! Who is it this year?" He asked.

"Um..... It's Pierre. Did you not just listen to him?" Angela replied perplexed.

"You mean that's not a woman?" Tony gulped sadly.

"No sorry Tony, you're out of luck. I think you need a cold swim to recover." Angela joked.

Pierre returned with a huge black suitcase trailing behind him. Upon opening it everyone gazed at the sheer amount of makeup and accessories that spilled out. Grabbing a pair of fishnet tights Pierre said "Who's first?"

Tony looked at the tights and backing up towards the rear of the group he went bright red with embarrassment.

Angela pushing herself forward shouted "Meeeee. I want to look like you Pierre."

Laughing and speaking under her breath Tink was heard to say "I don't think he's got enough make up."

Putting a fishnet stocking against Angela's forehead, cheeks and then shoulders, Pierre worked quickly to apply a combination of iridescent pink, purple and blue make up to create a rainbow scales effect along with pink, purple and blue eyebrows, finishing off the look with glitter. When he'd finished he found a bright pink wig and carefully tucking in Angela's short hair he turned to the group saying. "What do you think?"

Alice jumping up said "Amazing. Me next!"

Even Tink had to admit that Pierre had worked a mermaid miracle. By the time that Pierre had finished everyone looked totally different.

"We definitely need a group photo." Angela took control and ushered everyone together and those that had tails put them on before shouting "Mermaid Tails!" A passer-by was asked to take several photos. Nobody wanted to go swimming and ruin their makeup.

The professional mermaid of St Tresen arrived. Sitting on the top step of the Lido with her long dark hair flowing down her back, a metallic blue and shell mermaid bra edged with white pearls along with a large prosthetic metallic blue scale tail swishing in the water, creating a splash. After a while she dropped neatly into the water and pushing off from the side of the Lido the mermaid glided through her natural environment. Her tail glimmered like a rainbow after a storm and cut through the water propelling her forward. A local surfer who was a friend of the mermaid and also a photographer had joined her in the water to take photos, both above and below the water. The mermaid just hovered in the water her long hair flowing ethereally around her, eyes open as the surfer clicked away. She swam up and down the pool, rising to the surface and ducking down again, the scales of her tail glistening in the sunlight as she flicked it up when she dived down deep into the darker cooler water. The children and their parents watched from the sides wondering how she could stay under the water for so long.

After a few lengths she returned to the shallows of the Lido, waving at the assembled throng. Dozens of little children and their parents entered the shallows of the Lido. The mermaid swam back under the cordoned off area ready for photographs on the steps. Children and adults alike clustered around her trying to take her photo and shots with their children sitting or standing, next to the mermaid. She admired their costumes, making the children feel special, like they were the only one there. She certainly had a gift for talking to and encouraging children.

Before she got too cold, she wished the children good bye before swimming off towards the deep end and removing her tail then leaving the pool. Dressed back in her normal clothes she came to talk to the swimmers, admiring their own costumes and Pierre's make up style and fabulous outfit.

It had been a busy day at the Lido and in the café and the till receipts of both swelled the coffers.

Unhappy 1928

The autumn of 1928, she always remembered, were some of the unhappiest times in Liberty's life, while the summer of that year had remained some of her happiest memories. The fluctuation from the wonderful endless sunny days spent with Jack in the sea where real life had seemed to burst from every pore of her body to the depths of despair of not being able to go out to swim or see Jack. What was the point of carrying on? Having known real happiness; when she was deprived of it her situation was made so much worse. She lost interest in everything and everyone. She became miserable and withdrawn, sullen and inattentive. She couldn't shake off a cold, which had gone to her chest and then turned to influenza. Previously, an inquisitive and imaginative mind had made Liberty a rewarding pupil to teach but now the elderly Miss Scrivener, suffering from the after effects of the influenza herself, failed to inspire her protégé. She eventually spoke to Frederick, when he was home, but he was struggling, along with a lot of businessmen, investors and politicians after the Wall Street Crash in October, a million pounds wiped out from his own shareholdings. The price of tin had fallen and, in consultation with his managers, he was looking into more efficient ways of working and of cost cutting exercises, including the reluctant possibility of laying off some of his workforce. Miss Scrivener was left to decide what to do. Reluctantly she talked to Mrs Hitchens, recognising that she may be able to get Liberty to talk but Cook had no answers. It was no good asking Dorothy, while Daisy hadn't been replaced when she found herself in the family way after a dalliance with a farm worker from the next village. After many fruitless lessons and worried about the health of her charge Miss Scrivener in exasperation finally called the family Doctor.

Doctor Berryman had examined Liberty, charged a small fortune, and had come up with the diagnosis. "She's delicate." Her polio, he explained, had made her a weak patient, as evidenced by her recent outbreak of influenza. "She's to stay in her room, not to go outside, and not to be exposed to people with their diseases and infections."

When Frederick received the bill from the Doctor, he summoned Miss Scrivener immediately.

"I cannot get through to her." She defended herself. "She's always been such a wonderful girl to teach, she's intelligent and learns quickly. It's always been a privilege but in these last few weeks she has been unresponsive and uncommunicative. She seems to have lost her zest for life, her appetite is poor and she seems listless. Over the summer she had been so full of life, her eyes shone, she seemed even more inquisitive than normal and asking all sorts of things I couldn't answer about the world in general, politics, the economy and so on. There seemed such a transformation over the summer and now she's the opposite, withdrawn, as if everything is an effort. I didn't know what to do and I know you've been away so much with your work. I was at my wits end. I knew something wasn't right and so I called Doctor Berryman."

"Where were you when this swimming was going on? She's your responsibility and yet she told me she's been swimming in the sea over the summer. You know she's a delicate child and yet this has gone on under your nose. Leave me now and tend to your lessons with Liberty."

Miss Scrivener rose to her feet with an effort and stiffly left the room, shutting the door quietly behind her, tears in her eyes as she slowly made her way to her room.

Frederick looked at the ageing governess with fresh eyes as she walked away. Perhaps she was getting too old now to look after Liberty. He didn't know how old she was but she'd been governess to Maud, his sister, a generation ago. Maybe he'd asked too much or expected too much from her to run his house and be a governess to his only daughter, a daily reminder of the loss of his adored wife, Nancy. He sat and thought for a while, the Doctor's bill in front of him. He would ring Berryman and tear him off a strip. He lifted the receiver and started to dial the number but then paused. Maybe he was being hasty. It wasn't the Doctor's fault his child was delicate. He was used to making quick and accurate decisions when in business and in the House of Commons but occasionally some reflection, time and reassessment was needed.

Jetski

Peaceful and quiet with a high tide and a turquoise sea that looked like glass was perfect summer swimming weather. The seagulls were gently gliding in the thermals high above, enjoying the free flight without have to use any energy flapping their wings. There weren't any sailing boats out due to the lack of wind. The excitement of the Mermaid day seemed like a distant memory already and while the fundraising was gaining momentum Rachel felt that she needed some "me time" today. She was early today and decided to change first in the pool and walk around to Golden Rocks to enjoy some early morning peace and quiet. She had recently taken up meditation on Tom's advice after years of struggling with anxiety and depression. He had explained to her that the cold water swimming was so good for her that he wished he could offer it on prescription but found that most of his patients just wanted a quick fix or a pill. He had tried to explain to her that the immersion in cold water evoked a stress response but the more you swim in cold water the more this stress response reduces. He also went on to explain that cold water reduces inflammation in the body. He started to get a bit too technical and Rachel remembered telling him that he had lost her after the first sentence. What she did remember was the part about the friendship of a group of people also helped to improve depression and anxiety so she felt the swimming and the close knit group was a win win.

Rachel was also trying to live mindfully and to do her mediation but this was proving a harder challenge so by coming here today without the others she had planned on relaxing and bringing her focus to what she could see, hear and smell. Shutting her eyes she could feel the warmth of the sun sinking into her muscles and bones. It was early and the searing heat of the day had not arrived yet. It felt like a warm hug. Taking a deep breath through her nose the sea smelt fresh with a salty taste on the tongue. She could also smell a faint fish or seaweed aroma she wasn't sure. At first, she couldn't hear anything but as her ears started to tune into the sounds, she realised she could hear a faint hum and on opening her eyes could see a fishing boat leaving the port over to her right hand side. It was leaving a wake behind it. Shutting her eyes again she listened out for more sounds, really straining to hear as the day got started. It was so quiet and she realised she hadn't sat here before without people walking around and talking or birds screeching above. She began to feel relaxed but alive at the same time and thought to herself that she would do this again. Opening her eyes, she noticed a couple of kayakers quietly paddling, skimming above the water the bright red and green of their kayaks reflecting in the ripples and the water now looked like damaged glass. They were floating in silence and several cormorants were surprised as the strange coloured sea creatures snuck up on them causing them to take flight from their rocks where they had been drying their wings in the warm sunshine, looking like little dragons silhouetted against the bright backdrop.

Rachel enjoyed the moment before shutting her eyes again. In the distance she could hear voices too far away to make out any words. Drifting off into a relaxed state she became aware of another hum and glancing over to the port she could see that there weren't any fishing vessels leaving the harbour. Closing her eyes again she started to concentrate on her breathing. Slow rhythmical breaths, in and out. The noise was getting closer and it was starting to annoy her now. Opening her eyes, she could see in the distance, a black speck on the horizon that was quickly approaching. Thinking it was a small boat Rachel tried one last time to concentrate on her breathing, she knew the other swimmers would be here soon and wanted five more minutes. The boat noise was now sounding like the annoying high pitched whine from a mosquito circling your head looking for somewhere to land before biting you, getting louder as it nears your ear. She wanted to swat it and opening her eyes she realised it was a jetski. Still sitting, Rachel realised there were actually three machines racing across the bay, leaping up into the air from the waves they were creating. Using the swimmers' buoys as an obstacle course they were shifting their body weight to make tighter and tighter turns. The noise was so loud as they were so close to the land Rachel hadn't realised Tink and Sally had walked around the corner.

"Jetski wankers!" Tink said, startling Rachel. "Someone is going to get killed. They are too close to the shore and riding around our buoys. They're going so fast they wouldn't see anyone in the water."

"Is anyone swimming out there at the moment Rachel?" Sally asked.

"Not from here on the rocks." Rachel replied, standing from her comfortable seated position and squinting against the bright light as her eyes adjusted after being closed. "Unless someone has gone off the beach." She looked across towards the beach but wasn't sure if she could see anyone or not.

"Is that a swimming hat?" Sally pointed a bit further out. A green one? Over there. Look!"

Tink and Rachel looked and agreed that there was clearly a swimming hat quite close to the swimmers' buoys. The jetskiers were still weaving in and out of the buoys and jumping their craft out of the water.

"Oh my god." Tink said. "I do hope they're going to be alright! I'm so worried. This isn't the first time these wankers think it's completely acceptable to race around that without caring about anyone else. They should be the far side of the Beacon Pole or out on the opposite side of the harbour but way out, away from the surfers and kite surfers on Pencannock Sands. We had the same last year and the year before. The sun comes out and so do these tossers. Something has to be done. You think how many times we're out by the reefs looking for the urchins and starfish, underwater most of the time. We'd have no chance if one of those jetskis bombed across inside the Beacon Pole."

Bill turned up with Tony. Liz, Dawn, Cindy and Flo were just arriving too and there was a conflab about the jetskis. Bill had a pair of binoculars and took them out of his swim bag. He looked across and said that yes, he could see a green swim hat. "Could it be Ron? Doesn't he have a green swim hat and it looks like his swimming style too."

Ron Flowers was a long distance swimmer who regularly swam a couple of miles daily. He'd been part of a relay team across the English Channel two or three years back so thought nothing of spending an hour or so in the water. He had quite a distinctive front crawl swimming style with one arm that slapped hard down in the water each stroke.

"His kit isn't here though." Tink said.

"Maybe he's left it at the Trelyn end today." Tony added. "The wind is blowing towards Trelyn so maybe he wanted some resistance training this morning."

"He's waving." Said Bill, still looking through his binoculars. "And one of the jetskiers is waving back to him and pointing him out to the others. Looks like Ron, if it is him, is headed in closer to the shore now."

"Crisis averted for now, Thank God!" Tink said as the jetskiers made their way back in towards the harbour.

The swim was a bit tense that morning with everyone a bit wary in the water, in case more watercraft headed their way. The swimmers clustered in small groups to make themselves more visible. They always wore brightly coloured swimming hats anyway and some of them had inflatable luminous orange, pink and green towfloats. The sole topic of conversation was the behaviour of the jetskiers and it continued on the group's Facebook page throughout the day

It wasn't the relaxing mindfulness moment that Rachel had hoped for.

The following morning Rachel was awakened early with Tom thrusting a hot coffee into her hands. "Tink's gonna be on the radio in fifteen minutes. Pasty FM. She's on about the dangerous jetskis. Thought you'd want to hear it. I'll tune in at work just before my clinic starts. Gotta fly!" He kissed her and left.

Rachel took her coffee downstairs and tuned Alexa into Pasty FM. She normally preferred to listen to Radio 1 as a lot of her Zumba songs were played and she liked to dance along in the privacy of her kitchen while she was doing her housework or preparing food. She couldn't stand some of the presenters on this radio station who seemed to gear their shows towards her parents age group or sounded like they were country bumpkins who'd never heard a proper Cornish accent in their lives. However, it was great for local news, accurate weather forecasting, traffic delays and accidents across the region so Tom would often tune in before work to make sure his work journey wasn't going to be affected. If nothing of interest was on then he'd tune into talkSport.

The radio presenter read out the national and local headlines followed by a summary of the weather, overcast with a good chance of heavy showers, but light south westerly winds. "Stay at home day today." Rachel thought to herself, taking a swig of coffee.

And then "Today we have a local wild swimmer from Porthlowen, Isabelle Bailey, known as Tink. She's been having a problem with jetskis around the beautiful Golden Rocks which are situated behind the famous Liberty's Lido. So Tink, please tell me about the jetskis."

Tink was very eloquent and put the view point of the swimmers very clearly saying that it was only a matter of time before someone was seriously injured or killed, without some protection for the swimmers. She wanted everyone to be able to enjoy the water safely and for everyone to respect everyone else, that there should be some areas designated for swimmers, other areas for jetskis, surfers, sailing and so on as well as keeping away from the commercial fishing fleets of Trelyn. Maybe speed limits closer by the shore until they reached their specific designated areas. She argued her case well thought Rachel. She wasn't the usual grumpy Eeyore character that the others saw daily, that swore a lot and contributed little.

The radio presenter then moved to talk to the local harbour master, Fred Yeo, who said that his hands were tied as he could only advise jetskiers to restrict their speed or to only go to certain areas. They were required to give their names to the harbour staff when they launched. There were no specific laws that dealt with this, and each port had its own regulations, there wasn't a standard protocol that was UK wide. He did agree, however, that it was a problem and he recognised that Tink had a valid point.

A day later more footage of the jetskis appeared on the local TV news and this time Cindy was interviewed down at Golden Rocks. She said she was scared that she or one of her friends could be hurt or killed. She swam to relieve mental anxiety but this current situation was making her mental health worse. The mobile phone footage showed the jetskis coming in close to the rocks themselves, inside Beacon Pole and weaving through the swimmers' buoys. The hornets' nest was poked further when one of the jetskiers had managed to get on to the Cindy's Facebook page and ranted that the swimmers were all a bunch of ugly old dried up Grannies and the jetskiers had just as much right to be there as the swimmers.

The TV reporter interviewed the harbourmaster, Fred Yeo, but again he agreed there was a problem, his hands were tied and he appeared to not want to take sides in the argument. He did state though that the slanging match between the swimmers and the jetskiers wasn't helpful.

A week later a public meeting was called down at Trelyn Seaman's Mission where Tink, Rachel, Cindy, Diane, Michelle and Flo congregated in a café. Luckily Angela was away on holiday as she could be a bit like a bull in a china shop, not the sort of person needed where delicate negotiation and knowing when to shut up was a pre-requisite. Diane, as usual, was the scribe. Steph, who was the unofficial leader of the Ls, ran their Facebook page and organised a lot of events sometimes with other swimming groups around Cornwall and Devon, arrived at the café straight from work, munching a bag of crisps. Rachel felt sick and nervous and she was sure the others would feel the same.

The meeting was chaired by the Trelyn harbourmaster, Tim Matthews. He'd also invited the Falmouth harbourmaster and his counterpart in Porthlowen. The Commodore of the Sailing Club, Reg Kerris, arrived with a couple of club members, a handful of surfers, some with sails and kites too. The secretary of the Dive Club, Brian Collins, was present as was Freda Hoskins, the head and matriarch of the largest fishing fleet in Trelyn, a family business that had been part and parcel of the local scenery for a hundred years or more. A handful of locals made up the rest of the gathering along with retired PC Gordon Gage, who everyone called Green, a gentle giant of a man who had been the town bobby for over thirty years. Tim Powell, the coxswain from the RNLI was there too.

The meeting was well chaired. Tim Matthews invited the head of each group to have their say. "Keep it concise and factual please. Two or three minutes each. You'll all have a chance to have your say so please be patient."

Rachel was impressed by his management skills. When the conversation became heated or people interrupted, he remained calm, re-established order and did, in fact, allow everyone to have their say. It transpired that the sailing club, the diving club, the RNLI, the surfers, windsurfers and also the commercial fisherman had all had close encounters with jetskis, and other people who drove RIBs or speedboats irresponsibly. They all saw a need for some sort of rules and regulations but also agreed that everyone should be able to use the sea for either recreational or business purposes.

A couple of locals who owned jetskis said that they had as much right to be anywhere as the swimmers, sailors, and commercial fisherman. They said they were responsible, kept to the speed limit within the harbour, paid their dues and always kept away from known areas where groups of swimmers, sailors and fishermen were likely to be. They felt that the swimmers were to blame, swimming in dark colours, like black wetsuits, dark or no hats, and swimming far out towards and beyond the Beacon Pole. Tink and Stella took offence and rose to their feet, shouting and not doing the Ls any favours, Rachel felt. She just kept quiet.

Green intervened and got them to sit down. "Ladies. Please. The gents listened to you when you spoke and now you must listen to them. Without interruption!" he added, looking intently at Tink.

Fred Yeo outlined the rules in Porthlowen. "At high tide" he said "Myself and my staff come over to the slip when people are launching any type of craft and ensure that we have their names and addresses and we collect the harbour dues. We'll then advise them of the speed limits within the harbour and also of any activities that are on the water at the time, for example, sailing club nights. We advise them that they should stay outside the Beacon Pole and that the buoys are there as swimmers' markers and they shouldn't go near them."

Rachel and the others knew that this wasn't true as the harbour master was often conspicuous by his absence, and jet skis and other craft often launched without supervision or without making payment.

The Falmouth harbourmaster Phillip Carstairs, was invited to speak. A natural leader, who, when he spoke, you listened. His quiet but clear voice carried to the back of the room. Before being harbourmaster, Tim Matthews said, he had been in the SBS and had fought in conflicts all over the world. A no nonsense sort of guy, Rachel thought, the sort of guy that dealt in facts, got to the hub of the matter and got things done.

"What's the SBS?" whispered Diane to Rachel.

"Special Boat Service. An elite fighting team, part of the Royal Marines, a bit like the SAS but on water." She replied.

Carstairs brought a great deal of common sense to the meeting and spoke with calm authority. "You all have your reasons for wanting to use the water. Each of you feels that your own viewpoint is perhaps more valid than other groups. You all want to do whatever you want, whenever and wherever you want to but you all have to respect each other. We used to have a problem in Falmouth with jetskis and other such fast craft and believe me, the size of our problem was much greater than yours in Porthlowen and Trelyn. You'll know that we have huge tankers and Royal Navy vessels coming in and out of the dry docks, seven sailing clubs in the immediate vicinity, many types of commercial vehicles, water taxis, tourist trips, ferries and so on. There are hundreds of boats of all types moored up in the water between Falmouth and Flushing and there's several beaches too, which, like yours here, become flooded with tourists from April to October, many of which have the ability to launch jetskis and other such crafts.

Unfortunately, it took a death of a swimmer by a speedboat for us to deal with the problem that had been voiced by many parties with a vested interest in the use of the sea, similar to the different groups represented here...."

Tink was instantly on her feet, gesturing and shouting towards the jetskiers. "See. Jetski wankers. You caused the death of a swimmer."

The jetskiers were on their feet too. "It wasn't us. We're not to blame."

Both sides stood their ground hurling insults.

Tink was removed from the meeting by Green, quietly, efficiently and warned everyone else that any interruptions would not be tolerated and the perpetrator would be evicted.

Phillip Carstairs continued. "A particular individual had decided that he was going to do his own thing on his speedboat. He was a local so he had been identified on more than one occasion for speeding through the harbour, generally being unsafe, going too close to dinghies, sailing boats and ferries, swerving and creating waves which then disrupted them, and then going around to where the beaches were, going in too far and so on.

However, he ignored the warning, went out on his speedboat again one dull evening and unfortunately hit a swimmer, who was killed instantly. The swimmer was way out from the shore in a black wetsuit with a dark hat and no tow float or light and wasn't visible at all. The case went to court and the speedboat pilot was charged with manslaughter and sent to prison, but his sentence was reduced because the swimmer was partly to blame.

However, it could have been any fishing boat, ferry or other craft going about their normal lawful business but if swimmers chose to do what they want, without regard for their safety, then they run the ultimate risk." He paused to allow the severity and impact of his words to sink in.

"As we've been made aware of tonight, there are no specific maritime rules or laws that cover this. There are anti social behaviour laws which can be applied to individuals who continually act without regard to others. However, they don't apply out on the water. It's a land based law. We'd like the law to be changed and extend the anti social laws to say, 800 metres away from the shore. We've lobbied for a change in legislation with our local MP as well as maritime experts and various interested parties but as yet nothing has changed."

The swimmers and jetskiers were still looking daggers at each other.

"We had several meetings with many different types of leisure clubs and also businesses, all of whom use the water regularly. The upshot was that swimmers were given a designated area, marked by buoys about fifty metres off shore across Gyllingvase, Swanpool and Maenporth. They were to remain inside the buoys, with loads of notice boards warning people where to swim, where possible enforced by beach life guards. Kayaks, windsurfers etc were given specific areas to launch from on these beaches. All of the local sailing clubs, diving clubs, sub aqua clubs and so on were made aware of this, we went around to the marinas and got together with other harbour masters in those vicinities and again got more posters and boards put up. There was also a more visible presence of people checking and advising and thankfully we haven't had a repeat of this tragic accident but we are unable to police every single craft that goes onto the water. It remains incumbent upon us all to advise, to educate and not to put ourselves in harm's way.

Thank you for inviting me tonight." He concluded. "And stay safe."

The meeting broke up and the Ls met up with Tink outside who was still spitting feathers. "So! What did they say?" she interrogated them.

"Wait and see, basically." summarised Diane.

"Bloody typical." fumed Tink and stormed off in a huff. Rachel made her way home and outlined the salient points of the meeting to Tom. Another meeting had been pencilled in for October to see what progress could be made.

Promises

May half term arrived along with hot sunshine and lots of visitors. Rachel had worked hard to cajole the town people and businesses to donate promises and instant raffle prizes for the Auction of Promises. The Crowdfunder page had now reached £10,000 as the Lido had also started a "Buy a share in the Lido scheme." £25 would buy you a share so that anyone and everyone could buy a piece of the historic place. Lots of the prizes had been dropped off at the café and Rachel had spent several days either collecting more promises and then listing them and finishing off by putting them into envelopes or for those items too big she typed out the prize on a piece of paper before adding this to the envelope. In total she had nearly one hundred envelopes. Some items were going to be used as an instant raffle prize as they had already been collected. Things like chocolates, flowers and wine.

Bill arrived to help her. A seventy five year old retired Army officer he was very organised and he kept telling everyone he was very strong and fit. He had never married and you could see why. He was very regimented and controlling; even if you didn't want an opinion he would give it to you. He had sent Rachel several emails and spread sheets and had for weeks been trying to do a risk assessment for the night. She had struggled to keep his suggestions under control, exhausted by the amount of extra work he was trying to create. She had agreed that he could help her take everything to The Ship Pub early in the evening so they could set up and be ready.

He arrived in his black BMW and Rachel noticed it was so clean she could see her reflection in the bonnet. She was embarrassed when they arrived at her car to start loading the goodies and could see the look on Bill's face. There was sand everywhere from a recent trip to the beach paddle boarding along with towels and lots of spare clothing. She wished she had removed the bag of beach rubbish she'd collected the day before, after her two minute beach clean.

After loading up Rachel's car they then filled up Bill's and headed to the pub, meeting Tony, Sally and Diane who were all ready to carry in the gifts. Stan had put up two of his huge trestle tables to put all the prizes on, one for the auction and the second for the raffle. Rachel also had a box with all of the envelopes of promises which she carried in very carefully. She had made a list of everything before printing one hundred copies so everyone could see all the amazing donations and which people and companies had donated them before deciding which lots they wanted to bid on. Before placing the envelopes in the box she took several photographs of the groaning tables of prizes. Rachel liked to keep all the social media pages up to date so as to keep up the interest of businesses and people. She had some money already pledged against certain lots for people who couldn't make tonight as they were either working or away. Stan bought over a drink for her and asked if he could make her a sandwich. She gave him a big smile. She was famished having missed her lunch time due to getting everything ready

"Usual?" he asked.

"Oh please." she replied. Rachel was coeliac so had to be careful and Stan was a star, bringing her a cheese and ketchup sandwich on gluten free bread. There was still an hour before the Auction started so Rachel sat down and ate while the pub started to fill up.

"How did you get on at the Manor?" Tom asked Rachel. She hadn't seen him arrive but he pulled a seat up beside her, pint in hand. Tom was referring to her visit to see her elderly parents who still lived at Nancarrow House, although they'd taken over only part of the House, the former servants' quarters. The remainder of the House and Garden were open to the public for B&B, weddings, parties, antique fayres and a cafe. It was all run by Roger Evans, the efficient manager.

"Mum was on form. She gave me a bottle of her Gin to raffle, gave me £10 to buy her and Dad some raffle tickets and sent me down to see Roger. He's given me a ticket for entry for two to the House and Gardens followed by lunch in the cafe. Probably worth about fifty quid."

"Nice one Rach. Well done."

Eighty three year old Henrietta, Hetty, Liberty's only child had met Isaac Lockwood in the late 1950s and they'd married in 1961. She'd never worked while Isaac had been one of Frederick Nancarrow's business managers.

"How was your Dad?"

"Happy enough, considering he's eighty eight. He was asleep in front of the TV with half a pack of biscuits on the go. Apparently, he didn't come to bed until five this morning."

"Bet she wasn't happy about that. I take it they're not coming to the Auction tonight?"

"Mum would come but she can't really leave Dad, and if he came, he'd probably just fall asleep anyway. He wouldn't really hear properly, anyway would he?"

"I feel sorry for Isaac."

"Me too."

"Anyway. We got a couple of prizes from the Manor and £10 into the raffle kitty so I was grateful and I thanked her."

"She hoped we'd have a good evening and she wished you all the best for your compering job."

"Well thank you Hetty." Tom stood up.

Rachel wished Tom "Good Luck" as he picked up the microphone from Stan. There were easily two hundred people in there and the pub was getting warm. Flo had bought her fan and it was being passed around helping to cool everyone down. Windows were opened as Tom started to talk. He was a natural auctioneer, funny but calm, always getting the highest prices. He cleared his throat and got everyone's attention. "Thank you all for coming. Welcome to our Second fundraiser, after our success at the cake sale where we raised £1050.46. Thanks also to Stan for allowing us to take over the Ship tonight. Please dig deep and help us raise lots of cash to keep our amazing Lido Open."

The people of Porthlowen had been very generous. The lots consisted of holidays cottage weekends, a day's worth of gardening, car washing, pamper sessions, several meals in different restaurants, and even a boudoir photography session. Angela practically leapt up when Tom mentioned this lot, so much so that it was noticed by others. She was well renowned for encouraging everyone to swim naked and whenever a Navy helicopter flew over she would flash her breasts.

"I'm going to get this auction of promises off to start with this small but really really useful lot and living beside the seaside beside the sea we could all make use of this. So, lot one has been kindly donated by Graham's Garage and it's a complete car valet. Who will start me off with a £10 bid? Okay I have a bid on my left from Liz. Any advances on £10 please? This is for a full valet. That's inside and outside of any car. This would normally cost you £60 so come on guys who is going to give me another bid? Okay I've got £12 in front of me.

Come on come on. Any more? Any more? £15 I have. £18, £20, £22, £25." The bids kept on rising.

"£40." shouted a voice from the back of the room,

"£45." shouted another man.

"Any final bids?" Tom looked around the room and two hundred pairs of eyes stared back. Nobody put their hand up to bid any more. "Sold to the man in the red jumper."

Rachel was assisting Tom. Her job was to hand Tom the different lots and to record who had bid on which item so that they could pay at the end of the evening. The pub was so crowded that she couldn't get through the crowd and noticing her problems Flo signalled to Rachel she would cover the back of the room. Diane and Bill were going to be collecting the money at the end of the evening. Bill had created a spreadsheet and Rachel filled this in as the evening progressed. Tom knew he had a lot of promises to get through so in between the jokes he spoke quickly to keep everyone's attention and allow everyone to have time to get lots of drinks. During the half time break Alice and Sally went around and sold raffle tickets for the mountain of prizes on the second table.

When everybody had relaxed after a comfort break, Tom turned his attention to lot fifty five, the boudoir photographic session. "Okay girls. Oh, and gents, if you want to treat your other halves or maybe even have it done yourself, this next promise is an afternoon of hair, make up and then your own photograph session." The room became silent and a couple of the older members were asking what a boudoir session was. Tom looked slightly embarrassed and to start with he told everybody that the prize was worth £200. "I'm going to start the bid at £50, anyone? Just £50."

The room was silent. Some of the younger girls were giggling. they wanted to bid but didn't want to be the first.

Stan, the barman quipped. "C'mon ladies. If you don't start the bidding then I'm going to put in £50 and I'll have a dudeoir myself." The pub burst into laughter.

Angela stuck up her hand and shouted "£50!"

Diane looked at her agasp. "Angela! You do know what this is?" she asked.

Angela replied. “Yes of course I do. It’s not for me. It’s for my daughter. Her birthday is coming up soon and it’s too good a prize to not try and win it”.

Tom looked around the room and said “Thank you Angela for starting the bid at £50. Now who will give me £55?”

One of the young girls standing at the bar who had been giggling earlier stuck up her hand.

“Okay I’ve got £55 pounds. Who will give me £60?”

Another person shouted out and quickly the bids went up and up and Angela started to squirm in her seat and craning her neck to see who was bidding against her, putting in alternate bids quickly.

Tom said “I’ve got £150. are there any more bids? This bid is with the young lady at the bar at the moment!”

Angela shouted “£160.”

Someone from the bar shouted £170.

£180 came a cry from the back of the room,

“£190.” shouted Angela. She was almost jumping out of her seat.

“Two hundred pounds!” shouted someone by the pub door.

“Two Hundred and five pounds!” shouted Angela, then in her total excitement she then bid £210 pounds against herself.

“Okay.” said Tom. “Any more for this lot? “The bar was quiet so Tom bought down his hammer and sold the boudoir to Angela.

The swimming group looked to Angela, and Flo seeing that Angela was looking triumphant said “Your daughter is so lucky! Is this something she will like?”

Diane asked “Are you sure it’s not for you Angela?”

Angela gave a not very convincing full story about how it was definitely for her daughter.

Just as the next lot was announced Tink muttered to Cindy under her breath "The lady doth protest too much methinks."

Cindy nodded and rolled her eyes.

Nearly everyone in the pub that night bought one of the promises or won a raffle prize. By 10.30 Tom was sat at the bar quietly sinking a well earned pint from Stan. He was exhausted. The auction winners came to Diane and Bill to collect and pay for their promises while Rachel counted the money. Some of the other members of the swimming group started to clear up and slowly people started to drift away.

Diane, Bill and Rachel were still counting the money and adding up the spreadsheets to make sure that it all tallied when Tom bought them all a drink then came to offer his assistance.

"Thank you." said Rachel. "But I think we are nearly finished."

All three of them agreed that they had added up all the money and that they had got the same total.

"So how much have we made tonight?" asked Tom.

"Well." said Rachel with a big smile on her face. "I'm pleased to report that we've made £6583."

"Wow!" said Tom. "I thought we might make a couple of thousand but….., Bloody hell, that's incredible."

"It certainly is." replied Rachel.

On the way home he was chuckling to himself.

"What are you so happy about?" asked Rachel.

"Angela." He said simply.

"I know." Rachel said. "She really wanted that prize. She even paid over the odds for it."

"Yes. And everyone in the pub knew it." Said Tom.

"You didn't….?" asked Rachel smiling as the truth dawned on her.

"Yes. People were bidding against her that had no intention of buying it."

"You're wicked."

"All in a good cause." He defended himself.

Investigation 1928

Frederick thought about Liberty and how she'd shown herself to have a quick and intelligent mind. Her determination to read the Times, find out about the items in it and her grasp of some of the issues of the day. She'd known about Macdonald and the minority government, the Trades Unions and even the Olympics. That didn't show someone who was listless, withdrawn and uninterested in life. He'd been impressed, even astounded by her intelligence, even as he was berating her for swimming. She was right. Women did swim. Some women had those funny carts that went into the sea. He didn't know anyone who did. Who in their right mind would go swimming in the cold sea? But then he remembered when he was a boy he'd rushed into the sea, splashed about, kicked the waves, stayed in until, shivering, he was bundled into a warm towel by his Mother and she'd hugged him until he was warm again. Yes, he'd enjoyed the sea when he was a boy, perhaps it was only right that Liberty would want to be in the sea, she was a child after all, and while she'd had nannies and then Miss Scrivener, she'd missed her Mother's love too. He missed his wife as a companion, confidant and her own intelligent, quick challenging mind so it wasn't surprising, perhaps, that without a Mother, Liberty had somewhat forged her own way, surrounded by women but not a Mother. Not for the first time in his life he wished his dear wife was here to talk to and ask her advice especially where their daughter was concerned. He berated himself. Perhaps if he'd been here more, shown his daughter some love, talked to her more, found out her likes and dislikes, shown an interest in her studies. Was it too late? Perhaps he could make it up to her somehow.

He needed to talk to a woman, not Miss Scrivener as she was too old and also she hadn't married and had children herself. He wasn't unaware that Miss Scrivener had a soft spot for both him and Liberty but she was an employee at the end of the day just the same as Mrs Hitchens, who'd been kind to Liberty and had been a wife and mother herself but she was also the wrong person to talk to.

He vowed to make it his priority over the next few days to talk to someone to find out more about swimming. He had a vague notion that the Victorians had regarded godliness next to cleanliness but Liberty was clean enough. She had a modern bathroom attached to her bedroom and she went to church each week so that was alright. No. It was a woman whose judgement he trusted, one to whom he could talk to frankly, in confidence about Liberty becoming a woman, and also knew about the virtues of swimming. He'd played rugby at school, becoming a decent scrum half and representing the school on occasions. He knew that sport and exercise were good for both physical and mental strength, lessons learned on a sports field could be transferred to life itself so why not swimming? Both were Olympic sports, although rugby had been dropped for the most recent Olympics in 1928. His thoughts had gone off on a tangent. He brought them back to the present.

He would try and talk to Liberty and then he would find someone he could seek advice about daughters. But where to start? He cancelled his diary for a week, sent letters to London apologising for his absence from Parliament due to his sickness, ensconced Miss Scrivener next to the phone to tell everyone he was unavailable and summoned the Doctor. The business world could and would survive without him for a few days.

Liberty felt awful. It had been two months now since her Father had banned her from going out, to see the sea, to go swimming and especially, to see Jack. She was miserable. Every day she looked out of the windows of her room towards the sea, opening the windows to try and sniff the saltiness of the sea air. That autumn seemed colder, wetter and windier than any she could remember before. The heavy rain drops smashing into the windows of her room, occasionally turning to hail stones, the wind rattling the panes of glass, forcing its way into gaps in the roof and whistling with glee where it found them; and the grey and black clouds racing each other across the bay, each trying to outrun the other or be more ferocious in the intensity of the weather it carried. On rare days, the wind dropped, the sun came out, the sea became calm, as if teasing her of a memory of last summer. On dull stormy days Liberty's mood seemed as black as the rain filled clouds in the bay but on sunny days it was even worse. She spent days staring into space, lying on her bed, sat lifeless in a chair, tearful, frustrated, depressed and in pain from her weak leg, which then moved up to her hips and her back and then her neck. She moved less and less as each movement sent sharp pains and aches all over her poor body.

The Doctor had been summoned and came to the usual diagnosis. "She's delicate."

He prescribed laudanum, left his bill and drove off in his motorcar.

Jack waited for Liberty day after day and slowly realised that she wasn't coming anymore. He bathed alone, looking up in hope as anyone walked by. He was heartbroken and realised that he loved her. But she was a Lady and he was just a common miner. How stupid of him to think that she would fall for a man like him. But he couldn't forget her. He got on with his work, mindful of the warning he'd received only a few months before. He had responsibilities at home, to keep a roof over his family's head and put food on the table. He started courting Molly Masters, only kissing her when her brute of a brother was out of the way. He could do a lot worse, he kept reminding himself.

Dolphins

Low tide always made it a bit difficult to get in at Golden Rocks. There were only three concrete steps down into the water and after that there were uneven slippery rocks, many covered in sharp barnacles. This acted just like sandpaper on the skin so Liz had an idea how to get in. Both of her knees were damaged due to a motorbike accident in her early twenties and were now sore from arthritis as she became older. However, the cold effect of the sea water was a natural anti-inflammatory temporary cure and she was determined to get in to feel some release from pain.

Speaking to Heather, her swimming partner in crime, she said "I've got an idea that might help me get into the water".

"Oh no what's that? You and your ideas." replied Heather in her distinctive northern accent.

"Well when I was in bed last night, I was thinking about how I miss some of the swims when its low tide, so I got up and had a hunt around all my shopping bags. I found that the Lidl bag was the biggest and thickest." she continued.

"Ok?" said Heather slowly, "What are you up to now?".

"Well." continued Liz "If I sit on the bag, I can use it as a sort of mat and slide instead of getting scraped legs from the rocks, I think it might work."

Laughing Heather replied "You really don't cease to amaze me with your bonkers ideas. Go on then. I'm getting my camera ready for this!"

So, Liz picked up her thick plastic bag and walked down to the edge of the steps, placing it on the small ledge of smooth rock. She proceeded to sit on it and the rocks below her feet did look like a small slide. Holding on to the edge of the bag she slowly started to slide towards the water's edge. By this time some of the others had noticed what was going on.

Bill walking down to Heather was soon joined by Tony then Tom. "What IS she doing?" Bill asked Heather.

"You know Liz. She's desperate to get into the sea and will try anything." Heather replied.

The men stood and watched with Tom thinking to himself "Please no accidents today." He'd got a lunch date with Rachel later and was looking forward to trying out a new restaurant that had opened in Porthlowen and had been recommended by one of his patients.

Slowly Liz shuffled and slid, ending up in the water in a heap. Standing up she passed the bag back to Heather so she could tie it onto the railings.

Seeing the shopping bag Tony shouted to Liz "Every Lidl helps." before laughing.

Tom joining in started singing the Elton John classic. "It's a Lidl bit funny."

Bill just groaned and asked Liz "Are you ok?".

"Think that was a big success" She chuckled "Obviously other supermarkets are available!" She then ducked under the water and swam off. Like a mermaid or a seal, she might be clumsy on land but in the water, she was an effortless swimmer and could stay in for ages. It was unnatural.

As the wind direction was a westerly today it meant that Golden Rocks was really sheltered by the land. Further out to sea looked rough with waves breaking over the reef.

Angela and Alice were looking out to sea and shouting to the others, pointing. Liz could just make out what they were saying with the wind blowing around her swim hatted head.

"Dolphins! There's Dolphins!" Angela excitedly shouted. "Look. Over there."

Liz turned to look but could only see waves in the distance.

Angela was joined by Diane, Alice, Sally and Ziggy.

"Oh, my goodness there are loads." Ziggy said.

"Look at them jumping out of the water!" Alice agreed.

"One, two, three, four...... eight.....ten, gosh I can't keep up." Diane said. "Look everyone. There are dolphins. That's the biggest pod I've seen for ages."

Her enthusiasm was exciting the rest of the group and behind them were some tourists looking in the rock pools. Hearing all the noise they started to look out in the direction of the swimmers then on beyond them and out to sea.

Noticing them, Angela shouted over "There are Dolphins, a massive pod, can you see them leaping out the sea?" Realising they were foreign she started to mime dolphins jumping out the water with her arms before turning her attention back to the sea.

"Excuse me." said an American accent. It came from a tallish man in his thirties with dark hair and standing next to him was a woman of about the same age, shorter and blonde. "I'm looking through my binoculars but I'm not seeing any dolphins. Am I looking in the right direction?" He continued.

"They are there, out to sea" Angela replied "Maybe your binoculars aren't very good. I can see them leaping out of the water with the naked eye. I expect every time you look; they are under the water". She pointed "Look there's one."

"Nope. Can't see anything. Just waves." The man replied in his American drawl. "They must be hiding from us."

Angela now next to the man said "Let me have your binoculars and I will focus them for you. You've got to see this display."

"Thanks." Said the American, handing over his eye glasses.

Angela looked and fiddled, then looked again, before looking with her naked eye, back to the binoculars. "Oh sorry. They must have gone." she told him before walking back to the others, handing the binoculars back to the tourist.

She made her way quietly back to the excited group "Ummm I don't think they are dolphins, just waves." she said.

"But I can still see them." exclaimed Diane.

"Well it would appear that it's just waves hitting the reef."

There was a stunned silence before Alice burst into laughter, a real belly laugh, followed by Diane and then the others. The laugh was infectious, soon the women were struggling to breathe with Alice saying "Oh! My belly hurts!"

The poor Americans just looked at the gaggle of women.

Angela managing to compose herself said "We've not even got in the water yet and we're causing trouble."

Replying, Diane said "We can't even blame it on too much cold water affecting our brains".

"Think we need to get in the sea before we make ourselves look even more stupid." replied Alice. The group made their way into the sea still laughing. They were passed by Heather who'd finished her swim.

Liz drying herself was soon joined by Heather. "That was a great swim. I love it when its rough out to sea but so sheltered here." Liz said.

"Yes, but I'm feeling a bit cool now, 'that wind'. Wish I was warmer" Heather replied. "Mind you that reminds me. My neighbour gave me a telephone call last night. She asked me to come around as she was struggling with something. Well when I arrived, she was bright red and sweating. Turns out she had bought a new black shiny all in one PVC outfit to use for her webcam business and the zip had got stuck."

"What!" Liz said turning to look at Heather, her mouth wide open in shock. "You mean your neighbour I saw when I last came around for coffee. The one that popped in to borrow some milk?"

"Yes. That's the one." Replied Heather.

"But she's, well, really old and looked like she was about to go to church."

"Mmmm yes I suppose she did, well she has a nice little business 'entertaining people' but I did feel sorry for her. She'd been stuck in that outfit for three hours." Heather continued.

"She should have got in the shower to cool off." replied Liz laughing.

"Bet she didn't think about that!" Heather answered, giggling.

"Gosh you do have colourful neighbours. If something out of the ordinary is going to happen it's definitely going to happen to you" Liz said still smiling. "Oh I've got this image in my head!"

The two of them were sent into peals of laughter.

Reflection 1928

Frederick sat in his office and decided how to approach Liberty. Often in his business world he made snap decisions which would inevitably turn out to be correct. Sometimes, however, a more considered approach was necessary. He'd observed that Liberty rarely came out of her room these days and when she did, she looked pale and ill, she limped, her clothes looked creased and her hair was a tangled mess. He decided that a more caring and patient approach was required. A loving Father wasn't going to treat his only daughter in the same way he would as if she were one of the staff, or indeed his fellow MPs or other business leaders in London.

He walked slowly and quietly up the grand staircase, pausing a couple of times to get his thoughts in order. He knocked her door gently, no answer. He knocked again a little firmer and the door opened a crack. It hadn't been shut properly. He squeezed his head around the door and saw that Liberty was in bed. He entered the room quietly and shut the door carefully behind him. He walked slowly to the bed and saw that Liberty appeared to be asleep, her chest rising and falling, her breathing steady and deep. Her golden tresses were spread across the pillow and her pale, lily white skin was nearly as pale as the sheets underneath her. He turned around, as if to leave, not wanting to disturb her but then paused. He looked around for a chair and pulled it up alongside the bed. He sat and looked at his beautiful daughter as she slept.

"What have I done to you my girl?" he thought. "Could I have done things differently?" He looked at his only child, a younger model of his beloved wife. In his grief at losing the love of his life he'd omitted to look after the most important thing in it. He sat there for a long time, looking at Liberty as she slept, weeping quietly as he contemplated his life and her life too, virtual strangers living under the same roof. The tears relaxed him and in the quiet of the room he looked around, seeing it as if for the first time. The floor, the ceiling, the lights, the curtains and window. He stood quietly and made his way to the window where he could see a different aspect of the sea, the bay, the beach and the rocks. He sat on the window seat surveying his kingdom. For the first time, maybe since he was a boy, he looked properly at the colours of the sky, the clouds, the weak sunshine. In the foreground he could see the grounds of his estate, the trees, gardens and plants and he looked at the differing colours and how it contrasted with those outside. His own bedroom, and his office overlooked the port, where he always had one eye on the comings and goings of ships, boats, deliveries in, exports going out. The busy, busy port on one aspect and the tranquil, beautiful settings of nature on the other. He compared it to himself and Nancy. He was the busy, energetic, go getting, hard nosed businessman while Nancy had been a gentle soul. Kind, generous, patient, supportive but enjoying the quiet solace of nature in her sanctuary, her garden, but, he remembered with a grin, was well able to argue her case, stand her ground determinedly and make him see the other side of the argument. She had a fiery temperament on the rare occasions when it surfaced.

Liberty, had inherited much of her mother's quiet personality but the way she'd firstly noticed the headlines in the Times, then taken the trouble, effort and determination to find out what it meant, understand it and then discuss it had surprised him. While Miss Scrivener may have given Liberty the building blocks it had been Liberty herself who had been the architect, the designer, the builder, and the overseer of her growing confidence and maturity. And he hadn't noticed. Well, not really noticed. But then he thought back a few weeks and Liberty had been different. There had been something about her that he hadn't been able to put his finger on. Was it just that she was growing up? No she was still a child. No, she wasn't a child was she? How old was she now? Fourteen, fifteen next spring. If she was the daughter of a miner or fisherman, she would have been working for him for years. Some of the young lads in his mines were the men of their households having lost their fathers in accidents at sea or in the pits. Some of them were much better workers than some of the older men. There was fire in their bellies. And he remembered that some of his troops in the trenches with him in Ypres, in Belgium, had put their ages up from fifteen and sixteen to say they were eighteen to fight for King and Country. They were only boys but they were expected to fight like men and lay down their lives like men too. Fifteen year olds were definitely not children but not adults either as Liberty's twenty first birthday was still a few years away yet.

So, what was it about Liberty that summer? Her hair had shone brightly, her complexion looked rosy, she looked healthy and her eyes had life in them. She'd had an energy about her. And suddenly a picture of her coming into the dining room one morning for breakfast singing, humming, dancing and jigging one of those popular jazz songs that Daisy, the maid, would sing and hum irritatingly as she was dusting. He'd been reading the Times, peered over the top at her, she'd smiled engagingly at him "Morning Father." And danced the foxtrot over to her seat. That was it! She'd danced! No sign of limping. She'd danced! Little or no sign of the polio in her weak leg that day. And Liberty had been happy and alive. And now look at her.

He looked at the sleeping Liberty in her bed. Her hair was dull and matted, she looked pale, her closed eyes had grey bags underneath them. She looked lifeless.

The contrast was stark. It was black and white, night and day, chalk and cheese. She'd been trusting and opened up to him and told him she was going to the beach and swimming. So, was it just that? Swimming? Surely not. Maybe it was the nature but then she had the gardens and flowers like Nancy and she could walk along the promenade with Miss Scrivener, and with Tommy pushing the large perambulator because of Liberty's delicate leg.

He continued to examine his thoughts while watching his daughter sleep.

Solstice

"Who is going to the summer solstice swim tomorrow?" Sally asked the group. "The weather is looking good, hardly any wind and clear skies. "

"Mmmm not sure. I don't do early mornings." declared Cindy but always turned up every year.

Sally was a sixty eight year old hairdresser and still worked part time. She came across as looking fierce but was actually quite friendly. She was always changing her hair styles and colours. At the moment her blond hair was short on one side and graduated into a longer bob on the other side. Her shocking pink highlights started at her fringe and usually obscured her eyes like a sheepdog but today after her swim they slapped her face like pink wet worms as she walked back from the sea. Grabbing her towel she proceeded to pull down the top of her costume not bothering who was around and who saw before covering up and starting the drying process. Asking the others in the group about the early morning swim, there were lots of non-committals but there was always a good turn out and she had no doubt that with the forecast it wouldn't be any different. Finishing getting dressed she added her signature brightly coloured lipstick which on this occasion was shocking pink, completing her ensemble with a chunky pink beaded necklace. Sally carried on packing her bag before tying her glittery trainers onto the outside of her rucksack. Sitting down she started to put on her well used black lace up roller blades with bright green wheels that lit up as she skated along. Sally described roller blading as like floating, especially on a flat surface.

"It's like you have power and smoothness plus rhythm." She'd once said to Bill. "Rollerblading keeps me fit. How else do you think I get my peachy bum?"

Bill didn't know where to look.

Afterwards Sally was off to meet Andy her forty five year old "Toyboy", a local beach lifeguard and long-time friend of Stan from the Ship Inn.

It was a quiet start to the gathering at four o'clock the following morning. Everyone was still half asleep and subdued. So far there were about twenty swimmers who were huddled in groups talking quietly.

Liz started to speak "What's that rumbling noise?"

“Not sure” replied Flo “Sounds like a distant clickety-clack from a train.”

“Why would we be able to hear trains right over here? We’re miles away from the railway station.” Liz pondered.

“I think it’s getting louder.” Flo started to say before turning around as she feared ‘the train’ was actually nearly on top of them.

Everyone looked up and a silence fell over the swimmers just as Sally shot around the corner on her roller boots closely followed by Andy on his skateboard.

“God. You know how to make an entrance!” Cindy stated.

“Sorry guys. I feared we were late as I could see the sky was starting to get light.” Sally breathlessly said while sat on the floor pulling off her skates.

“Ok swimmers.” Angela shouted, trying to get herself heard over the sound of everyone talking at once. “It’s time. We need to get in the water and swim past those rocks so we get a great view of the sunrise. Let’s get some good photos.” and she started her descent into the water.

“Who knew there were two four thirties in a day?” Cindy uttered as she descended into the cold sea. Giving a small shiver she started to swim out, following the others. She was definitely not an early riser but she loved this time of day when she made the worthwhile effort to view the ephemeral glow as the moon went to bed and the world started to wake again.

The swimmers stopped in a group just past the rocks to face the horizon with their cameras poised ready. The sky started to turn a rosy pink before intensifying in colour to a deep crimson.

Rachel positioned herself further behind everyone so she could capture the dark silhouettes of the heads against the splendid sky. The clicking started as the sun started its descent upwards. With the back drop of equal parts blue with streaked pink and tangerine across the sky and the reflection in the sea it looked as if it could catch fire. As the sun rose a bit higher Angela and Alice started to do handstands in the water with Rachel taking more pictures of their legs silhouetted against the bright sky.

“Ouch” Alice shouted “something has just stung me”

“Whoa, me as well.” Angela replied.

Tony shouted over "Think we've swum into a shoal of blue jellyfish. It might be an idea to move or go back to land."

Cindy, fearing jellyfish, squealed and swam off first. It was a very fast swim back to shore. Several swimmers had small welts on their arms and legs that looked like nettle rash.

Tom always kept some antiseptic cream in his bag that had a slight numbing affect just for occasions like today.

The pink sky disappeared as the sun rose and the blue sky emerged from its slumber. The swimmers shivered on the shore as they supped their hot drinks and showed each other their photos after quickly getting dressed. It might be mid-summer but the early morning still held a chill.

Cindy reached into her bag, pulling out a flask and her ornate purple and silver Halloween goblet with intricate cat and bat designs on it. She poured in the drink from her flask and Steph turned to her and asked "Is that hot chocolate and alcohol?"

"Yes." Replied Cindy. "I need to warm up and the rum helps my nerves."

"Wow. You know how to live Cindy." Laughed Steph.

"I'm going back home to bed." Rachel yawned. "Night everyone. See you soon."

Talking 1928

Frederick sat down beside Liberty and watched her for a while, sleeping then on an impulse he leaned over and gently kissed the top of her head. She awoke slowly and sleepily, yawning and seeing it was him smiled gently. "Morning."

"Good morning my Darling." He replied gently.

"Won't you be late for work?" She stretched lazily.

"Not today. I've got more important things to do."

"More important than work?"

"Yes, I want to talk to you about swimming."

She looked horrified and pulled the sheets up to her chin.

Seeing her reaction, he apologised straight away. "I'm sorry. I don't want to upset you." He put his hand gently on hers. "Please let me explain. I've, um, been thinking." It was hard to talk to his daughter like this, to be contrite, and get her to listen, or at least try to listen. "I've been sat here with you for a long time."

"I know. I heard you."

"You did? Why didn't you say so?"

"I thought I heard you, but you were very quiet, then I knew it was you because I smelt you."

"Smelt me!" He snorted. "Do I smell then?"

"Not horrible." She giggled. "You smell nice and Fatherly."

He smiled. "What does smelling Fatherly smell like?"

"Like you."

"Oh well. That explains it completely." He chuckled. "Utterly logical." He shook his head. Children!

"I didn't tell you I was awake because I didn't want you to go. I didn't want to be on my own again."

Frederick felt awful. "I'm here now." He whispered. He cleared his throat "Shall we go out for lunch today?" He asked a little louder. "Just the two of us?" He looked at the pale forlorn figure in front of him. "If you want to that is?"

She looked at him quizzically for a quiet moment. "Yes please. I'd like that. Can we go in the motorcar? Just the two of us? You drive and I'll sit in the front with you."

"Yes, of course." He replied gently.

"I'll send Dorothy in to help get you ready." It was a statement not a question.

"No thank you." She said firmly." I can manage but you can help me to pick out a dress if you'd be so kind." She smiled.

"Yes I will, if you'd help me to pick out a shirt and tie to match your dress." He opened her wardrobe and held up a few dresses for her to choose. "It's cold outside but it is dry and sunny so you'll need to wrap up warm."

They decided on a pretty blue dress and Frederick left Liberty to wash her hair and get ready while he walked to the garage to bring the car around to the front of the house.

The postman arrived while he was outside the house, checking the car over, making sure that Tommy had cleaned it and that it was full of fuel. He sifted through the letters as he walked in through the front door and moved automatically towards his office. One of the letters didn't have a stamp but had an indentation instead. No. It couldn't be? He dropped the other letters onto the desk and turned the indented letter over. Sure enough, it had a red crest of Buckingham Palace on the reverse. He reached for the letter opener from its rack and was slitting open the envelope when Liberty entered the office.

"Ready Father?"

Lifeboat

The Royal National Lifeboat Institution is a big part of life in Porthlowen and its history dates back well over one hundred years. Generations of families had handed down their yellow wellies to younger family members to keep the tradition going, to help protect the local community, and those people above, on or below the sea who used it for leisure and for business.

Stan Trebilcock and his younger brother Mark were both volunteer Crew and been inspired to join by their Father Frank who had been the Coxswain of the Lifeboat on that fateful day twenty years before. Just before Christmas 1999 the Lifeboat had launched in near hurricane conditions to aid a boat with engine troubles. It had been one of the worst storms in living memory but when the call came from the vessel in distress the Lifeboat crew hadn't hesitated and gone to the larger ship's assistance. The weather had deteriorated further and both boats, together with all of their crews had perished in the cruel sea. Their father had received a posthumous Gold medal for his bravery and there was a plaque on the wall of the pub dedicated to that fateful night.

Mark was an electrician who worked for himself and was a keen surfer, the same as his brother. Standing at six feet tall with blonde hair, having been bought up close to the sea, everyone joked he'd been born wearing a wetsuit and he had owned a surfboard from the age of three, regularly winning prestigious competitions in his early teenage years. Mark always had a surfboard strapped to the top of his van ever ready for the ultimate wave. After his father had died and aged only fifteen he spent his last year at school being very angry and disruptive before leaving Porthlowen for a couple of years, surfing around the world and taking any part time job to fund his hobby, often wild camping on the beaches when he didn't have any money. Aged eighteen he'd returned to Porthlowen and started a four year electrical apprenticeship and joined his elder brother Stan as a crew member where he'd been ever since. Mark was single but very popular with girls. He had the kind of face that stopped you in your tracks. He didn't seem to notice the sudden pause in a person's natural expression when they looked his way. The sudden blush that accompanied it from the girls a big give away. The gold colour of his eyes were so unusual it was always a conversation starter, but Mark was so modest it made the girls fall for him all the more. With his tanned skin and almost perfect symmetrical face which looked like it had been moulded from granite, Stan always joked that there was a sudden interest in surfing when the girls realised that's where Mark could be found.

Stan and Mark were discussing the surfing forecast for the coming weekend, when the annual Porthlowen Surf Championships were being held and there was much anticipated excitement amongst the surfers as the conditions were looking favourable to awaken 'The Finders'. This was a reef that ran under the water out towards Porthlowen's headland. It was shallower than the surrounding sea and when the swell came in it broke over the reef producing much bigger waves. There was going to be an exceptionally high tide on Saturday lunchtime with plenty of swell forecasted, and the brothers were hoping for thirty feet waves. Mark had spent time in Portugal and Hawaii where he had surfed the big waves and was hoping that the conditions would be as great as the forecasters had predicted.

Stan had organised full staff cover in the pub for the weekend as the Food, Music and Surf Festival brought thousands of people into the town and was one of the busiest times of the year. He had had a busy few days planning and making sure he had plenty of stock so that the staff could run the pub during the day while he surfed. Mark and Stan lived in the big apartment over the pub, while their Mum, Beryl, lived next door in a cottage she'd bought soon after the tragic night when she'd lost the love of her life, Frank. It was a quiet Wednesday evening around six thirty and only a few of the regulars were in the pub having a post work drink. One of Stan's staff members, Gloria, wasn't due to start work until 7:30 when his RNLI pager went off, as did Mark's. The locals were used to this happening and one of them always stepped behind the bar to help out while Mark ran upstairs to grab his van keys and Stan quickly phoned Beryl next door that she was required in the pub and asked her to get Gloria to come in earlier tonight. The two of them ran out to Mark's van, wheels screeching as they accelerated away from the pub, doing up their seatbelts on the two minute drive to Porthlowen RNLI station, never knowing what awaited them at the station until they arrived.

They were both experienced crew but never ever took the sea for granted, as they had been taught by their Father, and in the back of their minds was always that fateful day. Jumping out of the van, they ran to the station and immediately dressed into their foul weather gear, drysuit with built in yellow wellies, helmet and life jacket.

The Coxswain was Tim Powell, a veteran lifeboatman of thirty two years. He was forty nine but looked a great deal older, his craggy features battered by the elements over the years. He'd been a lifeboatman at the time of the disaster twenty years ago but had unable been to go out on that fateful shout as he'd had a broken leg at the time. Feeling immensely guilty he'd immediately volunteered to become the Coxswain in the aftermath of the disaster and had proved to be an excellent leader on board. Dozens of people over the years owed their lives to him and his crew. It was his job to establish what the emergency was about, assess the conditions and choose the crew from those that turned up.

"What have we got Tim?" Stan asked as they changed.

"Couple of middle aged holiday makers who haven't turned up after an afternoon on the water in a red kayak. Their daughter has raised the alarm. Sea conditions aren't too bad and visibility is quite good so I'm not sure what's happened to them. They were heading down towards Lands End but we all know what the tides can be like there! And obviously the swell is starting to build towards the Surf Festival Weekend.

There were nods of agreement amongst the crew.

Stan was selected to go on the all-weather boat moored at the harbour pontoon, ready to go, while Mark joined the smaller inshore lifeboat which launched first and could go much closer into the shore and the coves. Two others joined Mark on the RIB which launched and left the harbour while the seven crew members of the all-weather boat slipped her lines and got underway, following the wake of the smaller and lighter craft.

The two boats worked in tandem while they searched for the missing kayak, even though the all-weather boat was much faster. It wasn't particularly cold for the time of year but with the evening sun starting to fall and its heat starting to diminish, all of the two crews knew the cooling breeze across the water would sap the energy of the kayakers. Even experienced kayakers could have accidents or come across unexpected conditions or hazards. The waves weren't particularly big but they were a little choppy, especially around the cliffs and rocks of West Cornwall.

More information came over the radio from the Coast Guard which stated that the kayak had been seen an hour ago on a beach that could only be reached from the sea. The incoming tide had now covered this beach so the inshore lifeboat headed towards the last sighting of the kayak, while the all-weather boat started further along the coast in the direction of the tide, both boats maintaining contact with each other and the shore.

Two of the crew members on Stan's boat had binoculars but everyone continually scanned the horizon, the cliffs, caves and coastline apart from the man at the helm, George Robertson, an accountant in his day job. Stan thought that it was lucky that there was good visibility this evening.

Suddenly Mark's excited voice came over the airwaves. "I think we can see them!"

Tim responded. "Well done Mark."

"Heading towards them now." Then a few minutes later he confirmed. "Yes I can see two people, one waving, the kayak has overturned."

Tim took the details and set a new course. "Let's hope they're ok." He muttered to Stan.

By the time that the all-weather boat reached the scene Mark's craft was alongside the red kayak. The bigger boat kept it's distance so as not to churn up the water and create waves which would hinder the rescue. With one of the crew at the helm Mark helped to pull the man, Robert, into the boat. Robert had managed to half pull himself into the RIB but his wife, Fiona, was cold and frightened. She was reluctant to let go of the upturned kayak.

Mark turned on the charm. "Come on my love. I'll come and help you." He lowered himself into the water and came alongside her. "On the count of three we're going to let go of the kayak and I'll hold you so you don't need to be frightened." He put his arm around her waist and swam to the side of the RIB where he lifted and Robert and the other crewman pulled, eventually dumping Fiona unceremoniously into the bottom of the RIB. Mark quickly pulled the upturned kayak towards the RIB where he and the other crewman were able to empty and lift it the right way up. Tying it to the RIB Mark pulled himself into the RIB as Stan's all weather boat pulled up alongside. After quickly checking that apart from being cold and wet the two holidaymakers were none the worse for wear. They were transferred into the larger boat, wrapped in towels and space blankets. The RIB followed, towing the red kayak.

Stan talked to the two of them as the boat made its way back to base. It transpired that they'd stopped on the beach to rest and to look around. Realising that the tide was coming in they'd launched the kayak successfully and were looking down into the clear depths below when a curious seal had suddenly appeared from nowhere, Fiona had panicked and had caused the kayak to capsize. They were quite a distance from the shore and beach by then, having been caught in a rip tide which took them out to sea. Both were grateful and apologetic and Stan reassured them that it all part of the service. As they recovered, they asked about his life in Porthlowen and he mentioned The Ship and as they wished the crew goodbye, once on the shore, safe and sound, apart from a scolding by their relieved daughter, they promised to visit the pub over the Festival weekend.

All that remained now was for the crews to hose the two boats down to get them clean and ready for their next shout.

Discussion 1928

"Look at this." Frederick said excitedly. "It's a letter from Buckingham Palace."

Liberty came over to his desk with a fascinated look on her face. "What does it say?"

"It says that King George the Fifth, the Queen Consort and Mary, the Princess Royal, will be coming to Cornwall on the Royal train. The King and Queen used to be the Duke and Duchess of Cornwall you know."

"Why are they writing to you?"

"Because." He said slowly. "There is a formal dinner on St Michael's Mount and The Princess Royal requires a dinner partner, as her husband is unwell and is unable to come to Cornwall."

"Bring the letter with you." She said enthusiastically. "And we can talk about it when we're out. How do I look?"

Frederick looked her up and down approvingly. Liberty had matched the pretty blue dress with a hat, gloves and a knee length blue coat with a fur collar in the fashion of the day. She still looked pale and limped a little as she moved but she did look grown up. "Very smart." He replied. "You look like a younger version of your Mother."

"Thank you. Let's choose your shirt and tie now and you can look very smart too."

The two of them had an enjoyable day out. Liberty liked being with her Father and they chatted about the dinner on the Mount. She liked sitting in the front of the motorcar and they drove to Marazion, overlooking St Michael's Mount. They wondered about its history. Frederick knew that the second Baron St Levan had been a brigadier general during the Great War.

"Do you know anything about Princess Mary Father?"

"Not really. I know who she is but I've not met her before." He had a distant look. "I'll have to find out as much as I can about her before I meet her. I don't want to appear uneducated. What ever shall I talk to her about?"

"There must be something about her in the Times or the Encyclopaedia Britannica surely."

"Let's not worry about her for now. I want to enjoy my time with you."

They looked out at the calm blue sea through the windscreen of the car, the waves gently washing onto the shore, some seagulls soaring over the bay, some calling to each other as they strutted up and down the beach, making a dreadful din.

"I wonder what they say to each other?" Liberty asked.

"I've never thought about it before. They're just birds."

Liberty pretended to have a conversation, changing voices each time.

"It's a nice view from up here." One will say.

"Where's the fish?" Another will say.

"Behave yourself." The mother will say to the young ones.

"What do I look like?" A young female will say as it preens its feathers.

"Very smart." An older male will reply.

Then Liberty mimicked the call of the gulls, shocking Frederick with the volume of the screech. They both laughed.

"That's better. You look happier." He looked at Liberty. "A little like you did in the summer."

She recoiled and looked away.

An awkward silence ensued.

"I was wrong. I want you to tell me why you were so different in the summer and now you're not."

"You wouldn't understand." She folded her arms and looked out of the side window. "And we were having a nice day." She sulked.

"I'm trying to understand." He said softly and patiently. "I just want you to be happy. I made you unhappy and I'm sorry. I'm not very good at this. Your

Mother was much better at this sort of thing than I am. And you are a woman, or will be very soon. I don't want to talk to Miss Scrivener or Mrs Hitchens about you. It's not the right thing and they are not young or a lady like you. And Dorothy is closer in age to you but she's just a working class girl." He placed a gentle hand on her shoulder.

Liberty sat in silence, staring out of the window. Not sure what to say. She'd enjoyed their day so far and she wanted more days like this. She wanted to talk to him and trust him but she was also mindful that he'd made her so unhappy and she'd felt like dying. She wasn't sure how much to tell him. Certainly not about Jack.

"Please Liberty." He said softly. "I want to do the right thing."

She turned to look at him and noticed the earnestness in his face. She hadn't seen him look like this before. She sighed, took a deep breath and said "Alright. I'll tell you but you're not to shout, not to interrupt and let me speak until I've finished."

Frederick took a deep breath, took both of Liberty's hands in his own and agreed.

Festival

Porthlowen Food, Surf and Music Mid Summer Festival was in its twentieth year and was now a well established international event bringing in around sixty thousand people over the three days. Originally it had started off as a small surfing event but had then started to attract some of the best surfers in the UK and then from further afield. Now it was a huge event, both in the surfing calendar and for the town of Porthlowen. Hotels, guest houses, campsites and Air B & Bs were all full. Pubs and restaurants would be rammed and the benefit to the local economy was huge. As well as the world renowned Surf Championships there would be theatre shows, family entertainment, food stalls along with street food vendors, parades, music of all types during the day and night and even a famous TV chef doing a turn in a huge marquee. The Surf Championships were taking place just along the coast at Pencannock Bay, a three mile beach of golden sands which at low tide stretched towards Porthlowen, while out to sea enormous waves and swell came in from far out in the ocean providing a popular surfing and kitesurfing spot. A small village of surfers' tents and camper vans would appear along the cliff top while yet more traders selling surf related clothing and merchandise parked up.

The first day of the festival was a Friday and started with a late night firework show and torch light procession. As it was mid summer it didn't get dark until late and so the fireworks didn't start until around 11pm with a huge bang to signal the beginning of the awesome light display. Tom and Rachel had met up with Dawn and Julie and their husbands for a couple of drinks at the Ship before congregating with hundreds of other locals along the sea front where a pontoon had been set up in the bay, and from where the amazing fireworks were launched. The display lit up the sky, reflecting over the bay and it was an incredible feast for the senses. Tom and Rachel ooooed and aaghed with the rest of the audience, agreeing it was a great start to the weekend.

Lots of the locals had got up very early to decorate Porthlowen with greenery tied to railings and lamp posts. Banners were created in workshops and then used to decorate the town and shops while some very large and very beautiful professional flags flew from the flag poles on the promenade near Liberty's Lido. These were always a feast for the eyes and this year was no exception. They were made of a silk material in bright colours of the rainbow. Diane always ran this workshop and this year she had dedicated the flags to open water swimmers. Each flag showed a different swimmer diving into the water.

On the Saturday the local Schools were involved in the street processions. It was like the Notting Hill carnival Cornish style with samba bands and other musical artists that provided the music for the three different processions taking part during the day. Each year the festival had a different theme and this year it was called "Under the Sea." The local Schools spent many weeks making brightly coloured structures and banners from willow canes and paper that the school staff and children carried, while wearing masks. They would all gather outside the Town Hall then proceed down the Main Street and back again as the crowds squashed in to line the street to watch, clap and cheer.

The Committee spent a whole year planning the next festival and followed a similar set up each time. The fair moved into the large car park by the boating lake. The recreation ground next to it lent itself to a large music stage and arena, with street food vendors and pop up bars spread out. Across the road from Liberty's Lido and stretching out along the promenade were many craft, clothing and gift stalls both inside a huge marquee and further smaller gazebos along the narrower parts of the promenade. Street entertainers amused the public with their performances

This year the Committee were taking further steps to make the festival environmentally friendly and sustainable. Liz was a member of the Festival Committee after becoming very concerned at the impact on the local area of last year's festival. Rubbish and waste that had been left on the streets and fields and then blown into the sea. For several days following the festival last year the Ls had retrieved and filled several bags with rubbish collected from the sea. The group had called themselves "Water Wombles" after collecting lots of the discarded rubbish. This had consisted of plastic cups and bottles, paper serviettes, food wrappers and lots of broken glass from bottles of alcohol recklessly tossed into the sea by festival revellers.

Tom wasn't on duty this year, as he had been for many years in the past so it was a new experience for just the two of them to wander lazily around the festival, experiencing its delights. They saw a couple of friends sat in the sunshine outside a cafe, which for one day only was able to put tables and chairs out into the street where normally cars, vans and buses rushed up and down. They joined their friends and talked while drinking coffee and watched the world go by, relaxing in the warm sunshine. People they knew came by and stopped to chat.

A group of men dressed as pirates walked past while three girls scantily dressed in brightly coloured samba dresses eased past in the opposite direction, attracting raucous comments from the pirates and ribald comments from the dancers. Laughter ensued from everywhere. A brass band started playing outside the church just down the road and gentle editions of popular music wafted up towards the cafe creating a pleasant ambience. Primary school children, dressed in fancy dress, having completed the previous processions or in town for the next one, ran around chasing and arguing with each other, wound up with excitement. Groups of teenagers tried hard to look cool, to impress, eying up boys and girls they fancied, shouting with bravado or giggling with embarrassment, mobile phones glued to their hands or ears. Harassed parents with kids of various ages manoeuvred buggies and pushchairs through impossible gaps trying to maintain a semblance of control over their offspring. Young couples held hands romantically and gazed dreamily at each other. Older couples held hands or arms in familiar companionship while pointing things out, chatting with each other and friends. Great grandparents pottered unsteadily on elderly legs, supported by each other and a stick, veterans of many festivals but still determined to experience at least one more time.

It was one of those weekends where anything goes, a relaxing, fun time where Porthlowen came out in force to enjoy the annual festival. Tom and Rachel, having drank their coffee, bade their farewells to their friends and moved to stand in the main street to watch the schools' procession amble in between the throngs of enthusiastic parents and grandparents calling and waving to their school age darlings. As usual the standard of models and creations that had been assembled seemed to surpass the previous year's efforts, and the colours, noises, music all added to a feel good vibration. Rachel recalled the many times that she had been one of those parents waiting in anticipation to watch young Poppy walk with her school in the parade and as Poppy became a teenager she was more reluctant to be included in a parade and was more likely to be found with her friends down at the fairground. So often Tom had been working, or on call for the weekend, sometimes down at the Surf festival or in his surgery so it was nice this year to be just like everyone else enjoying the festival in the sunshine. This was a time of year to catch up with friends that you only ever saw at the festival or in the local supermarket at Christmas, promising each time you saw them that "we must get together for a coffee sometime." But then not seeing them again until the next local celebration.

By Sunday evening, after the three days of the Festival, Tom and Rachel had enjoyed a wonderful weekend. They'd ambled around the stalls, stopped outside one of the pubs, standing and chatting to people who came and went, they'd grabbed a takeaway curry and sat on the sea wall, overlooking the tides.

They'd wandered down to watch the surfing for a while, soaking up the sun while relaxing on the beach, chatting to more people, sampling more ale and gin, slowly getting tipsy while listening to various bands and artists playing music. They'd got in a swim each morning with the others; they'd watched the TV chef demonstration and eaten in his restaurant with other friends. All in all, it had been a great, relaxing and fun weekend.

Honesty 1928

"It all started" She began slowly. "when I was looking around the garden at the trees and plants, birds and animals. Mr Rowe would point out the flowers and vegetables and fruit to me and then I would try to remember them. I'd look them up in the Encyclopaedia Britannica and also learn something about them and learn their Latin names." She looked at her Father. He was watching her and listening intently.

"Go on." He encouraged gently.

She laughed. "I tried to teach Mr Rowe the Latin names but he couldn't remember them. He knows so much though. About the animals and plants."

Frederick nodded. He hadn't really thought much about Mr Rowe. He tended to the estate with that boy. Benjamin was he called? He turned up day after day, throughout all weathers, always with a smile on his face, was reliable, had worked for the Nancarrow family for years and years, and Frederick realised he knew virtually nothing about the man. Liberty was teaching him a thing or two. He made a mental note to give Mr Rowe a pay rise.

"I started to look at the garden in a different way." Liberty continued. "Properly seeing things that had always been under my nose but never really looked at. The colours seemed to become more vivid and I started to notice the way things changed during the seasons. Some flowers come out in summer and different ones in spring and winter. I found it all fascinating." She paused for a few moments.

"What's wrong?" Asked Frederick.

"I'm just getting my thoughts in order." She replied. "So then I started to look outside of the estate and gardens. With my binoculars I could look one way, like you do, down into the Port with all of the vehicles coming and going, delivering things and taking things from the boats away. Then the boats come and go and there's different types of boats and ships, and cars and lorries. I could look out to the sea and see the sailing boats and the steam boats near and far. Then from the other side of the house and my bedroom I could look along the promenade, down to the rocks, the beach, the sea. And I noticed that every day the weather would be different, the tide would be in and there was no beach and then it would be out exposing the rocks underneath. I saw people walking, driving, riding bicycles along the promenade and um….."

"Carry on." Frederick said softly.

"I wanted to see it for myself so I um went outside the estate on my own." She took a deep breath and looked hard at her Father.

He nodded but said nothing.

"Each day I went a little further until I was down on the promenade." She breathed out a huge breath. "Then I sat on the rocks and just watched." Her stomach suddenly rumbled. "I thought we were going for lunch."

The quiet spell was broken. "But I want to hear the rest of your story."

"Can we go somewhere and eat and I'll tell you the rest then?"

Frederick was reluctant to stop the flow from Liberty but agreed and he drove to a cosy restaurant where he was known and asked for a private table in a quiet corner where they couldn't be overheard or interrupted.

Wombles

Everyone was talking about a TV program that was shown the night before called the Blue Planet. Living in close proximity to the coastline every one of the swimmers saw the amount of rubbish washed up onto the beaches or left behind after visitors had left. There was always rope, old fishing nets, plastic bottles and plenty of other litter, especially after a storm. The group was used to being 'Water Wombles' and daily collected rubbish from the shore line as well as the sea. They were proud advocates of the initiative called "Plastic Free Porthlowen," As well as raising awareness in schools some of the Ls had visited businesses to encourage the stopping of single use plastic like straws. This was set up to encourage shoppers in the town to stop using plastic bags and all single use plastic. Today however, they were discussing the wider implications of plastic on marine life.

Heather was talking to Cindy "Do you remember when we saw that seal with a plastic bag wrapped around its mouth?"

Cindy replying said "Oh yeah that was dreadful. I wanted to cry. I hope the seal managed to get it off and didn't die."

The local supermarket had swopped to small material bags with a draw string for fruit and vegetables and Heather had bought several and handed them out to the swimmers while saying "I thought we could use these to collect rubbish from the sea instead of stuffing it down our costumes. We can fill the bags and hopefully we can tie them onto ourselves. Might make it safer and more comfortable for us so no more scratches from tin cans and packets."

Heather was a dog rescuer and quite often had up to seven dogs living with her while she nursed then back to health before rehoming them. No matter what the weather was like she always turned up in her Wellington boots, having usually just walked her extended dog pack. She was always fundraising to pay for their food and vet bills. Lots of people would donate items to her that she would then sell, never spending any money on herself. Her one luxury, as she called it, was to join the Ls for a swim. Not in good health herself she always put the dogs in her care first and always said she preferred the company of dogs to men. Heather had had the idea of using large used empty plastic bottles with the tops left on but a small hole in the bottom and filling the bottles up with biodegradable dog poo bags. She had then gone around the town and tied them to lampposts to try and encourage the people of Porthlowen to clear up after their dogs. She knew how easy it was to forget or run out of bags to clear up dog poo when out walking the dog pack. This has been a huge success and it had encouraged other locals to also take on the role of supplying poo bags for others around the town. This had made a massive reduction of dog mess in the town. Heather had been in the local newspaper as well as local TV and this had really helped her fundraising efforts.

The group were discussing how they could reduce their single plastic use. A lot of them already bought their own hot drinks to have after swimming and Cindy suggested talking to Pierre about using their own cups when buying hot drinks in the Lido café. Maybe to encourage everyone, the café could offer a small discount to anyone who was prepared to do this. She certainly seen several disposable cups floating around the sea after being carelessly dropped or blowing out of full rubbish bins. Everyone who had watched the recent TV program about how long plastic takes to break down and how far it can travel in the oceans along with how much ends up in the stomachs of seabirds and fish was really worried.

Joining in the conversation Rachel asked Heather "Did you see in the local paper this week about the ten year old boy who they call 'The mini beach cleaner?' His Mum has set up a Facebook Page to show the huge amounts of rubbish that they collect each week." She carried on telling Heather plus Cindy, who had just joined them. "It's really clever. They make it into works of art then photograph it before disposing of all the litter. Sometimes he has made the rubbish into pictures and his Mum has started framing them and now they are selling them for charity. He's recently won a Young Person's Award towards conservation. I was thinking of asking the mini beach cleaner to come and help us publicise plastic free Porthlowen."

Angela listening to their conversation told the others that she regularly did beach cleans where they collected nurdles.

"What the hell are those?" asked Cindy. "They sound like a creature in a Harry Potter novel."

Angela continued to explain "Nurdles are plastic pellets used by Industry to make nearly all of our plastic products. Accidental spills result in large numbers of nurdles being washed into the sea. Marine life mistake them for food and the toxic coatings can end up in the food chain. Hang on, I think I have a photo from my last beach clean." She started to frantically scroll through her photos and showed them one of a glass jar full of tiny coloured round pieces of plastic. Putting her phone away she continued "I collected all of these about a month ago after taking part in The Great Nurdle Hunt organised by the local seal sanctuary. I can let you know when the next one is."

"Please do." replied Rachel.

"Everyone ready?" Liz asked "Let's collect more rubbish and enjoy our swim."

Due to the success of Plastic Free Porthlowen a film company had arrived for the weekend interested in how Porthlowen was managing the problem. They had filmed on the Sunday of the Festival around the town for their documentary and had arrived at Golden Rocks this morning just before the swimmers. As usual there was a huge amount of rubbish left behind after the weekend and this year there had been an offshore breeze which meant a lot of it had ended up in the sea.

Angela always being nosy, walked up to the three film crew as they started to set up and asked them "What are you filming?" in her usual know all and sometimes aggressive manner, her hands on her hips.

A tall good looking man in his mid-thirties with dark hair smiled disarmingly at her as he pushed his sunglasses onto his head, his colleagues supressing a smile as they continued to set up their equipment. "We're from Mountain Film Productions and we're making a documentary about the enormous amount of rubbish left behind by mankind. We're featuring Porthlowen in our short film."

"Well you've come to the right place." Angela announced. "We are the face of Plastic Free Porthlowen."

"Oh God, here she goes." Tink said.

Angela standing tall with her arms crossed continued to talk at the man. He was used to this as wherever they filmed people were interested. He'd also learnt to listen, as local knowledge was useful. He eventually tried telling Angela that his name was Matt, but didn't really think she had heard him as she was too busy telling him all about herself. "We're about to swim and give the sea a clean up of rubbish from the festival. I can already see lots floating on the surface." she stated.

Realising that this might be good footage for the documentary Matt asked Angela more about the swimming group. This was just what Angela loved, attention, but on this occasion, at least, it was a positive.

"Hang on." she said to Matt before striding purposefully towards the rest of the Ls, leaving the film crew alone to carry on setting up in peace.

"Listen everyone." she announced. "We're going to be filmed collecting rubbish today. My friend over there, well actually, he's a professional film producer you know, has asked me if I would like to be in his film, and, well, I said I would only do it if everyone else could also join in. I don't want to take all the glory you know." She finished with a wistful over the shoulder look towards the film crew.

Some of the Ls had some questions about the documentary, but Diane annoyed by Angela taking the limelight yet again asked "So what's your friend called?"

"Mmmm, well, mmmm, does it matter?" she replied "We're going to be in a film and it's so important to publicise the work we do to help the environment."

Tink being the furthest away from Angela muttered under her breath and giving Sally and Cindy a knowing look said "Yes so important to publicise the cause and not oneself."

As they started to laugh Angela shot them a look.

Matt, the film reporter and producer, walked along the concrete path over towards the group and introduced himself. He was around six feet tall with short dark hair, cut into a fashionable style. He asked if the swimmers were ok to be filmed, explaining that the program was being made for Channel 4 and was going to be aired in the Autumn. He continued saying they had already covered lots of places in the UK already. "We were just going to film the rubbish in the sea today but we would be really happy if we could film a couple of clips with you guys picking up the litter. Where do you get into the water?" he carried on.

Already for her swim Flo replied "Today as it's such a beautiful day we will be able to get in at the steps" she pointed and Matt followed her gaze.

Angela was faffing around talking to Alice "Gosh I hope I've got my new costume. I can't be on film in any old costume."

"You'll be fine in whatever you're wearing." Alice replied.

"I've got about seventy five costumes at home and I bet I've bought my worst one today." Angela hissed in a panicked voice. Noticing that Matt was now talking to Flo she quickly pulled up her costume and grabbing her gloves, hat and goggles pushed Alice out of the way as she practically sprinted over to him.

Usually the group managed to hold any rubbish inside their swimming costumes but there was so much today, after the festival that Tony had bought along a few net bags so that each swimmer could fill it up and not have to keep swimming back to land. The film crew started filming as the swimmers started to get in. Swimming away from the rocks they didn't have to go very far before Liz found a plastic bottle floating. Stashing it inside her net she swam after a soggy serviette.

Angela found a Coca Cola tin can floating just below the surface and held it up in the air before shouting over to the film crew. "Cooee look what I've found." The camera panned around to her just as she was pushing the can inside her costume, revealing just a little too much flesh.

The Channel 4 team filmed the swimmers removing plenty of rubbish from the sea. Plastic cups, straws, takeaway cartons and serviettes had blown into the ocean and the Water Wombles had been kept busy collecting everything.

Tony had been diving down to remove a glass bottle when he saw it! A grey hand poking out of the weed. Nearly swallowing water he quickly swam to the surface, the weight of his bag of rubbish nearly pulling him back down again. He couldn't be sure and dived down again but it didn't look like it was attached to anything. Calling Liz over Tony showed it to her. "What do we do? I don't want to touch it but we can't leave it there."

Liz put her head under the water to take a look at the hand before with a fresh lungful of air she dived underwater. Swimming gracefully through the water she held on to a piece of kelp that was attached to a rock which was close to the hand. This gave her some purchase to actually touch the thing! With her mind struggling to stay calm and her lungs now starting to burn she just grabbed at the grey hand before swimming upwards. Breaking the surface for an explosive breath of air she looked at what she had just bought up before starting to laugh, more out of relief than of shock.

Tony didn't see the funny side until she waved a grey rubber glove in front of his face. He couldn't make sense of what it was at first before realising that the severed hand was in fact a large glove probably thrown off a fishing trawler. "Well done Liz. That's one less glove for a dolphin to eat." He gave Liz a relieved look before joining her with a loud belly laugh. She placed the offending glove into her net bag. Flo and Michelle swam over to the two of them with their collections from the depths. As their nets were getting heavy they swam back to the shore and the film crew finished their filming by focusing on Tony's full net of rubbish and the five black bin liners that the Ls had filled from their morning swim.

Lunch 1928

As they perused the menu Frederick ordered drinks. Wine for him and lemonade for Liberty. "In London they have a drink called Coca Cola which has just come over from the United States of America. I don't think it's come to Cornwall yet but I don't think it will be long."

"What's it like?" Asked Liberty.

"Brown and fizzy, very sweet. I only tried it once and I didn't like it. I prefer wine."

"And whisky and brandy." Liberty added. "And coffee and tea."

"You're very observant." He laughed.

Liberty liked it when her Father laughed. It lit up his face and he didn't look so worried and serious.

Lunch arrived. Beef for Frederick. Chicken for Liberty. They tucked in hungrily.

"So, you were sat on the rocks on the promenade." Frederick encouraged. "Please continue."

"Yes. I sat on the rocks. The weather in the summer was hot, we had those few weeks where every day seemed to get hotter and hotter."

"Yes. I remember. It was horrible to have to wear a suit, tie, hat, and gloves. Especially in London."

"Miss Scrivener was affected by the heat and wasn't well during that time so that gave me more time to go off and I wasn't supervised or chaperoned."

She looked at Frederick, who had stopped eating and pursed his lips disapprovingly.

"So I sat on the rocks." Liberty continued hurriedly so that Frederick wouldn't interrupt. "And I watched and looked. I watched the birds, all different types. I watched the sea with its endless movement. I looked at the rocks, the rock pools and the different colours. I looked at the stones, and the weed and plants that are around the sea edge. I saw little fish and crabs and these plant type things that are actually animals, called anemones. I looked it all up in the

Encyclopaedia Britannica. I found that I relaxed as the more I saw the more I realised there was so much more to see. The colours were endless not just pink and green but so many shades of pink and green and all the colours of the rainbow. I found there was a whole world that I didn't know about and I just wanted to find out and see even more. It was all fascinating but more fascinating were the people walking up and down and I saw the children come to the beach and wash themselves. They laughed and called to each other. There were brothers and sisters, cousins and friends. Their Mothers watched the young ones while the older ones were together as a group, away from their annoying younger siblings." She looked at him closely as she said "I realised that most of the older children and even some of the younger ones work in your mines."

He jolted in his seat. She was right. They did. He was ashamed. He had lost his appetite now. He took a large gulp of wine and poured another glass.

He watched as Liberty continued to talk in between mouthfuls. "The children seemed to have so much fun in the sea and I wondered what it would be like so I found a secret spot, away from where anyone was watching and .." She gulped. This was the moment of truth. "I.... I um... took off my outer dress..."

He gasped but said nothing.

"Then I took off my boots and stockings and walked down to the sea edge very carefully, feeling the sharp stones and soft sand underneath my feet. Then I stood on the edge of the water and allowed the cold water to go over my toes. It felt amazing and it made my toes and feet really cold to start with but then I hardly noticed it was cold, maybe because it was so hot on the shore. I'd stand there for ages, feeling the water wash over my feet and ankles, and then I'd bend down and see the little creatures in the water, and I'd explore where the water had gone and left the rocks still wet. Each day I'd go a little further until the water was up to my knees." She looked at her Father who was listening with interest and had continued eating his lunch. "I found that when I closed my eyes and just listened, everything seemed to slow down and even stop. My breath was deep and I seemed to be part of the sea, the shore and the beach. It felt like I'd really come home. I really found myself. It was truly amazing." She decided to leave out the bit about Jack. "One day I ventured a little further and then I tripped over a rock and fell into the water. I went right underneath and I panicked and came out of the sea. I sat on the sea shore soaking wet, including my hair, shivering and my leg was cut. Then it poured with rain and I ran back home. That was the day I was wrapped up in a towel at the bottom of the stairs. Do you remember?"

Frederick shook his head. "No. I do not."

"I said I'd been asleep in the garden, had woken up when the rain started and then fallen over."

He looked at her strangely but she carried on telling her story, her chicken dish now finished.

Blood

Mike Higgins followed Tony out of the water. Debbie, his wife was a non-swimmer today, having revelled too much at the festival yesterday, and was happily sat on the side soaking up the sun. Mike stood on some pebbles just before getting out and going up the steps he suddenly felt a stabbing pain on the bottom of his foot. Thinking he had just stood on a sharp stone but already numbed by the cold, continued to rush towards his warm, dry clothes and his hot drink.

Alice, being the next swimmer to reach dry land, noticed the blood as soon as she reached the top of the steps. She followed the blood trail, being careful not to step in it. "Has someone cut their foot?" She called loudly. Feeling perplexed with the amount of blood, she couldn't understand how anybody hadn't noticed their injury. A pool of blood was now forming on the concrete floor below Mike. "Mike! You're bleeding. It's you!" Alice shouted. "Quick sit down."

Looking down Mike realised he had a deep wound sliced into the flesh of his right foot. It was heavily oozing blood and as the numbness from the cold started to wear off, he took a sharp intake of breath, the reality of the injury resulting in pain spiralling across his foot. He sat down heavily with a shock.

Bill, sprang into action, his previous Army training never far away. "Give me some space." He shouted as the Ls, alarmed by Alice's yelling, had grouped around Mike with concern, all shivering in their towelling robes. Wrapping Mike's foot in his blue towel to stem the flow of blood, Bill noticed that everyone else was still in various stages of undress so his quickest help was probably Debbie, who had rushed over and was now looking very pale at the shock of seeing her husband lying on the ground, blood everywhere, and with his foot elevated by Bill.

"Are you ok?" Bill addressed her. He hoped she wasn't going to faint or panic.

"Mmmmm. What's happened? Are you alright Mike?" Debbie replied her eyes fixated on Mike's foot and looking woozy.

Mike grimaced in pain.

"It's alright Debbie. He's just got a cut on his foot but can you run around to the Lido and fetch a first aid kit?" Bill continued. Blood started to soak through the towel and he pressed it firmly against the open wound to stop the free-flowing sticky red surge. 'This will need a stitch or three.' he thought to himself.

"Mmmmmm Mmmmmm" She couldn't answer and Bill could see she looked faint.

"Sit down Debbie!" he bellowed.

Tony walked up behind Debbie just as she started to crumple, catching her before she did, then laying her down carefully next to Mike. Taking off his robe he covered her up. "I can get the first aid box from the Lido if someone can look after Debbie?" Tony asked.

"I'm nearly dressed." Diane replied before continuing "You carry on Tony."

He sped off and arrived back out of breath, handing Bill the first aid kit. Mike was still in a lot of pain and the towel was now more red than blue. Debbie was sitting up and was being comforted by Diane. Bill opened the box and grabbing several pieces of gauze he replaced the towel and applied pressure, getting Mike to raise his foot higher by placing a couple of swimmers' rucksacks underneath his legs for support. "Tony look inside the box and hand me any bandages." Wrapping these around the gauze, blood was still seeping through at an alarming rate. He added more gauze, more pressure and more bandages until the box was empty. By this time several of the swimmers were dressed and offering to help.

Flo was frantically calling and waving to Tom but he was out of earshot with Rachel, Tink and Liz who were all diving off the reef, looking for starfish, urchins and anemones.

"Alice have you got your phone with you today? Bill asked.

"Yes, I have." Quite often the swimmers left their phones in their cars worried about theft from bags when swimming.

"Can you call an ambulance and explain about the Festival and the fact that the road is closed. Bill said "Tony, can you help me out by applying pressure while I think what we can do next."

Tom had finally seen Flo waving and had swam quickly back to the shore with Rachel following slowly behind.

"Mike's cut his foot and Bill's done some first aid on him." Flo met Tom at the steps and he hurried towards the patient. He took in the situation immediately with Tony putting pressure on the wound and Diane looking after Debbie.

Bill rose to meet Tom who asked "OK just fill me in on the details?"

"Mike has a nasty cut on his foot. I think he might have stood on some glass getting out. I'm guessing somebody must have thrown a bottle in over the weekend. I've asked Alice to call an ambulance."

"Okay let me have a look." Tom replied. "Well done Bill. You get dressed now as I'm going to need you shortly."

Tom could see that Mike was very pale and starting to shake with cold and shock, despite being covered up with several towelling robes. Rachel arrived at Tom's side and passed him a towelling robe to put on. Even though the weather was warm she shivered when she saw Mike's blood. Glancing over to Debbie, who was being comforted by Diane, Rachel headed back to her rucksack and quickly got dressed in case she was required to assist at all.

Every second Mike stayed there his heat was leeching away a few more fractions of a degree to take him closer to hypothermia with both the shock and the cold. Tom took his pulse which was now starting to slow down. He knew Mike needed to get into the warmth of a hospital. Bill took over from Tony, putting pressure on the towel on Mike's foot and he kept talking to Mike, reassuring him and making sure he was still awake.

"Where is that ambulance?" Tom said under his breath, as he got changed. "Debbie are you alright?"

She nodded, the colour returning to her cheeks.

Tom stood and addressed the assembled small group, concern for Mike etched onto their faces. "We need to get him to hospital quickly. If it was just the cut on his foot, we would be ok for a while but because he's been swimming, he's getting really cold and I'm worried shock and hypothermia are setting in. If we can get the wheelchair from the Lido before he gets any worse, we can wait there for the ambulance in the first aid room which might be warmer. Alice can you call 999 and get an update on how long the ambulance might be please? Rachel please can you go and retrieve the wheelchair from the Lido. Liz can you go with her to get people to move out of the way."

Liz and Rachel sped off through the crowds that had grown from just the swimmers to now festival goers walking around to take in views of the sea. 'Why did everyone seem to dawdle when you were in a hurry' Rachel thought to herself.

Returning with the wheelchair you could hear Liz before seeing her. "Coming through!" she shouted, her Cornish accent stronger than ever. "Thank you, my lover." she cried as she wove her way through and along the busy path.

Rachel was following as quickly as she could, pushing the empty wheelchair. She noticed that Tom's long-sleeved T shirt was now wrapped around Mike's leg so she handed him her pink hoodie to help Tom keep warm. It was a tight fit and his long arms poked out the end of the sleeves but he wouldn't care a jot. Parking the chair next to Tom and Bill she could hear them discussing how to get Mike into the wheelchair then quickly around to the Lido without further blood loss. Both highly trained in their own field she thought to herself that Mike was very lucky, if you could call it luck, to have cut himself while both men were present to assist and plenty of other swimmers to help as well. They'd come to the conclusion that the only choice was to pick him up, put him into the wheelchair and speedily get him inside the Lido and to some warmth. As soon as Rachel arrived, Tom, Bill and Tony lifted Mike as carefully as they could into the chair.

Tom could see Mike's lips were starting to turn blue and quickly checking his pulse he noticed it had slowed down even more. "It's really important we keep him awake" Tom said to Bill. "I'm getting worried now. Damn. Where's that ambulance?"

"Tony. Rachel. Can you clear a way through the crowds please, we need to move now!" Bill barked before getting behind Mike and with the utmost urgency started to push the wheelchair. Tom walked beside Mike, making sure he was alright and keeping people from getting too close. Debbie was still feeling a bit faint but walked slowly around to the Lido, accompanied by Diane and Alice. Flo, Angela and Liz brought some of the swimming bags around while Cindy, Tink and Michelle said they would stay with the remaining kit and look after it.

The Lido manager, Douggie, spoke to Tom as he entered the Lido, going the longer way around but down the slope following Bill. "The ambulance has been delayed trying to get here due to the closed roads and the volume of people. They've offered to send an air ambulance but I can't think where it would land as it's so busy."

“Ok.” Tom replied. “Thanks, Douggie.”

Mike was now lying on the bed in the first aid room and Bill had propped up his leg up once more. He was covered in many robes, towels and hoodies. The blood was again leaking through the layers after he’d been sat in the wheelchair, with his foot down.

“Bill. Any ideas?” Tom continued. “The ambulance is stuck. Is there any way we can clear outside the Lido and land a helicopter? Obviously, the Fairground is now directly outside where it would normally land and maybe the Police can help.”

Bill breathed out quickly before speaking, Tom could see that Bill was trying to assess the situation, his Army training being bought back into use. “What about the using the road that is already closed along the Promenade, it’s far enough away from the Fair and market stalls. If the police can shut it to pedestrians, I think it’s our only option. You stay with Mike and I will go and talk to the police.”

Bill returned quickly telling Tom that a helicopter was being sent and the road was being cleared. “How long do you think it will be?” Tom motioned before pointing at Mike.

“Soon was all they could say.” Bill replied.

Tom filled Debbie in on the details as she’d now arrived with Alice and Diane.

Rachel appeared with a tray of tea, coffee, sugar and milk. They handed it quickly to Debbie, then Tom, Bill and the others. “Courtesy of the café.” She said.

Liz poked her head around the door with her tin of swimmers’ cake. She offered it around. Everyone gratefully accepting a piece of the moist delicious bake.

The paramedics from the ambulance finally arrived with their gurney and carefully lifted Mike onto it. They liaised with Tom and Bill, quickly checked Mike over and then left the first aid room with a policeman who’d arrived to say that the Air Ambulance had arrived. Tom escorted Debbie to the helicopter and she gave him her car keys. He said he’d drop their car to their house along with their swimming bags. Rachel had Debbie’s number and they arranged that someone would come and collect them from the hospital once Mike had the all clear.

Tom, Bill, Douggie and Rachel sat in the first aid room afterwards, gratefully accepting another cup of coffee from Pierre at the café. Tink appeared along with Cindy and Michelle. They'd brought the rest of the swimming gear in from the rocks and deposited it in the first aid room. The rest of the Ls made their way home.

Matt, the film producer, popped his head in through the door. "I hope your friend will be alright. We carried on filming and so we'll really be able to hammer the message home about litter and rubbish in the sea."

Tom and Rachel left shortly afterwards and Debbie phoned a couple of hours later to say that Mike was OK but was being kept in overnight for observation and she thanked Tom, Bill and everyone for their kindness and told them that their son would collect the car keys from Tom later that evening.

Ice cream 1928

"For two or three days I didn't go back to the beach as I'd fallen over in the water and frightened myself." Liberty continued her story. "I couldn't swim but I'd seen much younger children than myself swimming so I thought that if I could learn about animals and plants, and learn Latin then I could easily learn to swim. I loved being down by the water, by the sea. I don't know what it was but something about the sea, the sea air, the waves, the nature, the birds, oh I don't know what it was but it made me feel differently to anything else I've ever felt before. I felt sort of quiet and peaceful inside myself. Almost as if I was a different person altogether." She went quiet as she looked at her Father, his lined face, his greying receding hair, his frown and worry lines across his forehead, the dark shadows of bristle across his chin and under his nose. He was waiting for more.

"After I'd been away for those days I felt as if I needed to go back, like an urge or an itch. I wanted to get back to the other me. The quiet, peaceful me. I walked over to the promenade and sat beside the sea, on the rocks, looking at the different colours and contrasting types of surfaces. I took my outer dress, my boots and stockings off and walked straight into the sea up to my waist and crouched in the water. It was cold initially but then I became accustomed to it, as I had with my feet before. I dropped down again and stood up, and again. Then I ducked down and stayed there, allowing my breath to return to normal, feeling myself relax inside and finding the peaceful part inside me again. I kept close enough so that I could touch the bottom whenever I wanted to and moved my arms like I'd seen the children doing, and then suddenly I was swimming. I was floating and moving a little. Then I forgot what I was doing and went under the water. I swallowed some water I think." She laughed. "I coughed, then I tried again and again and each time I swam a little further. Each day I went back and tried again and now I could swim. And every day seemed to be better and what was amazing was that my leg stopped hurting. My poorly leg stopped hurting. And I didn't feel delicate." She added firmly, nodding at the same time.

"And then I ruined it." Said Frederick in a whisper. He looked at his daughter in a new light. She'd become animated as she told the story, reliving and re-enacting how she felt, and he could see and sense the passion coming from her. Her eyes sparkled and she looked and sounded different. "I'm so sorry. You must get back to swimming as I can see it made you feel better. More than that it's given you a dream, a passion and it made you come alive!"

"Oh Father. Thank you." She rose from her seat in the restaurant, moved towards him and flung her arms around his neck.

"Would you like some desert?" A waitress appeared from nowhere and caught them unawares. Liberty removed her arms from her Father's neck looking self conscious while Frederick himself looked somewhat embarrassed.

"Yes please. Could I have some chocolate ice cream? Thank you." Liberty said, quickly recovering her poise. "Father?"

"Yes. I think I'll have some chocolate ice cream too." He couldn't remember the last time he'd had ice cream of any flavour and when it arrived he enjoyed every mouthful, remembering that there were a lot of things that he'd enjoyed as a child growing up that he'd forgotten all about. It had taken Liberty showing him a different perspective to reacquaint himself with these things. They left the restaurant and drove around in the motorcar for the rest of the day, talking about a lot of things. He talked about his childhood, his parents, his dear departed sister Maud. He told Liberty about her Mother, how much he'd loved her, how much he'd missed her. Liberty regaled him with stories, some that she'd made up about the people she didn't know on the promenade, she told him how Daisy used to tell Dorothy about Miss Scrivener behind her back. 'Yes Miss Scrivener. No Miss Scrivener. Three bags full Miss Scrivener.'

Frederick laughed, then told Liberty about some of his experiences in the Great War and how Rosina Hitchens had come to work at Nancarrow House.

She told him about mermaids and pirates, and kings and princesses, bringing the conversation back to the dinner at St. Michael's Mount and how her Father was going to accompany Princess Mary. How exciting. When they arrived back home it had been dark a long time and the winter evening had a chill in the air. Frederick parked the car and the two of them walked arm in arm back to the illuminated House. Liberty was tired now but she'd enjoyed her day with her Father.

"We must do this again soon." He said as he stopped at the bottom of the stairs.

"We must. Goodnight Father."

"Goodnight my Darling." He kissed the top of her head and she gave him a hug and she went to bed, sleeping soundly for the first time in many weeks.

Duckgate

With so many members there was always a birthday and even though they didn't need an excuse for cake this was always a time to over indulge with something a little bit special. Today was Diane's birthday and as she had not long had an operation on her foot the Ls chose a flat sandy beach to visit with easy parking and access. The girls helped Diane by carrying her swimming bag and the all important cake.

Liz bought her big pink folding chair so that Diane wouldn't have to sit on the sand and even though she was only going to paddle it would assist her to get changed as well.

Diane was so desperate to get back in the sea but had had to be very patient to allow her wounds to heal. Today was going to be her first dip post op.

Alice was excited to have cake and knew they were in for a treat as Diane's carrot cake was legendary in Porthlowen, very moist and incredibly decadent. She had won awards at the local farming shows in the past.

Walking across the beach in her birthday crown, Diane had added a seal picture to it, as was tradition when it was your birthday. Speaking to Liz, Diane said "I had to make some minor repairs to the crown as it was getting so heavy from all the additions and amount of use. We certainly have a lot of birthdays; especially in the summer months."

"Shall we sit over by the wall?" Angela asked. The wall was the start of the path going along the cliff top. There was a concrete slope there that joined the path. "It will give us a good base and stop anyone sitting too close. Mind you they will probably move as we are so loud." she continued.

The sand on this beach was quite a coarse sand made up of ground up shells and pebbles. The left hand side of the beach was sandy and as you walked across to the right it became stonier and on from there, at low tide, were many rockpools. Under the slope near where they were sitting was a stream that started at the massive duck pond by the carpark, travelled under the road and was fed through a tunnel before being released into the sea. To keep people safe, especially when the tide came in, the front of the tunnel had a metal grill attached.

"Let have a swim" Alice said, "Then we can have some cake, I forgot to eat breakfast today as I was so busy and I'm starving now."

"I'm hot as well." Rachel replied.

Tom was working today so the only 'Lads' were Bill and Tony. They joined the rest of the 'Ladies' having driven over together.

"Do you need some help Diane?" Rachel asked.

"No thanks. I should be ok if someone could walk down with me. I've got my stick for support. I just need someone to move it out the way of the incoming tide." Rachel walked down beside Diane and joined the others on the beach who were already getting changed into their cossies.

"Wow. That's some costume you've got there Cindy. Where is that from?" Angela asked.

"My friend has started making costumes from fabric that has previously had another life, like recovered fishing nets and other plastic from factories. It gets made into fabric and then she makes it into costumes and lingerie."

"That costume is so pretty and very vibrant." Liz said.

"Yes, it's beautiful and I love the brightly coloured jellyfish on it."

"It really suits you and if it helps the sea to have fewer micro plastics in it then it makes it a winner." Heather complemented.

"Aw thanks."

"Will she be able to make swimming costumes for others?" Angela asked.

"Yes. Definitely. She is playing around with fabrics and styles before she launches officially soon. I'm trying them out for her." Cindy replied.

"I'm happy to try them out for her if she wants." Angela stated.

"Me too." Agreed Rachel, and the others asked Cindy to mention the Ls to her friend.

Cindy promised saying. "I think I should be on commission."

Tony chipped in. "I'm happy to try some out too."

"Don't think this bright costume with jellies is quite your bag Tony." Cindy teased.

"Everyone ready?" Angela shouted while standing up, looking around at the group. "I'm getting a little warm and the sea looks very inviting."

Walking down to the sea Flo bent down to pick up a unusual shell on the tide line, putting it inside her costume to keep it safe. She was always picking up unusual pebbles and bits of drift wood to use in her crafts. Her husband worked away for several weeks at a time and now aged sixty she had retired from teaching. She spent lots of the summer months in her allotment and also ran a knitting club in the pool cafe during the winter. Angela had nicknamed it a 'stitch and bitch' club. But Flo preferred it to be called a 'knit and natter' club.

As she grew so many vegetables her lunchtime salad boxes were legendary, packed full of salad, grated root veg, onions, chillies and humous and usually taking Flo about forty minutes to eat as they were so full. Angela had joked that one of Flo's lunchboxes were a week's worth of vegetables for most people and contained about ten of her '5 a day.'

Flo was also the swimmers' go to person for knitted hats. Cats, polar bears, teddies all with ears. She had even made a knitted unicorn hat once and Rachel had had to stifle a laugh when she saw it, as the horn was, well, large and somewhat phallic!

"Knob head." Tom had whispered to Rachel the first time he had seen it. Rachel had collapsed into giggles.

Today, thankfully, the water was crystal clear and just how Rachel liked it, so you could easily spot the jellyfish and not accidentally swim into them and get stung. The beach was really getting busy now and was popular with kayakers and stand up paddle boarders.

Rachel spoke to Flo. "Isn't it weird that you now hear so many pumps going during the day blowing up the inflatables and SUPs, then also as the beach starts to thin out at the end of the day all you can hear is the sound of escaping air hissing. Just a couple of years ago that wouldn't have happened."

"Sounds like they have a problem with wind." Flo chortled. "Maybe they should change their diet?"

"Maybe they need to eat your massive salads Flo." Rachel laughed.

"Line up!" a familiar voice shrilled "Let's get a photo of the birthday girl and everyone else strike a pose. "Tits and teeth!" Angela was organising as usual.

"Oh dear. Why does she have to lower the tone?" Bill stated. "Whatever happened to cheese?" He carried on just talking to himself as everyone else was wading in.

Rachel helped Diane into the water while Alice ran back with Diane's crutch, placing it safely far enough up the beach so the tide couldn't claim it.

"Oh yes this is bliss." Julie said as she ducked down under the water.

Rachel agreed and swam strongly for a few strokes then duck dived to the bottom, spotting a small shoal of sand eels glistening in the sunlight as it pierced the water. She swam back to Diane to check that she was in and was ok. Diane tended to bob about for a few minutes as she wasn't a strong swimmer.

Julie also only tended to be in for a few minutes too so she and Diane stayed together before helping to get Diane's crutch and escorted her up the beach. Rachel swam deeper out to where Alice and Angela were ducking down and taking photos of each other. Bill and Tony sped past them, they'd be swimming a good mile or so as usual. Rachel swam over towards the shore, keeping her eyes peeled and looking left and right as she scanned the sea bottom where numerous species of weed swayed in the ever moving ebb and flow, attached to the rocks that formed the coastline. She startled a large green striped wrasse and it bolted into deeper seaweed cover. A large spider crab was on the edge of the rocks, where the sandy bottom stretched out into the bay. Rachel wasn't a fan of spiders on land and the large crab sent her imagination into overdrive. However, she dived down towards the crab to get some photos and it turned to face her and raised its claws towards her in self-defence. She took her photo, shuddered and swam away quickly. Ducking down into the weed, she grabbed hold of some strong looking kelp and pulled herself down. This was where the reef would reveal it's hidden treasures. She was looking for starfish, sea urchins and anemones mainly but would snap anything that looked interesting, "Purple Princesses" hopefully. Cindy, Flo and Heather were already on the reef and as Rachel came up for air, she realised that the other three were excitedly looking at something. She swam over and joined them.

"Compass jelly." Heather breathed as she emerged from the depths, gasping for air and pointing below.

Rachel put her head into the water and could see Cindy and Flo moving around the creature, snapping away with their underwater cameras. Rachel readied herself, took a big lungful of air and dived down, camera ready.

The colours of the Compass jelly were incredible. It's orange brown stripey markings gave it its distinctive name and it wafted up and down from the surface in its never ending search for plankton in the water. It had long brown tentacles that were below the familiar mushroom shaped body. Rachel described them as 'frilly knickers.' It's fascinating beauty was incredible and the four women kept diving down to get the perfect shot. After clocking a good half an hour in the water on her underwater watch Rachel was starting to get a bit cold and gestured to the others that she was going back in to shore. They agreed to follow her in, which they did, albeit slowly as they kept looking down at other rock faces to see what else they could see. The sea life at the bottom of the ocean was endlessly fascinating and sooo addictive. Rachel followed Alice and Angela up the beach towards the rest of the group and the birthday girl.

Back on dry land everyone chatted about their swims, the warm clear sea, the hot sun and trying to see their photos on their cameras but the sun was too bright to see the screens properly. They'd have to look later when everyone uploaded their photos to the group Facebook pages. They stood around in their colourful dry robes, supping hot drinks, warming up, chatting and laughing. Bill and Tony joined the women and as they were the last of the group to get back Diane unveiled her cake, paper plates and a knife.

"Form an orderly queue, behind me." Angela said.

Flo glanced at Rachel and rolled her eyes. "Unlike Angela to be first in the queue." She muttered under her breath.

Rachel supressed a smile and took her place in line.

"Just a sliver for me." Alice told Diane after she had cut a decent hunk for Angela.

Diane smiled and put a crumb on the paper plate. "There you go."

Alice huffed so Diane cut her a thin slice and moved onto her next customer.

The cake was heaven. "Oh my god Diane. That is so good." Rachel closed her eyes, savouring the perfectly moist carrot cake and the sumptuous thick sweet icing. It was just the tonic after being in the sea and ticked all the boxes. "You should be on the 'Bake Off.' This could be your signature bake."

The cake was quickly demolished and they all sat in the warm sun, dry robes now removed and dry multi coloured swimming costumes had replaced the wet ones from earlier. The group sat enjoying the company and the warm sun, looking out to the sea.

Rachel looked up as something had caught her eye. A little movement where the river ended and where the sea started. She could also hear something. She wasn't sure what it was but it sounded like a desperate cheeping. On the wall above the river end near the metal grid a couple of people were looking into the water. "Somethings happening in the water. I'm going to take a look". With that she got up and wandered down the beach with all the other swimmers watching her.

As she got closer, she could see a tiny duckling that had been washed down the river and was paddling frantically to get back up stream. Every time it made it through the grill its cheeps got louder as it echoed in the tunnel. Calling back to the group she shouted "It's a duckling. I think it's been washed down from the duck pond across the road."

Turning back around again she was startled to see Angela stand right next to her. "Whoa Angela. where did you appear from?" Rachel said. silently thinking to herself 'Did she fly down on a broomstick?' This old bird could certainly shift when she wanted to. It was a bit spooky.

"Right. We need to rescue the duckling." Angela said. Standing in her shorts and T shirt she started to strip off by removing her shorts so she could wade in. She tried to make a grab for the bird which swerved her and shot back up the tunnel entrance into deeper water and behind the grill. "Right I need to get in deeper." she said while removing her T shirt and standing there in her bra and knickers.

"Oh, ok Angela" Rachel replied "Would you like some help?" Some of the others had joined her.

"This poor little duckling is so scared we must rescue it. If it reaches the sea it's a goner. A seagull will eat it." Angela said looking at a couple of gulls watching from some nearby rocks.

"How can we help you Angela?" Cindy asked.

"Let's spread out in the water and see if we can herd it into a corner." Angela replied. The group paddled into the river and started to spread out, then closed in on the duckling but each time it dodged past one of them at lightning speed.

“Think we need a net.” Rachel said.

“I’ve got an idea.” Julie said and walked up the beach while the rest of them kept trying to catch the poor frightened creature. Walking back to them Rachel could see that Julie was carrying Diane’s crutch with a blue bag tied to the end.

“What in heavens name is that?” Angela asked. “Doesn’t matter. Just give it to me. Let’s see if it will work.” Leaning right over with the crutch in her hand, the rest of the group drove the duckling towards Angela. As she went to scoop it up the bag filled with water and it fell off the crutch. “This isn’t going to work.” She said.

“We need a net. I’m going to ask at the café.” Rachel said and walked towards the small beach cafe and kayak hire place.

“Ok this is weird request.” She asked one of the girls working in the cafe “But do you have a net?”

“Um no!” the teenage girl with dark hair and a nose piercing said snootily.

A deep voice came from the back of the kitchen “Ben does next door. In the kayak hire shop.”

“Ok thank you.” Replied Rachel.

Walking across the beach towards the shop she could see lots of bright yellow and red kayaks lined up on the sand with some more propped up against a fence. Wetsuits and buoyancy aids were hanging on a rail gently blowing in the soft breeze. A sign with a water sports menu was propped up against a small wooden hut advertising all the available sports. Alongside it was a battered but comfy looking beach chair but it seemed nobody was around.

“Hello!” Rachel called. She glanced over to the sea and wondered if the owner was out teaching or helping someone in the water. As she turned around, she jumped as she wasn’t expecting anyone to be there. In front of her was a man in his late thirties, tanned and athletic with a face that was very good looking but slightly weather beaten.

“Hi can I help you?” He asked.

“Um.” Rachel stuttered slightly startled, forgetting why she was there. “Are you Ben?”

He nodded. "That's me. Who's asking?"

Pulling herself together she remembered the poor duckling. "I don't suppose you've got a net, have you? The girls in the cafe thought you might have one."

"Yes. I have. Have you found a duck in the river?" He asked.

"Well yes we have. Is this a regular occurrence?" Rachel asked.

"Yes. I have rescued a few over the season. They are very fast." He said passing Rachel the net. "Would you like some help?"

"No thanks. We'll be fine, I think. There are several of us. Thank you for the loan."

"Can you bring it back here if I'm still open or drop it back to the cafe if not." He replied as Rachel set off down the beach again.

She felt slightly flustered and couldn't understand it. "Well he was cute." She thought to herself before thinking "I'm a married woman" before realising that she had said it out loud and felt her face turning red, hoping that nobody had heard. She picked up the pace, jogging back to the others remembering the poor duckling. Getting closer she shouted "I've got a net."

The group were waist deep in the water and Rachel heard Angela say "This isn't working. The poor creature is getting tired. Fabulous Rachel. Well done." She grabbed the net out of Rachel's hand. "This will do it. Ok everyone. Get into your places and drive the duckling towards me, I will scoop it out and then we can carry it back over the road to its mother in the net."

Diane, Heather, Flo, Julie, Bill, Tony and Cindy spaced themselves out with the poor little duckling in the middle cheeping despondently. Slowly they walked towards Angela in silence while she stood very still, net in hand. A huge crowd had gathered by the railing on top of the wall and along the beach. As the duckling neared her she swiped the net over it and then scooped down into the water. Grabbing the old heavy wooden net out of the water she looked down inside to find it empty. Looking closer down into the water she looked back into the net which had a string type material with large holes but small enough to contain a duckling safely. She looked back into the water and then all around her. "Where's it gone?" She spoke. "Can anyone see it? It must be here somewhere." She said to herself as she started to move in the water. "Where is it?" She shouted now starting to panic.

“It’s not here.” Diane replied.

“I can’t see it either.” Cindy said.

There was a deathly silence both from the swimmers and the crowd. Everyone apart from Angela.

Rachel was aware of high pitch moaning sounds but couldn’t work out where from until she looked at Angela who had gone an ashen colour and looked like she was about to faint. “Oh God” she was saying to herself.

“Angela, Angela are you ok?” Rachel said quickly walking over to her.

Angela look vulnerable and old. “I’ve killed it. Its last moments are going to be me bludgeoning it to death.”

“It’s ok Angela you were trying to help it.” Rachel tried to console her.

“I’m a murderer. I should have left it to swim back up the tunnel itself.” The others, walking from the river over to Angela, started to offer support.

Cindy walked past the end of the tunnel stopped and listened “I’m sure I can hear some cheeping.” She said to Diane.

Angela, on hearing what she said burst into tears before saying “It’s gone to ducky heaven. That’s the death cry you can hear.”

“No. I can hear it too Angela.” Diane said.

Rachel rushed to the top of the tunnel and saw the duckling being reunited with its mother.

Quacks and cheeps ensued while Angela sank onto a bench in relief. “I thought I’d killed the poor thing.”

Rachel grabbed the fishing net from Angela and quickly returned it to the kayak hire shop but the good looking, weather beaten man was nowhere to be seen. She went to the cafe and left the net there.

Analysis 1928

"Berryman here." The Doctor answered his telephone after Frederick Nancarrow had rang the house and spoken to his housekeeper. "How's your daughter? Do you want me to call to your house?"

It was a couple of days since Frederick and Liberty had been out for lunch. "I wanted to pick your brains about something."

"Fire away sir."

"Do you know anything about swimming?"

"I'm not sure what you mean." Doctor Berryman blustered. "I can't swim myself…"

"Health benefits and so on." Interrupted Frederick.

"I think it's beneficial, the same as any other exercise."

"In the sea?"

"Yes. I suppose so. It's very cold here I would have thought. People have swum since the beginning of time I would have thought although I cannot recall any particular passages in the Bible about swimming. They have swimming in the Olympic Games, of course, as well as many other sports. If you are thinking of starting to swim you may want to talk to someone who owned one of those bathing machines. I believe even Queen Victoria had one on the Isle of Wight."

"Did she indeed? Thanks for your time Berryman."

"Pleased to help." Doctor Berryman replaced the receiver not sure if he'd assisted or not, shaking his head. Frederick Nancarrow taking up swimming in the sea! At his age! Whatever was the world coming to?

Frederick sat at his office desk. So, the old Queen had swum in the sea. There really must be something in that. He recalled seeing the bathing machines along part of the beach many years ago. Did they still exist? He decided to take a stroll along the promenade and see for himself what Liberty had been talking about.

It was grey and blustery cold winter day in early December 1928 as he collected his coat, hat and gloves and strode out through the estate gates towards the promenade. It was cold and he'd shivered as he left his warm house, walking purposefully out of the grounds. He could smell the salty air as he walked towards the sea front, pausing to watch the waves crash into the rocks, the white spray flying into the air and the water splattering noisily across the dark coloured stones on the beach as the waves sucked outwards. He stood there for a minute filling his lungs with the cold damp air, watching and listening to the sounds of the surf. Far out to sea the grey sea merged with the same coloured sky while the coastline was white with the breaking waves. He walked slowly along the promenade, taking his time and looking at the scene in front of him, as if seeing it for the first time. He'd never given the sea a second thought, apart from as a means of making money. The tides and weather affected the ability of his boats and ships to sail, to land and to load and it was something he paid attention to but not noticing the sea for its own sake, what lived in, above and below its surface. White gulls soared above him, mewing to each other as they searched for food. Vehicles drove along the promenade in each direction while people went about their daily business, wrapped up in their coats, ignoring the tall stranger in their midst.

Frederick made his way to the far end of the beach where he noticed a couple of the bathing machines pulled to the top of the beach, far away from the advancing sea. They'd seen better days having been battered by the winds over the years, the wood rotting and the paint peeling. He was walking around them inspecting them when the door of one opened and a woman's head peered around the corner.

"Can I help you Sir?"

"Apologies Madam. I was looking at the bathing machines. I'd not really noticed them before."

"I'll give you the guided tour if you like, handsome gent like you." She smiled alluringly and winked at him.

He walked away quickly blushing, hearing her laugh behind him. He was firstly enraged. How dare she speak to him like that. Liberty certainly wasn't going swimming with a woman like that but then he slowed down, thought about what the woman said and chuckled to himself. The woman hadn't meant any harm. He slowed down and then halted, again looking out over the sea, the constant movement and noise, the grey choppy sea, the black clouds scudding across the sky, threatening rain he thought. It was time he got back inside out of the cold wind but he was curious about the bathing machine and the fact that the woman looked like she had been or was about to go swimming. He walked slowly back towards the bathing machines and waited until the woman emerged fully dressed with matching grey coat and hat, and a friend of hers emerged from the neighbouring machine, similarly attired but in black. He thought they were probably both in their forties.

"Ladies, may I talk to you for a minute please."

"Come back for your guided tour have you Sir? Bit late now. I'm fully dressed. You could have helped me with my dress." The grey dressed woman spoke.

"Please." He blushed again. "I just want to talk to you about swimming."

"Do you want to come swimming with us?" Black coat asked, laughing at his obvious discomfort.

"It'll cost you a cup of coffee." Grey hat flirted. "We're cold after being in the water and we always go to Cora's Coffee shop to warm up, although you could have helped me!"

Frederick wasn't used to being spoken to so forwardly by anyone. "I'll just settle for coffee thank you Ladies." He said quietly but firmly. "Please lead the way."

Cove

Rachel threw the swimming bags, packed lunch, drinks and beach gear into the back of the car. After a busy week she and Tom were ready to embrace the lovely summer day. She looked up, hearing the high-pitched screech of a buzzard loitering in the air scanning the ground for its next meal, lazily gliding, its magnificent wings stretched out, a dark shape outlined against the clear blue sky. Myriad house martins performed their aerial acrobatics chasing the omnipresent insects while in the distance she could a woodpecker's call, a laughing sound that reminded her of a kookaburra.

The buzzard suddenly dived bombed its victim, its wings a flurry of motion before it disappeared behind a hedge out of sight. Rising again slowly Rachel could see the buzzard had been lucky; as hanging from its mouth was a small rodent.

"Are you ready?" Tom disturbed Rachel's thoughts.

She turned and smiled at him before simply replying "Yep."

Shutting the front door Tom put his sunglasses on and climbed into the car.

They loved their days out with or without the swimming group and knew they were so lucky to live in such a beautiful area. Rachel had visited Wheal Rock Cove many times when she was growing up, coming with Liberty, Sarah and her parents for picnics and days out. Sometimes she would take a friend or two with her and they'd enjoy endless summer days followed by a barbeque, watching the sun turn into a red fireball before it disappeared into the matching coloured sea. She remembered learning to duck dive here, disappearing under the water and viewing fish, crabs, rocks and weeds. Her father had taught her to snorkel too and they'd spent many happy hours exploring under the sea together. She recalled that one day he'd gone out with a spear gun and had harpooned six or seven pollock or maybe mullet. The fish had ended up on the barbeque, mouth-watering fishy smoky smells wafting deliciously across the beach, day trippers casting envious eyes towards their makeshift kitchen. As the older generation became less willing or able to clamber down the cliff paths to the Cove the family days out continued with Tom, Poppy and sometimes other friends with their own young families.

Rachel and Tom walked down to the Cove accompanied by a sweet coconut smell hanging in the air. The bright yellow gorse flowers were now in full bloom and had started to warm up in the sunshine releasing their fragrant scent. A sea of golden bushes stretched as far as the eye could see, ending where the blue sky met the horizon. She could hear the buzz of insects both close and far away, feasting on the nectar in the yellow flowers, droning as they indefatigably pollenated the fauna.

Taking the narrow stony path from the carpark Rachel could see that several of the other swimmers were already on their way down to the Cove, their cars parked up in the rough gravel carpark. Swinging her rucksack onto her back she locked the car as Tom picked up his gear along with the heavy cool bag, containing their provisions for the day ahead. The beginning of their walk down to the cove was very narrow and she kept her arms close into her sides because, as pretty as the gorse looked, it had sharp thorns that would grab at your skin as you walked by leaving angry red welts on unwary arms and legs.

After five minutes the narrow track widened to join the coastal path and the views took Rachel's breath away. Many an artist had flocked to the area to sketch, draw and paint the stunning colours and light. The sandy cove and the surrounding seas reflected and scattered sunlight of varies hues. The direct light and reflected rays were ever changing and produced an almost magical ambiance even on winter days. The coastline of land, sea and sky had an ephemeral beauty that artists had captured on canvas and other materials, and then sold their work through the multitude of galleries in the area.

Tom and Rachel passed a derelict former fisherman's cottage. The thatched roof had long since blown away leaving ruined outside walls, a rotten door frame and a couple of broken windows. An old couple were sitting on a bench next to the building enjoying the warm sunshine, a cold drink and the sea views. The lady was looking through a new looking pair of binoculars.

"Hello." Rachel and Tom said in unison as they walked past.

"Morning. Beautiful day." The old man replied.

His wife smiled. "What time do the dolphins come out?"

Tom and Rachel stopped. "Sorry?"

"We were told we might see dolphins here but weren't sure what time they'd come out." The woman continued earnestly. "We bought these binoculars so that we could see them. I've never seen them before."

Rachel supressed a smile. "Yes. Well. You might see dolphins occasionally but they are wild creatures and they don't conform to a timetable."

The couple's faces fell.

"Never mind." Interjected Tom. "You could always look out for the penguins."

"Really?"

"No." he grinned. "I'm pulling your leg. Penguins live in the Antarctic. But there is plenty to see out there. Actually, if you look just down there, you can see a grey seal's head. You can see it's shiny head." He pointed.

Rachel looked too and helped the couple to see it through their binoculars, then pointed out some sea birds and some landmarks. They left the grateful couple peering out to sea.

"Silly season has started." Rachel chuckled. Tom agreed as the two of them continued their walk to the Cove.

As they neared the beach Rachel was feeling hot. Her rucksack had trapped the heat against her back and she could feel that her T shirt was damp. Standing above the cove she could see that the tide was low leaving the yellow sand glistening in the bright light and the sun baked rock pools exposed.

The swimmers had begun to group at the top of the cliff waiting for everyone to join them before they took a short scramble over the rocks and then down to the beach for a well-deserved swim.

This cove was Rachel's favourite place in the whole world. A place where she'd always felt safe and had lots of happy memories of family days out, swimming, snorkelling and rock pooling. A place where her mum had said she wanted to have her ashes scattered on her death. This to a six-year-old seemed aeons away and she remembered thinking about how they would get ashes to the beach in a huge wooden coffin. Would they be able to carry the coffin? Would it be on wheels? Not really understanding what ashes were. She could remember trying to work out how they could push the coffin off the cliffs and into the sea. Would it float or would it sink? In her mind it was a big worry for a six-year-old. One day they'd found a dead pig in the cave at the back of the beach and she wondered how it had got there; and in her mind the dead pig and her Mum's coffin became interwoven and it freaked her out. However, that was just one unhappy memory amongst the many many happy ones.

Taking a deep breath, she smiled looking down at the turquoise waters, feeling herself relax and the tensions in her body melt away. She couldn't wait to get into the clear sea. The rugged dark rocks on the way down to the Cove were smooth in parts, their roughness having been worn away by the elements and the many feet that had climbed down to the beach below. There were several places to sit on the wave cut rock platforms when the tide was in, but today the Ls had timed their visit for a low tide swim and then a sunbathe.

There were already a gaggle of children huddled around a couple of rock pools, nets in hands and buckets of water precariously balanced on the rough rocks. Squeals of excitement were heard as someone spotted a skulking crab or a bashful blenny under the seaweed and they all rushed over to help catch and land their victim.

Rachel fondly remembered how she had sat on the side of these same rockpools herself, using a towel to protect her legs from the rough barnacles, keeping as still as she could while trying to coax a fish out of its hidey hole using a dead limpet as bait, trying not to move but feeling her bum go numb underneath her. She had also introduced Poppy to the delights of the rock pools where there was always something exciting below the surface and every day delivered a different secret from the sea.

Carrying on down towards the sand she walked past another larger rockpool and looking down she saw her own reflection looking back at her as she peered into the still waters. A sudden flash of movement caught her eye as a small fish darted underneath the overhanging safety of a stone.

Tom had reached the beach and had spread out their large flowery beach mat, using stones to hold it in place. The two of them arranged their bags and staked out a little area for themselves. The sand was still damp from the outgoing tide and Rachel sat down with her back against the smooth slate and granite rocks, glad of a little rest and a cold drink, feeling the warmth of the rocks melt the muscles of her back. Shutting her eyes, she took a deep breath and enjoyed the moment, smelling the saltiness of the sea breeze and hearing sounds both near and far, the birds, the children by the rocks, the wind and the waves. Shutting out all the background noise she took a moment to enjoy her mindful peace as she took a sip from her bottle of water.

She blinked when she opened her eyes again and focused on what Tom was saying. The bright sun was shining straight onto her and using her hand she shielded her face as she reached for the sunglasses from the top of her head and looked at him.

“You ready for a swim” he asked, smiling at her and sticking his hand out to pull her up.

“Most definitely. I’m really hot from our walk down.” Rising to her feet she pulled her towelling robe from the bottom zipped compartment of her bag and lay it on the beach mat ready for afterwards. She was already wearing her costume which was probably one of the reasons she felt so sweaty. Unzipping the top pocket of her bag she retrieved her camera and goggles before looking for her swimming hat. She started to walk down to the sea following some of the others. The cold water was heaven on her toes as she reached the shoreline.

A couple of cormorants had taken off from the nearby rocks, probably disturbed by the swimmers, then landed a little bit further out on the sea, their descent sending out a little ripple in the mirrored water, which glistened and glittered in the bright sunshine.

Checking her camera was on and at the correct setting Rachel turned to take pictures of all the swimmers, the beach, the cliffs above and the cormorants before slowly walking into the refreshing water. Even though it was mid-summer it still had a bite, momentarily taking her breath away especially as she was so warm.

Rachel remembered that she although she had learned to swim in the Lido, it had been here in the Cove where she had become a really strong swimmer as her Grandmother Liberty had introduced her to the treasures below the surface. Initially Liberty had taken her out, probably too far for her eight year old capabilities, to look for purple starfish. She could still remember the argument that had ensued after the swim between her Mum and Liberty. Rachel had pulled her towel around her body tightly as she sat shivering; only hearing snippets of the adult conversation like “It was far too far, she’s only young and she’s only just learnt to swim.” And “Mum you can be so headstrong and annoying sometimes.” but all Rachel could focus on were the amazing sights of another world just below the surface of the big sea.

She had seen what Liberty had called “Purple Henrys.” They were incredibly bright and Rachel couldn’t believe that they were real when she saw them for the first time, clinging to the base of a kelp stalk. She had always thought this was a strange name for a starfish and in her head renamed them “Purple Princesses.”

After that first time Rachel and Liberty had swam together at this Cove and at many other places around the local coastline, sharing countless discoveries and evoking in Rachel a profound fascination for the sea, both above and below its surface, realising that when swimming just one hundred metres there could be a thousand different species of plants, animals, fish and creatures underneath her. Even though her Granny struggled to walk on the land as she became older, she turned into a Mermaid after entering the sea and young Rachel had thought that, on more than one occasion, she had seen a tail fleetingly flick up out of the water.

Today on the low tide Rachel was hoping to find some more Purple or even Orange Princesses and she knew exactly where they might be.

Tom had waited for her a few metres out to sea. As usual he'd dived straight into the sea as soon as it was deep enough to swim and forged a white channel of foam as he'd put his head into the ocean and blasted several dozen front crawl strokes. "It's really clear today." He said.

"Let's hope we find some goodies with this low tide." She replied as she caught him up.

Leaving the rest of the group, they turned right towards a large rock that was only visible at low tide. Liberty had taught Rachel that this was the first marker to aim for. With the rock behind them they then had to look up for a point that stood out and Liberty had said it was like an arrow pointing out the best place to dive down. Catching their breath from the swim across the small cove Rachel looked up at the rugged rock face that rose above them, feeling very small again all of a sudden, hearing her Granny's voice in her head. "Swim into the kelp forest and pull yourself down."

She looked down into the depths and saw the rocks, kelp and Tom deep below her. Checking her camera was still on the correct setting she put her head under the water to get her bearings. Today the water was crystal clear and with the low tide she really hoped to see something exciting. 'Come on Purple Princesses. Show yourselves.' she thought before taking a deep breath and duck diving towards the seabed. The kelp was thick at this time of year and Rachel was glad she had worn a neoprene glove to give her some grip and to avoid seaweed cuts. She didn't see much on her first few dives. It was all about acquainting herself to the sides of the rock face and finding her way through the weed. After a few dives it was as if her 'sea eyes' focused and all sorts of beauties became visible. The seaweed attached to the rock face was coloured pink, purple and orange and Rachel's keen eye soon had her first starfish, a large off white one. Needing to come up for air she hoped she could find her way through the forest again and was desperately trying to hold onto the tip of a piece of kelp as a marker. Catching her breath, she dived again and clutching her camera in her hand snapped away as she swam closer. It always seemed to her that once she had found one creature, they all seemed to come out to show off their beauty, colours and amazingness to her. Again and again she dived, rummaging around in the kelp and weed. She saw twenty or thirty differing coloured starfish alongside one or two tiny cushion starfish clinging to the underside of rocks and purple green anemones, their snake like tendrils swaying to and fro in the undulating of the moving waves. Sea urchins bigger than tennis balls littered the depths in greens, purples, pinks and blues, while green, red and pink stripy wrasse swam silently by. Lots of treasures but not the Purple Princesses today.

Tom was Rachel's timekeeper and always the voice of reason. After thirty minutes he glanced at his watch and called her. "It's time to head back to the shore before we get cold."

"Ok Tom, just two more dives." Rachel pleaded.

He had learnt that some days it was hard to get her out of the water as she could become lost in her own little world. A world where it cleansed her brain and she could forget her demons for a short time. So now having his doctor's head on he knew to call her earlier so the 'two extra dives' that always ended up being five or six allowed him to get her out of the water without succumbing to hypothermia.

Tom knew that he was marrying into a family of mermaids and Rachel had tempted him into the water like a siren sitting on the rock that day twenty five years ago, her long dark hair blowing in the breeze as the sun was setting.

Tom was a GP in a local practice and had come back home just a few months before. He'd been to the boys' grammar school in Porthlowen back in the 1970s and early 80s; and then had gone away to Uni in London to train as a Doctor. He had stayed there after he qualified. He'd enjoyed the bright city lights of London for a number of years and in that time had met, married and divorced a career lawyer who had dumped him for a cosmetic surgeon. The bright city lights lost their sparkle and he hankered after the fresher cleaner air of his home county. After moving out of his former marital home and spending a year in a bachelor pad a job opening had come up a surgery in Porthlowen when one of the GPs retired and Tom had jumped at the chance. He moved into his parents' house for a couple of months while he sorted himself out and got his bearings, then bought and moved into a small two bedroom cottage on the outskirts of Porthlowen. When not working Tom had joined a gym and got fit and discovered that long walks across the cliffs healed his mind and he felt like he found himself again, happier than he'd been in a long time. Rachel had assisted with his healing.

Tom had gone for an evening walk on a balmy late summer evening after a busy day at work to clear his head. The sun was starting to drop towards it's resting place in the sea, the sky starting to become tinged with orange and pink flecks. He was hot and was thinking of going into the water to cool off when he noticed a pretty young woman sitting on the rocks, basking in the warm evening sun. She smiled at him and he walked towards her. They got chatting and she stood up and announced that she was going into the sea to cool off and he was welcome to join her. Her dark brown hair caught the light when she moved her head, her green eyes sparkled with a zest for life and she had a healthy tanned glow with freckles across her nose and cheeks. When she smiled her cheeks had cute dimples in them and when she laughed it was infectious.

"I haven't got my swimming costume." He protested.

"Strip down to your underwear. I won't look." She laughed, flirting with him. She waded out in the sea to her waist and turned to face him, hands on hips. "C'mon in. It's lovely."

How could he refuse? He removed his clothes and noticed that she had her hands over her face but with her fingers open so she could still see him. He laughed and dumping his clothes on some golden coloured rocks just along from a bright white Lido, he paddled into the sea and eased into the cool soothing water. He swam towards Rachel who then challenged him to chase her. She let him catch her and then swam away again. After they'd got out of the water and dressed, shivering, they walked to a chip shop and sat close on a bench overlooking the sea, watching the sunset, talking and eating their supper. As they both had local connections, they had a few mutual acquaintances and had found it surprising that they'd never met before.

Tom found out that Rachel was a primary school teacher and had done her training at MarJon University in Plymouth. She'd been to the local private girls' school, paid for by Liberty, as that's where her Mother Hetty had gone too. She'd been living with Liberty at the time in the Manor, as she had split up with her boyfriend a year ago. She'd met him at teacher training and then they'd both worked at the same primary school in Porthlowen. They'd started to drift apart anyway and then he'd got a promotion as a deputy head out of county. Rachel hadn't wanted to move away so that was that. She'd never really seen him as the father to any children she might want to produce and they parted on amicable terms realising the relationship had ran its distance.

It wasn't long before Rachel had introduced Tom to Liberty, Sarah and her parents and the two of them had many happy days swimming and being out in nature with and without the family. They'd married a year later and Poppy appeared after another couple of years. Poppy could almost swim before she could walk and had followed in the family's mermaid traditions.

Back at the Cove walking out the water and seeing everyone eating and sunbathing made Rachel realise how long she had been in the water. She secretly thanked Tom for making her get out. Grabbing her robe, she quickly put it on and removed her wet costume. Despite the hot sunshine she started to shiver a bit. Sitting down she fumbled in her rucksack for her warm drink. Her fingers not working properly she struggled to open the lid, her teeth chattering with cold

"Rachel give it to me!" Angela said throwing her a look of disproval. "You always stay into way too long my girl!" she scolded as if Rachel was about five, pouring her a steaming hot cup of lemon and ginger tea. It hit the back of Rachel's throat making her hiccup but feeling the warm drink slide down into her body and sitting in the hot sunshine she quickly warmed up. Picking up her camera she pulled up the huge hood on her robe so she could look at her pictures with a little bit of shade.

"Any good photos?" Tom asked her.

"Think so but it's so bright and I need my glasses on to be sure" Rachel replied and she carried on. "I will look later on the laptop. I'm feeling hungry now and need to eat."

Tom passed her a box of salad and the cheeky chilli dressing he'd made that morning. She leaned back against the warm rocks and started to eat while watching a kestrel hovering above the group before it landed on the steep cliff above them and joined its mate. Rachel breathed in deeply and as she exhaled, she whispered the word 'Heaven' before taking a bite of her lunch.

Coffee 1928

As they walked towards the coffee shop, he found out that Grey hat was Ethel and Black hat was Joan and he admitted to being Frederick. Dreading what he may find inside he opened the door for the women and stepped quickly inside, hoping he wouldn't be recognised. Luckily it wasn't busy and he found a quiet corner in the pleasantly warm and cosy cafe. A large middle aged woman, with a round face, red cheeks and grey hair tied up in a bun, who he was introduced to as Cora, was friendly and polite and she offered cake too, which he accepted with good grace. The coffee was hot and delicious and the cake surprisingly tasty.

"So, how long have you been swimming?"

"Since childhood really." Ethel started. "Back then these bathing machines were all the rage."

"Even Queen Victoria had one, you know." interjected Joan.

"My Mother said 'If it's good enough for the Queen then it must be good enough for me.' So, my dear Father bought one for her and I used to swim with her and then when Mother became older and didn't want to use it anymore she just gave it to me."

"There used to be quite a lot of them here at the turn of the century." Joan said, stirring her coffee and adding three sugars. "I wasn't a swimmer then but I used to see them being pulled down to the water's edge and then pulled back again after swimming. I bought mine after a neighbour of mine became ill and wasn't going to use it anymore. We got chatting and she mentioned that she had one and I made her an offer about ten years ago and the rest, as they say, is history."

"What's the fascination?" asked Frederick. "And why do you swim in the winter when it's so cold?"

Ethel answered. "It makes us feel good doesn't it Joan?" Joan nodded, her mouth full of cake. "There used to be a few of us swimming but now it's just Joan and myself. I suppose for me it's just what I do. I get up and look out of the window and if the weather isn't too bad, I telephone Joan and we walk down together and come and have a look at the sea. If it's not too rough then we go in. We've got our bathing machines to change in and to keep our clothes dry. Of course, we can't take them down to the water's edge now. They've been here too long and neither of us own horses to tow them up and down."

“They’d probably fall to pieces if we did.” Joan added. “To answer your question Frederick, as Ethel said it does make us feel good afterwards. We look out and decide that we don’t really want to go in as it’s too cold or it’s raining.”

“And then we decide that as we’re here we might as well go in.” continued Ethel. “So we change in our bathing machines and then shiver as we hobble down to the edge. And then we decide it’s not a good idea.”

“And then we wade out shrieking at the cold waves as they come over our knees then our waist.”

“And then we plunge into the waves.”

“And we’re in.”

They both laughed.

Frederick looked at the pair of them, at one and then the other. He sipped a mouthful of coffee, noticing how their faces had come alive as they relived their experiences and remembering a similar sort of expression on his daughter’s face. Maybe there was something in this swimming caper after all. He tuned back into the conversation as Ethel carried on.

“So, we stay in for maybe ten or fifteen minutes, much more when the weather is warmer and we come out and our bodies are glowing.”

“Yes. Our skin is pink and we feel warm.” Joan said. “Then we come back to our changing rooms and get dressed and end up here for coffee and sometimes cake too.”

“We feel amazing afterwards. And we feel healthy and we don’t get colds and coughs either do we Joan?”

“No.” Said Joan simply finishing the last of her cake and draining her coffee cup.

“How do you two know each other?”

“We both lost our husbands in the Great War. They were twin brothers so we are sisters in law but we’ve been friends since we sat next to each other at Sunday school.”

“We’ve known each other nearly forty years.” Ethel said.

"Do you swim all year round?" Frederick asked. "More coffee?"

"Yes please." Ethel answered. Frederick summoned Cora over.

Joan carried on the conversation. "Thank you, Frederick. Yes. We swim throughout the year, weather permitting."

"It's horrible when we cannot swim. I need my daily swim to make me feel good. If I don't swim, I just don't feel the same and if I haven't been in the water for a few days because of storms or tides I get agitated and I feel like part of me is missing."

"And then eventually we get back in the sea and it's like coming home. It's difficult to describe."

"Even though in the winter it can be so cold it makes your fingers hurt and you cannot feel your toes afterwards." Ethel said.

Frederick looked at the pair of them. They did look well and both had a healthy complexion. Coffee arrived. He paid the bill and made his excuses.

"Remember me if you want that guided tour Sir." Ethel winked. "Anytime!" she added cheekily.

Frederick laughed. "Thank you for your time Ladies. Enjoy your coffee." He left the two of them deep in huddled conversation and shivered as he left the warm coffee shop. He meandered back to the two bathing machines standing defiantly against the winter elements, chuckling to himself at the two interesting characters he'd met.

Ball

The masked ball was organised for a Saturday night at the end of July. It was going to be held at the café and overspilling out onto the pool terrace. The theme was 1970's disco fancy dress with everyone wearing a mask. Pierre and Rachel had spent many evenings meeting up and several back and forth emails to organise the night along with Pierre's friend Summer, his and Rachel's Zumba teacher. Luckily the weather on the night was warm with hardly any wind and the pool looked stunning, lit up with twinkling fairy lights and ready to receive the partygoers.

Pierre was dressed in a tight silver catsuit, silver high heeled zipped thigh boots and a sequin jacket that was sparkling in the sunlight. He was also wearing a long blonde wig and he had decided not to go for a full mask and instead he was wearing festival stick on gems across his forehead, around his smoky eye makeup and finishing with long feather fake eyelashes and plenty of glitter. From behind he was a very convincing woman.

Summer looked at Rachel and said. "I could never compete with that could you?"

Rachel laughed and shook her head.

When Tony arrived, he said to Diane. "Gosh. Who's the gorgeous blonde in silver?"

Diane looked over then looked at Tony and started to laugh. "That gorgeous blonde is ...., oh shall I introduce you?' she said looking amused, walking towards Pierre.

"Yes please." Tony replied following Diane, puffing out his chest and holding his stomach in. "But she is quite tall though."

Diane gave the blonde a hug and then the blonde hugged Tony before saying "Hi Tony I like your outfit."

Tony took a step back and looked confused. "Oh!" He started to go red. "Thank you." He knew the voice, but it felt out of place. Suddenly realising it was Pierre he shuffled with embarrassment.

"Come on." said Diane laughing "I think you need a drink." and walked him towards the bar.

Pierre came to help behind the bar and went to serve Tony who started looking even more embarrassed. He wished he was wearing his mask. If Pierre noticed he didn't let on, always the professional. Tony reaching for his pint of local ale gulped several mouthfuls down at once.

The music of the night was from a local band called "Disco Inkernow." A five piece with three men, guitar, bass and drums while two women played the keyboard and led the singing. They played all the disco songs from the 1970's and wore amazing colourful outfits.

Diane could be heard telling everyone she still had her clothes from that time safely packed up in a trunk in her attic. She hadn't wanted to throw them away as they reminded her of such happy times living in London.

During the evening Pierre and Summer took to the dance floor and as they were both incredible dancers they soon got the crowd up and dancing, showing everybody simple dance routines.

Tony wasn't one to dance and when Pierre saw him sitting on his own, he sashayed over to him and asked him to dance. Tony nearly choked on his beer, looked like a rabbit caught in the headlights, didn't know what to do and before he could think clearly, panicked before mumbling something about his prostate and saying he needed the toilet. Walking off in a hurry he was cross with himself but was still embarrassed from earlier in the evening and didn't know where this behaviour had come from as he liked and admired Pierre. "Silly old fool." he said to himself'.

Tickets to the event were £25 each and included a pasty supper. The pasties were delivered hot by a local company who, most people decided, were the best around. Diane was always moaning that there should only be one type of pasty and that was beef skirt, potato, swede and onion with lots of seasoning. "I can't get my head around all of these new flavours, Mediterranean, vegan, chicken, and don't get me started on banana and chocolate flavour."

The band took a break while everyone was eating their pasties using paper bags to hold them. Pierre and Summer were chatting to people on the Lido terrace, everyone having a well earned drink. Some of the people already attended their classes so were used to the routines which helped to get everybody dancing. Rachel walked over to join the group with a pasty in one hand and a drink in the other. She was rather glad to get some fresh air as the café was getting warm after all the dancing. This was the last fundraiser that everyone had organised so far and Pierre and Summer were talking to some of their café and Zumba regulars about how much had being raised.

Rachel started telling them that there were only three months left to raise the total amount and so far only £80,000 had been raised from the £400,000 target. "I'm worried we are going to miss our target." she explained. "Everything has to be raised by 30th September. How the Crowd funder works is all or nothing, not a day over." She told the two of them, in between bites of her special cheese pasty, "I'm not sure what we can do next to raise more money. People are still buying shares in the Lido and we've still got three months of the entry fees and café takings over the summer but most of that will go in wages and running costs." She knew that this would be nowhere near the amount that they needed.

"Cooey." Angela's shrill voice broke up the conversation. She beckoned Rachel over, then started to introduce her to some local business people who wanted to donate to the fund.

This left Pierre and Summer chatting together just as the band started to play again, this time starting off with Abba's Dancing Queen. Summer grabbed Pierre and dragged him onto the dance floor. "I love this song." she shrieked.

The week before both of them had been to see the latest Mamma Mia film. They danced and turned, twisted and twerked to the seventies song only stopping at the end to get another drink.

Summer turned to Pierre and said. "I should use this song in my next Zumba class. We could use some of our moves and choreograph a little routine.'"

'Yes. Let's do it Summer." Pierre enthused.

Sitting down with their drinks they watched the other dancers. Summer took a sip of her drink, a large gin and tonic from a local distillery, savouring the citrusy taste. Turning to Pierre she said "We should do something to raise money. Something that involves dance and not just a sponsored dance but something even better'.

They both agreed to think about it, but carried on idly chatting and drinking.

"What about a Zumbathon with other teachers?" Pierre said. "This has been done before and we really want to make this a success and a huge money earner."

There was still so much more money to raise and they were both worried that the Lido wouldn't reach its target, Pierre wondered what would happen to the café and his job if the pool shut.

Summer looked really excited and turning to Pierre she said. "We should involve the whole community, especially those that use the Lido. Why don't we organise a Flashmob in the Lido to a popular piece of music, something like 'Dancing Queen' maybe. Everybody loves to dress up in 70's Glam. Look at them all here." She swept her arm around indicating everyone in the room wearing fancy dress and having a great time.

"Oh yes." said Pierre "What a great idea Summer. I can dress up as Meryl Streep and wear a long blonde wig."

Summer laughed. "Trust you Pierre!" then asked. "Do you think the others will dance? Rachel already goes to my Zumba class so I'm sure she will do it. Poppy too. And I'm sure some of the other Ls will take part. Angela and Alice are never shy, are they?"

They started brainstorming and the ideas just kept on coming,

"We should hold it here at the Lido." said Pierre. "On a Summer day during the school holidays when they'll be lots of tourists in town."

"We can teach everyone the routine in the evenings when I'm not teaching my classes." added Summer. "We will have to keep this really quiet so it comes as a complete surprise on the day."

They talked about outfits, who they could get to volunteer and then it occurred to them how would they actually make any money. They wouldn't be able to charge the people to watch as it was going to be a surprise.

"Maybe we can use this as a publicity event, not really a money spinner, but to get our plight out to the world". Summer explained to Pierre. "My brother James is studying media at University and is home for the summer holidays." She paused, thinking.

"Go on."

"Maybe he could film the flash mob and create a short film which could be used to publicise the Lido's fundraising plight. Wow. I've got so many ideas now I feel like my head is going to explode. Let's meet in the Ship on Monday night after my class but for now... let's dance."

Princess 1929

Saturday was the day Sir Frederick was dining with the King and Queen. At breakfast he was nervously glancing at the Times when Liberty came into the room. He looked up and smiled at her.

"Are you excited?" She asked, helping herself to a cup of tea.

"I cannot eat this morning." He admitted. "I've met the King once when I received my knighthood but there were lots of us receiving medals that day so he didn't talk, only to say 'Well done.' I've never met the Queen or Princess Mary. I won't know what to say to them. They won't be interested in the mines and my work I shouldn't think. Or politics." He shook his head and sank a large mouthful of coffee. He tried to focus on the Times.

"I'd like you to help me with something please Father." Liberty asked sweetly.

"Mm what is it?" He asked gruffly without looking up.

"Come with me please."

He exhaled a deep breath, closed his eyes and then looked up at his daughter who had stood from her place at the breakfast table. He rose and meekly followed her into his office where she had taken a volume of the Encyclopaedia Britannica from its place on the shelf. Liberty pointed. "Shall we read it together?"

She had opened it at the entry for Princess Mary. She was more excited than him at the prospect of her Father dining with Royalty. He smiled at her kindness.

"Yes. Let's find out about my dinner partner." He pulled up an extra chair so that Liberty could sit next to him.

They found out that Princess Mary was the King and Queen's only daughter. She was the Great Granddaughter of Queen Victoria. She was aged thirty one and had been married since 1922. She had two sons aged five and six. She had become a nurse and had formed a charity to help troops and she was president of the Girl Guides.

"What's the Girl Guides?" Liberty enquired.

“I’m not sure. Maybe if I get the chance, I’ll ask the Princess.”

The evening came too soon for Frederick. Liberty straightened his bow tie and smoothed his jacket. “You look very handsome Major Nancarrow.” She said admiringly as she handed him his gloves and hat.

“Thank you my darling.” He hugged her and kissed the top of her head.

“You can tell me all about it tomorrow at breakfast.” She said breathlessly.

He waved to Liberty from his seat in the motorcar as Tommy closed the door and drove off. Liberty went to her room and sat thinking about her Father meeting the King and Queen and Princess Mary. How exciting.

Secret

Summer arrived at the pub in her Zumba gear. Pierre hadn't arrived yet so she went to the bar to order a drink and talk to Stan. As usual Stan flirted with her. With her long blonde hair, slim figure and tight leggings she was a fit and attractive girl.

"Hello Sexy." He winked at her.

"Piss off Stan." she smirked. "Sparkling water, ice and lemon and the menu please."

"On your own?" he grinned, handing her the menu.

"Actually, I've got a date." She looked at the delicious offerings and opted for an open crab sandwich with a side of chips. (She always ate the same dish as she knew the fishermen, Mike. He was a friend of her mother's and she just couldn't resist the fresh shellfish.) She was really hungry having just taught two dance classes. She paid Stan for the food just as Pierre walked in.

"Hello gorgeous." Pierre beamed.

"Hi." Summer smiled.

"Oh. I don't mean YOU darling! I meant your handsome friend here."

Stan grinned. "Sorry mate, you're not my type." Pierre pouted and pretended to look offended. "I prefer blondes." He winked at Summer and disappeared to take Summer's food order into the kitchen.

Pierre watched him walk away, sighed, shrugged his shoulders and picked up the gin menu.

"Behave. You're married!" Summer laughed, playfully slapping him on the arm.

"Just window shopping!" Pierre laughed as he ordered a strawberry gin and tonic from Beryl, who'd been sent to serve him while Stan changed a barrel.

The two dancers wandered over to a table. Summer told him that she had ordered food but Pierre said he'd managed to eat something before locking up the café.

Summer clarified "I think we should decide on a date first, I've been looking at the Lido's website to see what they have on. I don't think we should do a Saturday as this is a changeover day for tourists and if we do it during the week lots of people will be working. So how about the Sunday afternoon on Bank Holiday weekend at the end of August as the Lido will be really busy. That gives us the time to organise the dance, the costumes and who will be willing to get involved. I still think we need to keep this really quiet."

Pierre agreed and took a sip of his drink.

Summer's food arrived and she took a couple of mouthfuls. "OMG.... total heaven. I've not eaten since this morning. Hang on I need to eat some more. You talk and I will just eat for a minute" she said before Pierre continued discussing who they thought would be most likely join in.

He pinched a couple of chips and dipped them in her tomato sauce as they spoke.

Summer thought that some of the Ls possibly would join them as they really cherished and used the Lido the most.

Rachel came into the pub, on her way home from the hairdressers, to pick up something that had been left for her. She came over to Pierre and Summer. "Thank you both for all your help at the masked ball last night getting everyone up and dancing. It was a fantastic success and we raised £1400 from donations, the raffle and ticket sales."

That's brilliant. Well done." Summer said.

"It's good but there's still a long way to go to get to the £400,000." Rachel replied despondently.

"How much do you still need?" Pierre asked.

"At the last count we had raised about £120,000 and I know that some more has been promised by some local businesses but it's not in the bank yet so I'm not counting those amounts until it's showing on the bank balance."

Pierre and Summer then told Rachel about their flash mob idea to raise the profile of the Lido via social media.

"Wow that's a brilliant idea." Rachel enthused. "Count me in. I'll help in any way I can."

“That’s why we’re meeting here tonight, to discuss our ideas.” Summer added.

“To be totally honest I was starting to get worried that we were running out of time and ideas and how we were going to let the rest of the world know about our little Lido. Rachel said. “Do you mind if I join you for a minute?” Sitting next to Pierre she asked them how it was going to work.

Summer replied. “We’re not actually sure yet. We were thinking of a Sunday in August, maybe Bank Holiday weekend.” While then explaining that they needed to keep it a secret as it had to be a surprise for the flash mob to work.

“Brilliant idea. Wow. Yes. That could work. Well done guys. I need to get home.” Rachel said as she stood up. “But keep me informed and if I can help then let me know.”

“Actually, you can.” Summer said. “We’ve decided that we would hold an invite only meeting. My place is too small so can we use your house instead of the pub or café so nobody will see everyone together and arouse suspicion?”

“Absolutely guys. I’m free every evening this week apart from Zumba so let me know and I will contact the swimmers. I think they will be interested.”

Summer replied “Oh fab. I will talk to some of my Zumba peeps too. I’m really excited now.”

Pierre checked his phone diary and asked. “How about on Thursday?”

‘Works for me. I don’t have any evening classes that day.” Replied Summer.

“Good for me as too.” Agreed Rachel. “So, shall we say 7.30PM?”

“Yep.” Both Summer and Pierre said together.

After Rachel had left Pierre asked “Can I organise the costumes?”

“Most definitely, but I’m not dancing in six inch heels!” Summer stated. “My Mum has helped out before with the wardrobe in the local plays and we might be able to find some costumes there. I will bring James along so everyone can meet him.”

With the enthusiasm of Summer and Pierre having rubbed off on her Rachel composed an email to send to the Ls.

Can you keep a secret?
Do you want to help raise the profile of the Lido's fundraiser?
Do you like fancy dress costumes?

If yes!!!!!

Come to my house on Thursday 1st August 7.30 Pm

PS It's a secret Sssssssh!!!!!!!!

Rachel

Advice 1929

"Major Sir Frederick Nancarrow!" Frederick was introduced amongst a long line of dignitaries and their wives. He bowed to the King, the Queen and then the Princess who looked enchanting in her white dress, tiara and glittering jewellery. She leaned forward offering her hand. "Good evening Major. Thank you for accepting my invitation at short notice."

He took her gloved hand gently and lightly kissed the back of it. "Thank you for inviting me, Your Royal Highness. I hope your husband is restored to full health quickly." He bowed again and moved along the line meeting his hosts Baron St. Aubyn and his wife, whom he'd met several times over the years at various functions. It had been the Baroness who'd thought of the Major when the Princess's husband had become ill. He accepted a drink from a tray at the end of the line and mingled nervously, sipping his drink carefully. Today of all days he didn't want to have too much to drink.

He noticed that the King and Queen had moved away from the Princess and he caught her eye. She smiled and he walked towards her, taking two glasses from a tray as her walked towards her.

"Would you like a drink Your Royal Highness?" He asked offering her a glass.

"Thank you Major." She smiled and accepted the glass. "I understand you are the Member of Parliament for this area."

"I am, for my sins Ma'am."

"You are lucky to be living in such a beautiful area."

"Thank you. Although, I confess, I often become engrossed in my work and forget to look around at the beauty of nature. My daughter reminds me to stop and look."

"She sounds wise. What is she called and how old is she?"

"Liberty and fourteen. Ma'am."

"What a lovely name. Is she in the Girl Guides?"

"No Ma'am. I confess I do not know much about the Girl Guides although I understand you are their president."

"I am. It's to encourage girls in the same way as the Boy Scouts to get out into nature and develop outdoor skills, camping and fires, patrolling, marching, wearing a uniform, developing leadership skills, healthy in body, mind and spirit, that sort of thing."

"It sounds like something Liberty would be interested in. I'll talk to her and see if there is a group that meet locally."

Just then they were called through for dinner and they made their way together through to the dining room, following the King with the Baroness; and the Baron escorting the Queen. Frederick accompanied the Princess to her seat then took his own, opposite Mary.

Frederick found himself next to a portly dull elderly wife of the retired member of Parliament, Sir Peter Trevithick, to his right. He tried to engage her in conversation several times but her answers were monosyllabic. He thought she had a hearing device in her left ear as he could see a wire trailing down her neck so maybe she was deaf and just struggled to hear him. She concentrated on her food and tucked in heartily.

To his left was a pretty young woman in her early twenties who giggled vacuously every time he tried to talk to her and nibbled sparingly at her food, pushing it around her plate during the various courses until it came to the sweet desert which she ate hungrily. She was pregnant and was expecting her first child in the next three months. Her husband sat to the right of Princess Mary and monopolised the conversation without saying anything of great importance or interest. He was Lord Grey, the eldest son of a rich hereditary Peer from the North of Cornwall who had inherited his title a few months ago after his Father had died of a heart attack, and had then married the cause of the heart attack, a maid who was expecting his baby and was now Lady Grey.

The former Member of Parliament Peter Trevithick and Frederick had tackled each other across the benches in the Commons and in the hustings locally. There was a certain amount of animosity between them as Trevithick, distantly related to the famous locomotive engineer, had been the incumbent Liberal MP for over twenty years before he'd been usurped by the younger, more dynamic and energetic mine owner, soldier and businessman Major Frederick Nancarrow. They disagreed on most things politically and he tried unsuccessfully to goad Frederick into declaring political support for various issues of the day. The food was excellent, the wine was splendid and apart from Princess Mary the company was stifling and dull so it was with relief when it was announced that coffee would be taken in the adjoining room. Frederick accompanied Princess Mary from the dining room and as she made her way to the window to overlook the dark sea she commented again how lucky he was to be living in such a beautiful area.

"My Father loved coming to Cornwall when he was the Duke here." She said. I remember when I was a young child coming here and swimming in the sea with my brothers. We had one of those old fashioned bathing machines to change into our bathing costumes. It was great fun."

"I was speaking to some local ladies about their bathing machines only last week." Frederick replied. "They looked quite old and weather beaten. The machines I mean, not the ladies." They both laughed. "They swim all year round."

"How extraordinary." Said the Princess Royal, laughing. "Far too cold for me."

"Yes. I thought so too but Liberty confessed to me that she had swam in the sea during the Summer and Autumn, unbeknown to me. She said it made her feel…." He paused, somewhat embarrassed."

"Go on." encouraged the Princess.

"Made her feel more alive. You see she had Polio as a child and has always been delicate, and since her Mother, my wife, died I've always tried to protect her."

"Understandably." Murmured Mary. "I was aware of the passing of your wife. I'm very sorry to hear about her." She continued. "I do believe that there has been some research into the benefits of swimming."

"Yes. I spoke to the Doctor about Liberty as she'd become somewhat withdrawn and quiet after being so effervescent, vivacious and somehow more alive during those months. I'd initially put it down to her growing maturity but I now realise there was more to it than that. She was missing the swimming. The Doctor said what you have just indicated, in that there are certain benefits of swimming. The women I spoke to with their bathing machines certainly looked healthy, although I'm no expert. I understand that your Great Grandmother Queen Victoria had a bathing machine on the Isle of Wight."

"She did indeed." Mary agreed. "So, the answer is to get a bathing machine for your daughter and she can swim with your ladies."

"That's a good idea Ma'am."

"That's settled then."

"But..."

"Yes?"

"I'm sorry."

"No. Go on. What is it?"

"I'm concerned that there are storms and waves and then there's the privacy and safety concerns."

"Ah yes. I do see. That wouldn't do at all" Then she smiled. "The answer would be to swim in a Lido." She pronounced it 'Leedo'.

"I not aware of that word Ma'am. Lido?"

"It's an Italian word meaning beach or shore from the Latin "Litus". Now it means an open air swimming pool. There are one or two already in this country that I'm aware of. It could be open all year around, it would be safe from the waves and storms. It would have changing facilities. And your Liberty would be safe. Liberty's Lido. Yes. I like the sound of that."

Coffee arrived and Frederick escorted the Princess to her chair, next to her Mother while the gentlemen retired for brandy and cigars. Frederick stood alone sipping his brandy and pondered over the Princess's words. A Lido. That was the answer.

But how to do it?

Mystery

The next day was a Tuesday and there was quite a queue outside the Lido. The Ls started to arrive and met in their usual corner. Everyone was talking about the mystery email, what could it be? What did Rachel have in mind? Everyone was trying to decide was it a fancy dress party, a play, a pantomime or a fashion show? Diane wondered if it was swimming costumes through the ages. Whenever anyone walked past them, they would stop talking. Everyone agreed that they would all be going and whatever it was they would be supportive.

"Unless." Alice squirmed. "It's a naked calendar. Then I wouldn't be able to do that."

Bill looked embarrassed. "We wouldn't do that sort of thing in the Army. Good grief."

Tony replied "I'd be quite up for that."

Angela retorted "Trust you!"

"Bring it on." Tony shouted, 'I've got a lovely tow float that needs blowing up."

"I'll get Pierre to help you Tony if you like?" Steph said innocently. The group roared with laughter.

Tony went red and kept quiet.

Alice looked at them in horror before walking off while saying 'Oh my god. This is too much. I won't be able to look at my tow float in the same way. I don't do naked in public. There must be better ways to make money."

'We don't know it's a naked calendar yet." Sally gently reassured her.

Diane intervened. "The memo asked if you like fancy dress. So, we won't be naked. Thank God."

Tink told everyone that she wouldn't be going as she didn't want to socialise or dress up and as she had bought her shares that was her contribution!

When Rachel arrived, she addressed everyone. "Quiet guys. You're talking very loudly. We're supposed to be keeping this quiet! Remember?"

"Oh sorry. We forgot in the excitement." replied Liz.

Alice came bounding over, not hearing what Diane had just said. "It's not a naked calendar is it?" she blurted loudly. "Like that film? You know the one. Where we are just covered with bits of swimming equipment." Her voice getting higher and higher as she started to panic.

"Sorry Alice but I'm not saying anything here at the moment. The walls have ears, but I would never ask you to do something you don't feel comfortable about, but to reassure you, it's not a naked calendar. Please just come to the meeting." Rachel replied.

Rachel realising everyone was going to give the game away before they had even had the meeting rallied everyone up to set off for their swim. The bright colours of the costumes and the number of swimmers always drew attention especially when they walked out of the gates of the Lido onto the pavement by the main road and then along the promenade. They looked like a weird cult who were having a day out from their institution. They walked the short distance around to Golden Rocks.

"Is that a new costume?" Alice said to Angela, breathing easier now she knew she didn't have to get naked

"Oh, this old one? No. I just pulled it out of my basket of cossies. I had a bit of a sort out. I counted eighty five. I think I'm going to have to started hiding them from Gerry as he keeps asking me the same question and is getting suspicious of any packages I keep getting. I got around that by telling him it's his birthday soon and to stop asking questions. I now need to start buying him some gifts but I think he will get even more suspicious with extra items arriving."

"It is a lovely costume. I did think about buying it for myself when I saw it on the net the other day. I thought it was a new season one." replied Alice.

"Oh, is it? Gosh you sound just like Gerry. Are you two in cahoots?" Angela retorted looking annoyed.

It was low tide today which meant they had to clamber down the rocks to get into the sea. It was best to wear beach shoes as the rocks could be slippery in parts, the roughness having been worn away over the years by surging seas. However just as you got to the bottom of the rocks there were lots of acorn barnacles which acted like sandpaper to the swimmers' skin. It was never a problem when the tide was in but on a spring tide it was very low and the swimmers had to gently ease themselves into the water, scraping limbs and digits as they entered the sea. Some avoided low tide swimming, much preferring to keep their skin intact.

Tink loved low tide as it meant she could swim out to the reef to photograph the urchins, starfish and other creatures. She stood on the water's edge looking out to sea, the breeze gently blowing her wild long curly hair. Looking like a mermaid she was often heard to say, "I prefer the water creatures to people." Tink also loved pink. Her hat, goggles and swimming costumes were all bright pink. Someone once referred to her as Barbie, getting a 'fuck off' as an answer back. Those who knew Tink found this funny and said she should be an evil Barbie if ever there was one! Tink always swam on her own. She thought the others were pathetic and sad taking pictures of each other in the water and that photos of nature were the only way. Nobody was allowed to talk to her when she was 'in her office.' Everyone had learned to ignore her grumpy attitude but nobody could deny that her photographs that she sold in her gallery were amazing. She had recently had an exhibition in London and had taken her framed photographs and paintings of the sea along with what lay beneath, like seals, jellyfish, urchins and all the different colours of starfish she'd found. She'd even had one published in National Geographic magazine once. If you left Tink alone on a low tide she was always happier just doing her own thing in the water, gathering more photos. She was a bit like a wasp's nest, poke at your peril!

Feasibility 1929

When Liberty woke the following day, her Father was already at work in his office. He decided not to tell her about the Lido idea for now. He wanted to do a feasibility study, cost, design, location, funding and so on, plus he had to continue to manage his business empire.

He gave Liberty a brief rundown of the evening. She wanted to know about what Princess Mary was wearing but he hadn't really taken much notice other than it was a white sparkly dress and she wore some jewellery. He did mention that they'd spoken about the Girl Guides and that was something that Liberty didn't know much about but was interested to find out more and to perhaps see if there was a local group that met. He said he'd see if he could find out some more information.

Over the next few weeks Frederick made some enquiries and visited a couple of open air swimming pools around London. He spoke to the owners and architects of these pools and obtained some ideas as some of the challenges but also benefits that were involved. He was directed towards an architect of some renown who had made his name in the Art Deco area of building and was now based near Truro. Frederick invited him to come to Porthlowen to see if he could come up with some ideas.

William Branigan was a tall erect man with grey hair and a carefully trimmed handlebar moustache who looked with interest at the area around the Port, shoreline and promenade, asked poignant questions and left promising to return with sketches and options together with some provisional costings. Frederick thought he could work with the man and together they would to be able to come up with a scheme that he could put to some potential funding partners.

Branigan returned with some rough plans and they discussed them in Frederick's office, taking the plans down to the beach and Frederick could see in his mind's eye the pool taking shape as the architect described his creation referring to his drawings. They agreed to take it to the next stage and Frederick would pay for detailed plans, measurements and costs to be drawn up ahead of a scheduled meeting with the Town Council, various wealthy businessmen and dignitaries.

Fredrick was somewhat nervous as he stood up to thank the chairman for inviting him to speak. He introduced William Branigan, who stood and presented his plans for Liberty's Lido earnestly and eagerly. He was an eloquent speaker and Frederick was proud of his man. He could see some nods of approval while some pursed lips and shakes of heads indicated that not everyone was on board with the vision. While Frederick could see the plans come to life as Branigan expanded on his outline drawings, it was obvious that there was likely to be some opposition. Branigan was a visionary in his field and while it was obvious he knew about building projects and the technical side of what he was doing he was no salesman. Branigan sat down after his presentation and looked around expectantly at the audience.

"What is the cost likely to be?" One member asked.

"What is the time scale?" Another interjected.

"What is the point?" A third man added.

Frederick and Branigan rose together and answered the barrage of questions that seemed to fire at them from all four corners of the room.

"What if it's delayed?"

"What if there's an over spend?"

Ongoing costs, storm damage, rich girl's play thing, white elephant, blot on the landscape, modern monstrosity. So many questions and statements were flung across the room. Frederick and Branigan argued their case vociferously. In desperation Frederick gave them his vision. He would pay for half the building costs and he would release shares to investors if the Council put up the rest. He argued that it was right for a new modern twentieth century stylish designed building to be built that would put Porthlowen on the map. It would bring people to the Town and to Cornwall in general, it would generate some jobs directly to the Lido itself and to the wider Town too. It would be part of the Community and would provide a legacy to the area for generations to come. "For our children, grandchildren, their children and beyond." He finished.

The vote was close but at the end of the meeting the Chairman announced that Fredrick's idea had won the day and gave the go ahead for the building of Liberty's Lido.

Flashmob

Everyone was intrigued about Thursday's meeting and arrived one by one. After Rachel had served drinks, she took a deep breath. "Thank you for coming tonight. As you know we have had great success with our fundraising so far. However, we really need to up our game and get more national publicity. So, Pierre and Summer have had an amazing idea and I hope you will get behind them."

The room was silent

"Over to you guys." Rachel said.

Pierre took the lead and explained about doing a Flashmob and that their idea was to use Dancing Queen by Abba and other upbeat songs, with the pool as their stage.

Blank faces looked back at him!

"Ummmm. What's a Flashmob?" asked Liz.

"I told you it was about nudity!" chimed Alice. "I'm not flashing anywhere!"

"I can't dance and I'm definitely not doing anything naked. Plus, my hip wont cope with that." said Diane

"Is it Zumba?" interrupted Dawn.

Everyone started talking at once.

Pierre stood up as he couldn't be heard trying to establish order. He failed. He put two fingers into his mouth and let out a piercing whistle.

Silence.

"Ok so now I've got your attention I can start to explain all about Flashmobs. They've happened all over the world. Summer? Maybe we should show them a You Tube Flashmob dance video first?"

"Yep just loading it now. Hang on." replied Summer.

Pierre carried on talking. "Don't worry. It's not an Olympic sport. Summer and I will choreograph a simple repetitive routine that everyone could manage. Dance is a beautiful way to deliver your thoughts or a message."

"Ok gather round." Summer ordered as it appeared on Rachel's TV screen. "I've got it loaded. It's a Flashmob from an international train station. They're dancing to the Sound of Music."

"Wow." said Flo after the video had finished. "That is so inspiring."

"Well we couldn't do that. It's so professional." Alice replied.

Pierre calmed them down while Summer said "We will rehearse at my studio in secret. I already have an idea and Pierre and I have created a simple dance, maybe if I explain it will help. People would be placed around the Lido dressed in normal summer clothes so they wouldn't look out of place. We can sit down or be chatting with friends, like on the You Tube video. Everyone would have bright large coloured silk scarves hidden, maybe they could pretend they were towels and sit on them."

Twenty pairs of eyes stared back at her.

She continued. "Pierre and I would start dancing when the music begins. Look watch this." She leant over to Pierre and grabbed his hand. In Rachel's cramped living room it was a tall order to show the dance and not trip over legs as everyone was jammed in like sardines. "Sally pass me a scarf please. They are in my bag nearest to you."

Sally slowly unzipped Summer's bag and pulled out a soft bright pink silk scarf. Handing it to Summer she was heard to say "I don't like delving into other women's handbags. It feels so wrong."

As Summer and Pierre started to dance, they could only manage a few basic moves due to space. After nearly tripping over Bill's legs they gave up.

Summer carried on explaining "So after Pierre and myself start then others would stand up at set places and times around the pool and follow each other while trailing their scarfs behind them high up, like this." She demonstrated by putting her arms in the air above her head. "Until we all gather together for the finale." Summer explained how her brother would video it, making it into a short film.

There was a buzz as everyone started to talk at once again until Bill said "How would this make money and what about the risk assessments for this?"

Diane rolled her eyes and gave Sally a look; one that Rachel saw, so she decided to speak up. "Well." she said. 'It's a good point that Bill makes. There aren't any direct ways to make money, like the cake sale or the promise auction. However, this is to raise our profile. We will share it on You Tube, Facebook and other Social Media. We are looking for sponsors to donate money and for other people who want to buy shares. At the moment we are a small seaside town and our audience is only locals and holiday makers."

"So, do you think that we will make lots of money?" Alice questioned.

Still the voice of doubt, Bill had lots of questions. "What if someone falls? Or trips over their scarf?

Rachel trying to ignore Bill's negativity replied to Alice "This isn't a cast iron way of making money but without raised awareness of the Lido in the media I'm very worried we won't make our target."

Pierre piped up "Come to Summer's studio on Saturday afternoon as she doesn't teach at that time and we will show you our ideas and we can all start to practice"

Angela had been very quiet throughout the whole talk and Rachel had forgotten she was there. "Are you ok Angela?"

"Well of course I've been in a Flashmob before and it was a total failure. We all looked stupid and I told them all it would fail!" She carried on "And I won't be dressing up in anything nylon. It's just too cheap, too fake and too flammable!"

Rachel had a sinking feeling in her stomach but before she could intervene Angela drew breath and addressed the whole group "You're all going to look silly and I'm not going to be part of it. I'm going. I've got more important things to attend to." She stood up, grabbed her coat and walked out of the room, leaving the Ls looking at each other in silence.

Rachel didn't know whether to feel relieved or worried. Angela could be very persuasive and a lot of the others always took her lead as they'd learnt that this was easier then crossing her. At least if Angela wasn't involved it would make it much simpler and Pierre and Summer would be able to pull it off but having said that the whole idea of a Flashmob was to have lots of people involved.

Rachel quickly called an end to the meeting, reminding everyone to keep it a secret. Alison and Diane along with Bill also said their goodbyes and left quickly, following Angela up the garden path. Ziggy, Sally and Liz followed and Rachel could see a group had gathered outside her house having their own private meeting. This worried Rachel and she knew Angela could be extremely persuasive and her way of going about it was not always ethical.

Tom arrived home from work asking Rachel how the meeting had gone. Casting his eye back down the garden path then back to Rachel he could see that Angela had ruffled feathers. Rachel replied “I’ll tell you later”.

Opening 1931

Liberty awoke at around six o'clock on Sunday the first of September 1931. Today was going to be a fun day. Nervous, scary, exciting but hopefully fun too. Today was the day that Liberty's Lido was going to open. The King, Queen, Princess Mary, her husband and children were all going to be there. The whole Town would be there along with the press and television cameras. Wide awake now Liberty pulled back the curtains to a completely blue canvas of sky with not even a tiny white cloud as a contrast. She opened the window and sniffed the cool fresh air as it entered her room. She padded across and pulled on a dressing gown and slippers and ran a brush through her hair. She walked downstairs and saw her Father in the dining room.

"Morning Liberty."

"Morning Father. Couldn't you sleep either?"

"No." He admitted, pouring some coffee for her.

"Thank you." She said, holding the cup in both hands, feeling the warmth and enjoying the aroma of the fresh coffee. "I feel nervous."

"I do too. Meeting the Royal Family, Princess Mary, her husband and her children. How gracious of them to come and open the Lido."

"Yes. What an honour."

Liberty dressed carefully later that morning. The day was warm and she looked stylish and elegant as she wore a yellow dress with matching hat. She packed and unpacked her swimming costume, swim hat and a robe several times to make sure she hadn't forgotten anything. There was a towel and a hairbrush too. She handed the bag to Dorothy, who was going to be her assistant today and would help her to get ready to swim later that day. Dorothy was as pleased as punch and looked very smart in her Sunday best.

Frederick looked Liberty up and down approvingly and offered his arm for her to hold as they made their way through the front door, walking down the drive of the estate and out onto the short walk to the Lido. His tie and pocket handkerchief had been picked out by Liberty and matched the colour of her dress perfectly. Dorothy followed a short distance behind them carrying Liberty's swimming bag. Flags and brightly coloured bunting decorated the white walls of the Lido and Liberty could see members of a brass band waiting to one side. They would be entertaining the crowds later. Crowds of people thronged the street, waiting for the gates to open. Today was free entry to the Lido, everyone welcome. Lords and Ladies, men and women and their children. Frederick and Liberty stood outside the white painted metal gates underneath the sign that boldly proclaimed "Liberty's Lido" while cameras whirred and flashed. The gates opened and the manager of the Lido ushered them in, Dorothy included.

The Manager Matthew Thomas was introduced to Liberty, and he gave them a guided tour showing Dorothy where to leave the bag. Liberty was to have a designated changing cubicle for later, the blue doors of the cubicles the same shade as the colour of the sky above. Frederick heaved a sigh of relief as he looked around the Lido. There had been months of building works, delays for weather and workmen strikes. A team had been on bonuses and working around the clock to make sure that everything would be ready for today. One couldn't afford to keep Royalty waiting. Only yesterday there had still been some unfinished work and last minutes hitches but it had been completed with only hours to spare this morning. They finished the tour standing on a higher deck surveying the pool below them with the sea behind them.

"Well done Mr Thomas." Frederick said shaking the Manager's hand.

Liberty tuned out of the men's conversation and looked at the contrast of the bright white walls of the Lido with the richness of the blue sky above. The water in the pool was as still as a mirror and reflected the brightly coloured flags and bunting as well as the blue doors of the cubicles. The diving board stood proudly at one end of the pool and it also had a mirror image reflection. It was peaceful inside the Lido and the only sounds were those of the hubbub of the gathering crowds outside. The sun shone brightly and Liberty could feel it's warmth as she looked down at the scene below. What a wonderful creation it had been and she was so grateful to her Father for having the drive and ambition to see it through to its completion. She walked slowly around the Lido on her own soaking up the peace of her surroundings. She returned to her Father who had now been joined by several prominent local VIPs and the architect William Branigan.

"Delighted to meet you." Branigan said shaking Liberty's hand. "I am so glad that the Lido has been named after you. It's an honour to finally meet the name behind the creation. What do you think?"

"It's wonderful. Thank you for your design. It truly is magnificent."

The band were setting up on one of the balconies, looking very smart in their uniform, making an out of tune din as they readied themselves. They stopped practicing as Frederick, Liberty, Branigan and the other dignitaries walked to the gates and stepped outside them. A Royal Blue ribbon was hastily tied across them. Liberty looked around at the crowds standing patiently, waiting for the Royal Family and caught sight of a familiar face. Jack. He was beaming from ear to ear as he saw she was looking at him. She smiled widely at him and went red.

Practice

Saturday 3PM arrived and it was just Rachel, Pierre and Summer at the dance studio. They started to show Rachel their ideas for a very simple walking dance and Summer had brought several large silk scarves that her Mum, Ruth, had stored in the attic.

Rachel said "Where is everyone? Have either of you to had any notifications from the others saying if they're coming or not?"

Neither Pierre or Summer had heard anything from the swimmers but Summer replied, "I've heard from some of my Zumba members, at least four, and they should be here by now, I'm surprised they're late".

Diane arrived breathlessly saying that a lorry had blocked the road and everyone was on their way up by foot but were having trouble finding parking spaces, especially as it was summer season. Pierre looked at Rachel and she could see that he was relieved as people started to arrive. There was Flo, Sally, Alice, Michelle and Heather and many of the others joining Diane and some of Summer's Zumba dancers too. In all there were about twenty people.

Cindy arrived a bit later apologising that she'd only just left work at her friend's boutique shop and was looking a bit flushed after rushing. She took off her pink hoodie to reveal a T Shirt with the words 'I'm A Cunt' emblazoned across the front.

Alice took a sharp intake of breath as she noticed the words.

Cindy noticed that Alice was staring at her chest and then remembered what she was wearing, laughing it off with a single line. "My best friend bought it for me." She knew that Alice was easily offended but she didn't let it get to her. Cindy was a unique member of the Ls. She regularly coloured her hair and today her hair was bright pink. She knew she was outside the norms of society and that some people must meet certain expectations in order to fit in but Cindy used her body as a way of visibly expressing her life. She was overheard telling Tink one day "Just like someone who redecorates a room because they are fed up with how it looks, I use tattoos and piercings to change my looks and 'redecorate.' I hope that one day someone will dry out my skin and use it as an art canvas."

Rachel looked around the room at everyone who had arrived and kept finding herself looking at the door waiting for Angela to make a late entrance, keeping the limelight on herself again. The group was split into two with Summer and Pierre each teaching their group some of the basic steps

Pierre and Summer had marked out the floor with masking tape in the shape of a circle, to represent the pool, in the middle of the room and then marked the name of everyone's position with a cross and placing a piece of paper with names written down. This seemed to make it easier as people started to see it taking shape in their minds.

As Pierre was usually one of the last to leave the Lido, with the café being open longer hours, he had secretly met Summer there one night at dusk so they could practice and see if, logistically, it would work. She had filmed them on her phone as she always found in her classes that a visual helped people master the steps in their own time at home. Just making a few tweaks, they had also snuck into the Lido late the next night to practice.

Pierre had bought sustenance today in the form of a huge carrot cake, everyone eyeing it eagerly on the table when they arrived.

"So, if we practice first then we can enjoy Pierre's scrummy cake while we discuss outfits and have a break in about an hour." Rachel said.

"If you find your names on the floor this will give you an idea of where you will be starting in the Lido. Just like in the You Tube video; everyone will have a starting place." Summer directed. "I'm going to start with Pierre and we will walk through it without any music so you can hear me. If it makes it easier I can give you all a cue today".

"Yes please" Diane replied.

Pierre and Summer started by humming the song to give everyone some musical help. As they walked around she called out people's names but found they jumped up, startled like rabbits caught in the headlights, and had forgotten what to do. Bill and Tony got confused about what their first steps were and Diane and Flo bumped into each other and had to be helped to their feet. There was lots of laughing, swearing, chatting and post mortems after each run through.

After about five practices Summer thought to herself "It's like herding cats. Are we actually going to get this perfected?"

Looking across to Pierre she mouthed "We need cake!"

"Let's have a break everyone." Pierre shouted, clapping his hands loudly. "Well done."

"Thank goodness for that. All this getting up and down is putting pressure on my bladder" Bill said as he headed in the direction of the toilets.

While they were enjoying the cake the door of the hall opened and in burst Angela, but she looked somehow different. Her hair and make up looked like she was just about to go onto a film set.

"Hi Angela." Summer called across "Wow. You look amazing. We wondered where you were." She carried on. "Have you come to join us?"

"Well I don't want to intrude but, well, I thought with my dance background I'd be able to help you." replied Angela.

"Dance background my arse." Diane whispered under her breath to Cindy "She's only come to have a nose and she's too frightened of missing out."

"Why is she dressed up like a dog's dinner? Cindy whispered back.

"I reckon she's had that boudoir session. You know the one she auctioned for a couple of months back and paid over the odds for."

"Wasn't that for her daughter?" Cindy smiled cattily.

"Apparently not!" grinned Diane.

"Would you like a slice of cake Angela? We were just taking a break." Summer offered.

"Well I don't normally eat cake, as my body is a temple, but I suppose on this occasion it would be rude not to, thank you." Quickly reaching for the offered slice she continued. "I don't want to interrupt anyone. Just carry on and I'll sit here quietly, and if I can offer any help just ask."

"Ok guys. Is everyone ok and ready to start again?" Summer called out.

Bill slowly getting to his feet moaned, "Gosh I'm feeling rather full. That cake was delicious."

"Well you did have two slices Bill." Sally gently pulled his leg.

"Let's start at the beginning again, this time with music." said Summer trying to establish control.

"One, two, three, four." shouted Pierre as Dancing Queen started to blast out and everyone geared up to do their bit.

"Again." shouted Summer after the first time. "We're getting there now." She kept encouraging and working around the Ls pointing, directing and offering advice. "If you do it like this. Well done."

"Gosh I think I need more cake." Michelle said to Cindy wiping sweat from her forehead after another hour of practice. "I'm friggin' knackered."

Michelle was sixty two and a retired teacher who still taught private lessons for children after school. In her spare time apart from swimming she was a member of "The Pirateers" a three girl dance troupe who performed at pirate days both locally and nationally. Describing herself as a bit clumsy, she bought the fun element to the group dances and the Ls always turned up to her local performances, even though they could be a bit cheeky and made Bill blush. He was still talking about the balloon popping dance! And it had made his day when Michelle had sat on his lap dressed in a burlesque pirate outfit.

She had recently joined and become a member of the group, having found them by accident. Newly divorced and finding herself disorientated and feeling topsy turvy in a world suddenly devoid of sense and reason she had felt torn in two and no idea where to go next. She had taken to walking the cliff paths with her dog, feeling nature's healing energy. Sitting on a beach one day while taking a well earned breather she watched a group of swimmers enjoying the water. On an impulse she walked over to them and struck up a conversation with Angela who she thought she had recognised from visiting the cafe by the Lido in Porthlowen. Rachel had been there that day too.

"Oh yes that's me, always around the Lido and in the cafe, my second home." Angela bragged. "Been going there for years. Ever since I was a child." She continued. "So you say you're fairly new to the town? Thought I hadn't seen you before. I know everyone."

"Umm well I've been living here for a couple of years, our paths just haven't crossed, that's all." Michelle answered. "So, can you tell me a little bit more about your swimming. I'm looking for a new challenge as I've had a change in circumstances and have read lots of information in the press about the health benefits."

Rachel fearing Angela could put Michelle off quickly explained about meeting in the Lido at around 10.30 every morning. "You're very welcome to join us."

So Michelle had gained her swimming legs and become hooked, also enjoying the social side to the group.

Michelle was also owner of Willow, her faithful hound, who was the group's unofficial mascot. Willow was always present on swimming days at Golden Rocks. She would sit on the rocks watching everyone in the water or would wander off to find a comfy coat to sit on if someone had left one out. Willow would sometimes join Michelle in the water on hot days but was usually curled up asleep on a towel waiting for her mistress to return and open the doggy biscuit pot. One of her favourite pastimes was to sit at people's feet waiting for food to drop, always hoovering up after everyone.

"I can't believe it takes me so long to learn the dance." Cindy whispered to Michelle.

"Do you want to come over to mine tomorrow so we can practice in the evening? Maybe if we have a couple of glasses, we will be able to think clearer and if we finish off the bottle then we won't care." Michelle replied with a wink.

"Sounds like a plan." Cindy nodded.

Becoming aware of loud tutting coming from the direction of Angela they both looked across to see her staring at them with a look on her face like she was sucking on a lemon.

Cindy not one to take any crap from anyone just pushed back her shoulders, stuck her boobs out and made sure Angela could read her rude T shirt. The shocked look on Angela's face told Cindy her message had been received loud and clear. Angela pursed her lips even more and pretended to busy herself by pushing a stray lock of hair behind her ear, only looking back at Cindy when she had composed herself, while Cindy gave her a knowing smirk.

"Ok everyone. Thank you. Let's leave it there for today, you've all worked really hard. Well done. Please can you make next Wednesday evening at 7PM?" Summer said distracting Cindy. "Remember to keep it a secret."

Everyone clapped and whooped.

While the Ls and Zumba dancers gathered up their belongings Diane noticed Angela had rushed up to Summer and was busy talking. "Oh god. Do you think Angela is trying to worm her way in?" she said to Liz.

"Probably. She never likes to miss out and after everything she said about how Flashmobs being rubbish." replied Liz.

"Right I need to go." Diane said "Things to do. See you in the water soon. Cheery bye everyone." she called as she left.

After everyone had left, Summer started to pack up her equipment. Turning to Pierre she asked "How did you think that went?"

"Mmmm Ok, I think. We're going to have to do a lot more rehearsals. Oh my god what have we started, Summer?"

She looked at him, shrugged her shoulders and puffed out her cheeks, exhaling a large breath.

"What did Angela want?"

"Well she wants to join in." Summer replied.

"Thought as much. Well we can add her in. To be fair were bound to get someone drop out so the more the merrier." Pierre carried on. "I'm shattered, that was mentally exhausting. Fancy a quick drink to talk tactics?" He said and putting an arm around Summer they walked outside into the late evening sunshine and headed towards the Ship.

Over their drinks Summer said that she had roped in her Mum to help make some scarves for everyone. The scarves would be bright and in a variety of colours and she'd also made a list of accessories to wear with their swimming costumes and bikinis, such as sunglasses, sunhats, sarongs, cover ups and so on. "The brighter and more glamorous, the better." She concluded.

"Of course, darling." Pierre agreed. "Absolutely."

Ceremony 1931

At midday the church clock started chiming and on the twelfth stroke a black Rolls Royce pulled up outside the gates of the Lido. The mayor of Porthlowen, splendidly dressed in a scarlet frock coat and a tricorn hat stepped forward and opened the car door. Prince Mary's husband emerged to cheers and he leaned in and offered his wife his hand. The Princess looked elegant in a fashionable summer dress of pink and she smiled and waved to the crowds. A second Rolls Royce pulled up as the first one drove away and again the Mayor opened the door. King George V stepped out and waved at his subjects who cheered and waved Union Jack flags. The Mayor assisted the Queen who then stood beside her husband acknowledging the throng.

The local VIPs had formed a line and the King, Queen and Royal entourage moved towards them. Liberty was so nervous; her heart was beating loudly in her chest and she thought everyone would hear it.

Frederick was first in line and he bowed deeply as he shook the King's hand.

"Major Sir Frederick Nancarrow." the Mayor indicated.

"May I present my daughter Liberty, your Majesty."

Liberty curtsied perfectly as she'd been practicing for weeks.

"Enchanting." murmured the King as he moved down the line shaking hands with the local VIPs and William Branigan.

Liberty curtsied to the Queen who moved down the line silently and again to Princess Mary.

"Delighted to finally meet you Liberty." enthused the Princess Royal. "Your Father told me so much about you when I met him two years ago. I thought you were wise then when he told me about how you tell him to take time to look at the sea and nature. It's lovely that the Lido has been named after you. I'm looking forward to seeing you swim later."

"Thank you, Your Royal Highness." Liberty smiled and curtsied. She couldn't believe the Princess had spoken to her.

King George V stood at the gates of the Lido, he turned and looked back at the crowds waiting for his wife and daughter, who joined and then flanked him.

The three of them stood side by side smiling and waving to the cameras. At a suggestion from Princess Mary both Frederick and Liberty joined the Royal Party, Liberty standing next to the King.

The King was handed a pair of scissors, took a step forward and the gathered crowd went silent. You could have heard a pin drop. "I declare Liberty's Lido open." He said simply, cutting the blue ribbon. The crowd cheered and the huge white gates were opened while the band started playing a joyful uplifting tune.

The manager Matthew Thomas bowed and shook the King's hand. "Welcome to Liberty's Lido Your Majesty."

Branigan took the King on a guided tour of his creation, pausing to describe and point out various aspects of the design, while Matthew Thomas followed them, interjecting when asked. Frederick accompanied the Queen while Liberty was asked to walk with Princess Mary. How exciting. Initially Liberty was nervous but the Princess had a calm demeanour and a way of putting people at ease. They talked about the sea and the glorious day. The Princess talked about her children, two boys aged seven and eight. They ended up on a high balcony overlooking the Lido and the sea beyond. Mary closed her eyes and looked up at the sun, feeling the warm rays on her face.

"You are lucky to be living in such a beautiful part of the country Liberty."

"Thank you, Ma'am."

The rest of the Royal party and VIPs joined them and took their seats in a temporary stand with a canvas roof to protect them from the heat of the sun.

At a sign from Matthew Thomas the first of the crowds were allowed in and as Liberty looked, a sea of people walked down the steps and took up positions around the pool. No-one was allowed into the water.

Liberty was accompanied by Dorothy to her changing room where she changed into her swimming costume.

"Oh, Dorothy I'm so nervous."

"You'll be fine Miss Liberty."

In the cubicles next to Liberty she could hear voices. These were synchronised swimmers and exhibition divers who were going to put on a display for everyone.

The crowd and band went silent as the King stood and projected his voice across the Pool.

"Welcome to Liberty's Lido. I give you Miss Liberty Nancarrow."

The crowd cheered as Liberty walked to the water's edge. She felt self conscious in her swimming costume and hat. She stood on the pool side and dived gracefully into the cold water with barely a splash, swimming gracefully across to the opposite side where Dorothy was waiting with a gown and a towel. She looked up at her Father and Princess Mary who were stood together clapping her and both beaming, she looked in the opposite direction and her eyes met Jack's. He was clapping and beaming too.

Unbeknown to Sir Frederick and Miss Scrivener, Liberty had continued to learn to swim with Jack throughout 1929, 1930 and 1931 and had even learnt to dive. She was now almost as strong a swimmer as he was

It was the best day of Liberty's life.... So far!

Beach

No matter how long you live in an area it seems there is always a little beach or cove just waiting to be discovered. Liz and her husband Dennis had stumbled across a near empty beach on one of their many and varied cliff top walks. They'd walked around Wreckers Point and then discovered Sanctuary Beach. With softly rolling sand dunes, tall whispering marram grass waving in a light sea breeze and clear turquoise seas gently lapping against the rocks and multiple rock pools just waiting to be refilled had inspired Liz to share it with the other swimmers and so they had arranged an Ls day out away from the Lido. She was intrigued by the name and had done some research. True enough it had been one of the infamous areas where wrecking had taken place. The Point itself looked a little like Lands End from the sea and numerous ships had fallen victim to strategically placed lanterns which had drawn the sailors onto the wicked rocks where the ship became stricken and the booty was plundered by locals. The sea bed was littered with pieces of old ships and some of their less than valuable contents.

Gathering in the meeting point car park the Ls started the ten minute walk across the cliffs down to the beach. There was only a couple of other cars in the near deserted car park. Angela stopped on the way to take a photo of the bright pink foxgloves in the foreground, with golden sand, blue skies and wispy clouds in the background. For those wanting an ice cream, coffee, fish and chips, toilets and other facilities these were provided in a former fishing village, now dedicated to the congregation of tourists, a few miles away, but Sanctuary Beach was a quiet cove in all its natural beauty, far away from the hustle and bustle of the holiday trade.

The cliff path gave way to a steep track before reaching the beach. A small sign attached to a metal pole read. "The whole of this beach is for everyone's enjoyment. In the case of harassment or offensive behaviour, please ring the local police on 101."

"Liz where are you taking us?" Diane looked up warily from the sign and across to Liz

"Oh, um did I not say?" Liz replied looking embarrassed while carrying on walking so that Diane couldn't see her blush. "This beach is popular with naturists, but don't worry there is a large rock about three quarters of the way up the beach with a white cross on it. That is the divide between those that want to wear clothes and those that are happy to swim in their birthday suits"

"Oh!" was all Diane could reply.

"But don't worry about that, just look around you, isn't it simply stunning?". Liz continued.

Tony catching Liz up said with a smile on his face "I think I'm going to like this beach. I've just read the sign.". He winked at her.

"I think you might be disappointed if you think you are going to see lots of scantily clad beautiful women. When Dennis and I were here it seemed to be mostly men walking towards that end of the beach." she chuckled.

Tony sighed with disappointment.

Throwing their rucksacks down at the back of the beach there was evidence of an old bonfire. A circle of blackened stones, partially burnt wood and charcoal had been left and a slightly smoky smell wafted towards the Ls.

Looking up Liz could see that some of the vegetation on the cliff side had been burnt but looked much older that this fire. "Such a shame that someone would light a fire so close to the cliff and then allow it to catch alight. This is how gorse fires can start, not to mention the carnage to any little rodents or birds living there. Shall we move down the beach a little? You never know if any broken glass has been left under the sand."

"Well as its our first time to this beach we need a group photo." Angela was herding everyone into a line in front of the sea. A passing beach goer was asked to take the photo before everyone turned and entered the sea.

"Oh my! It's so lovely in today. This is just what the doctor ordered." Rachel shouted looking over at Tom.

"He certainly does." Tom replied before splashing her.

Swimming straight out from the beach with Tom following her, Rachel paused to take a breath and looked back towards the beach. "Aaagh." She shrieked. "Something touched my leg", she panicked. Thinking it was Tom who had been close by, she thought to herself it was his hand that had caught her. Glancing over her shoulder she realised he was a good ten feet away. "Oh god" she thought to herself "What the hell was that?" It had been solid. Was it a seal? It definitely wasn't seaweed or a rock but had felt rubbery. Lots of thoughts were going through her head. Rachel had a vivid imagination that could often work overtime. Was it a body?

Shouting to Tom to come over, he turned and could see she looked scared. Sprint swimming over to her he asked "What's wrong? Are you ok?"

"Something touched me!" Treading water, she was obviously frightened.

"Have you looked under the water?" Tom asked.

"No. Aaaggh! It's just touched my foot again. You look. I'm too scared." Rachel had a deep fear of death and bodies. This had started around age eleven after she had been to the beach with her parents. A body had washed up and even though Rachel had never touched it she could remember that the colour of the skin was grey and it had given her nightmares for years. Now as an adult it only took something like this to catapult her back to age eleven again.

Looking under the water, it was incredibly clear and Tom could see what had bumped into Rachel. Lifting his head out of the water he looked across at her and with a reassuring smile he said "It's a Barrel Jellyfish. Wow it's the first one I've seen this year. It's massive. No wonder you were worried."

These jellyfish didn't come every year so it made it all the more special when they did. A huge mushroom shaped bell with eight frilly tentacles below, they could grow really large and up to thirty five kilograms in weight. Luckily, they weren't stingers like some of the others that the Ls sometimes encountered, especially the potentially deadly Portuguese Man O War. Rachel put her head under the water and could see the jellyfish swimming off into the distance. Feeling much braver she decided to swim after it, fishing her camera out from inside her costume. Swimming above, below and to the side of the jelly she took lots of photos and as it swam towards the bottom she dived down and followed.

Tom followed them both and took photos of Rachel swimming with the huge beautiful creature. He surfaced to draw breath as Rachel also came to the top. "Can you take some photos of me as well please?" He asked.

"Of course, hold on let me catch my breath." Rachel replied.

Angela had noticed that they were diving above something and quickly swam over to see what it was. She never wanted to miss out on getting a perfect photo to send to the Open Water Swimmer magazine. "Oh my goodness its huge." She shrieked. "That's the biggest Jellyfish I've ever seen. Taking control, she said to Rachel "Dive down I'll take a picture of you near the Jelly."

Obediently Rachel dived down coming within touching distance but feeling too scared to actually touch it.

“Right my turn” Angela bossily told Rachel, “I’m going to touch it so make sure you get a good photo. I’m not sure you’re in the right place there with the light, can you move over there?”

“OK.” Rachel replied and just went along with Angela’s orders.

Tom gave Rachel a good luck thumbs up and swam off to see what else he could find.

“Are you ready Rachel?” Angela yelled before diving deeper and closer to the jellyfish. Down she swam before she put out her hand and touched the top of the large creature, quickly turning to look up at the surface in the direction of Rachel before smiling.

Rachel pushed the shutter several times hoping she’d got a good shot so she could be released from her ‘duties’ and go for a swim, thinking to herself as Angela swam back to the surface “Even under the surface this woman smiles and poses.”

“Did you get the shot?” Angela shrieked as her face hit the surface.

“I’m sure I did.” replied Rachel. “I’ll show you the pictures when I’m back on the beach. I’m off to catch up with Tom now.”

Rachel moved away at speed as she knew from previous swims that she would end up getting cold taking photos of Angela and not having a proper swim herself.

Catching up with Tom he said “Well done. You’ve done your duty!”

Rachel just shook her head and swam closer to him. “God she’s intense! Have you seen anything else?”

“Actually yes, there’s a Crystal Jellyfish around here somewhere. I’ve been trying to take a photo but as it’s transparent I keep losing it. Let me see if I can find it for you”. With that he put his head under the water while lying flat on the surface.

“Wish I’d bought my snorkel.” Rachel said to Tom when he surfaced. “I can’t hold my breath like you can. Bloomin’ asthma.”

"Yes but you do well." beamed Tom, "The swimming really helps you. Remember what you used to be like years ago."

"I know" Rachel grinned before continuing. "It's just when I see something interesting under the water and I have to come up for a couple of breaths and then when I look under the water again, I've usually lost it".

"I know it's frustrating but you do really well, especially in the winter and you always seem to take better shots than me" Tom said. "I don't seem to be able to find that Crystal now and I'm starting to feel a little chilly. Shall we do a slow swim back to the beach and see if we pass anything interesting on the way?"

"Yep sounds good." Rachel replied.

Walking up the beach the sand was really warm between Rachel's toes. She was feeling a bit cold and was glad to put on her towelling robe and remove her wet costume. Sitting down on the warm sand she reached for her flask of hot lemon and ginger drink. She could feel the heat transferring from the sand to her body, slowly warming it up like a lizard.

Michelle had come out of the water just before Rachel and Tom, and was starting to get dressed. Taking her robe off she went to spread it out on the beach before lying on it. "Eeww! What's that?" she exclaimed while looking down.

"Is that chocolate?" Alice asked.

"Can't be I've not eaten any and my robe is clean on today".

"Oh god" Sally joined in the conversation. "Look! Where you've been sitting. Is that dog poo buried in the sand?"

"Nooooo!" Michelle exclaimed "That's really gross. Dirty people burying it under the sand and not taking it home with them. I'm a dog lover but even this is turning my stomach. I can smell it now. I need to clear this up." Folding up her robe she carefully placed it into a dry plastic bag and reaching into her rucksack pocket she produced a spare poo bag before scooping up the offending mess. "Luckily I've always got plenty of bags for Willow. Everyone. Make sure you're not sitting on any more." Michelle told the group.

"Well that's really put me off my lunch." Alice said before carrying on, "Shall we all move to a new spot as that's all I can smell and focus on now?"

“Yeah good idea.” Angela agreed.

After moving a little way down the beach Rachel tried to change the conversation by pointing out the heat haze. “Look across the beach. You can see the shimmering waves of heat rising in the distance. Its making people walking along the beach look funny, wobbly looking. It feels much hotter all of a sudden and the sand is burning my feet.”

“Time to put up the parasol.” Liz stated. “I’m melting and I want to eat my lunch without my sandwiches turning into toasties”. Unpacking her brightly coloured parasol she secured it into the sand. Willow walked over, plonking herself next to Liz for shade, ever hopeful for food. Laughing, Liz looked down at Willow before saying “You know the best spots dear Willow. I bet your fur coat is too much in this weather.”

While eating lunch the conversation turned to the story behind Wreckers Point, Liz telling them all how she’d looked up its history and there had been an argument about whether wrecking had been a good or bad thing for Cornwall.

“It’s harvesting, pure and simple.” Tony said.

“It’s stealing.” Alice countered. “It belongs to someone else and you’ve taken it. You wouldn’t steal crops from a farmer’s field that he’s harvested. Would you?”

“Course I wouldn’t. But this is different. You’d eat a fish that you’d caught from the sea, wouldn’t you?”

“Yes. But that’s not owned by anybody.”

Flo entered the debate. “I think there is some old law that things washed up on the shore are like ‘finder’s keepers’

Alice pouted. “But I still think it’s stealing.”

Tony asked her. “So, you find a tenner on the floor. Do you keep it or take it to a police station?”

“Keep it of course.”

“But is that stealing or finders keepers? You see my point Alice?”

"But I disagree with wrecking, luring ships onto rocks and then wicked men plundering the wrecks, killing poor unfortunate souls and so on."

"There's a big difference between plundering a natural shipwreck, and the contents of a ship washing up on the beach, or instigating a shipwreck by luring ships onto rocks." Flo said.

"Attitudes have changed now." Tony said. "But a hundred years ago or more it was seen as fair game, a way of life and everyone was in on it from poor people to the rich landowners.

Tom intervened. "Do you remember when those containers got washed up on the beach in Devon or Dorset a few years ago? The locals took the contents of the containers including motorbikes. I don't think that much was actually recovered by the police."

The conversation moved onto the comedy film Whisky Galore where crates of whisky had been washed up on a Scottish Island Coast and the customs man was trying to find the whereabouts of the missing crates by talking to lots of drunken Scotsmen.

The rest of the day was spent sunbathing, dozing, relaxing and even double dipping before the Ls returned to their cars and went home in the warm evening sun.

"That was great." Rachel said to Tom as he drove them home. "I enjoyed that."

"Yes. Can't wait to look at the pictures of the Jellies properly."

Sure enough, once they were home, they had amazing pictures of the Barrel Jellyfish which they sent to the Outdoor Swimmer magazine. Rachel's one of Tom was published. Angela's wasn't!

Promotion 1931 - 1933

In early 1931 Jack was summoned to Sir Frederick's office. Jack was petrified that Liberty's secret had been rumbled. Frederick had been impressed by the hard work and maturity that Jack had shown and was promoted not once but three times, earning his way out of the gut-wrenching poverty of his parents' and grandparents' generation. New developments were being built in Porthlowen and Jack became one of the first of his generation to be able to buy his own house, which he lived in with his mother Agnes, and his brothers and sisters.

Now aware of the reliability of Jack Pender and his leadership skills Frederick came to rely on the common sense and straight talking of his shift manager and, although young, in 1933 was given the title of manager for the whole of Wheal Trencrom. Frederick felt he could rely on the honest answers of his young manager rather than other managers who told him what they thought he wanted to hear. Jack was a true leader of men and he could inspire the workers by being one of them, never forgetting his roots but he was also able to rub shoulders with the middle and upper class members of Porthlowen.

It was a tremendous honour and still Frederick knew nothing of the relationship between Jack and Liberty. They met in secret whenever they could and Liberty had helped Jack's education by discussing the issues of the day that she learnt from the Times as well as reading and writing. His quick, lively enquiring mind quickly grasped the important facts and they often argued vehemently about their polar opposite viewpoints; he from his working class side and she from her privileged background. However, this only served to strengthen their own relationship and Jack's ability to manage the mine.

Unicorns

Tom pumped up the last of four massive inflated Unicorns. There wasn't any electricity by the Lido to do this, so he'd had to do this at home. He had retrieved them from the back of the garage from a box buried under everything that had been hoarded over the last few years.

Rachel and Poppy were getting ready while Tom lined up the Unicorns by the car. Walking back into the house he could hear Rachel and Poppy shrieking with laughter and was only aware he had walked through a cloud of glitter when he saw that he was covered in it. "Poppy, you can't wear this it's bad for the environment." he said.

"It's ok. I bought it at a festival and it's biodegradable, anyway I'm not wearing it but you are!" Poppy replied looking at his sparkling face. "Come on Dad get ready."

"I'm nearly ready. Just need to put my pink wig on."

"Do you need a hand with your tutu and wig?" Poppy gently teased Tom.

"Ummm no. I think I can manage. I can't believe I agreed to do this. I hope none of my patients see me floating on a unicorn."

"Don't worry Dad. They won't recognise you when I'm finished." Poppy replied.

"Great." groaned Tom.

"Ok before we leave, we need a family selfie for my Instagram." Poppy announced. "C'mon Mum."

"Ummm no Poppy I have a reputation to keep as a sensible person." Tom replied.

"Too late Dad. I've done it." laughed Poppy.

"Right everyone let's go." Tom continued. "Poppy you get in the car and I will start to load the unicorns around you. I hope they all fit in."

"Why have we got four Dad?" Poppy asked.

"I said I would lend one to Diane." Tom replied. Two were squeezed into the boot with much pushing and a quick slam of the door. "I think I will have to put two on the back seat with the bases meeting in the middle of the car. Then the heads can lie down with one on your lap Poppy."

"Ok you sure they are going to fit in?" Poppy asked from her seat inside.

"Actually, I'm not sure now that I can see how big they are next to the car."

"Pass me one and I'll pull and you push. If you open the window then shut the door carefully I'll stick the head out." Poppy directed. "Ok shut the door and put the last Unicorn in the other side, open that window as well and I'll pull that one in too."

Tom did as he was told, ramming the last inflatable in. "Oh god." he groaned "What have I started?" He looked at Rachel who in turn looked at his Volvo estate and then back at Tom before raising her eyebrows and jumping into her seat.

"Well I'm ok in the front." Rachel said. "Are you ok Poppy as I can't see you? Can you breathe alright?" Rachel shouted into the back of the car.

"Yes. All ok from the cheap seats." Poppy replied.

"Let's go." said Tom as he started the engine and put the car into first gear. Slowly going down their drive and just clearing the hedge at the bottom they headed for the Lido.

Driving slowly around the narrow Cornish lanes, keeping to the middle of the lane so the unicorns wouldn't get snagged on sharp hedges, was ok as it was early so they didn't meet any other vehicles, but as soon as they reached the outskirts of Porthlowen and Tom could speed up the unicorns came to life. They seemed to get partly sucked out of the window as if they were straining to look around and then their heads started to bob in the wind.

"Tom. We seem to be getting strange looks from people." Rachel said, looking up from her phone.

"Really I can't think why." Tom replied. He and Poppy started laughing.

"Mum have you forgotten the Unicorns?"

"Oh yes I've been so engrossed checking my emails I'd completely forgotten them." Rachel answered back.

"It's ok Mum, I'm back for the summer now. Dad doesn't need to be your handler for a few months."

"You cheeky mare!" Rachel retorted indignantly before they all started laughing. "Quick Tom there's a parking space over there." She pointed excitedly.

Tom just managed to manoeuvre into the space, allowing extra room on either side for his precious cargo. Getting out in his pink wig, tutu and tights he was just trying to retrieve a unicorn from the side door to allow Poppy to get out, when a voice behind him shouted "Alright Doc?"

He turned around to see one of his patients standing beside his own car, holding a parking ticket. "Whass on?" The elderly gentleman continued looking Tom up and down before carrying on "Tis none of my business what you get up to in your own time is it." the gentleman carried on as if it was the most normal thing in the world, placing his ticket in the windscreen, locking his car and walking off, looking back chuckling to himself.

Rachel and Poppy had stayed laughing in the car leaving poor Tom outside on his own.

'Oh great!' he thought to himself. 'This is going to be all over town later.'

Poppy was now free to get out of the car and Tom turned to her before saying "No one will know you, they said. No one will be able to tell it's you Dad in a long pink wig, they said. Well Poppy they can!"

Poppy yanking the other Unicorn out of the car replied "Just an average day Dad. Just an average day. Come on. I'm desperate for a swim." Swinging her swim bag onto her back she grabbed a Unicorn by the neck and walked off in the direction of the Lido.

Tom gave Rachel a defeated look as he followed Poppy.

Tom lined up the four unicorns outside the changing cubicles before putting his bag on the seat at the back of one of them. Retrieving Poppy's discarded bag from the floor before someone tripped over it he placed it in the changing room next to his own. Noticing a huge spider sitting in its web in the corner at the back he quickly swopped the bags over before he had to deal with a sobbing screaming wreck who couldn't even mention the 'S' word. He knew another of the group was on their way as he could see a unicorn head moving along the wall outside the Lido. Down the steep steps to the Lido came Angela her pink wig blowing in her eyes and nearly tripping up.

"Morning!" she shouted as she retrieved pink hair from her mouth.

"Morning Angela. Would you like some help?" Tom asked.

"Oh yes, Tom, Please." Angela gushed. "Please can you take my 'Fanny' for me."

"What?" Tom said taking a step back.

"My Fanny! If you could grab her, I'd be most grateful." Angela said thrusting the unicorn in his arms.

Rachel was following her down the stairs and watched amused as Tom went bright red and did as he was told. Placing her own unicorn down next to Poppy's she joined Tom on the bench. Smirking she asked "Seen any lovely fannies lately Tom?"

"I'm not really sure what was going on there." He said bemused. "What's she talking about?"

Well….." she said slowly enjoying the moment then nodded in the direction of Angela's unicorn and to where she had written in pink permanent marker the words 'Fanny' at the bottom of its neck.

As the penny dropped, he looked towards some of the other unicorns and saw that they also all had names. Floosie, Sugar Tits and Jezebel. Relieved he then said "Please don't name ours I'm not sure I could cope."

"I won't, but I can't promise that Poppy won't."

Tony did his daily head count, commenting that the collective noun for a group of unicorns was a blessing.

"Well I'm a blessing in disguise Tony!" Tom laughed.

Today with the warm sunshine and a promise of a fun day there were thirty Ls at the Lido. Nearly everyone had bought a unicorn and they made an impressive sight all lined up in front of the cubicles. Many of the visitors were taking photos of the pink wig wearing swimmers. Angela was organising everyone to sit on their Unicorn in a long line for a photo session. The bright colours were amazing but there was a strong smell of plastic in the air from the inflatables.

"Oooh that reminds me." Diane said to Michelle before continuing "I've got a deflated flamingo for you. I love that you repurpose these plastic monstrosities into amazing bags. Next time you have time can you make another mermaid tote bag please? My sister is so jealous of mine and I promised I'd buy her one."

"Gosh, yes no problem, I was so busy over the winter making bags I've nearly run out of plastic but will be able to stock up now the summer is here and everyone is using their lilos." Michelle replied.

Everyone had managed to sit down on their unicorns but Alice wasn't the only one wondering how she was going to get off it. Having had a hip replacement over the winter she still found getting off the floor difficult. Now she was trying to negotiate not only getting off the floor but also straddling an inflated Unicorn that every time she tried to put her hand down to get any purchase it quickly disappeared deep inside the plastic, causing her to lose her balance. Now starting to get hot and frustrated she could see that everyone else was up and chatting and it seemed to her that nobody had noticed the trouble she was having. Trying to roll over a bit to give herself some momentum she tried one last time but only ended up rolling off the unicorn and landing at Tony's feet with her legs in the air and having scraped the skin off her elbow.

"Alice are you ok?" he asked, "Let me help you up." He reached down and helped her to her feet.

"Thank you." Alice replied. "I seem to have cut my arm on the rough surface." she continued.

By this time everyone was looking over at the commotion before Julie walked over with a tissue to help dry Alice's cut. Tom came over to check that she was alright.

Angela had been the first person to notice Alice's struggle and was secretly taking photos, not realising that poor Alice was really stuck. "I'm so sorry Alice, I didn't realise you were so stuck, I just thought you were just messing about, I wouldn't have taken photos of you if I thought you were really hurt." Angela said.

"Those photos better not end up on Facebook Angela." Alice said crossly, thinking to herself that Angela only would have thought. 'What a great photo opportunity.'

"Oh no don't worry. For your eyes only Alice." Angela replied smugly.

Tom accompanied Alice to the First Aid area of the Lido and quickly cleaned her cut and put a plaster on it.

Douggie came around with his clip board and the attention turned to him. "Ok everyone I've got a list of today's races and events. We've got fastest woman and men's race on a unicorn, plus a children's race. £5 per entrant and £2 for children and students. If you want to enter come and find me by the kiosk so I've got your names. There's face painting, hair plaiting and some kids' games, plus several bands playing over the day. Also, Pierre has worked hard and got lots of excellent cakes and exciting dishes in addition to all of the normal food in the Cafe. I saw him returning from Trelyn earlier this morning so fresh mackerel is on the menu today. Eunice has baked extra pasties today too. Let's try and raise as much money as we can. We're nearly at full capacity already and its only eleven o'clock."

Tom looking over towards Rachel asked "Are you going into the women's race or just here for a float around?"

"I'm not sure, I'm a bit nervous and want to see who the competition is as I don't want to get killed especially if Poppy and her friends are in it."

"Ok fair enough." Tom replied "I expect they will be."

Rachel continued "I'm going to ask Douggie if he will do just an Ls race, I'm going to look for him. Do you want a coffee?"

"Yes please and a slice of coffee and walnut cake. I think I need to keep my strength up for the race." Tom replied.

"God you're so competitive, it's just like sports day all over again when Poppy was at primary school and you always wanted to win the Dad's race."

"No point being on the start line unless you're in it to win it." he countered.

Lining up at the start line were thirty five men all keen to win, all sizing up the competition, testosterone and banter aplenty.

Rachel laughed to herself. 'Why do men always take it so seriously? Have they forgotten they are sitting astride unicorns?' She looked for Tom in the crowd and recognised him from his bright coloured trunks against the white of his inflatable unicorn. Some of the male lifeguards were also in the race leaving the female lifeguards on duty.

Poppy came running over. "Is Dad racing?" she asked.

"Yep. Him, his unicorn and his ego are all lined up at the start." Rachel replied, pointing him out.

"Gosh Dad is going to get annihilated. See those three there, they are Surf Life Savers and go to the gym every day." Poppy told her Mum adding. "They're probably about half his age too."

"Poor old pensioner." Rachel laughed. "Well he's only 'in it to win it' so he says. At least he's up for a challenge." Rachel continued.

"Yeah right. Up to die I think." Poppy said as Douggie stood up with his clipboard in one hand, a starting gun in the other and taking it all very seriously.

"Ok we want a clean race, so get ready for the starting gun" he said. "One, two" bang!!!!! The bang was an explosion of white water mixed in with unicorn heads and various peoples' arms and legs frantically paddling and splashing. Most unicorns had started on "One!". Nobody seemed to emerge from the splash at first as unicorns hit and bounced off each other like dodgems at a funfair. Slowly people got control of their inflatables and started to go in the right direction. A young lad, tanned with long blonde tousled hair started to pull away from the pack. Poppy recognised him from college and surfing as she started to cheer. "Come on Josh."

Rachel was still scanning the crowd for Tom, who was lost in the middle of the abyss of inflatable unicorns.

"Who is that out in front?" Rachel asked Poppy.

"Josh." she replied simply.

"Isn't that the one you fancied at college?" Rachel asked innocently.

"Mum! Be quiet! There are lots of people around and someone might hear. Anyway, he has a girlfriend!" Poppy said exasperatedly then pointed. "There he is, there's Dad. C'mon Dad!"

Yes, Go Tom!" Rachel shouted, grateful for the change of conversation.

The race resembled a strange rugby scrum with all the unicorns in a pile, some were going backwoods or sideways and most people didn't look like there were in control at all. Douggie blew his whistle as the leaders crossed over the finish line. It looked like Tom had only just made it half way around the course.

Poppy dived in and swam over to Tom. She jumped on the back of his unicorn and tipped him in. Tom appeared next to her before pushing her head under and both got out of the pool laughing. "Don't think Unicorn racing is your thing Dad."

"No." he agreed nursing a couple of bruises from the encounter.

The Ls only race was a non starter as it was only Rachel, Julie, Dawn and Mary who'd expressed any interest. In the end they'd just gone for a ride around the pool, chatting, sunbathing out on the water and generally having a fun time. People of all ages swam, jumped, splashed and paddled with or without their unicorns.

The day continued pleasantly. Tom was torn between Pierre's fresh mackerel salad but he'd already got an order in for one of Eunice's pasties. In the end he had both, taking the pasty home for later, or the next day. The fresh mackerel was unbelievably good, so tasty as it had only been swimming a few hours before. Rachel agreed with Tom that it was delicious while Poppy was happy with her pasty. As the day progressed and the sun's heat started to diminish in intensity several of the Ls retired to the Ship including Tom and Rachel. Poppy was meeting her mates in town somewhere.

Rachel had a phone call from Douggie later that evening to say that the Lido had had one of its busiest days ever with over six hundred people coming in throughout the day. Rachel knew that people had been queueing on the steps to come into the Lido, waiting for other people to leave. The café had been rammed all day and evening too. I'm clearing up and then I'll be in to help Pierre to cash up. I'll let you know the final figures later."

"Brilliant Douggie. There's a pint here with your name on it when you're ready, Tom says."

It was just before closing time when Douggie came to collect his pint, Pierre accompanying him. Both looked exhausted.

Tom quickly got them a drink. "Well done chaps." He toasted them.

"We've made over four thousand pounds today." Doggie said simply.

Rachel hugged him and Pierre. "You've done so well. I'll update all of the social media pages later to let everyone know. A good addition to the coffers."

Eligibility 1933

Frederick Nancarrow held a party to find Liberty a husband in 1933, on Liberty's eighteenth birthday. In his opinion they were eligible bachelors but to Liberty they were boring, empty headed and rich. The suitors left empty handed and disappointed.

Dancers

"Ping, ping, ping."

Rachel's phone was coming to life and it wasn't even seven in the morning yet. She sat in the garden enjoying the early morning warmth of the sun as she sipped her morning coffee. In the distance she could hear a bee buzzing around the honeysuckle collecting nectar, its hairy yellow and black striped body blending in with the yellow sweet-scented flowers. Picking up her phone to read the messages she knew what it would be about.

A group chat had been created weeks ago and titled 'Fundraiser' in case any innocent person had seen the sheer volume of messages toing and froing between the group. There were already twelve notifications that day.

The first one was from Alice who had decided she couldn't go ahead today as she was so nervous. The thought of it had sent her to the toilet and this worried her even more, as they were all wearing swimming costumes later. The next six notifications were from the rest of the group offering up their sympathy with Angela offering to lend her a brown and black costume and long sarong if she felt she could manage the dance.

Alice was cross with herself as she suffered from 'nerves' as her Mother had called it and really wanted to take part.

Summer and Pierre had both replied saying it was ok and they totally understood. They left it that if she felt better a bit later then she was most welcome to join in or even just come for support or to watch and cheer everyone else on. The final few messages were just a few of the group checking in and discussing how amazing the weather was.

Tom walked from the kitchen into the garden with his mug to sit opposite her at the table. "I'm going to cook breakfast in a minute. Can I tempt you with some bacon and eggs, mushrooms, tomatoes, toast, the works?"

"No thank you Tom. I've had a banana and I'm feeling a little nervous myself. I only hope I don't forget the steps." Rachel replied, smiling at her husband.

"You'll be fine. It's only a bit of fun to hopefully raise the Lido's profile." Tom said as he grinned encouragingly across the table.

"I hope I can suck my tummy in, dance and smile for that amount of time". Rachel carried on.

"What? What are you talking about?" Tom quizzically looked at her.

"You know Summer's brother is going to be videoing it and, well, I want to look my best. Well as best I can in a swimming costume at my age" Rachel explained.

"Rachel you always look amazing." he said while giving her a big hug. "I need some food. What time is the living dead up?"

"Living dead?" Rachel repeated. "Oh, you mean Poppy. Who knows, as she went out last night. I heard her get in around one. "

"So what time are we leaving?" Tom asked.

"Doesn't really matter as the Flashmob isn't until this afternoon but I would like to go for a swim this morning. It might settle my nerves a bit, then maybe some lunch in the cafe" she suggested.

"Great idea. Pierre always has some good specials on at the weekends, hopefully some more of that mackerel" Tom stood up and headed into the house leaving her quietly thinking about the day ahead.

Over the past month there had been several practices for the Flashmob but slowly the swimmers had become dancers, of a sort. The routine had come together but there was still a massive room for improvement. It had been hard work and stressful getting the Ls to commit to dance practice. Most of it had been left to Summer as Pierre was in his busiest time in the café, working long hours and making sure that income was maximised there. The practices had been at Summer's studio and not all of the swimmers turned up to every session so it was with a certain degree of trepidation that Rachel approached today.

Her thoughts slowly turned into a rehearsal in her head. She shut her eyes and could picture where everyone was standing around the Lido. Then her mind went blank and she started to panic. "What if I can't do it, or I bump into someone or I trip up and fall into the water?" Her mind was racing and she found herself shaking her head as if trying to remove the negative thoughts from her mind.

Taking a couple of deep breaths, she recounted her therapist's words "Rachel you can't crystal ball everything!"

Taking another deep breath Rachel decided to move out of her comfy chair by the table and walk around the garden to clear her head. Walking towards the sweet peas she could smell their heady fragrance. It was almost intoxicating and decided that as she hadn't cut any for a couple of days, she would get a pair of scissors from the kitchen and fill a jug so as to keep them flowering. Anything to keep her mind occupied.

The evening before, Summer had sent out a 'last minute details list reminder.' Rachel had made sure all of their costumes were ready along with flip-flops and flower rings for her and Poppy's hair along with anything else they needed.

"Ok I'm ready." Tom called from the front door. He had been outside to open up the car and place his swimming rucksack in the boot.

"Yes. Just coming, Gimme ten minutes. I'm going to leave Poppy a note to say where we are. I hope she can join us for lunch." Rachel continued as she closed the front door and walked across the gravel pathway towards the car.

There was much excitement at the Lido as the swimmers prepared for their morning swim. It was difficult not to blurt out about the Flashmob and more than once Tony's booming voice had been a bit too loud before Angela had exclaimed "Tony Ssssh."

Trying to change the conversation Rachel shouted above the noise "We're going to the cafe for lunch if anyone wants to join us. Pierre is working there this morning and Summer said she and her brother will arrive just after lunch for a 'swim'".

"This is so hard to keep quiet." Flo gushed, "I would like to join you Rachel if that's ok?"

"I will as well." Angela said.

"Me as well." said Liz and everyone else joined in with a "Might as well" or "There's no point going home." comments.

"We wouldn't look so out of place if we're still here at lunch time." Bill stated. "Plus, I happen to know Pierre has made a huge homity pie which he is serving with salad on the menu today and that's one of my favourites." he said eagerly.

"Ok if that's everyone staying then I will reserve some tables outside and get a menu so we can pre-order to save time. Twelve thirty ok with everyone?" Rachel asked. Everyone agreed.

After an excellent lunch, the homity pie ticking all of the boxes, they went back to the Lido's changing cubicles and found that it had now become very busy due to the hot weather with its fiercely loyal community of regulars joined by today's casual visitors. The water in the Lido forming a kaleidoscope of blues enticing the hot sunbathers in to cool down.

So as not to draw too much attention to the group they sat down on the wooden benches and slowly one by one, they got changed before walking to their starting position taking any deckchairs, props and towels with them. With it being so busy they blended in. However, some of the spots that had been mapped out by Summer were already taken and this sent a couple of the swimmers into a spin with the changes.

Summer had just calmed them down when Alice arrived "Yay you made it!" Summer exclaimed as she walked over to her, "Are you feeling better?"

"Actually I am. Much better. I was so nervous this morning." Alice thanked her.

"Does that mean you're here to join in?" Summer whispered.

"Yes. I think I can manage it." sighed Alice.

"Great. Thank you. I was so worried about you this morning. When you're ready then go strut your stuff girl." Summer said in an American accent giving Alice a reassuring hug.

"Oh ok." Alice blushed slightly as she put her bag down and went to get changed. Emerging wearing a pink swimming costume and matching sarong tied around her slender hips, she set off around the Lido carrying a stripy towel.

Once everyone was in position Pierre and Summer quickly scanned the Lido and Summer looked over to see if her brother, James, was in the right place. He was on the Lido's top sun terrace overlooking the sea at the farthest point from the main entrance. She hoped people would just think he was taking photos of the sea. He had also roped in a friend, Harrison, to help out and he was already on the other sun terrace by the entrance. Summer phoned James to check that he was ready before making a second phone call to Douggie as he was going to control the outdoor PA system. Both Summer and Pierre were wearing long towelling robes as if they were about to go swimming. The only thing different that any eagle-eyed person might have seen was that Pierre had six inch heels on, but it was busy and nobody seemed to notice.

The Lido normally only played music outside when there was a specific function on so when Madonna's "Vogue." started to play, some of the locals looked around in surprise. Summer and Pierre took the lead from the music and started the Flash mob by pulling off their robes and flinging them into a changing cubicle. Summer was glad to remove hers as she was dressed in a tight lycra, silvery green sequined catsuit, under a silver sarong and the added extra towelling layer in the twenty-five degrees heat was getting a little sweaty and she could feel a bead of sweat running down her spine.

Looking over at Pierre she smiled taking in his costume which he had kept secret. "Wow." She mouthed.

His body-hugging costume which made him look even taller had silver padded shoulders and small round mirrors sewn on everywhere. It certainly was a show stopper. Gazing at Pierre she found herself so enamoured by the extravagance of his costume she nearly missed her musical cue. The sun was reflecting off the mirrors and sequins and she wished she'd worn her sunglasses. His outfit needed a health warning. Walking barefoot, the ground below Summer's feet had absorbed the heat from the sun and she was glad there were plenty of wet areas where swimmers had left the pool, dripping their way back to their belongings.

Involved with chatting or eating, or swimming with their children the crowds of people only slightly registered the music at first. As the music continued people began to look up from their books and conversations were put on hold. A group of teenagers started to point and others followed their gaze. Summer and Pierre's sparkly costumes now starting to stand out from the normal array of swimwear and summer clothing. Summer had choreographed a routine just for the two of them that fused Zumba and a Street Dance vibe lasting a couple of minutes to really get noticed. It was an up-tempo song that had a few people clapping, swaying and moving to the beat. It was an amazing dance routine and Rachel was mesmerised, especially by Pierre wearing his six inch heels and channelling his inner Beyonce. She'd have broken her neck just wearing them let alone dancing a complex Street Dance. The music seamlessly transitioned into Abba's Dancing Queen as the two dancers trailed their lightweight sarongs behind them and reached Rachel first. Onlookers watched on but had no idea what was going on and what was coming next. What first seemed like a random dance of happiness by Summer and Pierre started to grow. Having been sat ready on her towel Rachel had, today, worn one of her 'special' costumes used for dressing up and probably not really suitable for swimming in. With bright blue and green iridescent mermaid scales it shimmered in the sunlight and as the duo walked towards her, she got to her feet, pulling out her hidden green sarong and leaving her towel where it had been placed. Seamlessly two became three as the dancers moved perfectly to their choreographed moves.

The music continued and out of the corner of her eye Summer saw her brother behind the camera above them. Starting to relax and enjoy herself she smiled at Pierre and Rachel as they carried on. The crowd was starting to take notice that this wasn't just a normal afternoon and were getting to their feet, some looking confused and others smiling. The group moved slowly around the Lido as more onlookers got out their cameras and phones. What the crowds didn't know was that the show was just about to get started.

The dancers were joined by Summer's younger sister, Saffron, wearing her trademark baseball cap and baggy checked shirt tied around her middle, her blond haired pony tail bobbed as her dance moves rivalled that of her elder sister.

After "Dancing Queen" came "Walking on Sunshine" followed by "I'm so excited" by the Pointer Sisters and many other tracks from the movie Flashdance.

Sitting in her deckchair Angela looking ever the coiffured glamour puss wearing a gold lamé swimming costume and gold sequinned flip-flops. She had somehow found a pair of gold framed vintage sunglasses. Reaching under her deckchair she grabbed her gold crown and placing it on her head she stood up, releasing her side tied gold sarong giving it a quick shake she joined the others.

Diane had her deckchair facing the dancers so she could watch, nervous she might miss her cue. She had already had had three costume changes due to stage fright and modesty and was now wearing a black costume patterned with bright pink flamingos and a skirted bottom. She had been sitting wearing a very large pink sunhat to partly protect herself from the searing sun but also to be incognito. Standing up she stumbled before sitting back down again. She had become stiff sitting there for so long and found it slightly difficult to prise herself out of the deckchair. Giving it one last heave, it wasn't the elegant start she wanted but she adjusted her hat and unhooked her pink sarong from the back of her chair. Shuffling from her arthritis she walked towards the others before she was able to start moving with more ease.

Now everyone was watching the group, clapping, some jigging to the music and some singing along with the words of the popular songs. The dancers moved towards Tom who was leaning up against the Lido wall. Tanned, toned and wearing a green pair of trunks he had refused to wear anything glittery after the unicorn day but did agree to carrying an emerald green sarong. He was glad he had spent the winter in the gym pumping weights and he felt comfortable in his body but was really out of his depth with anything dance related. Poppy had once tried to show him how to twerk at a Christmas party and had given up declaring he was a 'Dad Dancer.' He'd nearly put his back out! Trying to look cool but failing, he fell in line next to Rachel hoping she would give him some confidence but really wishing it was over.

The expanding dancing group moved towards Bill and Tony who had decided that the only way they could take part was as a duo and this worked out well. They could stand near the entrance and not look out of place while chatting together. Bill had asked what he should do about their sarongs as it would look odd standing there holding them. Tony had suggested they could place them in their swimming trunks and pulling them out just as the dancers reached them before being told off by Angela who had pointed out there would be a very large bulge and what if pulling out the sarong allowed something else to escape and how they didn't want any nudity, before Diane had carried on the conversation saying they didn't want to attract the wrong type of people. Looking at the approaching dancers Bill was heard to say to Tony "Good grief, Pierre looks like a disco ball." Bill and Tony taking their role really seriously, carried on dancing past the main entrance with Harrison filming their every move. Not sure whether to smile and trying to concentrate, Bill remembered Summer's words "Block them from your mind. Walk with your head held high and just relax. Nobody wants to see you marching around!"

Stepping out of their cubicles Cindy and Michelle continued to wow the crowd. Wolf whistles and cheers were heard as they emerged. Cindy had gone all sexy 1950's with her pink hair styled into Victory Rolls to add a touch of glam. Her vintage floral swimsuit looked very sophisticated and matched her bright pink wedged sandals. Her well arched brows hardly moved as she winked at Michelle and they start to dance. Michelle complimented Cindy's look as her costume was white with a bright red cherry pattern and matching red flowers on her head. The two of them elegantly moved and joined the growing dance group.

Now they reached Poppy, who was dressed in a sequin covered jumpsuit she had worn previously at a festival, her long blond hair flowing down her back. Her silver and white sarong hung from her hand as she started to weave a tapestry of movement. She surprised Rachel, and everyone else, with a cluster of energetic and stylish shapes and moves, clapped, whooped and encouraged by Summer and Pierre, who'd obviously planned this.

Virtually everyone was up on their feet now, beaming smiles on their faces, cheering, clapping and waving. Rachel loved to see the effect that their dance was having on the visitors to Liberty's Lido. A thought went through her head that she wondered what her Grandmother Liberty would have made of all of this. Probably joined in she decided.

Alice and Flo joined the rest of the dancers and then moved onto Sally, who had wisely decided not to use her rollerblades on this occasion. The final dancers to join in were Heather, Julie, Dawn, Steph, Linda, Mary and Sandra. They had been patiently waiting on the white concrete steps in the quieter part of the Lido. They joined in with enthusiasm as the music once again came back to 'Dancing Queen' and the whole entourage arrived back at the start, after having danced an entire circuit of the Lido. They now all did the same routine, the music reaching a crescendo and the dance its climax.

The crowd cleared a space for them to finish and as the music ended the dancers sank to the floor to signal the end. They stayed like that for a few seconds and then there was a huge cheer from the audience, lots of clapping, shouting, whistling and it was all over. Rachel looked around her. They had done it. The assembled assorted group of mostly middle age and retired swimmers had done it. A Flashmob. Who would have believed it? Everyone was hugging everyone else. Some were crying. Someone later described it as a feast for the senses, a painting that had come to life.

The Lido was buzzing like a beehive with excitement and the dancers gathered together for an excited group hug before pulling apart and shouting "We did it."

"Oh my God. That was so much fun. I feel I could do it all again". They strutted around the Lido like peacocks, having had their ten minutes of fame.

Rachel hugged Tom "Wow that was amazing. You were so good Tom. Gosh I need a drink. I feel so alive." She talked faster and faster before releasing Tom and hugging someone else. She was almost delirious. Rachel looked up to see Summer hugging her brother James before he and Harrison disappeared into the crowd.

The rest of the day was spent at the Lido, enjoying the comments from the spectators, congratulating each other, soaking up the atmosphere and generally, Rachel thought, it had been one of the best days of her life. Several of the swimmers retired to the Ship and Rachel and Tom had no hesitation in joining them where they endlessly relived their exploits and when Dancing Queen had been on the jukebox for the umpteenth time that evening, Stan called time on the shenanigans. Liberty's Lido Ladies and Lads, feeling slightly the worse for wear, staggered home or arranged taxis.

Guest 1934

Jack Pender became a frequent guest at Nancarrow House during the mid thirties at the request of Frederick. As one of the managers there were often meetings at the House to which his attendance was required. Instructions were sent to Mrs Hitchens that there would be guests for dinner. Liberty had been introduced to the managers by her Father and Jack had been no exception. They pretended that they hadn't met before as Frederick introduced them to each other.

The morning after Jack's first invitation in 1934 Liberty asked her Father about him, saying that he looked familiar and she was sure she may have seen him at the Lido or around the Promenade. Frederick gave Liberty a brief description of Jack's background up at the mine, and how he'd been promoted over older and more experienced men but that he regarded him highly.

There were often lively discussions at the dining table and Liberty would contribute and participate in these discussions. Initially Frederick had been reticent to include Liberty but as she'd proved many years before she was more than able to hold her own in conversations about various matters. Jack didn't contribute much at his first couple of invitations but as he became more accustomed to being included, and his advice sought, he confidently discussed, argued and defended his corner, even against Liberty. Frederick had chuckled inwardly when Liberty and Jack had an animated discussion to the exclusion of the other guests at dinner. He had to declare a truce between them and decided that if it had been a boxing match and he'd been the referee then the result would have been a draw.

The following morning at breakfast Frederick asked Liberty her opinion of Jack Pender.

"I think you've got a good manager Father. He seems to know his mind, despite his humble beginnings and argues his point well even though I don't always agree with him."

"I'd noticed." He smiled.

Flat

Life felt a bit flat the day after the Flashmob, the Bank Holiday Monday. Rachel had the hangover from hell. She was tired, her feet hurt and it was all a bit of an anti-climax after the day before. Tom had annoyingly declared himself fine after a huge fry up, bacon, sausage, eggs, beans, loads of toast and copious mugs of coffee. The smell of it alone was enough to make Rachel urge and she went outside to get away from the malodorous pong but the sunshine was too bright and she slunk off back to bed with a pint of water and a couple of paracetamol. By midday, after a sleep, Rachel felt a bit more human and with tea, toast and some more water inside her she was more of less ok. She checked her social media which was full of comments about the Flashmob yesterday. She still had to pinch herself that they had actually managed to do it. There were a few videos that had been posted by locals of the dance but as she scrolled down through the mostly great comments, she was saddened to see that the Facebook trolls had criticised them saying that they were all crap granny dancers and words to that effect. It certainly took the gloss off the fun they had all had yesterday and suddenly her hangover came back.

"Have you seen the email from Summer? Tom asked.

Rachel flicked to her email app and saw that Summer had invited everyone to the Ship Inn at seven thirty that evening to watch the little film. James and Harrison had speedily put it together as they had been concerned that others would post parts of it on social media and detract from their own impact. The pub had a huge screen in a back room that was used for showing sporting events. Rachel replied to Summer that she and Tom would be there but then she sat there and felt a bit apprehensive about it.

"C'mon let's go and have a quiet afternoon away from the crowds." Tom suggested having packed their swimming bags. Go and jump in the shower and I'll pull a salad together that we can take with us."

"Ok thanks. There's half a cold chicken in the fridge that we can take. I need a swim but can't face the Lido today."

"Me too. That's what I thought."

Rachel and Tom spent a gentle afternoon ten miles up the coast, the cold water instantly washing away the remnants of last night's alcohol. Rachel found she was hungry after her swim and tucked in ravenously to her meal.

“That feels better.” Tom said after finishing his food.

“You’ve already had a huge breakfast.”

“I know. But I needed that swim and then something healthy to eat.”

They relaxed in the warm sun and chatted amiably, enjoying the peace and quiet of the small cove.

Premiere

Rachel and Tom gathered, along with the others, in the back room of the Ship later that day just before seven thirty, having showered and changed once back home. James and Harrison were at the back of the room, along with Stan, having sorted out the lighting and sound previously. Summer, Pierre and Poppy were sat together, as were Alice and Angela, as usual. Rachel noticed that Millicent, Nigel and other members of the Lido committee were sat in a small group too. Even Doris!

Rachel took a seat next to Flo and when Tom arrived with a large sparkling water for her, she whispered "I should have had a large G&T. I'm not sure I'm ready for this."

"You'll be fine." he replied giving her shoulder a squeeze. He took his pint and stood at the back of the room along with Bill, Tony and Douggie.

Stan stood at the front just after seven thirty and the room went quiet. "Everyone here?" he asked.

There was general assent. The room went dark and the screen came to life to murmurs from the assembled group. For a couple of seconds there was a blank white screen and then there was some gentle music, Fleetwood Mac's "Albatross." Tom told Rachel later, as the camera panned around in the distance, the azure blue sky, the shimmering sea, and it followed the flight of a lone seagull as it flew over the empty Lido. The camera captured the contrast of the white seagull and the white walls of the Lido and their reflections onto the sapphire coloured, mirror like surface of the water inside it. The film moved then went to an image of the painted white metal gates with its name plate "Liberty's Lido." and the blue sky through the gate posts. The music then changed to a popular tune from the 1930s and the still photo of the white gates went to black and white. There were images of King George, the Queen, Princess Mary and various local dignitaries of the day. There was actually old movie footage of the King declaring Liberty's Lido open. And, Rachel was pleased to see, pictures of her Grandmother Liberty with the Royals and then moving film of her diving into the water on the opening day nearly one hundred years ago. The music then changed again through the forties, fifties and so on with a few photos of people enjoying the Lido through each decade and a tune from that time too up until the present day. Black and white stills moving to colour as time progressed, hairstyles and clothing changing through the years.

The music then stopped for two seconds and in the pause there was a photo of the sign announcing the date of the closure of the Lido.

Important Notice.

Unfortunately, due to the lack of funding the Lido will close permanently on 30th September 2019.!!!!!!!!!!!!!!!!!!!!

The audience booed.

The music started again, excerpts of Pink Floyd's Money and Abba's Money Money Money, accompanied by photos of the Cake Sale, the Auction of Promises, Unicorn Day and so on with a running target of money raised, still showing a substantial shortfall. And then Madonna's Vogue started to play, to cheers from the Ship's audience. Rachel's heart was in her mouth. The film then zoomed in on Pierre and Summer starting their complex routine, with shots of surprised looks on visitors faces. Rachel cringed as she watched herself dancing as she joined the dynamic duo. The audience sang, clapped and cheered in the room in the Ship as the film worked its way around the Lido and the other dancers joined in, the music and video interspersed with shots of the smiling faces of the watchers of the dance. The music and dancing on screen finished to whoops, shouts and cheers and then "Again. Again." And "Encore."

James reran the film and everyone clapped and cheered again and then ran it one more time.

Rachel didn't know what possessed her but she suddenly stood up and made her way to the front of the room. "Thank you to James and Harrison for making such a great movie. Thanks boys. It's an amazing tribute to the past, the present and hopefully the future of Liberty's Lido. My Granny, Liberty, would have been so proud of what you've done."

The room went wild as the throng clapped and cheered the two lads. They accepted the thanks humbly and embarrassedly.

Rachel continued. "Thanks also to Summer and Pierre for the choreography and for their incredible patience in getting us all to be able to dance."

Everyone clapped and cheered again as Pierre did an elaborate bow, always the showman. Summer accepted the plaudits nonchalantly but secretly she was pleased.

"And thanks to all of you for taking part and also coming tonight. Now to the important part." Rachel continued seriously. "James will upload the video to the Lido Facebook, Twitter and Instagram feeds, as well as to You Tube so we need you to like it and share it to everyone you know. It will have a link to our fund raising page, how to donate, Gift Aid and so on. This was an amazing day and an amazing film but if the Lido closes on 30th September then it will all be a waste of time. Together we can all do this." She went red, and sat down to a standing ovation and huge applause.

Later when most of the others had left, James and Harrison were tidying up their kit, and Summer, Pierre and Poppy were chatting quietly Tom approached Rachel and she gratefully accepted the large G&T he offered her.

"Thanks. I needed that."

"Thought you might. You were great. Great dancer too!"

"Shut up." She said, playfully slapping his arm.

Proposal 1935

A few days later when Jack called at the house to see Frederick, he'd been delayed so Liberty invited Jack into the drawing room and they sat chatting, while Dorothy brought coffee, until Frederick arrived. Frederick saw as he entered the room that the two of them were getting on well. He'd noticed that Liberty often hadn't got on well with other young and eligible men when they'd come to the house or out socially but with this young man it was different. She seemed to chat in a relaxed manner and she looked alive when she talked to him. He'd noticed this first when the two of them had argued over dinner.

He had to examine his conscience. This boy was from a working class background yet he, Frederick, had grown to like and respect Jack. He wasn't just a good worker; he was a good manager too but would he make a good husband for Liberty? Husband? What on earth was he thinking? They hadn't been courting but he could see that Liberty seemed happy. He wished he could have talked to Nancy about affairs of the heart. Jack seemed honest but would he make Liberty happy? The men that Frederick had thought would be eligible had been sent away hastily by Liberty but there was something about Jack Pender that was different.

Jack also had to examine his conscience. He loved Liberty, and he was sure she loved him too, but what would Frederick say? What would his boss do? If he played his cards wrongly then he would not only lose Liberty but his job and his home too. His Mother and siblings still relied on him. He had an internal discussion in his mind as to how to proceed. He really didn't know what to do.

Liberty too was in turmoil. She loved Jack. She'd always loved Jack, since he'd rescued her from the sea all those years ago and she wanted to marry him but would her Father approve? She doubted it. Although Frederick liked and respected Jack, that was as an employee, a big difference to being a son in law and possible future father to Frederick's grandchildren.

In the end, the matter was taken out of all of their hands when, early in 1935, Frederick was approached by a recently widowed rotund, balding, middle aged landowner and businessman Donald Brown, who had made his money in the brewing industry. He needed a new wife to look after his brood of four children since his wife had died. Frederick had met him a few times at business meetings and they'd chatted amiably enough over the years. Frederick received a phone call from Brown who said simply that he'd like to meet Frederick as he had a proposal for him which he, Donald, thought may be mutually beneficial.

Frederick invited him in on a wet and windy February afternoon, taking his wet coat and hat and given him a whisky, offering his condolences on the demise of his late wife. Brown got straight to the point. "I'd like to ask for your daughter's hand in marriage."

Frederick spluttered into his drink in shock. He hadn't expected this. "But..." he started.

"It makes perfect sense to me." Brown continued. "My children need a mother to care for them and your daughter comes from good stock obviously......."

Frederick interrupted him, making up his mind quickly. This fellow was talking about his daughter as if she was a prize exhibit in an agricultural show, he didn't love her, or care for her. The man was also middle aged, only a couple of years younger than Frederick himself. "Unfortunately, my daughter is already betrothed to another gentleman. She is in love with him, and he with her, and they already have my blessing, so you see....."

Brown apologised profusely, went puce and emptied his glass in a rush. "I'm sorry, I appear to have made an ass of myself. Of course, I understand completely I just thought...."

He left the house quickly, grabbed his still dripping coat and hat from the stand, tripped over his feet as he exited in haste and ended up sitting on the moist step. He stood up rapidly as his backside was now soaking wet. It was a comical sight and Frederick roared with laughter at the man's obvious discomfort and soaked demeanour, from his warm and dry vantage point inside his home, as Brown jumped into his car and sped off.

Liberty heard her Father laughing and entered the drawing room. "What are you so happy about?"

"That man asked for your hand in marriage and I sent him packing."

"Without consulting me?" Liberty looked at her Father sternly.

"It's Donald Brown, he's been here a few times for meetings and for dinner. He wanted you to be the mother of his four children as his first wife has recently died and he was describing you as if you were breeding stock. He doesn't know you, or care about you, or even love you. He was sincere in his desire to marry you, but as a business transaction."

"I know him. Ugh he's revolting. He's old...... and he's fat!"

"So am I." Frederick said, patting his stomach.

"Yes, but you're not revolting." she smiled at her Father, not denying the fact that he was old OR fat. "What did you say to him?"

"I told him you were betrothed to another man who loved you, and you loved him and I'd given my blessing."

"And did you have 'another man who loves me' in mind? One that I love too?" she looked coquettish.

"Yes." Frederick looked at Liberty sheepishly. "I think that your young man, Jack Pender, should come and ask me an important question. Don't you?"

"Oh Father. Thank you." Her face lit up with a beaming smile and then she burst into tears and she hugged him so tight he thought his neck would break.

Happening

Rachel slept better that night and woke refreshed and ready for the day. She scanned her social media accounts on her phone eagerly in the morning and saw that many of the dancers had already shared the video, tagging others in it, some of them retweeting it on their Twitter account. James and Harrison had uploaded a shortened version of the video, with mostly just the Flashmob part but it still gave a powerful message about acting now or losing it forever, with a link to the fund raising page, and another link to watch the full video on YouTube. It was still so strange to see herself dancing on the film. Even Trelyn RNLI had shared it on their feed.

Tom was off to work while Rachel was going to meet some of the Ls down at the Lido. Poppy was still in bed when Rachel left the house. The weather was dull with a slight wind as she got out of her car and made her way across the road to the Lido but at least it was dry even though the visibility wasn't fantastic.

"Not feeling the love today." She said to Alice as they put their colourful towelling robes over their swimming costumes and walked together with a few of the others.

Tony overheard her. "You'll be alright once you're in."

Alice agreed with him. She nudged Rachel as they noticed a group of Japanese tourists looking oddly at the assorted towelling dressed group. "We must look like a group of aliens or something." She laughed.

Rachel smiled at the tourists as they walked past, some smiled back. There about ten or twelve swimmers disrobing as Alice, Tony and Rachel rounded the corner of the outside wall of the Lido and joined the others.

Flo pointed out a seal's black shiny head in the distance as the group started to undress. "I hope it doesn't come too close. They scare me. Those teeth!" The seal looked at them curiously but decided not to play today and swam further out to sea. Rachel was relieved. She loved the seals but not when they were circling underneath her like a silent submarine, bumping her feet, popping up suddenly and making her jump.

The waves gently sloshed into Golden Rocks creating a slight swell as they ebbed and flowed. A couple of cormorants sat on top of some rocks and watched as the Ls queued in a line to get into the water, many of them faffing as usual before they took the inevitable plunge into the cool sea. After the first couple of minutes Rachel relaxed in the water and felt the muscles in her stomach and neck unwind. She lay on her back and looked up to the grey overcast skies above, taking a deep breath. That felt better. She swam with Cindy and then they chatted as they bobbed in the waves before exiting the water, quickly drying themselves and making their way back into the Lido.

Douggie was talking to some customers but he made his excuses and came over to see Rachel. He wanted to discuss the Flashmob and the video. He'd obviously enjoyed being part of the group, and as part of the Trustee committee, as well as an employee of the Lido he wanted it to succeed.

Rachel heard her name being called and turned to see Pierre making his way towards Douggie and herself. The three of them discussed the day of the Flashmob, the showing of the video in the Ship last night, and the sharing of the film on social media.

"We'll just have to wait and see now." Rachel finished the conversation, excusing herself to go and get dry and warm. "I'll be up for a coffee and some cake shortly Pierre."

She checked her phone once she was dressed and saw a text from Poppy saying she was on her way down. "I'll meet you in the café." She texted back. "Pierre has made your favourite cake. I'll get you a piece." She got a thumbs up in reply.

Poppy breezed into the café. "Have you seen this?" she asked without preamble, tucking into a huge chunk of red velvet cake with her fork, sliding her phone across to Rachel.

"Hi Mum. Are you ok? Yes thanks. I am, loving daughter and thanks for asking. Thanks for the cake Mum. You're welcome Poppy. Hope you enjoy it."

"Whatever!" Poppy rolled her eyes. "Are you gonna look or what?"

Rachel sighed and took Poppy's phone. It was the YouTube video of the Flashmob. "So? What is it I'm looking at?

"The views." Poppy said in an exasperated tone through a mouthful of cake, rolling her eyes and gesturing with her fork. "Obviously."

Rachel hadn't looked there before but saw that the video had five thousand views.

“That’s good. Shows that people are looking at it. Just need them to put their hands in their pockets now. Thanks Pops.”

“Thought you’d be pleased.” Poppy said smiling, finishing the last morsel of cake and standing up. “I’ll see you later. God that cake was sooo good.”

“Did it even touch the sides Poppy?”

Marriage 1935

In September 1935 Liberty became Mrs Pender in a quiet ceremony. The two of them moved into Nancarrow House and in August 1936 she presented Jack with a beautiful baby daughter and Frederick with his first Grandchild. She named the baby Henrietta. It was the happiest time of Liberty's life.

Publicity

Rachel's phone pinged with a message from James to say that the Cornishman newspaper had contacted him as they'd seen the video and wanted to meet her, himself and some of the other dancers down at the Lido, to discuss the Flashmob and the fundraising efforts. She rang them and arranged a date and time, quickly clearing it with Douggie, as the manager, and some of the Committee members first.

Three days later the paper came out with a great photo of the Flashmob on the front page together with the headline "Save Liberty's Lido." On page three there was a photo of "spokesperson" Rachel together with a few lines that she had said about raising the profile of the Lido, raising money to keep it open for current and future generations. Rachel thought she looked awful. Tom reassured her that she didn't. There were photos of Summer and Pierre together, looking photogenic and fabulous as always, with quotes from them too. James had got in on the act, lending his support and lots of his photos of the dancers and spectators were at the bottom of the page. There was also a photo and message of support from a TV chef, Peter Donnelly. Originally from London, he'd come down for a surfing holiday with a couple of mates and their girlfriends to spend a week in three camper vans overlooking the beach at Whitesands, the scene of a summer surfing festival back in the nineties. They'd gone swimming in the iconic Lido one day when there was no surf and he'd remembered the pool from those days. His girlfriend had become his wife and he opened a string of boutique restaurants across the country, all bearing his name, one of which was just a few miles from Porthlowen, up on the North Coast of Cornwall. Rachel and Tom had taken Poppy there for her eighteenth birthday. Rachel was glad that he'd lent his support to their campaign but they were still woefully short of their target of £400,000.

A week went by and each time that Rachel went onto Facebook she could see that there were more and more likes for the Flashmob video, on both the Lido's official page and also the shortened version that James and Harrison had made. Both the Lido's and her own Instagram account was much the same, more and more people were following the posts.

She noticed that the Lido was now being followed on Instagram by a local Olympic Gold medallist from the 2012 Games in London. She had been at school with Summer's younger sister, Saffron, and they'd remained friends. There was a gold post box stationed just around the corner from the Lido in honour and recognition of the achievement of Sarah Miller who had won the

800 metres swimming title in an Olympic record and then followed it up with a couple of world titles and retained her Olympic title four years later in Rio. Since then she'd married a famous TV personality and retired from swimming competitively to start raising their family. She'd actually learned to swim in the Lido and so made an impassioned plea for support amongst her followers that by keeping the Lido open may uncover a future Olympian from Porthlowen. Her husband, Chris Cousins, had actually got even more followers on Instagram than Sarah and he had also posted about the Lido on his account. He knew a couple of local actors who were now working in America, one had been in a Hollywood movie alongside Tom Cruise. The actors too had used the Lido when they'd been children and young adults before their big break had taken them away from the town.

Another weekend came and went. It was the first week of September and the kids went back to school on Tuesday 5th. Poppy was due to go back to Uni in another week and Tom would drive her back as there was a Trustees meeting that evening when the main item on the agenda was the closure of the Lido on 30th September and the discussion about the finances was worrying Rachel. Was all the fundraising that they'd worked so hard to achieve going to go to waste?

During the following Monday night Rachel hadn't slept well at all, worrying about what she would say at the meeting as well as thinking that Poppy would have forgotten something. She guessed the other committee members would be feeling downbeat too. Tom, as usual gave her encouragement, said she'd done her best, kissed the top of her head and went to start his breakfast, after consoling her with a steaming mug of coffee.

Poppy was disorganised, as usual. "Mum have you got....? Do you know where .... is?"

Rachel drained her cup and helped Poppy and Tom to finally get out of the door, an hour after they should have gone.

She sat in bed looking at her social media. The weather was awful that day. High winds, high tides and heavy rain. She looked at the Lido website saying that it was going to shut the pool today although the café would remain open. She looked out of the window and decided that she'd stick around at home doing household chores, cleaning, batch cooking and sorting out odds and sods that had been pushed to the back of the queue over the sunny summer days. She ramped the radio up, started emptying the fridge then prepping and concocting delicious dishes. She was absorbed in what she was doing she didn't register her phone ringing initially. She yelled at Alexa to stop and took her phone into the lounge. The display said No Caller ID. Probably her Mum, who had steadfastly refused to change this facility on her own phone despite the many times that Tom, Rachel and Poppy had tried to explain that they wouldn't answer as it could be a scam. Rachel had only answered it this morning as her Dad had been a bit under the weather recently.

"Hello."

"Is that Rachel Roberts?" an unfamiliar man's voice asked.

"Yes. Who is this?" Rachel said warily, suspecting a scam call, or someone trying to sell her insurance or double glazing.

"This is Martin Jones. I'm the producer of West Country news. Hello. Are you there?"

Rachel had gone silent momentarily. "Yes. I'm here. Sorry."

That's alright." Martin said soothingly. "We've seen the video about Liberty's Lido on social media and wanted to come down to the Lido to do a piece about the pool, the fundraising, meet some of the dancers and so on. I'm guessing you're the right person to talk to about this?"

"Yes. I suppose I am." She said, finding her voice. "When were you thinking of coming down?"

"Friday morning if that's ok? The weather forecast looks alright for filming. We'll send a reporter, a camera man and a sound engineer. We'll do a few interviews, including with you, and we'll want to meet some of the dancers too so we can get some shots of them. Ten o'clock alright? "

"Yes, of course."

"Can I have your email address and I'll send details over to you, contact numbers and so on."

"Sure." She gave him the information. "Thanks. See you then." She put the phone down, her hand shaking and sat for five minutes gathering her thoughts. She wouldn't ring Tom and Poppy just yet. She checked on the oven and washing. All in hand. She quickly made a list of people to phone and started working her way through them. Bill, Douggie, Millicent, Nigel Merlo-Banks, Summer, James and Pierre. They were all enthusiastic about the visit of the TV company and they agreed to discuss this in more detail at the Trustee meeting that evening. Rachel had already cleared with the committee members that Summer, James and Pierre could attend. Douggie, Millicent and Nigel readily agreed but Bill, as usual, had something to say about it being "highly irregular." She'd left him until last, even though he was the chair of the Trustees, knowing what he'd be like.

"It is a highly irregular situation Bill." She shut his protests down, agreeing with him. "But this could give us great publicity and maybe stop the Lido closing. We've only got just over two weeks to get the rest of the money in. We need all the help we can get. That Flashmob with those three's help has really got people talking about the Lido. They're young, dynamic and energetic. They are the real future of the Lido, not you, not me. They'll be the ones bringing their children and grandchildren here long after we've gone."

"I see your point." He conceded.

The committee meeting that evening was short and to the point. Bill opened the meeting, welcomed the newbies and quickly referred to the treasurer, Millicent, who announced that the turnover of the Lido had increased and this had been as a direct result of the measures put in place by Rachel, Douggie and Pierre previously. She pushed around printouts of the figures, reminding Pierre, Summer and James that this information was strictly confidential. She started to go through and explain the figures. The pool itself was open longer than in previous summers which had given early morning and evening swimmers a place to swim when tides and sea conditions weren't viable. These same people also used the café more as it was open longer hours. Although it had been stressful organising more shifts for café staff and life guards the result was putting money into the Lido's coffers. Walkers, tourists and workers had been using the café for breakfasts, lunches and evening meals as well as for drinks, ice cream and cake.

With Rachel and the others reaching out to the tourist business sector there was more awareness of the Lido with posters and leaflets now adorning guest house, hotel, B&B and campsite windows, walls and desks. The leaflets offered two for one deals, weekly season tickets, free coffee or tea or ice cream and so on. Douggie and Pierre agreed that all of these had increased foot flow into both the Lido and the café. Entrance numbers were up and these people were then spending money in the café. The average sale value had also increased. So, in short, more people all spending more money had had a positive effect on the profitability of the Lido.

Both Douggie and Pierre had deputy and shift managers for their respective areas of responsibility and this had eased their load a bit, allowing them to manage more. Increased turnover had also increased costs, especially staffing but Millicent was confident that with careful management and the new more effective use of the Lido and its facilities it would create a sustainable business model beyond the 30th September. The colder, darker winter months would create additional challenges but the Lido had events planned, the meeting room would be used for local groups and the café would work in conjunction with the events and the groups.

However, although the crowd funding was working, was clearly having some effect and the fact that the donations had been steadily rising, they were still nearly two hundred thousand short of the target with just eighteen days left. Millicent paused to allow the figures to sink in.

"We're not dead yet!" Quipped Nigel bringing the Monty Python quote to Rachel's mind.

She smiled "Absolutely."

Bill invited her to speak. "Thanks Bill." she said getting to her feet. She gave a quick outline of how the social media campaign was gaining momentum with some celebrities now following them, and publicising the plight of the Lido. Bill and Millicent looked a bit blank so James gave them a quick layman's explanation of how social media worked. They still looked a bit vague but realised the essence of what he was saying, the fact that more and more people knew about the fundraising problems with the Lido.

She then gave a quick outline that West Country TV were coming down to interview her and some of the others. "Let's hope this further spreads the word." She finished and sat down.

Wartime 1939

In 1939 Hitler invaded Poland and Britain declared war on Germany. Jack immediately volunteered to join up, along with most of the town, including his brothers. Jack was killed on the beaches at Dunkirk in 1940 when Liberty was just twenty six. She was heartbroken and never married again. It was the worst time in Liberty's life.

Filming

Luckily Friday was bright and sunny, little wind and it looked like it would be ideal for filming. Rachel felt too sick to eat breakfast and couldn't settle to anything. Her swimming bag was packed very early and she was down outside the Lido gates well before it opened. Douggie saw her waiting outside and quietly let her into a side entrance. She took a phone call from an unknown mobile number. It was Jessica Higgins, a name that Rachel recognised, from West Country TV. "We're just about to arrive. Can you let us in please?"

A van pulled up outside the Lido, Rachel introduced Douggie to Jessica, who introduced the two Lukes, the cameraman and sound guy; and herself as Jess. They all helped load the gear into the side door of the Lido and one of the Lukes went to park while the other four carried the gear into the café. Pierre quickly organised coffee for all of them, putting it through as expenses while Jess outlined her plan. "Ignore us. We'll just set up, walk around, taking some views, sampling the atmosphere and we'll talk to a few people. It'll be on the local lunchtime and evening news later today."

Douggie excused himself to go and supervise opening up. James, Harrison, Summer and Poppy arrived together. Rachel swore that Poppy fancied Summer's brother James. She could do worse Rachel thought. He seemed a nice guy, friendly, smiley and quite good looking. Jess and the Lukes started sorting their stuff while Rachel went over to the cubicles to dump her swimming bag and wait for the Ls. Most of them usually arrived around ten thirty for an eleven o'clock dip. She noticed that one of her initiatives had paid off, a poster on the back wall of her changing cubicle was advertising a local campsite. The campsite had paid £100 for the privilege and that was £100 closer to the £400,000 target. But they were still only half way there. She sat in the quiet fresh morning sunshine thinking about it.

"Penny for your thoughts." Bill arrived, prompt as always.

"Just thinking about how much we've still got to raise."

"I know. We've done well but still got a long way to go."

"Let's see how much response we get from the TV people being here today."

"Where are they?"

"In the café setting up. They'll walk around later, probably get us all jumping in or something. "

Flo arrived with Angela, then Tony and then Steph. The others arrived in dribs and drabs. Jess sauntered over and talked to the group. "OK we want you all to jump in together from the far wall." She pointed.

"But we always get in here." Angela interrupted, pointing to a point just below the cubicles.

"It's the best angle for the camera with the sun's position." explained Jess smiling. "It also gives us a better view of the whole Lido. But you get in wherever you like. We'll be over there with the rest of your group."

Angela looked sheepish.

"Then we'll talk to a few of you." Jess continued in her professional manner. Rachel noticed that the two Lukes were talking intently to James, Harrison and Summer. Poppy was loitering in the background, listening intently. "So, if you'd all like to make your way over there and we'll be ready to go in about ten minutes. I'll do my introductory piece then the camera will swing over to you guys who will be standing on the edge ready to jump in. I'll count 3 2 1 Go and you all in jump in on 'Go.' When you've finished swimming come back out this way and I'll talk to you. Alright? Any questions?"

"Yes. I can't jump in." said Diane, walking stick in hand.

"That's all right lovely. You can go in down the steps just beforehand and be in the water near to where everyone jumps in. Is that ok?"

"Yes. Thank you."

The swimmers went to their individual cubicles, emerged in their bright swimming costumes, with their colourful swim hats and goggles on their heads and made their way slowly over to the start point. There were about fifteen of them today.

Jess was over there already with the Lukes, microphone in hand. The group stood nervously on the edge, listening to Jess go into professional mode.

"I'm here today at the famous Liberty's Lido in Porthlowen. It was opened in 1931 by King George V and has been an iconic landmark on the Cornish coast for nearly one hundred years. Will it be here in another one hundred years?

Only time will tell but there is an important deadline hanging over this beautiful Art Deco building. Unless £400,000 can be raised by the end of this month then the pool will shut, the developers will move in and a piece of local history will be lost for ever. Don't forget that this is the place where Olympic champion swimmer Sarah Miller learned to swim and maybe by keeping this place open we can unearth another swimming superstar. The very first person to swim in the Lido in 1931 was Miss Liberty Nancarrow, and it was her that the Lido was named after. Behind me are a group of swimmers that meet here every day throughout the year, come rain or shine. They're called the Liberty's Lido Ladies and Lads or the Ls for short. One of them is Rachel Roberts and she is the granddaughter of Liberty Nancarrow and the chief fundraiser on the Trustee Committee of the Lido. We'll be talking to her in a little while. Many of our viewers will be aware of the Flashmob that's been circulating on social media over the past few days and we'll be talking to some of the swimmers and dancers that participated recently too. But firstly" She turned to the swimmers. "3 2 1 Go!"

The Ls jumped in with a huge splash and there was the usual shrieking as their warm bodies hit the cold water. They swam around for a few minutes, Rachel dreading having to talk while she was wet and being on TV in her swimming costume. One or two of them got out and Jess spoke to them, while the Lukes hovered with their camera and microphone. Angela was the first one out and Rachel could see her animatedly talking and pointing to things around the pool.

Reluctantly Rachel swam over and exited the pool. Jess thrust a microphone towards her. "Here we have Rachel Roberts who is the granddaughter of the Liberty that the Lido is named after. Rachel. How do you feel about the Lido shutting? Do you think that it is a fitting tribute to your Grandmother Liberty?"

"We're not shut yet. Rachel replied firmly. "My grandmother may have been the first swimmer but I certainly don't intend to be one of the last. I learnt to swim here as did my daughter, and I hope that my grandchildren and their children will also be able to enjoy this wonderful place. Lots of local children have learned to swim here too as well as tourists on holiday. Families have been enjoying this place for decades and will continue to do so. There really is nothing like it in Cornwall and providing we can raise the rest of the money it will continue being a legacy to my grandmother Liberty for future generations."

"Thank you, Rachel." Jess turned to face the camera again. "In these days of increased awareness of mental health issues and the reported benefits of cold water swimming for physical and mental health it is vital that the pool remains open for everyone forever. If you want to donate to the Lido's fundraising cause then please follow the link at the bottom of your screen now."

This is Jessica Higgins for West Country Live at Liberty's Lido, Porthlowen."

Death 1962

In 1962 Major Sir Frederick Nancarrow died after a short illness. He was seventy seven. A popular man, honoured by the town and remembered fondly by his only daughter, Liberty Pender.

Aftermath

"Well done Rach. You were brilliant." Tom said later as he watched it on TV later. "You really got your message across. I thought Pierre and Summer did well too."

"Thanks. Yes, those two did well." Rachel said, embarrassed

Tom agreed. "You all did your bit. You've done your best. I think that Jess and her boys did a good report and the fact that it had the fundraising link across the bottom of the screen throughout the piece should help too. It was great that they managed to get hold of Sarah Miller and Chris Cousins too and they also said the right things. I bet the only person who didn't like the report was Angela."

Rachel laughed. "Yes, she won't be happy she wasn't in the limelight."

"You definitely said the right things. Liberty would have been proud of you. And we're all proud of you too. Even Poppy!"

Rachel's phone rang. No caller ID again. She left it and it went to message. She listened to the message. "It's Mum." She rolled her eyes. Probably her moaning about Dad eating biscuits again." Poppy's eighty eight year old Grandad was always hungry but he wasn't well and he was very old and if he ate biscuits, so what? Did it really matter?

"Hello Mum." Rachel rang back. "Yes, we've just watched it too. What did you think?" She listened for a bit, nodding and adding "uh huh. If he wants to eat biscuits Mum then just let him. Bye." She hung up.

"Mum and Dad have just watched West Country news and saw the bit about the Lido. She thought I came across quite well but then went on to say that, of course, my public speaking manner had been inherited from her."

"Of course." Agreed Tom. "And I take it your Dad has now bought shares in McVities!"

"Other biscuits are available. Don't forget, Tom." She laughed.

At swimming the following day. Rachel was inundated with comments about seeing her on the TV. Most of the group were pleased with the coverage, Tony asked for her autograph and Angela ignored her. She saw Pierre in the café after her swim and he gave her a big hug. "You were wonderful Rachel."

"You were too, you and Summer." Her phone rang. "Hi Millicent. Yes, thank you. I guess this is what it's like to be famous."

Millicent had complimented her on the TV performance. "I was just ringing to say that the article on the news last night has resulted in an increase in the Lido pot. We've had over fifty thousand pounds donated since lunchtime yesterday when it first went on TV. That's extraordinary."

"Wow." Was all Rachel could manage. "I'll tell the others. Thanks Millicent."

'You won't believe this" beamed Rachel before continuing "Our fund has increased by just over fifty thousand pounds since yesterday's News report".

"No way" Pierre grinned, "Fifty thousand pounds? That's incredible. Fifty thousand pounds." he kept repeating it as he tried to digest the information.

"I'm going to put a post on our group chat to let everyone know" Rachel exclaimed to Pierre as she found her phone at the bottom of her bag. "I feel like we're finally getting our message across. If people see that others are backing the Lido, I'm hoping it will give others the confidence to donate and support us."

Looking on Facebook back at home later Rachel could see that Cornwall Live had picked up on the story and were showing the Flashmob video. Astonished she saw there were twelve hundred likes and it had four hundred and fifty comments, starting to read some she was encouraged when people had left comments of encouragement, some said they had donated and there were a few very upsetting comments from some who said it was a drain on already stretched resources and the money would be better being spent on keeping toilets open or having more police officers on the beat.

Tom, walking into the kitchen could see that Rachel was upset and looking over her shoulder read some of the comments himself. "Rach. Ignore them. There will always be haters. Look at all the good comments. The fact that we have raised fifty thousand pounds in twenty four hours is awesome."

Tom's last few words were hardly heard by Rachel as her phone started ringing. She answered absent mindedly, not really looking at the display.

"Hello can I speak to Rachel Roberts please." the voice said.

"Hello. Yes. This is Rachel."

The voice continued "Hi this is Jade Smythe. I'm one of the producers on 'This Morning TV.' We have seen your Flashmob video on Twitter and YouTube, as well as the local West Country article and we'd like to invite some of you into the studio next Friday if that's ok?" Rachel quickly put her phone on speaker phone so Tom could also hear and he quickly walked back towards Rachel and listened as Jade continued.

"We are really interested in your cause as we have been covering Mental Health Week and the fact that cold water swimming is helping people with anxiety and how being part of a social group helps to combat loneliness we really resonated with your story and how the whole community are coming together to help. Holly and Phillip will interview two or three of you and then we want all of you to do part of your Flashmob dance. So, what do you think?"

Rachel stunned into silence tried forming the words but nothing would come out.

"Hello are you still there?" Jade asked

"So sorry about that. I am totally flabbergasted and I was unable to think straight for a minute. We never expected to have so much media presence, which is a good thing, but your telephone call caught me unaware. What did you have in mind?"

"I totally understand." Jade continued "Shall I put it in an email so you can digest it all and if you have any questions then just give me a call. I will add my telephone number along with my assistant Scarlett's number too."

Hanging up Rachel looked at Tom slightly stunned before they were dancing for joy around the lounge then collapsing onto the sofa and hugging each other before Rachel shouted "We're going to be on TV. OMG what will I wear? I think I need my haircut." Rachel felt wonderfully alive. "Tom, I need to go shopping!"

"Aren't you forgetting something first." Tom exclaimed trying to get his wife to calm down and hear him. "We need to tell the others first"

"Oh yes." Rachel effused "So we do. Oh my god we're going to be on TV." She blew out a huge breath before writing a quick note on the group chat.

This Morning TV program requests the pleasure of The Lido Flashmob dancers on their program on Friday. More details to follow #werefamous #flashmob #thismorning

Birth 1966

In 1966 Liberty's first and only grandchild, Rachel was born, in the height of the Swinging Sixties and just a few days after England had lifted the Football World Cup. Liberty was fifty one by now and still a regular swimmer in the sea around the Lido in the summer and inside the Lido when the weather or tides were against her.

Train

"I still don't know why we have to catch such an early train." Cindy said sleepily at 5.55 on the Thursday morning. She took a sip from her takeaway coffee with two extra shots in it. "Maybe this'll wake me up a bit."

The plan was to get up to London for some sightseeing and shopping before taking in a show, Mamma Mia obviously, and then visiting the studios tomorrow morning before returning home straight after being on the TV. Poppy, Harrison and James had skived off from Uni for a couple of days to be involved.

Michelle, who was sat next to her, agreed but then pulled her coat over her head and told Cindy to wake her up when they reached Paddington, after telling her that she'd need to be up early again tomorrow morning to be on TV.

Tony was moaned at by the whole group when he opened a pack of homemade still warm egg sandwiches, took a huge bite and then announced he was looking forward to meeting Holly. "I really fancy her." he said.

"Don't think she's gonna fancy you Tony, stinking of bloody egg sandwiches for fuck's sake." Cindy groaned sticking her nose into her coffee cup hoping the strong coffee smell would obliterate the overwhelming pungent smell. The rest of the group laughed at Tony who looked offended but he carried on tucking into his breakfast. Cindy looked like she was going to be sick.

Rachel pitied the rest of the travellers in their carriage. She knew that the Ls could be loud and raucous when they got together. Loud conversations and laughter often accompanied the group, as did rude words. She wouldn't be surprised if someone fell out with someone else today. As with any group there were plenty of egos and personalities that sometimes clashed. Occasionally it was like herding cats. Despite the early hour and the pervading egg smell, when James and Harrison returned from the buffet car with bacon rolls for themselves, Summer, Pierre and Poppy, the delicious smell wafted towards Rachel and she couldn't resist. She made her way to the dining car and ordered some food and coffee. What was it about travelling early that made you want to stuff your face?

"God I'll probably eat my body weight in food by the time I get home tomorrow." She mentioned to Dawn who was sat next to her, passing her a bacon roll and cup of tea.

Dawn tucked in. “Never mind. You don’t do it every day.”

Rachel knew that before long Liz would be passing around huge slices of swimmers’ homemade cake. She’d already spied a big tin foil package in Liz’s bag.

Steph had made them all laugh by telling them about her ninety seven year old grandmother. “In the summer when it’s raining Grandma likes to go out into the garden and take all of her clothes off so that she can feel the rain on her bare skin. Luckily, she lives in the middle of nowhere. I asked her what does she do if the gardener is coming around and she replied ‘Oh it’s ok Stephanie I stand sideways so he can’t see the front.’ The group roared with laughter. Steph’s Grandma was certainly a character. She’d been in the WAF during the Second World War where she’d met her Wing Commander husband, Steph’s Grandad.

The journey passed uneventfully and the train arrived at Paddington with the swimmers all still talking to each other. Cindy, never an early morning person, was fully awake and charged after four cups of coffee and three visits to the loo. Michelle woke up after Cindy nudged her. Tony had consumed his egg sandwiches. Liz’s cake was all gone and Rachel was starting to feeling nervous about being the main spokesperson for the group and hoping she wouldn’t come across as an idiot on TV.

The motley crew assembled on the platform and Rachel took charge. She didn’t know why she did but someone needed to as otherwise they’d never all get to the hotel together. “Are we all here?” They had to get the Tube first, something she was a bit dubious about, not being particularly familiar with it. Luckily Harrison was at Uni up here so the group listened and then followed him. Finally, the group arrived at the hotel without anyone becoming detached from the group. After quickly booking in and dumping her overnight bag Rachel hooked up with a group of four others, Dawn, Steph, Mary and Julie. Poppy was going to go with the young ones, James, Harrison, Pierre and Summer. Some of the others were doing their own thing while Tony was heading over to the Natural History museum, not being a fan of shopping.

“Your mission, should you choose to accept it, is to shop till you drop girls.” laughed Julie.

“Mission accepted, destination Oxford Street.” grinned Dawn heading back towards the Tube station. The others followed. A few hours later, heavily laden with shopping bags the shoppers arrived back at the hotel. A quick change, and then into a restaurant across the road with the other swimmers and a trip up to the West End to watch Mamma Mia completed a fun day. Dancing in the aisles was compulsory!

Trustee 1981

In 1981 Liberty Pender became one of the founding members of the Lido Committee, along with Bill Chamberlain, Millicent Angove and four other local residents. There had been a threat of the Lido shutting because of the growth of leisure centres in Cornwall. It was in danger of becoming an expensive "white elephant" so Liberty had set up her own trust fund that would donate £20,000 a year ad infinitum.

Television

The following morning, footsore from all of the walking around the shops, bleary eyed from a combination of a late night at the theatre, lack of sleep in a strange bed and an early start the day before, Rachel stumbled downstairs to another early breakfast, this time in a hotel. Poppy and Summer had been sharing a room and followed her into the dining room. She joined them at their table until Poppy pulled a face and said they were saving a place for the boys. Rachel rolled her eyes and went to sit with Tony, Linda and Mary. She forced her breakfast down, feeling excited but nervous and a bit sick.

Cindy was the last down into the foyer of the hotel, moaning about yet another early start however looking TV ready, her bright pink hair caught up in a fishtail plait with tousled sections at the front, eliciting a catty comment from Angela. "I hope you haven't got that awful T shirt on today?"

"I was thinking of buying you a present from the same shop yesterday Angela?"

Everyone's bags packed and shopping bags full of the results of yesterday's trip to Oxford Street, apart from Tony. Taxis came to collect the group and take them the short distance to the ITV studios where they disembarked and went together into the impressive foyer. They were greeted by a stylish young woman called Scarlett and taken to a room where they were offered drinks and refreshments and divested themselves of their coats and bags. A bathroom was off to one side.

An attractive fashionable woman entered the room, tall with brown hair styled into a pony tail who Rachel thought was mid twenties. She was holding a clipboard and smiled at the group. "Good morning everyone. Welcome to ITV. I'm Jade Smythe and I'm one of the producers of "This Morning." In a few moments Scarlett will take you around and give you a short tour of the studios. Your slot will be at around eleven thirty and you'll meet Phillip and Holly quickly just before they go on air at ten o'clock. I'm looking for Rachel Roberts."

"That's me." Rachel half raised a hand. "Hi."

"Hello. We spoke on the phone" Jade said smiling at her. "We want you on the couch, then Phillip and Holly will talk to you and ask you some questions about the Lido, and the fundraising plight, the fact that you're Liberty's granddaughter and then introducing the Flashmob. Who did the arrangement and choreography for the dancing?"

"That was me and Pierre." answered Summer gesturing towards Pierre.

"What's your name?" asked Jade. Summer gave it to her.

"We'll get you to answer some questions on the couch too." Jade continued. "Now do we have the people who filmed the Flashmob and launched it onto social media?"

James raised his hand from the back of the room as did Harrison.

"Hi guys. We also want one of you to answer questions please."

Harrison indicated. "That'll be James. I just helped to film the dancing."

"Ok then James." Jade made a note on her clipboard. "So, Holly and Phillip will ask Rachel, Summer and James some questions while they'll be some photos shown and a little bit of the Flashmob too then we'll move the camera shot over to where the rest of you will dance and perform some of the Flashmob for about a minute. After Scarlett's tour you'll be brought back here so you can practice if you need to and change into your dancing clothes. OK. I'll see you later and Scarlett will answer any questions you have." She strode purposefully out of the room.

"I feel sick." Rachel said to Scarlett.

"You'll be fine. Holly and Phillip will make you feel at ease. Just be clear and concise and make sure you get your message across."

Rachel smiled weakly and disappeared to the toilets again. She didn't feel much better when she re-emerged. She felt jittery. She'd drunk too much coffee this morning. Her phone pinged. It was Tom wishing her good luck.

She quickly rang him. "Tom. I can't do this. I feel sick."

"You'll be great. Just be your fabulous self. I'll be watching and I've set up the TV to record it too."

"Thanks." She hung up feeling worse.

Her phone rang again. It was Millicent. "Good morning Rachel. Good luck. I was just letting you know that we've had another ten thousand pounds come in over the last couple of days so if they ask you a figure you can say that we've raised two hundred and seventy thousand pounds."

"Brilliant, that's great. Thanks for that Millicent."

Scarlett gathered the group together. "Ok keep close. Please leave your handbags and phones in here. The room will be locked until we get back. The group chattered excitedly but followed Scarlett down a vast long corridor. Rachel thought, not for the first time, that the Ls were like a group of school children let out for a day trip.

Scarlett stopped outside a door and told them all to be quiet. "Lorraine Kelly is on air in here. I'm just going to poke my head in to check and then we're going to go in and just stand quietly at the back. Just follow me in single file and one of the team inside will shut the door behind us. Please do not talk."

The dancers watched Lorraine in action for a few minutes until Scarlett then gestured to them to leave. Once the door was shut Scarlett took them down to another room. "This is the "Loose Women" Studio." She indicated. There were a few people milling about but none of the stars of the show. Finally, they got to the "This Morning" studio. It was a hive of activity as it was due to go on air in about twenty minutes. "Wait here a minute." Scarlett said and disappeared, reappearing shortly with Phillip Schofield and Holly Willoughby.

"Welcome to London." Phillip said smiling warmly at the group. "I know your Lido. I went there a few times when I was a boy." Rachel knew that he'd lived in Cornwall during his childhood. "I was sad to hear about the fact that it could close if you don't raise the money. Let's hope we can raise the profile." He turned to talk to James and Harrison, Summer, Pierre and Poppy, talking to the boys about the filming and the social media launch while Holly took the rest of the Ls onto the studio floor, pointing various things out including where the majority of the group would be while Rachel, Summer and James were talking to the famous couple.

"Which one of you is Rachel?" Holly asked as they stood by the couches.

"Me." Said Rachel stepping forward, her heart beating so loud she would swear that Holly could have heard it.

"Hello Rachel." Holly smiled warmly. "So, I'll start by asking you some questions about the Lido, about the fact your grandmother was the Liberty that the pool is named after and a bit about the fundraising so far. Alright? Don't be nervous." She turned to Tony. "And what's your name sir?"

He told her. "So, you're the elder statesman of this group of lovely ladies?"

"Well someone's got to keep these women under control." Tony looked at Holly with puppy dog eyes.

She winked at him. "In my experience Tony, it's usually the other way around." Tony blushed like a beetroot. The dancers laughed, Holly smiled and said she'd see them all later. Phillip joined her and the two of them walked onto the TV set.

Scarlett led all of the group back to the room with all of their bags in. "I'll come and collect you again at about ten past eleven. Make sure you're changed and ready to go." The door shut and they were left alone again.

"See the colour of your cheeks Tony." Cindy laughed, pretending to warm her hands on his face.

Tony went red again. "Oh. She was lovely, wasn't she?"

"Maybe you should have offered her one of your egg sandwiches." said Cindy, sending the room into guffaws of laughter. Poor Tony.

Summer took charge, clapped her hands and shouted for everyone to listen. "We're going to run through the short Flashmob dance. James has edited the music for about a minute. Poppy, Pierre and me will do the start to "Vogue" like we did down at the Lido. Rachel you'll then join in as before and then we'll switch to Dancing Queen and all of you will join in together including James and Harrison. Harrison will do Bill's part with you Tony so you won't be dancing alone ok?"

The music started from James' phone and Summer walked through the dance, then again and again. After a few times of everyone dancing she then stood to the side and watched it, Poppy and Pierre dancing together. "Again." She said. "Remember to smile." At last she was satisfied that the dancers looked alright.

They all changed and photos were taken, selfies were sent and the group was ready. Jade re-emerged and asked for Rachel, Summer and James while Scarlett took the rest of the Ls back to the studio. The threesome were taken to a side room to have studio make up applied. Rachel though she looked hideous. And then Jade took them to the couch next to where Holly and Phillip would sit. There was a report from an earlier outside broadcast being shown on the TV and then there was going to be an advert break. Phillip and Holly sat on the couch and looked at the cameras.

Holly started. “Down in the far west of Cornwall in the town of Porthlowen there is an art deco building known as Liberty’s Lido that was opened by King George V in 1931. Sadly unless £400,000 can be raised by the end of September the pool will be shut forever. In an effort to raise money a swimming group known as Liberty’s Lido Ladies and Lads participated in a Flashmob dance which has gone viral on social media after being on local TV and in the press. Some of you may have seen it. In the studio today we have some of the swimmers and they’re going to be dancing for us a little later after we’ve spoken to three of their members who were instrumental in creating the Flashmob. You’ve been to this pool haven’t you Phillip?”

Phillip took over. “Yes, I went there a couple of times in the summer when I was a boy. It’s a great place. I remember swimming in the natural sea water and thinking how cold it was but these days with all of the knowledge of the health benefits of cold water swimming on both physical and mental wellbeing maybe I ought to rethink that.”

Holly continued. “Here we have Rachel, who is the Granddaughter of the Liberty that the Lido was named after. Rachel how do you feel about the threat of the Lido shutting?”

Rachel’s heart was in her mouth. “Well obviously it would be a very sad day for Porthlowen and for West Cornwall in general if this iconic building was to shut but we’re not dead yet. My grandmother taught me to swim in this Lido and Sarah Miller, the Olympic swimming champion, learned to swim here too as have many generations over the years. It’s such a feature of the town and has been for nearly one hundred years. We want to make sure that it stays open for at least another one hundred years.

“So, what fundraising have you done so far? asked Holly.

“Well as of this morning we’ve raised £270,000. This has been as a combination of initiatives locally like an auction of promises, cake sales and so on, as well as spreading the word locally, pushing local businesses to sponsor and promote us and changing the way that the Lido operates, longer opening hours in the cafe, offering the facilities for local groups to meet.”

"So, Summer what inspired you to come up with the idea of a Flashmob?" Phillip enquired.

"I'm a Zumba teacher and I was looking through videos on You Tube trying to get some ideas for new dances for my classes with my friend Pierre, who is the manager of the café at the Lido. Pierre and I were looking and a video came up of a Flashmob in a shopping centre, and I thought it would be a great idea and fun to do one at the Lido. Pierre agreed and we then thought it would be a great way to showcase the Lido too. Pierre and I started to think about a routine but we needed a cameraman to record it so I talked to my brother James here, who is doing photography, film and music studies at Uni."

"Ah yes James" Phillip nodded towards him before continuing "The man who is responsible for uploading the video, you must be really happy it has gone viral and been retweeted by so many famous people."

James looked a little bit embarrassed before replying "Well, yes, um, I never expected the response. When I checked earlier today it has been retweeted fifty thousand times and the You tube video has been watched by nearly one million people. I'm blown away and happy I could help raise to the profile of the Lido. Please please please support our appeal by going onto our crowdfunding page."

The camera panned back to Holly who said "We are going to watch the Flashmob now as these three join the rest of the dancers. While you watch, details of how to see the full video on You Tube which contains old clips from the Lido; and also, how to donate to their crowdfunding campaign will flash up on the screen. Good luck everyone and we hope you meet your target."

After everyone had danced the people in the studio clapped and cheered. The Ls were led off by Scarlett and they could hear Holly and Phillip saying 'Oh Wow that was so good. Thank you to the Liberty's Lido Ladies and Lads and just remember to support them by following the link showing now at the bottom of the page."

Back in the room, reunited with all their bags they had a group hug and a whoop for joy. There was excited chatter amongst them all. Phones were ringing and pinging with good luck and well done messages from friends and relatives.

Rachel's phone started ringing. It was Tom. "Well done darling. You were amazing. I'm really proud of you."

“Thanks Tom.” she managed to answer before bursting into tears.

“Mum what’s wrong?” Poppy asked before taking the phone from Rachel.

“Dad what’s happened as Mum has burst into tears! Is there a problem?”

“Not this end Poppy.” Tom faltered.

Still holding the phone Poppy turned to Rachel saying “Mum?”

Rachel still crying managed to blub “I’m ok. These are tears of happiness and relief.” Pulling herself together she continued “I think all the worry, all the fundraising and all the memories of Granny have just hit me and I started to feel very overwhelmed.”

Poppy, hugging her Mum, held the phone to her ear before saying “Its ok Dad. Mum is fine we’ll call you in a little while.”

“What you need darling is a Crispy Crème Doughnut!” Pierre broke the mood. “I’m buying us a bumper box for the journey home as I think we all need a sugar hit and we’ve a train to catch. Let’s get this show on the road.” Leaving the studio, they all jumped into taxis heading for Paddington Station and doughnut heaven.

Seated on the two o’clock train everyone was silent, too tired to talk and quietly contemplating the morning, doughnuts having long been consumed. James was on his phone answering emails and texts before he checked his earlier tweets about being at This Morning and sharing group photos of Holly and Phillip with the group. “Wow we’ve had loads of support. Rachel can you check in with the crowdfunding page please?”

“Yes sure, Oh My God, this can’t be right, it says we’ve got three hundred and sixty thousand pounds…..”

“What!” Angela responded “Show me Rachel, that can’t be right!” as she leaned forward and snatched Rachel’s phone off her. “Wow. Yes. It’s true. Sorry Rachel.” She handed the phone back.

“We’re nearly there everyone.” Rachel announced to the group to another cheer. “Just another forty thousand to go.” So near and yet still so far she thought to herself.

They'd just gone over the Tamar bridge into Cornwall when Tom texted her to say that he'd just started watching West Country news and there was going to be a bit about their "This Morning" exploits. He was recording it but he'd film it from his phone too and send it through to her. Twenty minutes later the film came through and everyone huddled around the phone to watch it. Typically, they went through a tunnel and then they were in an area with no signal. When the clip came through it was buffering and so it was ages before they could watch it.

"Oh, this is so frustrating." Angela scowled as she watched the circle going round and round on Rachel's phone.

"I need to see it." Cindy said continuing. "I hope they caught my best side and I don't look fat."

"You never look fat." Rachel told her.

"It's playing, Ssh everyone." Said Angela as they watched the thirty second highlighted clip.

Rachel broke the silence "Well done everyone. It's now in the lap of the gods and the public to dig deep into their pockets and donate. I'm exhausted and can't wait to get home."

Baby 1998

In early 1998 Rachel married Tom Roberts, a local GP, and in November of that year they announced the birth of Poppy, Liberty's great grandchild. Liberty had reached the ripe old age of eighty three and still went swimming in the Lido or the sea most days, although her arthritis played her up and she needed a stick, and also help from her friends to get her in and out of the water. She took The Times daily and she and Sarah continued to work on the crossword after swimming while drinking their warm up coffee, occasionally laced with a healthy dose of brandy.

Target

"I need a swim." Rachel rolled over in bed while speaking to Tom as he got ready for work.

"I bet you do. Have fun. I'll message you when I've finished around lunchtime and I'll see what you're up to. I'm going to be late so gotta go. Have a look at the fund total. I think you'll be happy." He said as he kissed her good bye.

Getting up she silently walked downstairs, an inner monologue playing out in her head, Coffee first? Crowdfunding first? Deciding she could wait a couple of minutes longer she made a coffee and retrieved her phone from its charging cable sat, at the old oak kitchen table before logging onto the fundraising page. "Four hundred and thirty five thousand pounds. What, that can't be right!" Logging out of the page she logged back in and the figure was still the same.

Taking a sip of her coffee Rachel took a moment for the news to sink in. She breathed a huge sigh of relief then she burst into tears. They'd done it. She couldn't believe that they'd reached their total let alone exceeded it. What an emotional roller coaster.

Her phone started to ring. It was Millicent. Rachel wiped her eyes with her dressing gown sleeve.

"Good Morning Rachel, I hope you've recovered from your trip?" Not allowing Rachel time to answer she continued. "I'm guessing you've seen the crowdfunding page?"

"Well yes, I have but I'm overwhelmed. How has the total increased so much overnight?"

"My dear girl, you've done it. You, the Lido and the Ls are famous. You're all over the newspapers and the internet."

"Thank you, Millicent." She paused. "I have a confession to make."

"Yes?" Millicent encouraged gently." Go on."

"Sarah wanted me to take her position on the board but she also left me £50,000 in her will to go into the Lido funds. I spoke to Joseph Baker just after the announcement that the pool may close and he suggested that I kept quiet about the money until it's future was secured as he thought that was what Sarah would have wanted. She wouldn't have wanted the money to be wasted unnecessarily and it would have gone to another charity if we hadn't been successful."

"I agree entirely. Sensible decision. Exactly what Sarah would have wanted." Millicent said in her no-nonsense manner.

"So, I'd now like to donate the £50,000 but anonymously if possible."

"I'm sure that won't be a problem. Leave it with me. I'll sort it out for Tuesday's meeting. Don't forget will you. We need you just as much moving forward with your ideas and passion. I won't tell them where the money has come from, don't worry. Sarah definitely made the right choice in proposing you as her replacement on the Board. Liberty's Lido is safe for now."

"Thank you, Millicent."

"No. Thank you Rachel. Porthlowen is so very grateful to you all. Liberty would be so proud of you for your courage and determination. You really are so like her. Well done."

Millennium 2000

Liberty announced that she was tired after staying up late to watch the millennium celebrations and went to bed. She didn't wake up. She was a couple of months shy of her eighty fifth birthday. She was missed as a Mother, Grandmother, Great Grandmother and as a friend.

Saturday

Rachel packed her swimming bag, dressed herself in a new brightly coloured summer dress that she'd picked up in London and hurried to the pool. As she got out of her car the warm sun was beaming down on her from a cloudless blue sky. She stood silently for a moment outside the white gates of the pool pausing to look up at the sign above the entrance. Liberty's Lido.

She smiled as she walked under the sign and through the gates. "I hope I did you proud Granny."

THE END

Printed in Great Britain
by Amazon

49171324R00200